ESCAPE TO EDEN

PRAISE FOR *ESCAPE TO EDEN*

"*Escape to Eden* is a wild ride. From the shiny sterile halls of the Institute to the filth-ridden underground tunnels, the chase to survive keeps the adrenaline rush on high while still pulling at the heartstrings. Rachel McClellan draws a world with all the glamour of Panem and the horror of the Hunger Games, giving us a heart-wrenching story of family ties and hope in the bleakest of times."
–**Jane Houle**, award-winning author of the Ryan Chronicles

"In *Escape to Eden* McClellan crafts a perilous future where radiantly hued eyes hold beauty, power, and terrible danger."
–**Catherine Stine**, Amazon bestselling author of the Fireseed novels

"A science-fiction thriller set in a dystopian society that is terrifying in its depiction of man's search for perfection. From the first page, I was rooting for the unknown girl to escape and hooked on finding out what happens to her as she discovers who she really is and what the world has become. Rachel McClellan's writing is fast-paced, clever, and compelling. Addictive!"
–**Debbie Herbert**, bestselling author of *Siren's Secret*

"*Escape to Eden* is a fast and furious ride that grabs you from the first page and won't let you go. There are superpowers, action, romance, and plenty of adventure, but the best part of the book is its rich and inviting heart."
–**Aimee Easterling**, Amazon bestselling author of the Wolf Rampant series

"Action, intrigue, mystery, and . . . a compelling main lead. That's what it takes to make an excellent story. And that's what *Escape to Eden* by Rachel McClellan is. Don't sit this one out."
–**Kyoko M.**, author of the Black Parade novels

RACHEL MCCLELLAN

ESCAPE TO EDEN

SWEETWATER
BOOKS
An imprint of Cedar Fort, Inc.
Springville, Utah

ISBN 13: 978-1-4621-1777-2

Published by Sweetwater Books, an imprint of Cedar Fort, Inc.
2373 W. 700 S., Springville, UT 84663
Distributed by Cedar Fort, Inc. www.cedarfort.com

LIBRARY OF CONGRESS CATALOGING-IN-PUBLICATION DATA

Names: McClellan, Rachel, 1977- author.
Title: Escape to Eden / Rachel McClellan.
Description: Springville, Utah : Sweetwater Books, an imprint of Cedar Fort,
   Inc., [2016] | "2016 | Summary: When seventeen-year-old Sage wakes up in a
   hospital with no memories, her only clue the words "Run now!" written on
   her hand, she must figure out why most people would kill to get their
   hands on her.
Identifiers: LCCN 2015032099 | ISBN 9781462117772 (pbk. : alk. paper)
Subjects: | CYAC: Genetic engineering--Fiction. | Diseases--Fiction. |
   Science fiction. | LCGFT: Science fiction. | Action and adventure fiction.
Classification: LCC PZ7.M4784139 Es 2016 | DDC [Fic]--dc23
LC record available at http://lccn.loc.gov/2015032099

Cover design by Rebecca J. Greenwood
Cover design © 2016 Cedar Fort, Inc.
Edited and typeset by Justin Greer

Printed in the United States of America

10 9 8 7 6 5 4 3 2 1

Printed on acid-free paper

To Ashlyn
who has the strength and courage of a thousand ninjas.

The world is yours.

CHAPTER 1

I may be the dumbest person in the world. That's what I think, anyway, when I see these awkward hands resting on my stomach. Awkward because I don't recognize them when I should; they're attached to my body. But the lone freckle just beneath my third knuckle is as foreign to me as my name.

Clueless as I am, I'm still able to process my surroundings. I am in a small room with a single door opposite me. A bedside table with a lamp on its top is to my left. There are no windows, at least not that I can see. There are a couple of large plastic squares on the wall that may be covering some, but I can't be sure. Everything in the room, including the walls, is painted a bright white, which makes me think of snow. I can make that connection, so I'm not stupid, but why can't I remember my own name? That seems like it should be an easy enough thing to remember. I also can't remember where I'm from, or how I got to this wintery place.

What I do know is that a few minutes ago I was sleeping. When my eyes opened, I discovered a thin white sheet draped over me that provided little warmth. I'm wearing a light blue gown. I'm young, probably sixteen or seventeen. And I'm a girl.

My first thought was that I was dead, but when I move my arms to my chest, my muscles are stiff. I'm pretty sure dead people don't have sore muscles. So I'm alive, which is good, but I still don't know what's wrong with my mind. I wish I could look inside my head or move things around to see if anything is broken, or if my brain has turned to mush. Then I would be dead—all that mashing around. Maybe I am dumb because I'm thinking about

1

this stuff when I should really be trying to figure out where I am and why.

I bring my knees up, my feet sliding across a hard mattress beneath me, and turn my head slowly. My neck is stiff too. On each side of the bed is a metal rail with white buttons at the top. One of them has an arrow pointing up. I press it, and the top of the bed rises, moving me into a sitting position.

Was I in an accident? I try to remember, but my mind is as blank as the walls.

There are no sounds and the room smells like . . . a chemical, but I can't recall which one or why the scent is familiar. I don't like it, so I open my mouth to breathe.

Another button on the bedrail draws my attention. At its center is a black image of two people. I press it. Images appear in a big square on the wall opposite me. This I do remember. It's a Wall Television. I've seen it before, but don't remember where, which frustrates me something awful, because if I can remember a stupid WTV, I should be able to remember my name.

On the screen, two people talk—a man and a woman. I stare at the woman first, because she's both striking and strange-looking. She doesn't have hair on her head, more like fur. It's long and red, like a fox's tail. Her face is white, so white it's almost translucent. A blue vine-like line beneath her skin pulses across her forehead, but what's odd is it looks like the vein has been strategically placed to look like some sort of a crown. Despite the peculiarity of it, the woman is beautiful, like an antique doll.

At first, the man next to her looks normal. He's not. His black hair is too shiny, too fine looking, like spider silk, and seems to float above his head, swaying slightly whenever he moves. And his eyes—they are a sickly pale yellow, though his tanned skin tells me he's healthy. His whole appearance contradicts itself. He, too, is strangely handsome.

I think I've seen them before, or at least others like them.

I touch my own hair. It's plain brown and hangs straight to my chest. There is nothing remarkable about it, maybe a bit wiry, but I don't think that's a good thing.

The couple's lips are moving. I inspect the metal rail and find

2

another button with the image of a speaker. I press it. The woman's voice, deep and sultry, breaks the silence.

"—biggest event of the year. It's where we give back to those who are suffering."

The man nods. "And there's been a lot of suffering. The president himself has given up his portion of oDNA for a week."

"So generous. A true leader. Meanwhile, he asks all of us who are able to give up a one-week supply of oDNA. This may frighten some, but we have to remember that this is for the poor who can't afford it. The Institute is making this event bigger and better than ever before. In fact, they plan on auctioning off a new serum that's rumored to enable men to live to the age of thirty-five. Can you imagine?"

The man chuckles. "That would be something indeed."

A clicking draws my attention to the door. I shut the WTV off and place my hands in my lap. It's then that I notice the edge of a deep purple bruise showing beneath the sleeve of my cotton gown. It looks fresh, but I don't have time to examine it before the door opens.

A frighteningly thin woman walks through the door, and I choke on a breath. She is tall, almost as tall as the door she just came through. More disturbing is her forehead; it sticks out at least three inches past the rest of her face, overshadowing her dark eyes. Someone else might try to hide this with bangs, but this woman wears her hair short to her chin, parted in the middle, accentuating her strange bone structure.

The woman makes eye contact, and her tight lips twist up. The motion is not friendly. Her long fingers hold a paper-thin silver pad. "You're awake."

I speak, and my voice cracks as if I haven't spoken aloud for a long time. "Where am I?"

She comes to my bedside, looking me up and down. "What do you remember?" Her voice is colder than the room.

I try to think, but something blocks my thoughts, especially when I try to gain access to personal information. "Was I in an accident?"

I stare at her head, which I do know is a rude thing to do, but

I can't stop. Something tells me, an instinct perhaps, that I need to be nice, even flattering, to this woman who shows off her odd forehead.

The woman presses buttons on the silver pad, then her eyes meet mine. "You're staring."

"I'm sorry, it's just . . ." I try to figure out where I should go with this. ". . . you must have a really big brain. It's beautiful."

The words just tumble out, and they feel right, so I don't question them. I hope this isn't me being dumb.

The woman smiles, a genuine one, and her chin raises. "I'm extremely intelligent."

"You must be. I've never seen anything like it."

"Of course you haven't. You're an Original, an oddity that shouldn't exist."

This alarms me, and I forget the flattery. "An Original? What's that? And who am I?" I begin to think maybe I shouldn't be here in this place that looks and feels like winter without the snow. "Who are you?"

The tall woman moves to the foot of my bed. "You may address me as Ebony Branson. I'm the chief Techhead here at IHRD in Boston."

"What's IHRD?"

"The Institute of Human Research and Development." She clicks on the pad again. The action is silent, but there's something about the way she moves her fingers, all sharp and clicky, that I don't like. I don't think this woman is a nice person.

"How did I get here?"

She doesn't stop clicking. "My people found you in the woods, abandoned and starving. It's rare to find one of you, but you're lucky we did and not others."

"Why?"

She gives me a look but doesn't stop poking at the silver pad. "Because you're ugly and unremarkable," she says matter-of-factly. "People don't like your kind. You're a reminder of what mankind used to be—weak and unremarkable. Do you understand?"

Something tells me to agree, but what I really want to do is ask for a mirror.

"Yes, ma'am." I resist the urge to touch my face to feel for a deformity or maybe a patch of scars.

My response pleases her, and she smiles and tilts her head, like she's about to do something she wasn't planning on doing. "I would like to show you someone. Please tell me if you recognize him."

I sit up. "Where?"

Ebony presses a button on the pad. The white wall to my right shimmers a bright blue until it turns into a giant glass window. On the other side is another room identical to mine, except sitting cross-legged on the floor is a boy with blond hair. He looks young, his face toddlerish with smooth pale skin and big blue eyes. But his height makes me think he's older, maybe eight or nine. His gaze drops from the ceiling and turns toward me. He stands slowly.

I pull back the sheet covering my legs and move to the side of the bed, wincing as I do so. My muscles ache bone-deep, but I want a closer look. I stand, take an unsteady step, and then another. I manage to make it to the glass wall.

"Do you know him?" Ebony asks.

He is a beautiful boy, but very thin and almost sickly-looking. I try to recall anything familiar about him, but I can't. "No, ma'am. Who is he?"

"We don't know. We found him close to where we found you. He's like you, but even less intelligent."

I flinch at that.

She stares at the boy. Her nose turns up like the room smells bad. "He doesn't speak, and his brain appears," she pauses, "broken."

I look back at the boy. He is moving toward us. He stops directly in front of me, only an inch of glass between us.

Ebony steps back as if she might catch whatever she thinks the boy has. "It is a shame that he has been allowed to live."

I don't say anything, but I raise my right hand to the glass, spreading my palm against its shiny coolness. The boy stares at me for a moment before his eyes go to my palm. He raises his arm, and for a second I think he's going to mirror my action, but then he points at something on my hand.

5

Ebony clears her throat and the wall shimmers again into a solid white.

"What will happen to him?" I ask. I turn my hand over where the boy had pointed.

"He will remain here for study and tests until we can make a decision what to do with him."

In very small letters the word *Now* is written on the tip of my right pinky.

"And me?" I ask, afraid of the answer. "What will happen to me?"

"No harm will come to you. We only need to study you. Ensure you are healthy and well."

Carefully I turn over my left hand so Ebony doesn't see.

My left pinky has a word on it too. It says *Run*. I turn my hands inward until my fingertips are touching. Together the words say:

RUN NOW.

CHAPTER 2

Run now.

My pulse races reading these two small words. Is it my handwriting? I don't know. It could be, but even if it isn't, I feel strongly that I should follow the command. Another instinct.

I turn my gaze to Ebony. "It must be difficult for you."

"What's that?"

"Being around someone like me." I nod toward the wall. "And him," I say. "It must take great strength."

"It is difficult. But one grows used to it. We must remember that charity is an important human characteristic."

"You are very kind."

She clicks a few more times on the pad that seems to be an extension of her hand and then looks up. "I must go now," she says and then hesitates. "Do you need anything?" she asks. The words seem difficult for her to say, like they're too big for her mouth.

I lower my head. "I am a little hungry."

Ebony clickety-clacks onto the pad again. "It is not your scheduled dinnertime yet, but perhaps a little pudding. Would that be nice?"

"It would make my day," I say with my face turned down, hiding my expression.

"Tomorrow we'll see if you can't have a cookie." She seems pleased with herself as she strides out the door, which closes firmly behind her.

I put my fingers together again. *Run now.*

A whirling sound captures my attention, and I turn around. Next to my bedside table, a small white panel in the wall has opened. Just inside the space is a cup of chocolate pudding and a rectangular plastic wedge for a blunt spoon. As soon as I take them, the wall's panel snaps closed.

I abandon the pudding and the wedge on the table, wondering why I asked for it in the first place. And why did I feel it was important to flatter Ebony?

I sit on the bed and ponder my situation. I can't remember anything personal, yet I feel a familiarity to things around me. And I'm not actually as shocked as someone in my situation should be. I think of the words on my fingers. I think of the way I handled Ebony, and I think of why I wanted something to eat. The world around me makes no sense to my foggy brain, but something deeper, my instincts, seem to know something I don't—what to do.

So I surrender myself to them.

I glance around the room, this time noticing two security cameras in the corners. There's nowhere to hide. I pick up the plastic wedge and pudding and climb back into bed. I eat it there, the thin sheet pulled up to my waist. As I eat, I pretend my eyelids are growing heavy, and by my last bite I feign exhaustion. I lower the top of the bed, pull the sheet to my shoulders and close my eyes. The empty pudding container and spoon are covered with me, like I forgot about them.

Pretending to shift in my sleep, I sneak the wedge into my hand. It's a slow process, but eventually I manage to snap it lengthwise, giving me two pointed shards. I slip one into each hand, then wait several long minutes before I move. When I do, I turn over and open my eyes and yawn widely.

Sitting up slowly, I keep my hands close to me, away from the camera's view. I rise and walk around, appearing to be bored. I stop near the door and sway back and forth like I'm dizzy. Without warning, I drop to the floor. I make my arms and legs shake; saliva drools from my mouth.

Like I expect, the door opens within seconds. Although my head shakes as if I'm having some sort of fit, I take in everything I can about the young woman who comes in to check on me. At first I think she's like me, plain and unremarkable. I feel a spark inside, and my chest swells like I might cry with joy, but I don't have time to wonder why.

The woman is different, or maybe I should say normal. I'm the odd one. I see the unusualness in her dark purple eyes, which tells me something, but only my instincts know what. I wish they would be a little more helpful like jogging my memory of who I am, but my instincts seem hardly compassionate. I know this because they are telling me to maneuver the sharp point of one of the wedges face up in my right hand.

The woman lifts my head, trying to get it to hold still, but I make sure she can't get a good grip. She's yelling for someone to help, but says it so fast, it's like one giant new word. I can tell she's never dealt with the problem I'm giving her, and she's about to have a major anxiety attack because of it.

That's when I strike. I hit her hard in the back with the point of the wedge, a blow directly to her lower spine just above her pelvis. It won't kill her, but it will temporarily paralyze the lower half of her body.

While the woman collapses to the floor, I jump up. "Sorry," I say, because I do feel bad that I hurt her (she may be a very nice person after all), and I rush out the door. A cold breeze blows up my skimpy gown.

I'm at the end of a long, wide hallway the same white as my room, but the ceilings are significantly higher. I take note of this. For some reason it makes my stomach churn. I dread finding out why.

A woman in an all-white dress with a black sash around her waist sits at a desk. Two tall male Techheads—they have the same peculiar forehead as Ebony—are approaching the woman's desk, but are still several yards in front of me. Just beyond them is a tiny woman walking with the boy who had been in the room next to mine. She's a good inch shorter than him and he's small.

An alarm goes off. Red lights flash on the ceiling. All eyes go up—then focus directly on me. I run. I run the only direction I can go and hope my instincts will continue to act as my brain, which really could be mush at this point.

The tall Techheads stretch out their arms to trap me, but I

don't slow. Instead I grab a stack of papers from an empty desk with one hand. With my other hand I grab an electronic pad similar to the one Ebony had earlier, and I am mindful to keep my fingers pressed together on the plastic picks.

Just before I reach the Techheads, I toss the papers into the air. The muscles in their long, expressionless faces pinch and tug, and their eyes dart around. They are all about order, not chaos, my instincts say. One yells in frustration and begins grabbing at the falling papers. The other Techhead does the same. They've lost sight of me.

I rush past them and focus on the nurse now standing behind her desk. Her hair is long and black with silver streaks. I suck in air, fear clenching my chest. I don't know why. I just know she's dangerous.

The woman stares at me, concentrating. Her pale gray eyes begin to light up. My instincts tell me I don't want them to get brighter. Something very bad will happen if they do.

I raise the silver pad and flip it hard. It twists through the air and hits the nurse square in the eyes. She screams and covers her face. I am surprised by the accuracy of my aim. I keep running.

The dwarfish woman and boy are standing still, watching the scene play out. I have no fear of them and sprint past, toward the exit ahead.

The boy makes a sudden noise, like he's hurt. Over my shoulder I see his eyes are wide and full of fear. My mind, not my instincts, tells me to keep running, but I stop. I look from the boy to the exit. Going against all rationale (but what is rational about anything that is happening right now?), I return and snatch the boy's arm. Now we're both running, but he's not as fast and trips. I scoop him up. He wraps his arms around my neck, his legs around my stomach, and buries his head into my shoulder like he's done this a million times before. I run fast, grateful that the boy is small and light

I'm almost to the exit when the floor begins to shake underfoot. There are two closed doors ahead. One of them is huge and tall like the ceiling. I slow just as the door explodes open, spraying debris everywhere. I screech to a halt and stare at the massive figure before me, understanding now why the ceilings are so high. This man, this creature, wouldn't fit otherwise. He is not only tall but wide, almost touching each side of the hallway. The black shirt he's wearing barely contains his muscles. If he shivered, his shirt would tear. He has thick red hair like a doormat, and his black eyes are too close together. He laughs, staring down at me as if I'm about to be his new chew toy.

"Where you go, Ugly?" His voice booms out each word deep and loud. He is definitely not one of the Techheads. And he's rude.

My thoughts race and spin as they try to figure out what to do next. I worry that my instincts seem to be hesitating.

The massive man has a small head with a red face on top of boulder-like shoulders, and long arms that extend down to chubby fingers. The zipper on his pants is open and yellow beehives are printed on his black underwear. Then I notice his legs, which I expect to be like tree stumps, but they are much smaller than the rest of him.

My thoughts come to an abrupt halt. I know his weakness.

When he takes a step toward me, I race straight for him, holding the boy tighter to my chest. His arms swing to grab me, but I turn sideways and slide on the floor directly between the creature's legs, coming up behind him.

He can't bend well—that's his weakness. He glances over his shoulder, confused. A surge of triumph races through me, but then I remember I still don't know who I am or why this is happening to me. I just know I need to run.

I slam open the EXIT door. Stairs lead up or down. My instinct tells me to run up, so I do.

The alarm blares loud enough that I can't hear my own breathing. My chest heaves up and down, and I start to feel the weight of the boy. The further up I go, the heavier he becomes.

There's movement in the stairwell beneath me. *Hurry.* My legs burn, yet somehow I block the pain and keep going, as if I've done something like this before.

I reach a door with a long sunlit window. I stop and set the boy down, my eyes searching all around the doorframe—for what, I don't know yet. I open the door and look up. That's when I find what I've been looking for. At the top of the doorframe is a small black box no bigger than the end of my thumb. In its center is a pin-sized glass circle.

I remove the makeshift plastic pick from between my fingers and wedge it into what I now recognize as a sensor. Anyone who comes after us won't be able to open the door because the covered sensor will think that something or someone is on the other side. The bad people coming after me will have to wait for security to turn off the alarms altogether, allowing them to manually open the door.

I call them bad people, but I could be the bad one—I'm the one escaping. But I don't feel like the bad one. I took no pleasure in hurting those two women.

I pick up the boy. He wraps himself around me again as I close the door tight. Turning, I am accosted by the bright sun overhead. I raise my arm to shield my eyes. The rooftop resembles a city park. Groups of trees, many of them cherry trees with branches full of pink blossoms, and green grass give way to paved walking trails. Benches and wooden tables have been placed next to the trees providing shade to whoever might want it. No one's wanting it right now. It's about 2:00 in the afternoon by my quick calculations.

I sprint across the grass to the ledge of the building and peer over a four-foot stone wall. We're very high up, maybe eighty stories. A six-lane, black-as-night road weaves between buildings far below. Small, sleek automobiles glide across its smooth surface, barely making a sound. The structures nearby are the exact height of the building we're standing on. They are full of windows, broken up by lines of silver metal, creating a large grid.

Their roofs are similar to this one: landscaped parks with cherry blossoms and metal benches. The buildings are too far to jump to, however, and when I look to my left, I discover a metal walkway crossing to the nearest building. Beyond, similar walkways connect the entire city.

The door I just came through rattles loudly, and the boy clings tighter to my neck.

"It's okay," I say and take off running toward the metal path.

The pounding grows louder on the door. They mean to break it and not wait for security. I have only moments.

I stop before crossing the walkway. I realize they'll expect me to go this way. Others will be waiting for me on the other side.

"We're going to have to hide," I say to him. "Can you do that?" He doesn't answer but he moves his head in agreement. This little boy is smarter than I think. Any other child in this situation would probably be frightened and cry for their mother, but he seems to know how much harder it would make our escape.

A few trees are close by, but they are much too small to climb, let alone hide in. I keep looking. Dotted across the roof are rectangular aluminum boxes about my height. I sprint to the nearest one and set the boy down. The glass front displays food and drinks—not what I'm interested in at the moment. I run my fingers all around the back of it. At the bottom is a panel. I discover a metal button on each side and push it. The panel pops off, giving access to some kind of electrical box inside. The space isn't big, maybe a foot deep and three feet high. Room for one small boy.

I turn to the boy and place my hands on his shoulders. "I'm going to hide you inside here. Do you understand?"

His blue eyes aren't looking into mine; they are looking just above at my forehead. His expression is blank, giving me nothing to go on about how he might feel being stuffed in a small, dark space. Out of time, I simply pick him up and place him inside. He hugs his knees to his chest and rocks slowly.

"I'll come back for you." I smooth his blond hair. "I promise."

As I slide the panel back into place, my heart lurches painfully. A child this young should not have to go through something like this. I hesitate by the box until an explosion and plume of smoke billows from the rooftop access door. I'm on the run again.

I sprint to the suspended bridge, praying I'm not seen, but I don't run across it. Instead I jump over the edge and flip beneath the long walkway. I resist the urge to scream, unsure of exactly what I'm doing, but underneath my hands grab onto two long cables running the length of the bridge. I wrap my arms around them, then my legs, my back to the ground.

I tell myself not to look down. I fail. Hundreds of feet below me is the smooth black road, a steady stream of cars skimming across its surface.

What a horrible way to die.

CHAPTER 3

A fierce wind twists between the buildings, swinging my body on the cables like a plastic sack caught on a wire. After sliding further down on the wires, I hold my breath and close my eyes. There is a commotion above me as people search for the boy and me.

"She's got to be here!" It's a man's authoritative voice. "Look everywhere."

"You four go next door," someone else says. Their running footsteps echo on the bridge. The movement rattles the metal, shaking the wires I'm gripping.

"Over here!" a man yells.

I open my eyes. Metal scrapes on metal. Suddenly I'm more frightened at what I hear than I am of falling.

"I found one!"

Several voices talk at once, but all I hear is a child whimpering. *The boy.* I move to leave my hiding spot, but logic stops me. I don't know who this boy is, and besides, what can I do? I was lucky before, but now I'm out of ideas. Later I will return for him. When I know more. When I know who I am.

My heart aches when the boy cries louder. I shut out his voice and focus on the shrill sound of the wind. On the soft whirring of the vehicles below. On the sounds of footsteps slowly retreating back inside.

Hours pass, and my muscles are burning hanging onto the cables. I've shifted positions dozens of times to keep them from seizing up, but that is no longer effective.

The sunset provides a temporary distraction, sinking in swirls

15

of reds and oranges, then draining away until all that is left is black. I hang on in the darkness and the silence.

Very slowly, I begin to inch my way back to the end of the bridge. My muscles won't let me move any other way. The cables tear open blisters that have formed on my hands. I grit my teeth and continue forward. When I reach the end, I drop my feet, and dangle next to the side of the building, so high in the air. This time I don't look down. My muscles tighten for a few seconds and relax. They shake as I step upon a narrow lip of the bridge attached to the skyscraper. Painfully, I climb back onto the rooftop, and crouch low, hiding in the shadows.

No one is around. I'm tempted to return to where I hid the boy, just to be sure, but I spot a camera above the door pointed in that direction, like they expect me to come back for him. I purse my lips together. Later.

Bending low, I scamper across the bridge to the next building. I'm sure there are cameras there too, but shadows are my friends, my only ones, and I keep to them.

I stop next to the rooftop door and search all around. It doesn't have the same security as the Institute's. I open the door, careful not to leave blood from my palm on anything. No alarm goes off so I slip inside.

This building smells different, like beef stew with carrots and potatoes. A rumbling creates a pit in my stomach. I follow the scent down two flights of stairs until I hear voices. Through a window in a door, I spot rows and rows of room dividers, sectioning a massive room into small offices. In each cubicle sits a person with a headset. I squint to see if maybe they are like me. Their foreheads are, but the only way I will know for sure is if I see their eyes. I'm struck by what my memory is choosing to remember. Why can't I remember the important things? I look down at my thin blue gown, at the bruise on my arm, and touch it lightly. Whatever happened, whatever put me in that place, it was bad. My heart, the way it feels as if there's a great hole directly in the center, is my witness.

Just then the door opens. I stumble back, caught unaware. Just as surprised, a tall man with dark hair and eyes the color of gold meets my gaze. I wait for his reaction. He stares for what feels like forever. My nerves can't stretch any tighter. Finally my shoulders slump. I am completely exhausted.

"Help me?" My voice is small.

He turns from me to look up and down the stairwell. When he looks at me again his amber eyes turn a soft caramel. He is not like me.

"What's your name?" he asks.

I open my mouth, hoping my mushy brain will have dried out a bit, but a name never comes. I shake my head beginning to breathe heavily.

"My name is Anthony." His eyes flicker to the purple stain on my skin. "Your arm. May I see it?"

I hesitate, waiting for my instincts to guide me. Anthony is older than me, mid-twenties, perhaps, tall and well built with thick brown hair.

"You can trust me." His eyes hold mine, his voice as smoothly modulated as music.

When an instinct doesn't come, I raise my arm. He carefully lifts the wide sleeve of the gown and studies the bruise. "We have to get you out of here," he says looking up. "Now."

"Where?" I ask, but I'm too tired to care. Too tired to even think.

Anthony says nothing. He frowns, the first real expression I've seen on his face. He opens the door a crack and peers inside the giant room with all the people. "My office," he says. "It is along this back wall in the corner." The frown is gone, his face again smooth. "I'm going to distract everyone. When I do, I want you to cross quietly to it. Do you understand?"

I nod. For the first time since waking today, I take a deep, full breath. Someone is helping me.

He searches my face. "You're going to be okay," he says, "but no matter what happens, don't let anyone see your eyes."

I nod again. Eyes are important.

Anthony walks into the room and crosses to the far side. "Everyone, I'd like to make an announcement. May I have your attention, please?"

All heads swivel in his direction and when they do, I sneak in. I stay close to the wall and try to act invisible.

"Our daily quota has been met for twenty days in a row. Because of this success, I am allowing you all to go home early."

There's a buzz of voices and a few hands clap. I'm already inside his office, crouched on the floor. The room is gray, and a black desk takes up most of the space. Papers rest on top, neat and organized. A framed slogan on the wall reads: "MyTalk: Your Voice Matters."

Anthony speaks again, "It is Friday night. I would like you to all," he pauses only briefly, "to go have fun."

The voices grow louder, but I don't hear anyone moving.

"I'm serious," he says. "Leave or I'll change my mind."

This time people move.

Several minutes go by before I take a chance and peek between the crack in the door. Most everyone has left, but a few people are gathered around Anthony, talking and laughing. They are beautiful people, perfectly symmetrical faces, smooth, flawless skin, some dark and some light. The eyes of two of them are the same gold color as Anthony's.

I duck back when Anthony glances in my direction. "Go home. Have a good weekend," he tells them.

Soon there is only the sound of footsteps approaching the office. Anthony enters the room and closes the door.

"Everyone's gone," he says. "You're safe."

He studies me for a moment, and I wonder if he thinks the same thing about me that Ebony thought, that I am simpleminded and plain—ugly. I have the urge to shrink into the wall.

"The Institute's Security searched this building several hours ago," he says. "They didn't say for what, but it was for you, wasn't it?"

"Yes."

"Where have you been hiding?"

I open my palms and stare down at the raw blisters. "Under the bridge. Hanging on the cables."

A vertical line appears between his dark eyebrows. "You hung on this whole time?" He reaches into a lower drawer of the desk. "I only have a few," he says as he removes something small and clear, then he comes over to me and bends down. "We'll put them on the worst ones."

I hold out my hands, and he covers a translucent material over the wounds that have blood oozing from them.

"Thank you."

He smiles. It transforms his face into something bright and welcoming. "You must have many questions. I am wondering why you're not asking them."

"I don't know what to ask first," I admit. "Everything is so confusing."

"Here, have a seat." He gently helps me off the floor and into his chair. Every muscle in my body fights the movement, and I wish I could lie down, but instincts, or maybe just common sense, tell me there isn't time for that, and won't be for a long time.

"Can you start by telling me what you remember?" he asks.

I inhale deeply. On my exhale, I say, "I woke up in what looked like a hospital room. I couldn't remember anything: not my own name, or how I got there, or where I'm from. There was a woman there who called herself a Techhead."

At this Anthony straightens, no longer leaning against the desk. "Did she tell you her name?"

"Ebony. She was really smart and was monitoring me or something. She said it was to keep me safe."

The muscles in his jaw tighten, but a moment later his face is smooth again. "What happened then? How did you escape?"

"I'm not sure." I shake my head. "Something inside me, an instinct, told me to flatter her." I search his eyes for a reaction, but they give nothing back. I speak faster, telling him about the words on my fingers, the plastic spoon, about knowing how to paralyze the woman with the purple eyes, how I ran into the hallway and knew how to stop the lady with the white eyes, and how I knew about the giant, deformed man.

And I tell him about the boy.

My throat feels swollen all of a sudden. I should've done more to help him. I finish by telling him the boy was taken while I hid under the bridge.

He is back against the desk, studying me, his arms crossed to his chest. "An amazing story," he finally says.

"You don't believe me?"

"I do. It's just remarkable that someone with no special abilities," he pauses, then continues, "can do what you did."

"But how did I? And why do they want me if I'm as unremarkable as Ebony said? Why am I so different from you? From them? And where am I?"

Anthony lifts his hand to silence me and smiles once more. "Let me answer what I can. First, you're in Boston. You have just escaped from the headquarters of the Institute of Human Research and Development, a near-impossible feat, I might add. Obviously you have been well trained. You may not know who you are, but someone taught you the layout of the Institute, taught you about the different races, their weaknesses, their strengths. The training has been so ingrained into you that when you feel threatened, your instincts, as you call them, take over. As for why they want you, you're different. An enigma they'd like to get rid of but can't because they need you."

"What do you mean?" A cold breeze—at least I think it's a breeze—chills me.

Without saying anything, Anthony removes his suit jacket and wraps it around me. "Over a century ago, closer to two centuries, the world was a perfect place. No wars, no illnesses, prosperity for everyone." He scoots more onto the desk, his legs dangling. "It was like this for a long time, but then man grew bored. You see, man by nature is a conqueror, so in a peaceful, illness-free world, what is man to do?"

He pauses, still looking at me. I'm not sure if he's waiting for me to answer the question, because I can't. My brain is still mush.

He continues, "With nothing to conquer, man turned on himself, searching desperately for a way to make us perfect. They created the Institute of Human Research and Development to search for ways to eradicate what they thought to be the weaknesses from human DNA, like being short, overweight, bad-looking, and so on.

"The experiments with DNA started out small. Scientists were able to locate certain genes, the intelligent gene for example, and replicate it. They injected it first into newborns and, with some refinement, the experiments turned out to be a success. So they searched for other positive DNA traits to duplicate. When they were combined, they called this prime DNA. The rich paid enormous amounts of money to alter their children to be the smartest, fastest, prettiest kids around. It did not take long before others had access to the scientists' research, much of it illegally. Criminals sold it on the black market. Some unscrupulous researchers, utilizing animal DNA, created whole new breeds of humans.

"A gulf opened between the altered and the unaltered population. To combat such an imbalance, the government issued a mandate that all schoolchildren would be injected with doses of pDNA to help them be the best they could be. It was believed at the time that this would solve the imbalance and cure the problems inherent in human behavior. Two generations passed before we started to notice complications. People began dying early from diseases no one had ever seen before, making the population decline rapidly. We call it the Kiss."

I shiver at the name.

He looks back at me. "After a century of mass pDNA injections, humans became a genetically altered species. One that dies at a very young age. Scientists tried to fix the problem by adding synthetic DNA, but that only gave us abnormal abilities, some of them extremely dangerous."

The woman with the white eyes, I think.

"But for the majority of us, it is nothing so extreme. Amber eyes are the result of our ancestors complying with what their government required of them. A lot of us have developed minor enhanced abilities, but nothing to brag about. There are others, however."

"Like Ebony and the people at the Institute," I say.

"Yes."

"Why do they want me? I'm obviously nothing special."

"On the contrary. You're very special. Your DNA hasn't been altered; you are pure. An Original.

"The Institute seeks your kind because your DNA delays the

Kiss for a time, allowing them to live longer. They take it from you, out of your bone marrow," his eyes shift to my arm, "and combine it into a special formula they call oDNA, or Original DNA. Only the richest of the rich and very important people, such as government officials and Institute employees, are given those doses."

"Why doesn't the government change things? Surely the president can do something."

He laughs; even his laugh is smooth sounding. "The government is controlled by the Institute. They are the ones with the power because they control who gets oDNA. Years ago we had a president who tried to pass a law that would allow anyone to get oDNA at an affordable price. The Techheads threatened to destroy all their research and data if the law passed, so the government backed off. You see, no one has the brainpower to duplicate Techheads' work, and Techheads are too proud to ever share their knowledge. That leaves the entire human race, what's left of it, at Techheads' mercy."

"And what about people like me? Originals? Where are they?"

Anthony exhales slowly and shakes his head. "Those who have survived have either been taken by the Institute or are in hiding."

"And society is okay with this?"

"I wish I could say no, but you have to understand that this is a very different world. With people dying as young as they do, people have fallen into a survival mode. When the Institute tells people that Originals are kept in a safe place, that they are taken care of and have a great life, people don't question them. Nobody wants to know the truth. Everyone just wants to live as long as they can."

It's too much for me to take in. Maybe if I can remember who I am and where I came from, I might be able to better understand what he's saying, but right now it sounds like I've awakened into a world where no one cares about anyone else, or what is happening. If the dream was a paradise, the reality feels more like a hell.

"And my memory? Did they permanently mess it up?" I ask.

"I believe they gave you a drug that temporarily blocks your memory. They do this to Originals to keep them calm through the testing."

"Testing?"

Anthony nods. "A great deal of testing. All kinds, some of it quite painful. Before your DNA can be sold, they need to know if you have any defects, or the potential for defects."

I rub my arm. "So I'll get my memory back?"

"I think so. In time."

I breathe easier, but his answers have me wondering about something else. I look at Anthony, his creaseless white shirt and sharply creased slacks.

"Why are you helping me?" I ask. "Aren't I worth a lot of money? And won't anybody who helps me get into big trouble?"

He smiles. "For a long time the Institute has said they are close to finding a cure, a breakthrough that will return our DNA to the way it was. A growing number of us no longer believe them." He lowers his feet back to the floor and leans against the desk. "We think the only way to fix the human race is to start over. Find Originals and protect them. They are our future. It's not a coincidence that I work here next to the Institute."

"How many Originals are there?" I want him to say thousands. I want him to say that they are all around but just keeping a low profile. I want him to make me feel like I'm not alone. He doesn't.

"In my lifetime, I've only met six. But that doesn't mean they don't exist. Many of them are in hiding."

"Have others escaped from the Institute like me?"

"One. A year ago."

I lean back into the chair, letting his words sink in. A feeling of hopelessness smothers me, making it hard to breathe.

He says, "You're very lucky, you know? But something tells me luck had nothing to do with it."

I open my mouth to say I don't feel very lucky when a pounding on the door has me off the chair and backing into the corner.

The Institute. They've found me.

CHAPTER 4

I press my back into the wall until it hurts.

"It's okay," Anthony says. "I asked someone I trust to come help us. You have nothing to fear."

I start to protest, but he's already opening the door.

A girl pushes herself the rest of the way in and says, "So what's so important that I had to come all the way over here on a Friday night? You know it's my only night to wear a dress—"

The words stick in her throat when she sees me in the corner. She looks younger than I am, but by the confidence in her voice and her stance, standing tall with shoulders back, I think she could be older. Her wavy blonde hair goes past her shoulders and contrasts with her short black dress. Her eyes are amber colored like Anthony's. She carries a black bag over her shoulder.

"Her eyes," the girl says and looks at Anthony. "Is she—?"

He nods and turns to me. "This is Jenna. She's here to help."

"Thank you," I say and smile.

"Don't thank me yet. I haven't agreed to help anyone." Her eyes jump to Anthony. "This could land me in a lot of trouble, you know that, right?"

Anthony nods, but he's smiling.

"And it may surprise you, but I'm already not liked in most circles. Some people, men specifically—"

"I'm very aware of your lack of likability."

"Don't interrupt me when I'm talking. Men don't like me because I speak my mind. Smart people feel the same way. It scares them. In fact, the Institute could be watching me right now."

"Nobody cares about a thirteen-year-old girl with an attitude."

She huffs. "Well they should, because I'm dangerous."

Jenna hands him the black bag and turns to me. "What's your name?"

"She doesn't remember yet," Anthony answers for me.

Jenna looks down at the bruise on my arm as if she knows the reason for my temporary amnesia. For some reason I'm embarrassed and avert my eyes.

"So what should we call you?" she asks.

I shrug.

"You have the same brown color of hair as my old dog. He was shy, too. How about Patch?"

"Don't name her after your dog." Anthony unzips the bag. "She'll remember her name soon enough." He hands me clothes and shoes. "Put these on. We're going to have to move fast."

Jenna and Anthony turn around so I can change. I stare at their backs, wondering how I ended up in a position where I had to undress in front of strangers. But then I remember the Institute, and experience a jolt of fear. I dress quickly.

"Where are you going to take her?" Jenna whispers, but the room is too small for me not to hear.

"To The Rapture. I'm hoping Bram will know what to do. She's not safe in the city."

"Won't that be dangerous? Sixers have been known to go there. If they see her—"

"Then we can't let that happen, right?"

"What's The Rapture?" I say as I pull a black t-shirt over my head. It's too big and the white leggings are too small. I look like I'm wearing a short dress with tights. At least the sandals sort of fit as long as I don't have to run.

Anthony swings the backpack over his shoulder. "It's a night club not far from here. The owner is sympathetic to Originals."

"What are we going to do about her eyes?" Jenna asks. "They're such a dull green, like that moldy color in my toilet. Eww."

"Jenna," Anthony warns, but she keeps talking.

"People will recognize her for what she is miles away."

I reach up and touch near my eye, wondering if they really look that bad.

Jenna comes to me. "Maybe if we fix her hair."

She uses her fingers to fluff my long hair to the side, even pulling parts of the top down in front of my eyes. I can barely see through it.

Jenna laughs. "You look ridiculous."

I smooth back my hair, not seeing the humor in the situation.

Anthony hands me a black hat with red flowers on its side. "You look fine. Just keep your head down and don't look at anyone. If it was daytime I'd never take you out, but I think you'll be okay at night. You ready?"

I pull the hat down low over my eyebrows. "I think so."

"You've got to be pretty scared," Jenna says. "Are you scared?" She's smiling big, her cheeks puffed wide.

"Leave her alone," Anthony says and opens the door to peek out. "It's empty. Let's go."

We move into the large space of office cubicles. I feel exposed being out in the open and step closer to Anthony.

"Did you bring your car?" Anthony asks Jenna.

"It's on the street, but can't we just walk? It's only a few blocks."

"Better to keep her hidden as much as possible."

Anthony leads us into the same stairwell I came from earlier and heads down. I hesitate on the first step, knowing the last thing my body wants to do is walk flights of stairs, but, seeing I don't have a choice, I hurry after him.

"You have a car—and drive?" I ask Jenna.

She scowls like the question is the dumbest one she's ever heard. "Of course. Don't you?"

"I don't know," I admit. The only thing I remember about cars is what I saw from hundreds of feet in the air.

"Because humans die so young, the legal age for an adult was moved to twelve," Anthony explains. "We needed more people in the work force. That means they need the ability to drive."

"How old are you?" I ask him, and wince at the pain in my tired legs.

"Twenty-six."

Jenna snickers. "Anthony's so old he used to ride a train to school."

"Just because you're legally an adult," Anthony says to her, "doesn't mean you have the maturity of one. Trains stopped running over a hundred years ago."

I look over the railing and grip it hard. So many stairs.

Anthony and Jenna continue to verbally assault each other as we hurry down the steps, but neither one seems to be offended. They make me think of how a brother and sister might interact, and I wonder if there's someone I'm close to in the world. This thought creates a pit in my stomach.

It takes us fifteen minutes to reach the bottom. My muscles scream, but I won't show how exhausted I am. I need to be strong for these people who are helping me. Anthony opens a door, and a gust of wind nearly takes my hat off.

"Hold on, Patch," Jenna says and laughs. "You might blow away."

I press the hat to my head, and choke at the coldness of the air as it rushes into my lungs. The streets are clean and shiny, almost as if they've been polished, and thin strips of grass and trees on each side of the street have been meticulously groomed. Every few seconds a car, sleek in design, drives by. Everything looks perfect. No blemishes. No scars.

"Where's your car?" Anthony asks.

She points to the corner. "And don't even think you're going to drive, old man. I don't want you getting crusties all over my seats."

"Let's hurry," he says.

I walk faster to catch up, but Jenna lags behind, staring longingly at a clothing store across the street. Inside the glass window, a mannequin wears a long black dress that's open on the sides. It sparkles with jewelry.

Anthony and I reach the car unnoticed. Only a handful of people are on the streets and most of them look uninterested in us.

Except one.

A man across the street with blond hair. He's facing our direction, leaning against a light post. He doesn't look much older than me. I wish I could see his eyes.

Anthony attempts to wait patiently for Jenna, but his hand is gripping the handle of the door tightly. "Take your time, Jenna!

We're in no rush," he calls. His gaze flickers to the lone man.

"Life's too short to rush," Jenna says when she reaches the car. As soon as she touches the driver's side door, something clicks, and she opens it. Anthony opens the passenger door and motions me into the backseat. I scramble in and turn around to look at the man. He's gone.

"Drive," he says. "Fast."

Jenna doesn't question. The car's engine comes to life when she wraps her hands around the steering wheel. The tires don't squeal as the car shoots forward.

"Drive six blocks then backtrack to The Rapture."

She does as he says, never saying a word. I glance behind us several times, not able to tell one pair of headlights from another.

"Pull into the alley and park," Anthony says.

Jenna drives into the dark alleyway and parks next to a shiny metal container the size of a small tree. The top of it reads, "Waste." There is nothing else around us. The long strip of space between the two shiny metal buildings is free of clutter and debris.

At Anthony's insistence we wait in the car until he feels it's safe for us to go. Several minutes of darkness and silence pass, turning the air into a heavy pressure on my chest. It's as if the whole space has swollen like an invisible bubble that seems to smother my face. Sweat breaks on my brow, and my breaths become shorter and shorter. An image of a sealed coffin comes to my mind, making my heart race. I try to calm down, but the suffocating feeling only grows.

I place my hand on the door handle, ready to burst free from the vehicle, but Jenna's voice stops me.

"You're being paranoid, Anthony. I'm going in." She opens the door and closes it behind her without waiting for a response.

Anthony sighs but follows after. He opens my door and startles at the sight of me. "Are you okay?"

I jump from the car and take a deep breath. Air fills my lungs, pushing away the smothering blackness. "I'm okay. Just nervous."

"Don't worry. Just keep your head down and stay close."

The alley is quiet, but as soon as Jenna opens a side door into the silver building next to us, I'm accosted by loud music—a beat that matches my heart rate. I inch closer to Jenna until I run into her.

She shrugs me off. "Personal space here, Patch. What's your problem?" She walks though the door, her eyebrows drawn together.

Anthony shakes his head. "Don't worry about Jenna. She's been through a lot, and it's made her rather cold toward others. I know that shouldn't be an excuse, but believe me, she's better than most."

The inside of the Rapture is dark, occasionally lit up by flashing lights. It's a big space with high ceilings. Tables line the walls, each one holding a single candle with a very realistic flame. Jenna nudges me and points up. I follow the direction and flinch when flames suddenly engulf the ceiling. Jenna laughs, and I realize these flames are fake too, a special kind of hologram. They flicker and jump like real fire, but when I walk beneath them there's no heat. Then they disappear as if extinguished only to return moments later.

Anthony finds what is probably the only empty table in the whole place pressed against a shiny steel-looking wall. It's black and narrow with two square, metal stools on each side. "You girls wait here. I need to find Bram."

"I want to go too," Jenna says. She's on her tiptoes, trying to look over the heads of the nearby crowd as if searching for someone she might know.

"No. I don't know if he will be alone. You need to stay and watch . . ." He looks at me and hesitates as if he's not sure what to call me. Finally, he says, "Patch."

He disappears into a dark tunnel to my right before Jenna can argue, but as she drops onto the stool, she says, "I'm not a bloody babysitter."

"You don't have to stay with me," I say, growing tired of her attitude.

She rolls her eyes. "Yeah, right. We're going to have to watch you like we would a baby. And wipe your nose and change your diapers. Poor, poor Patch."

Heat rushes to my face. I've never been spoken to that rudely.

I don't think anyway, but if I have, I'm pretty sure I didn't take it.

I lean over the table and say, "I mean it. I don't need you. I escaped from the Institute without you holding my baby hand, didn't I?"

Jenna smirks. "Look who suddenly has a backbone? And you're right. I didn't hold your hand, nor would I ever want to. I'm out." She stands and says over her shoulder, "Wait here."

I stare after her, wishing my glare would burn a hole in her back. She disappears into the swarms of people, bouncing up and down like she plans on having the time of her life. I lean back against the cold steel wall and cross my arms to my chest. Periodically a flash of light shines into the crowd, and I think I catch sight of the back of Jenna's blonde hair.

I pull my hat further down over my forehead to shade my eyes and survey the people in the room, specifically looking at their eyes. Most of them glow a bright maple color, but others flash a bright green, yellow, and even purple. I'm instantly afraid of the ones who don't flash gold, but I'm not sure why. I slide my hands into the sleeves of the black shirt, and hunch lower into the seat, wishing I could melt into the hard metal.

All of a sudden I shiver, the kind of shiver that makes me know I'm being watched. I look around to find the reason for the hair on my arms standing to attention. Across the room is the tall, dark outline of a man. Lights flash over him, illuminating electric blue eyes, making me think of lightning. I feel the power in them as strong as thunder. He sees me watching him and moves forward.

Straight for me.

CHAPTER 5

He moves slowly, deliberately.

I search the crowd, my fingernails digging into the bottom of the chair, but it's metal and doesn't give. Jenna and Anthony are nowhere to be seen. I look back at the approaching man, hoping an instinct will kick in as to what I should do. Nothing comes. Maybe he's harmless, I hope. But the way he's moving through the crowd, not touching anyone, slipping through them like a ghost, makes me doubtful.

I stand up, contemplating my options. Follow Jenna into a crowd of dangerous people or after Anthony into a black tunnel? Despite my earlier aversion to being in a dark space in the car, I decide to follow Anthony.

I move to take a step, but the man is suddenly upon me, his hands on my shoulders, pressing me to the wall. The stool is in my way, making my feet slip, but I don't fall because he's too strong. I stare at the ground, afraid to let him see my eyes.

He takes hold of my chin with a cold and firm grip. "Look at me," he says.

When I begin to struggle he presses harder on my shoulders until I cry out in pain.

"Look at me or you'll regret it." His voice holds a threatening note all the way to his fingertips.

Because nothing comes to me as to what I should do next, I do what any sane, life-wanting person would do: obey. I stop struggling and slowly meet his gaze. His incandescent blue eyes hold even more power this close, and a shiver shakes my whole body, but he doesn't notice.

"Your eyes," he says, frowning. "Are you an Original?"

I don't answer. I'm too afraid of being sent back to the Institute.

He glances all around us while still maintaining his tight grip. "Who sent you? Is this a test? Answer me!"

I gasp when the pressure on my shoulders becomes too great. "You're hurting me!"

He searches my eyes, his dark eyebrows drawn together. The rest of his face is shadowed from the lights above, or maybe that's just what he is—an extension of the darkness, some abnormality that shouldn't exist.

His grip lightens, but he still holds me against the wall. "Why are you here?"

I try to look beyond him, hoping to see Anthony or Jenna, but he is blocking my view of anything else. A thought comes to me, not so much an instinct, but more common sense. He is a man after all.

I bring my knee up between his legs hard. His steel blue eyes widen, and he falls to the floor moaning. I scramble around him and dive into the crowd of moving bodies that's like a turbulent river, twisting and swirling. I spin around until I'm spit out the other side, next to a bar lit up by the same illusion of fire that's on the ceiling.

The music is louder here, and it vibrates my insides. Someone grabs my arm. I breathe a sigh of relief, thinking it's Jenna by the smaller grip, but when I turn around there's a girl with black, spiked hair. I think it's spiked anyway, but as I look closer I notice that the four-inch spikes are actually horns lining the center of her head all the way down to the back of her neck. Her eyes shine nothing, only blackness, and this lone fact, not the spikes on her head, terrifies me to the bone.

"Sorry, I thought you were someone else," she says and is about to let go of my arm, but at the last second she sees my face. "Hey, what's wrong with you?"

I stutter as I try to think of something to say.

She frowns and her eyes turn darker, if that's possible. "I think someone's looking for you."

"She's with me," a voice says from behind. The voice is loud enough to be heard over the blaring music.

I spin around, almost running into the man who had me pinned to the wall moments ago. He's standing beneath a glowing light now, revealing that he's just a regular man, or really a boy. He looks only a little older than me, with hair as black as the shadows he just came from. He's tall and wearing a long, dark leather trench coat that fits him snugly across his wide shoulders. Like everyone else, his skin is flawless, but I do discover a flaw amongst his perfectly broad chin and high cheekbones. His nose. It's crooked. I find it oddly comforting to find fault in a world that seems so perfect.

"How can she be with you?" The horned girl says, sneering. "You're never with anyone. And what's with her eyes?"

"She's tripping on something. Addict." The muscles on the side of his face bulge, exposing a dark vein running the length of his neck. He looks ready for a fight.

I remain quiet, not sure how to react. My instincts, however, know to stay away from the girl with the horns.

"Let's go," he says and faces me the other direction. To the other girl, he says, "See you around, Spit."

I don't look back and let the boy push me back into the waves of people. I keep my eyes down. I can't forget that I don't belong here.

When we reach a break in the crowd, I spin around and say, "I have to go back to the table."

He shakes his head and continues to push me across the room and to the entrance of a long hallway. He's strong, stronger than a normal man. I sense it in the way his arm is nudging me forward, gentle like he's afraid I'll break in two if he's not careful. I bet if he wanted he could toss me to the other side of the room. I have to find Anthony.

"Stop, please!" I say again.

He cuts in front of me so fast that I stumble back. "It's not safe here for someone like you, don't you understand? What are you even doing here?"

His features have softened, but there's still a sharp edge. The kind only deep pain creates. I wonder if I have the same expression on my face because I feel pain inside me too, but don't know what's created it.

He sees my hesitation and possibly my fear. "I'm not going to hurt you. I'm not like them." He motions to the crowd over my shoulder.

"Then what are you?" Words are all I have to go by with this boy. I'm hoping I'll be able to discern the truth.

He frowns, like he's not sure how to answer the question. "I'm just me," he says. "I don't belong in this world. Neither do they. But you"—he swallows, his Adam's apple going up and down—"you belong."

But I don't belong, I want to say. Not even close. Instead I blurt, "I escaped from the Institute. A man named Anthony brought me here so he could talk to someone named Bram."

The boy stiffens and clenches his jaw. "Come on," he says. He guides me into the same dark hallway Anthony disappeared into moments ago. It smells like sweat and fresh paint, and the air is sticky like it's been sitting too long with nowhere to go.

The boy stops at a door and swings it open wide without knocking. "Did you lose something?"

Anthony turns around. His eyes go from me to the boy.

"How could you leave her alone out there?" the boy asks.

"Calm down, Colt," Anthony says. "She wasn't alone. Jenna's with her."

Colt looks around sarcastically. "Do you see her anywhere?"

"Where's Jenna?" Anthony asks me.

"She had to go do something, but I'm fine. It's okay."

Colt scowls. "It's not fine. Spit saw her."

Anthony's eyebrows lift, and he looks at a man who is sitting behind a desk. "Bram?"

Bram, who looks a little younger than Anthony, rises. He's not tall, but he's well built and has eyes a soft caramel color. He circles around his desk and comes toward me. I back up.

"Don't worry, girl. I mean you no harm." He grips my chin lightly and stares into my eyes. "Remarkable." He lets go and steps back. "You must protect her no matter what happens. It's up to you. I can't help. I'm sorry."

"What? Why? That's why I came here!" Anthony says.

Bram shakes his head. "The Institute is watching my every move, even at my house. She's not safe with me."

"Then what am I supposed to do?"

"Leave. Right away. If Spit's seen her, then others may be on their way." He goes to his desk and scribbles on a piece of paper. "Go to this address. You'll be safe there for a short time."

He tears the paper in half and writes something else on the bottom portion. "And here's the code to get in. You keep one and give the other to Jenna. I'll contact you soon with where to go next and how we can get her to Eden."

My head snaps up. "Eden?"

Something about the name sparks a fleeting memory. I struggle to hang on to it, and then, just like that, it's gone.

Bram gives the papers to Anthony who, in turn, gives one to Colt instead of waiting for Jenna.

Colt raises his hands, refusing to take it. "Whoa! I can't take that. I'm staying out of this."

Anthony says, "Colt, I need your help. She needs you."

"Sorry, but you've got the wrong person."

"No, we don't. You brought her here. You could've just as easily taken her to the Institute and received a huge reward."

Colt steps toward the door. "I can't just pack up and go."

"Why not? What's holding you here?" Anthony asks.

The room is quiet yet loud at the same time. I don't know what to think. Colt had felt so threatening before. Had he really been trying to help me?

Bram sits down. "Why would you trust him, Anthony?"

Colt glares at him. "I can be trusted."

"Then prove it," Anthony says. The room goes from heavy to aggressive.

The tension breaks when Jenna appears in the doorway. "There you are, Patch! I've been looking everywhere for you."

Anthony grabs her arm. "Why did you leave her? What were you thinking?"

She shakes his hand off. "She told me to. Said she could take care of herself." She notices Colt. "Maybe I shouldn't have left. I didn't realize a snitch was in the house."

I take a small step back; my stomach churns as I realize that two people now have both said they don't trust Colt. I need to keep my guard up with him.

Colt moves toward Jenna, but Anthony steps between them. "We have bigger things to worry about, Jenna. Spit saw her."

Fear replaces her smirk. "Then what are we waiting for? Let's bolt."

Anthony turns and addresses Colt one last time. "Are you going to help?"

Colt hesitates, probably afraid. They probably all are. I may not know them well, but I know their lives aren't any more valuable than mine.

I clear my throat before I speak. "It's okay. He doesn't have to come. None of you do. You've already helped me so much. I don't want you putting your lives at risk anymore. If you can just give me directions to get out of the city and to this place called Eden, I can make it on my own."

The room does the whole quiet/loud thing again, and I squirm under their intense stares. Colt's stare is especially uncomfortable, like he's seeing beyond my eyes and all the way inside me to a place I don't even know about.

"Let's go. Now," Colt says, making me think he saw something.

CHAPTER 6

After leaving Bram's office and hurrying down the hall, Anthony pushes open a back door leading into a different alleyway than the one we parked in. It's as clean as the one before and smells like lilac bushes. I look around for them but see none.

"Wait here," Anthony says and jogs to the corner of the building.

I stand close to Colt and Jenna, glancing sideways at Colt. He's looking down the alleyway, opposite of Anthony. His whole body is alert and tense.

"Thanks," I say to him, my voice low.

"Don't thank him just yet," Jenna mutters, and again I wonder what Colt has done to make her hate him so much.

Anthony jogs back. "The Institute is here."

"How many vehicles?" Colt asks.

"Just two, but more will be coming. Jenna, can you bring your car back here?"

"On it." She sprints down the long alleyway the way we just came.

My head spins, and I nearly stumble as I realize how close to the truth my earlier statement was—their lives are at risk because of me. "Anthony, I mean it. Just tell me where to go. I can find my own way."

"Nonsense. You would never make it. At least not until your memory comes back."

"Where do you think she came from?" Colt asks, his voice low.

Anthony rolls his shoulders back trying to relieve tension in them. "From a raid. Nothing else makes sense."

"Raid?" I don't like how the word fits in my mouth.

Colt's shaking his head. "But they didn't find anyone at the last one. At least that's what I was told."

"When was their last raid?" I ask. My stomach feels rotten and twisted inside. I inhale deeply to smell the lilacs.

"A month ago," Colt says.

"Do you think—"

"It wasn't you," Colt interrupts. "No one was there." The way he says it, all forceful, makes me think he's trying to convince himself more than me.

"Then where did I come from? Where did the boy come from?"

"What boy?" Colt asks.

I explain about the boy, remembering how he had held me around the neck. With every word, the sick feeling in my gut spreads until I think I might throw up.

"I talked to Bram about the child," Anthony says. "He knows someone at the Institute who will find out more."

"Can I stay in the city until I know he's safe?" I ask.

"No. It's best we get you to Eden as soon as possible."

"Eden," I say. "You said it before. What is it?"

"The only safe place for Originals. Its location is secret. I don't even know where it is."

The sounds of tires squeal from around the corner. I expect to see Jenna's car, but it isn't. Not even close.

CHAPTER 7

A vehicle approaches us fast. It's a small sports car that looks as liquid as black ink. Beneath a streetlight, the metal shimmers, making me think it can change its shape.

"Run!" Anthony grabs my arm and pulls me forward, but within a few steps I'm already ahead of him, fear overriding my stiff muscles. Colt is faster and leads the way deeper into the alley.

"Where do I go?" Colt calls.

"Ashton Street," Anthony says.

"See you soon!" Colt turns into an adjacent alley, leaving us alone.

I stay close to Anthony, my heart pounding louder than the sound of my over-sized shoes slapping against the shiny pavement. One of them flies off, almost tripping me, and I quickly abandon the other and run barefoot.

The shimmering vehicle is almost on us when out of nowhere Jenna's car appears, blocking its path. I expect to hear metal crunching against metal, but when I look back the hood of the ink-colored car looks like it's buckling even though it hasn't touched anything. It must be the cars reaction to stopping suddenly.

"Get in!" Jenna yells.

I barely get the door closed before tires are clawing at the road again. I wonder if they'll leave a mark against the perfectly constructed pavement. Anthony and I look back at the black car. It's following behind us dangerously close.

"It's just a tag," he says. "I don't think anyone's in it."

"But how do we lose it?" Jenna asks.

Anthony swivels forward in the passenger seat, rubbing the

back of his neck, but doesn't say anything. I'm still staring at the vehicle; its hood shimmers again as if it knows I'm watching. There's something familiar about its behavior. I think hard until my brain hurts.

"We need a charging station," I say. Another instinct.

"What are you spouting?" Jenna asks, eyeing me in the rear-view mirror.

"A charging station. You know, for cars. Surely there are some around here."

Jenna lets out an exaggerated sigh. "Balls, Patch! Of course I know what a charging station is, but what good will that do?"

"If we can reverse the cables and shock the power system in your car—"

"It will reboot the whole system, dropping the tracking," Anthony finishes, his voice excited.

Jenna turns a corner sharply. "And you say you can't remember anything. Are you messing with us?"

"I can't explain it. I don't have control over the things that come back to me."

Anthony taps on a lit-up screen on the dashboard. "Talk about it later. Let's just get to a charging station before a real vehicle with a lot of angry Institute employees shows up."

"Sure thing, boss," Jenna says, swerving the car left. She swats at Anthony's hand. "Quit messing with that thing. I know where I'm going."

In a matter of minutes she pulls up to what looks like a closed auto repair store. Out front is a metal box that says: "Free Charge."

Anthony's out the door before the car comes to a complete stop. I open mine and hesitate. The shimmering black car has followed us into the parking lot. Its headlights bathe us in an accusing glow.

"Hey, Patch!" Anthony calls. "I'm not sure if I know what I'm doing."

I jog over and inspect the box. It's a shiny silver with a red button on its side. Only one cord comes out of it, a metal clamp at its end.

"We need to open it," I say.

"How?" Jenna asks next to me.

Anthony runs his hands all around the box. "It's solid."

"So bust it open," Jenna says. "And hurry. We probably have less than a minute."

Anthony straightens and sucks air into his lungs in a slow inhale. He holds his breath for a few seconds and then, in a lightning-quick move, smashes his fist into the side of the box. The metal buckles under the pressure.

I jump, startled by the violent action.

"Again," Jenna says.

Anthony duplicates the process and on his exhale punches a hole right through the metal. He reaches in with his hands and begins to tear at the box until there's a gaping hole in the back.

He wipes sweat from his brow with the back of his hand and says, "Now what?"

"Impressive," I say and bend over to peer inside. There are two small metal squares side-by-side with wires attached to each of them. On one of them is a plus sign, and on the other a negative. I need to switch the negative charge with the positive.

"Attach the charging clip to your car," I say to Jenna while I set to the task of switching the wires. It takes me a few seconds to locate the right ones, a green and yellow wire. They come apart easily, and I reattach them into the other's location. After double-checking my work, I say, "Press the button."

Just as Anthony reaches to touch it, I shout, "Wait!"

Inside, at the back of one of the small boxes, I notice a white switch. I flip it up. Had I not done this, I would've fried Jenna's car. "Okay, now!"

Anthony pushes the button but nothing happens. At the same time there's a humming sound, faint at first, but definitely growing closer.

"They're coming!" Jenna says. "Why isn't the car rebooting?"

Anthony rushes over to where the metal clamp is attached to Jenna's bumper and wiggles it around. "Try it again."

I hit the button and look up expectantly. The sound beyond the buildings in front of us grows louder, and the ground rumbles beneath my feet. I'm not sure what's approaching, but my racing pulse tells me I don't want to find out.

Just then Jenna's car powers down. A few seconds later, lights flicker and come back to life.

"Get in," Jenna says.

I'm already halfway into the car. The sound approaching is almost deafening. I expect to see some giant machine on wheels rounding the corner at any second.

"Let's see if your little stunt worked," Jenna mumbles as she presses on the gas.

The car darts forward, leaving the parking lot. Anthony and I turn around to watch the tracker car. It doesn't follow.

Jenna laughs. "I can't believe that worked! Maybe you're not the dummy I thought you were."

"Just drive," Anthony says before I can say anything. "Fast." He's still watching behind us. After a few blocks he turns back around. "That was close."

I shake my head, bothered by something. "We may have gotten away, but won't the tracker have already sent information about this vehicle to the Institute? They may have already traced it back to Jenna."

"Not mine," she says. "It's my mom's and registered to her old boyfriend's address. We also have different last names."

Anthony taps his fingers against a center console; they leave prints against a shiny surface. "She's right, though. It's only a matter of time before they discover your mother has a child. They'll start an investigation and discover who you are."

"Then I'll report the car stolen. This might surprise you, but I am a wonderful actress."

"That might work," Anthony says and lets out a long sigh as if he's just realizing how complicated getting me out of the city will be. I really hate that I'm so dependent upon them. They're taking huge risks for me, a perfect stranger. Somehow I need to find a way to repay them.

After a few seconds of silence, I ask, "What was coming toward us? The rumbling?"

Jenna and Anthony exchange glances.

"The Institute," he says. "They come with one of their massive transport vehicles. It has to be very large to hold their soldiers."

"The trollmobile," Jenna says. "Packed with mutants."

I remember the tall beast in the hospital. "Monstrous chests and small legs?"

"Yes, that sounds right. How did you know?" Anthony asks and swivels around in his seat to look at me.

"There was one at the Institute where they were holding me."

"And you got away from him?" Jenna asks, her eyes wide in the rearview mirror.

I nod and sink into the seat.

They're quiet for a minute until Jenna says, "So how'd you know to do that thing with the charger?"

"I don't know."

"Come on, Patch," she says, "You can tell us. We're pals now, right?"

I don't say anything because I'm not sure how I feel about her, but we're definitely not pals.

Her eyes narrow in the mirror. "I think you know more than you're saying."

"Leave her alone," Anthony says staring out the window. "She's had a difficult day."

That is one way to put it, I guess. I ignore Jenna and ask him, "How did you smash through that box?"

He keeps his back to me as he speaks. "All of us with gold eyes have some kind of genetically enhanced ability, some more than others. I can exert great strength but only in short bursts. Any longer back there and my arm would've given out."

"What about you?" I ask Jenna.

Her jaw tightens then relaxes. "Let's just say that when they were handing out special abilities from the DNA pot, I got the crud on the bottom that has to be scraped off."

"That's not true," Anthony says. "Your ability has helped us many times."

"Whatever." Jenna's quiet after this.

I stare at the back of their heads, wondering what it would be like to have a special gift, something that sets you apart from others. "What about Colt?"

Jenna chuckles. "Colt's a real freak, a one-of-a-kind. Where is he anyway?"

"He's meeting us there," Anthony says.

"But doesn't he have the code to get us in?" Jenna asks.

"Yes."

Although they didn't answer my question, I stay quiet, listening to their conversation.

"And you trust him to show up?" Jenna asks again.

"He'll be there."

Jenna snorts. "You have too much faith in him."

"Some would say I put too much faith in you."

She laughs like it's the dumbest thing she's ever heard.

"Why don't you like him?" I ask.

"He betrayed us," she says.

"What did he do?"

"Enough," Anthony says. "It doesn't matter. He's different now."

"Sure he is. If you ask me, he's just a typical Noc. Not even their own mothers trust them."

I lean forward. "What's a Noc?"

Jenna glances back at me. "A Nocturnal. Their DNA has been mixed with—"

"Turn here!" Anthony says, startling Jenna. She turns the wheel hard, and I slide sideways along the leather backseat.

"Park in that alleyway," Anthony points to her left.

She pulls in and turns off the lights. We sit in the darkness. The only sound is my breathing, which begins to quicken. I focus on my sore muscles to provide a distraction from what feels like a heavy blanket wrapping around my chest and smothering my face.

"So how long do we wait?" Jenna asks.

"He'll be here," Anthony says.

Just then a crashing sound rattles the top of the car, and I lay flat, afraid the roof might collapse.

"What the?" Jenna says and peers upward out the window. She moans loudly. "I'm going to kill him!"

Jenna exits the car. I'm slower to go out, since I'm trying to catch my breath.

Colt jumps from the roof of her car onto the ground while he pushes his arm through the sleeve of his long jacket and pulls it the rest of the way around him.

"You are so dead," Jenna says, storming over to him. "Look at my car!"

Colt glances at a dent in her roof. He doesn't grin, but there's a twinkle in his eye. "Did I do that?"

I look at the crumpled metal then look up. The building next to us is at least twenty stories high. Where did he come from?

"I hate you," Jenna says. She reaches into her car and presses a button near the ceiling. I back away at a sudden humming sound. The metal on the top of the car vibrates for a few seconds before the roof smooths itself back to normal. I stare in awe.

"Pretty cool, huh?" Colt asks. His tone is light, but he still wears a serious expression like he's expecting a fight at any moment. I wonder if he knows how to smile.

"Over here," Anthony calls. While I wasn't watching, he'd moved to the end of the alleyway.

I follow after him. It's dark, but I don't have to worry about tripping over anything. The alley is also freakishly spotless, making me uncomfortable.

Behind me Jenna says to Colt, "Just give us the slip of paper so you can leave. I know you don't want to be here."

"You don't know what I want," Colt says. "You never have."

"Oh please. As if you've ever wanted anything beyond food and money. You're the shallowest person I've ever met."

"Better shallow than a narcissistic drama queen."

"Be quiet, you two," Anthony says, over his shoulder. "We're here."

I look around, searching for our destination. A quiet street lies in front of us, and on each side are more of the same tall rectangular buildings. Perfectly neat and orderly. In some of these, faint light of those still awake shines out tinted windows.

"Where?" Jenna asks.

Anthony walks around the corner and stops at the shiny side of a smooth metal building.

"There's no door," Jenna says.

"The symbol," Colt says behind us. "Eden."

I follow Colt's gaze. Just above my line of sight there's a small drawing etched into the metal: a wide tree with full branches, twisting and curling. Two of the branches make a complete circle around the tree. Anthony runs his finger over the symbol. A blue light appears at the ground and races up to make the shape of a door. Beneath the circle a keypad appears.

"Read the numbers," Anthony says.

Colt reaches into his pocket and removes the slip of paper Bram had given him. While he reads, Anthony punches in the numbers. "33, 14, 74, 21, 16."

The door opens.

CHAPTER 8

I nside, hurry," Anthony says and glances around.
I walk in first to the darkened entryway. A smell reminds
me of cranberries.

Jenna elbows me out of the way and says, "Move it, Patch."

Anthony's voice sounds through the darkness when the others
have come in and the door has closed behind us. "Lights on."

The room lights up. It's spacious, more so than I expected. The
walls are a pale green. Simple, square-shaped furniture fill a large
living room. The others walk past me.

An office is to my left. I glance in, careful to inspect the place
that is to protect me from the Institute. A lone brown desk sits in
front of a giant picture hanging behind it. It's of a man with dark
hair, light brown, normal-to-me eyes, and a smile. He is an Original, like me. Something about his smile draws me in. While the
others explore the rest of the apartment, I continue to stare at the
portrait. The painting is encased by a heavy silver frame. At the
bottom a plaque reads "Howard P. O. Edmonds." I grimace. The
name feels off. He doesn't look like a Howard. I move closer and
reach up, my fingers tracing the lines on the man's face.

"What are you doing?"

I turn around. Colt is standing in the doorway. He removes
his long jacket and tosses it into an empty chair. In this faint light,
his black hair shows a hint of red.

"This man," I say. "Do you know him?"

He's quiet for a moment before answering. "He's an Original
and a brilliant scientist. He's been trying to find a cure for us for
years."

"He looks familiar." I keep looking at the man, waiting for my memory to unfold itself and reveal my life, but it remains locked.

"So you really don't remember anything?" Colt walks into the room.

His powerful presence sends a chill up my spine the same way it did at the Rapture. I admit, it frightens me a little so I subtly step away from him.

"I feel memories floating around," I say, "but there's a fog preventing me from seeing them. Does that make sense?"

"It's the drug." His eyes flicker to my arm, then move to my hands, which are still raw from gripping the cables. "You must be exhausted. Why don't you get some rest?"

"So what are we supposed to do here?" Jenna says from the hallway.

"Wait," Anthony responds. "Go find a book to read."

He walks into the office with Colt and me. Jenna lets out an exaggerated sigh as she follows after him.

"Hey, Colt," she says when she sees us by the painting. "Feeling guilty?"

"Shut up," he says to her.

I turn to Colt. "Have you met him?"

The muscles around his jaw bulge. "No."

"How about you, Anthony?"

He's quiet for a few seconds then says, "I met him once."

Colt tilts his head then points at the bottom of the painting. "Look at his name."

"Howard O. P. Edmonds," Jenna reads, looking over our shoulders. "So? It's a dumb name."

"Read it again," he says.

I say it in my mind. And then I get it. "Hope," I say.

Anthony turns to me. "What did you say?"

"The first letter in each name spells 'hope.' Is that what you're talking about?" I glance at each one of them. By their silence and the way their eyes are connecting, I feel like I'm missing something.

"This is stupid," Jenna says. "I'm getting something to eat."

Anthony calls over his shoulder, "Do it quick. We may have to leave at a moment's notice."

"Patch needs to rest," Colt says. The name Jenna gave me sounds so wrong on his lips.

Anthony looks at me as if waiting for me to agree with Colt, but I don't say anything. I want nothing more than to sleep, but if it isn't safe, I won't complain.

When I don't answer, Anthony leaves the room saying, "We'll rest until dawn, but then we've got to go."

From the kitchen Jenna says, "We can't just leave, Anthony. Our lives are here, our jobs."

"You don't have to come, but this is what I've devoted what little life I have left to. You know that."

Colt leaves me to join them, but I stay back, lingering in the doorway of the office, unsure if I should be listening to what feels like a personal conversation. The three of them stand together, looking like a small family.

"But you can't just leave me!" Jenna says. "What will I do?"

Anthony smiles. "I'm sure you'll find someone else to irritate."

"But I want to irritate you."

"Then you'll have to make a decision. What about you, Colt? I could use your help."

He shrugs. "I've got nothing better to do."

"Oh great," Jenna says. "Now I have to go. Someone has to protect you from him. He might betray you."

"Stop that," Anthony says, scolding her like a father would.

I leave the man in the portrait and join the others in the living room.

"What about the boy?" I ask, remembering the way he had screamed when the Institute took him away.

"Who?" Jenna asks.

"There was a boy in the hospital with me. Just a child."

"Don't worry," Anthony says. "Bram will figure it out, but my responsibility is to you. We'll get you to Eden where you'll be safe."

He disappears into a doorway, which I assume leads to a bedroom.

I think of the boy, how scared he must be feeling right now. I hope he's okay.

Jenna returns to the kitchen. "There's pizza. You hungry?"

"Cook two, I'm starving," Colt says.

"I wasn't asking you," she says. "Patch, you, hungry?"

I nod, my stomach tight with hunger pains.

Anthony returns carrying blankets. "There's two beds in the bedroom. Jenna and Patch can sleep in there. Colt and I can sleep on the couches."

"Actually," I say, "can I sleep in the office?" For some reason I want to be near the man in the painting.

"Are you sure?"

I nod. Out of the corner of my eye I sense Colt watching me. I resist the urge to look over and instead go into the kitchen to help Jenna.

"Here," she says and hands me a long, metal tube. "You can cook it."

I turn the device over in my hands, trying to figure out what I am holding.

Jenna removes a pizza from a refrigerator and places it on the counter. "Get to it," she says. "I'm starving."

"Right." I look at the rod again, pushing all around it, but nothing happens. I try touching the end of it to the edge of the pizza, thinking maybe it will sense the dough or something. Really, I have no idea what I'm doing.

Jenna laughs. "Serious? You can break out of the most secure place in the country, but you can't cook a pizza?" She takes it from me. "What is wrong with you?"

I step back, too hurt to think of a comeback. I wish I knew what was wrong with me.

Jenna raises the rod horizontally above the pizza and tightens her hand. A blue light appears along the length of the metal. She scans it across the thick layer of dough and cheese three times. By the time she's done, the pizza is cooked. She glances back at me. "Was that so hard?"

Colt walks into the kitchen and pushes past her to cut a slice of pizza. "Why do you have to be such a conker, Jenna?"

I'm not familiar with the term, but by Jenna's reddening face, I know it's an insult.

"Don't call me that," she says.

Colt takes a bite. "Then stop acting like one."

Anthony looks up from an electronic device in his hands. "Hurry and eat and then get to bed. You're going to need all the rest you can get."

"Better do what he says and eat," Colt says to me. "And fast before Jenna wolfs the whole pizza. In addition to being a conker, she's a huge porker."

Before I can respond, both Colt and I are ducking from a flying cup. It hits the wall behind us.

"Jenna!" Anthony says.

"Did you hear what he just called me?" she says, another cup gripped tightly in her hand.

Anthony sighs. "The last thing I need right now is to supervise a bunch of kids. Grow up, both of you."

"Whatever." Jenna takes a plate of food and walks into the bedroom. She slams the door behind her.

Colt chuckles, but still there's no smile.

"I expect more from you," Anthony says as he passes by Colt on his way to the kitchen.

Colt mumbles something through a bite of pizza in his mouth.

Anthony takes a slice of pizza into the living room and sits on a chair in front of a paper and pen. Every few seconds he scribbles a word like he's making a list of some kind.

I stay where I'm at, standing beneath a fluorescent light. Their interactions are so strange to me, yet familiar somehow.

"Here," Colt says and gives me one of his slices. He walks away and sits across from Anthony.

I quickly take a bite to prevent a long string of cheese from falling to the ground. As soon as I taste it, my stomach demands more. I eat three more slices, careful of the open blisters on my hands. The heat from the pizza stings my open wounds. When I'm finished I turn and see Anthony and Colt staring at me.

"How long has it been since you last ate?" Anthony asks.

"Ebony gave me pudding earlier today. I don't remember if I was given anything before that."

Anthony shakes his head. "Maybe it's best if you don't remember. The Institute is known for its cruelty."

Colt sets his plate of his half-eaten pizza slice on the cushion next to him and returns to the kitchen. He looks inside several cupboards, shoving cans of food this way and that, until he removes a small white box.

"This will work," he says. "Come here, Patch."

I hesitate because I hate that name.

"You can choose a different name if you'd like," he says as if he's read my mind.

I go to him. "It's fine, I guess. There are worse things then being named after a dog, right?"

His eyes meet mine. "You're hardly a dog. Give me your hands."

I don't move. I'm too distracted by an unfamiliar feeling in my gut. It's like my stomach has flipped in the most pleasurable way, warming my insides.

"Your hands," he says again. "I need to put medicine on them."

"Oh," I say and open my right palm.

"Those look bad." He twists a lid on a small tube and squeezes a clear, gelatinous substance out the tip. "Rub that around, and then get your other hand."

I do as he says, trying my best not to flinch as the medicine is burning something fierce.

"It hurts at first, but it really speeds up the healing process," he says.

I meet his gaze. His blue eyes seem to shimmer, reminding me of the colors of the inside of a shell just beneath a tide pool.

A tide pool.

I remember the ocean. The sounds, the smell.

"What is it?" he asks.

Realizing I'm still staring, I glance away. "The ocean. I think I lived by the ocean."

"You're getting your memory back," he says and hands me the ointment. "Put a lot on."

"Thank you."

Ten minutes later I'm lying on the floor in the office, staring at the man in the painting.

"You don't have to sleep on the floor," Anthony says as he walks in.

"It's okay. I don't mind at all."

He squats down. "Everything's going to be okay, I promise. Soon you'll remember who you are, and we'll be out of the city and on our way to Eden. And who knows? Maybe you'll know someone there."

"Maybe."

He straightens. "Get some sleep."

Before he turns off the light manually, I say, "Thank you, Anthony. For helping me."

"You're welcome."

The lights go off. As soon as they do, a soft glow appears at the base of the floor near the door. I can barely make out the outline of the man in the painting. I close my eyes and see him. His brown eyes, the slight smile. I think I hear him laugh. This makes me think of Colt, whom I don't think knows how to laugh, and I wonder why Jenna hates him so much. I remember his eyes and think again of the ocean.

This is what I'm thinking of when I fall asleep. In my dreams I feel the ocean's foam swirling around my ankles, cooling my skin. Waves crash to shore, tirelessly battering the earth. There's a forest nearby with old, tall trees. I run into it laughing. There's someone else there too, chasing me. They giggle. It's a child's laugh.

But then there is no laughter.

I'm with someone else and we're boxing. It's a faceless man. He's teaching me to fight. Where to punch, where to kick. I'm tired, but I can't stop. There's a sense of urgency pushing me harder and faster.

The scene changes; I'm back at the ocean. Resting, watching waves crest and then fall. They never give up their motion. The sand is cool between my toes when I curl them. I'm not alone. The giggling child is here too. It's a boy. A beautiful boy as still and serene as the forest at our backs. I feel such pride when I look at him. Such love.

My heart stops beating, and I wake up screaming. Anthony and Colt come rushing into the office, both of them commanding the lights on.

"What is it?" Anthony says. "What's wrong?"

I look at the man in the painting; there's a pain in my heart so great I think I'll crumble into pieces.

"I'm so sorry," I say, my eyes tearing.

Anthony takes me by the arms. "What's wrong?"

I meet his eyes. "The boy at the Institute."

Anthony frowns. "I know. Bram is going to help him."

"He's my brother. And I left him. I left him alone!"

CHAPTER 9

I lean against the wall, sucking in great breaths to try and break the invisible band crushing my chest. I left my brother! I wipe at the tears on my cheek with the back of my hand. The man in the painting stares at me, accusingly. *I'm more disappointed in myself than you could ever be.* Out loud I say, "I'm sorry. I didn't mean to."

"Why do you keep saying that?" Colt says, looking from the painting and then back to me. This is the first time he's spoken since finding out about my brother. Anthony left a few minutes ago to call Bram.

"I made a promise to him," I say.

"To your brother?"

I shake my head. "To him." I nod at the painting.

"This man? But how do you even know him?"

I inhale deeply. It's a shaky breath. My memories have all returned—how Max and I were captured, our time at the Institute, and my life in hiding . . . much of it is painful.

"He's my father," I say.

His face goes pale, much paler than it already is. "Howard is your dad?"

"That's not his name. My dad's name is William. William Radkey."

He doesn't seem to hear me. He's staring at the painting, his expression pained as if he's just been poisoned. "I need to tell Anthony. Wait here." He walks to the door, but before going through he places his hand on the doorjamb. Without turning, he says, "Patch, I'm sorry."

"For what?"

He leaves without answering. I go to stand but wobble a little, my head spinning. How much sleep did I get? I glance at the clock. Only a few hours. It's not even dawn yet.

I go after Colt, still fighting for breath. My brother's all alone. Because of me. I think back to when I'd had a small moment of clarity just before they dosed me with a new round of anti-memory serum. I had actually been in the same room with Max drawing. Ebony was watching us interact, probably making sure the serum was working on both of us. Max didn't seem to recognize me, but when his hand brushed mine as he reached for a marker, the fog in my brain lifted. I tried not to show it, but Ebony must've noticed. I saw her moving behind the glass to come into the room. I reacted quickly and wrote the words "Run Now" as small as I could on my pinky fingers. Thank goodness no one had noticed.

Colt is in the kitchen next to Anthony, who is speaking low into an earpiece wrapped around the top of his ear. "—need to know what time it starts—" he's saying when Colt tugs on his arm.

"You're going to want to hear this," Colt says.

Anthony looks from me to him. "Get me what you can," he says. "I'll see you soon." He reaches up and removes the earpiece. To Colt he says, "What is it?"

Colt shakes his head. "You'll never believe it."

I look from him to Anthony, still confused, and wonder what my father has to do with all this and why his picture is on the wall. And then there's Colt, who acts like he knows him, but that's impossible.

"You know Howard?" Colt says.

"What about him?"

"He's her father."

Anthony's mouth opens. He blinks once then walks by me and goes into the office.

"Come on," Colt says, and we follow after him.

I wonder again about my father and how they can know him. Growing up I rarely saw other humans. It was always just my dad and Max and me. But then I remember my mother and my legs go weak. *My mom.* I touch the wall to help steady myself. I can't think about it right now. I can't think about *her*. Too much pain. I force my legs to move. To go forward.

Anthony is staring at the painting. "Your father is Howard Edmonds?"

"His real name is William Radkey," I say. "Please tell me what this is all about."

Anthony lowers his voice and speaks to Colt. "No wonder she was at the Institute and not at Enfield."

My head feels like it's going to explode. "Enfield? Would someone please explain to me what is going on?"

Anthony is the one to answer. Colt still looks sick and pale. "Enfield is a place where the Institute holds Originals, but you were being held at the Institute's research department because of this man." He points to the picture. "Your father has saved countless lives, or prolonged them I should say. And not just Originals, Primes too. The Institute's been looking for him for a very long time." His eyes flash to Colt's and Colt looks down.

I'm curious about the exchange, but before I can say anything, Anthony asks, "Did you know this about your father?"

I think back. "He had a lab next to our home that he'd work in a lot. And a few times a month, he would travel to the city to, according to him, help others. I always assumed it was for illnesses, but nothing of this magnitude."

"Tell her, Anthony," Colt says.

I look at Anthony, waiting for him to speak.

It takes him a few seconds before he says, "Your father isn't just a scientist. He's HOPE's founder."

"Hope?" I ask, thinking of the initials of the name on the painting.

"It stands for Helping Originals Protect Eden. Remember how I told you about the growing number of Primes who believe Originals are the only way our world can survive the future?"

I nod.

"It was your father who organized us, making us the first group to challenge the Institute. They'd love nothing more than to destroy Howard, I mean William, and they'd do anything to accomplish this goal. Anything." He's looking at me like he's waiting for me to connect invisible dots.

The dots connect into something ugly and cruel. "Max and I. They know we're his children."

Anthony sits on the corner of the desk. "You're probably the most valuable Originals they've ever captured. Not only could they sell your DNA for top dollar, but they can use you as leverage to get your father to turn himself over."

I think of my father. "He will never do that."

Anthony's eyes flash back to the painting. "What happened that day you were taken?"

The day we were taken. I swallow, but there's no saliva in my mouth and the air gets caught in my throat until I cough. "It was morning. We were in our home, a small log cabin in the woods near the coast of Maine. I was cooking breakfast while my brother, Max, stared out the window. He was watching my father walk into his lab." I take a deep breath. "Then there was this horrible sound. It was the same sound we heard at the charging station."

Colt and Anthony look back and forth, communicating silently.

I continue. "My father had taught me what to do if someone ever found us. I was supposed to run to the coast where we kept a boat. From there I'd sail to a nearby island. But I didn't do that. I had to make sure my father was okay." My body loses some of its strength. I lean into the wall to keep me upright. "When I opened the door to his lab, my father was escaping behind some secret wall I didn't even know existed. It closed. I was calling my father's name, and he still closed it without a single word to me. That's when we were captured." I look up at Colt. "That was about a month ago. The raid you talked about, someone was captured: me and my brother."

Colt clears his throat, but doesn't say anything. He still won't meet my eyes.

"My father," I say, "do you know where he is?"

Anthony stands. "Your father is fine."

"Where is he?" Pieces of a puzzle I don't want to solve are slowly coming together.

"I believe he's in New York City."

"Did he say anything about his children being captured?" I ask the question, but I already know the answer. The puzzle has come together. It is ugly and something I don't want to look at.

The room is quiet until Anthony says, "I'm sure he had his reasons why he didn't."

A little color returns to Colt's face. "What reason would that be? Had we known, we could've grabbed them on transport or at least used our connections inside the Institute to make sure they were okay." He shakes his head. "But what's even dumber is why they were in the forest to begin with. They should've been at Eden, not in the woods all alone without any protection."

This was something I had also debated with my father for the last two years. "He didn't feel the time was right."

"You knew about Eden?" Anthony asks.

"I wanted to go there. I asked all the time, but my father always said it wasn't safe yet. He never said why." Because I don't want to think about my father's decisions, I quickly change the subject.

"When did you meet him?" I ask Anthony.

His gaze drifts above my shoulder as if he's seeing through to another time. "Years ago his medicine gave my wife three more years to live." He blinks and clears his throat. "I better wake up Jenna," he says, and pauses. "Patch, don't worry. We'll get Max and get you to your father."

"My name's not Patch."

He and Colt both look at me.

I lift my chin. "It's Sage."

CHAPTER 10

"Get up now, Jenna," Anthony says inside the darkened bedroom.

Colt and I sit on the couch. Colt is quiet, lost in his own thoughts, and I'm lost in mine. I'm thinking of how I can get back inside the Institute to get Max. My brain, no longer trapped in a fog, is working quickly, calculating different scenarios. None of them are promising.

"Why is it I never get any sleep when I work with you?" Jenna says. "Give me five minutes and I'll get up."

"You better or I'm coming in with a bucket of water."

"Ugh. You're so cliché."

Anthony closes the door. "I don't know why I put up with her."

"So what's the plan?" I ask.

"I'm going to meet Bram soon. When I get back we can discuss what to do."

I stand and pace the floor. "I can't just wait here. I have to do something."

"The safest place for you is here. Just be patient."

"How? Max is surrounded by strangers in a world he doesn't understand. And who knows what they're doing to him? I have to go."

"Listen to me. You can't help him if you get captured again. Just wait. We'll come up with a plan. We'll save him together, but we have to know all the facts."

The door behind him opens.

"Save who?" Jenna yawns. She's combing her tangled hair straight.

"Her brother, Max. He's the boy that's at the Institute," Anthony says.

She removes some stray hairs from the comb and says, "You left your kid brother with Techheads? That's cold."

I cross the room in three steps and slap her hard, surprising everyone in the room, especially myself. "I am tired of your insults," I say, my face only inches from hers. "You know nothing about me or what I've been through."

"Boo-hoo," she says, gritting her teeth. "You've had a hard life. We all have. At least you get to live long enough to see yourself get varicose veins. Sheesh. You're so emotional," she says, raising a hand to touch her cheek. "I don't know how you're going to survive this world."

"Is that what I'm going to have to do? Become emotionally dead? If that's what you are, then you're already dead." I turn around and catch Anthony with his mouth open. "When are you meeting Bram?" I ask.

"I have to call him first and let him know about your father. It complicates things."

Jenna drops into a nearby chair, still touching her cheek where I slapped her. It's bright red. "Her father? Why would Bram care?"

"Howard Edmonds is her father," Anthony says and positions the earpiece behind his ear again.

"William Radkey," I clarify, but no one notices.

Jenna slowly turns to Colt, her eyes big. "*The* Howard Edmonds?"

"Not now, Jenna," Anthony says in a warning tone.

"But this is huge!"

"I said later." His voice is firm and Jenna doesn't argue. "I have to make that call.

Anthony walks into the office and closes the door.

Jenna eyes Colt for several seconds like she's itching to say something, but then she turns to me. "So apparently you've got your memory back. What's that like?"

She doesn't call me Patch or anything else, which is nice for a change, but her voice still reeks of sarcasm.

I think of all that I remember. Only one word comes to mind.

"Painful."

My gaze meets Colt's. This time it's him who looks away.

"More emotions. You're boring me." Jenna stands and goes into the kitchen, muttering under her breath.

I don't get upset. I have more important things to do, like trying to save Max. I sit in the chair Jenna's just left, my knee bouncing. There must be something I can do. I imagine the layout of the Institute. I know it inside and out because my father had me memorize it every week for the last year. In case. He had me learn a lot of things. In case. His lessons were grueling, almost cruel, especially after my mother. Things would've been so different if she were still alive.

"Tell me about your childhood," Colt says suddenly. His eyes are a softer blue, like the color of the sky on the edge of a cloud.

"Like I said, I lived near the coast. In Maine. It was an amazing place. For the first seven years of my life it was just me and my mom and dad, then she had Max. I loved having a brother, someone else I could confide in." The motion of my leg slows to a steady rise and fall, like the swells of the ocean. "My parents were great teachers. They taught us everything. How wonderful this world is and how important the people living on it are. But then my mother died. I was twelve." Colt doesn't say anything so I continue.

"One day I came back from spending the night on the beach with Max, and she was just gone. My father had already buried her. He never talked about it. All he would say was it was a horrible accident." Even Jenna has stopped chewing her cereal from the kitchen to listen. Colt shifts in his chair.

"My parents died when I was young too. And Jenna's dad died." The words bring pain to his face, and I wonder how many times he's said them aloud.

Jenna swallows and adds, "Moving on from depressing stuff, did you ever leave your home? You know, get out a bit to see the world?"

It takes me a moment before I continue. "I knew about things in the world, but never experienced it firsthand. Only watched it on television. I wished I could be a part of it, but I knew I'd never be accepted. I was obviously different, not special."

I laugh a little, imagining all the times I'd paint my hair or try to lighten my skin with powder to hide my skin's imperfections.

"That's where you're wrong. We're not special." Colt motions between Jenna and him. "We're freaks of nature, a science experiment gone wrong."

"Speak for yourself," Jenna mutters.

"If it were up to me," Colt continues, "I'd completely wipe us all out, leaving only people like you, Originals, to start over and make this world a better place."

Jenna laughs. "Then it's a good thing no one cares what you think."

A shadow passes over Colt's face. "One of these days, Jenna—"

"What?" she asks. "What are you going to do? Turn me over to the Institute?"

Colt stands suddenly. "I'm warning you!"

Jenna sets her bowl onto the counter and walks over to him, smiling. The action's not friendly. "Don't threaten me. We wouldn't be in this mess if it wasn't for you."

"What is she talking about?" I ask.

Colt doesn't answer, but his face is pale again.

"Yeah, Colt," Jenna says. "What am I talking about?"

"This isn't the time—" he starts to say, but Jenna cuts him off.

"No. I'm not letting this go. The piper has come and now it's time to pay." She turns to me and opens her mouth.

"Jenna, don't!" Colt says.

She doesn't stop. "Colt is the reason the Institute has your brother."

"I don't understand," I say.

Colt leans back into the sofa, his expression stone.

Jenna crosses her arms, looking pleased with herself. "Almost a year ago, Colt turned your father into the Institute in exchange for money. They had your dad for several days until he escaped, but in the process a Canine bit him. That Canine eventually tracked him back to your house in Maine where you were captured." She is watching Colt as she speaks. "This is all Colt's fault. And with that"—she curtsies to Colt—"I leave the room." She walks into the office where Anthony is on the phone and closes the door.

I stare after her, trying to absorb everything she just said. My father had been captured. He escaped, but a Canine had bit him. I know what a Canine is: a Prime with an unusual taste for blood. Once they've tasted the blood of their prey, they can track it anywhere. No wonder my father never stayed home much, especially this last year. But in the end it still wasn't enough.

Turning to Colt, I ask, "How much?"

His eyes meet mine. "What?"

"How much did they give you in exchange for my father?"

He hesitates like he doesn't want to answer, but he does. "A grand."

I fight back the urge to cry. "So you traded the life of a human for a thousand dollars?"

Colt's mouth tightens and his features sharpen. "Looks that way, doesn't it?"

I don't know how to respond. What world did I step into where a person would trade the life of another for money? I turn away from Colt, unable to look at him.

"Time to go," Anthony says as he walks out of the office. He seems to sense the tension in the air. "What's going on?"

Neither Colt nor I answer. Jenna walks out of the office to stand next to Anthony. "I can tell you."

"What about my brother?" I ask quickly.

"Max is still at the Institute, but they're moving him for the event in two days."

"What event?" I ask.

"It's a yearly fundraiser where wealthy Primes raise money for those who are close to dying. They even donate a vial of their own precious oDNA for a week."

I remember the conversation I'd heard on the Wall Television at the Institute. "But why would they take Max there?"

Anthony doesn't say anything and doesn't look at me either. It's Jenna who answers. "He's on display. Buyers like to meet their future donor, like one would when picking out a prized pig. And believe me, your brother is going to make them a lot of money when everyone finds out who his father is."

Although I don't say it out loud, I wonder if that's true. Ebony thought Max was broken and so might other Primes. Max *was* different from everyone in this world, but he was hardly broken.

"How long can an Original live while their DNA is being sucked out of them?" I ask.

Anthony says, "It's not them taking DNA that's harmful, that's the easy part. It's all the testing and experiments they put Originals through. The Techheads deny the experiments for the public's sake, but we have strong evidence to the contrary."

"So how long does my brother have?"

The room is silent. It's Colt who eventually decides to be the bad guy.

"No one knows for sure, since we don't know what they do with the bodies, but we've heard the average life span is six months, probably less for a kid."

I sink into the chair, feeling the blood drain from my face. Why didn't I know any of this? My father sure didn't skimp on any of my other lessons.

"We'll get him back," Colt says, his voice hard. "I promise." He looks at me for the first time since our argument, but I have to look away. What little I know of him makes me want to keep my distance.

Anthony clears his throat. "Bram's going to help a little. Not as much as I would've liked, but he's giving me some things that will help us go unnoticed once we're inside the pavilion."

"But how do we get inside?" Jenna asks. "The place is going to be crawling with mutants."

Anthony shakes his head. "That's going to be the hard part."

"Where did you say it was?" I ask.

"The Oscar Johnson Pavilion. It's a big building on the edge of town. Real fancy place."

"I know it," I say.

Jenna scoffs. "How could you know it? You never left your cottage in the woods, remember?"

"My father taught me the layout of every Institute building he knew of, including the OJP. For example, I know their security is tight. They change their passcodes twice a day and only three people know them. I know the guest list to get into their events will be digital using those same passcodes. We're not getting into that party. At least not through the front doors."

No one says anything for several seconds, and I look down, embarrassed. It probably does seem strange that I know all of this random information. At the time my father taught it to me, I thought it was odd too. Not so much anymore.

"Then how?" Colt asks.

I look up. "In the basement. Security is minimal. There's a water drain. If we go through the tunnels—"

Jenna waves her arms. "Stop right there. We are not going through the tunnels. No way, no how."

"She's right," Anthony says. "We won't get past the Junks."

"Not to mention the dreaded mutated alligators," she adds.

Anthony snorts. "That's a myth. We only have to worry about Junks, which is plenty."

The term stirs a memory within me. Junks are human addicts who injected all kinds of pDNA, both human and animal. The result was disastrous and over time they mutated into smaller creatures devoid of human reasoning. The Institute tried to eradicate them, but they escaped into the tunnels beneath the city, making it near impossible for the Institute to find them all.

"Meat," I say. "Raw meat. They like it and it will buy us some time."

Jenna laughs. "You want us to feed them? Look, I know you've been living under a rock your whole life so I don't want to be mean, but you're a twisted nut job! No one, and I mean no one, goes into the tunnels."

I stand and curl my hands into fists. "I didn't ask for your help, you prepubescent teen."

Her eyes narrow. "What did you call me?"

Anthony laughs and I think Colt smiles but just barely. I take a deep breath and step back. "The same goes for the rest of you. I will get my brother back. No one has to risk their lives for us."

"I already made my decision a long time ago," Anthony says. "The human race needs to be saved. Now let's go. Bram's waiting. Colt?"

"I'll stay with Sage," he says.

My eyes go to Colt, but he's not looking at me. After what Jenna told me, I'm not sure I should be alone with him.

Jenna scrunches her nose. "Who's Sage?"

"I am," I say, expecting some kind of insult from her.

She shrugs. "I like Patch better."

I ignore her, something I'm getting used to doing, and say to Anthony, "Are you sure it's safe? Maybe it's better if I stay here alone."

Jenna smirks knowingly at Colt.

Anthony furrows his brow, his gaze going back and forth between Jenna and Colt as if he's trying to figure out what's going on between them. "No, Colt's right. You're much safer with him. You can trust him. I promise."

I swallow the lump in my throat. Anthony may trust him, but I can't dismiss the fact that he so easily turned in my father, which eventually led to my and Max's and capture. I'll have to keep my guard up around him.

I take a deep breath before asking, "When you're at Bram's, can you ask if there's a way I can speak with my father?"

"Sure," he says, but the way he says it makes me think it's not possible, which is disappointing. I want to know why he didn't try to find Max and me.

"Are you staying or coming?" Anthony asks Jenna.

"For now, going," she says. "It's too stuffy in here."

"I'll be back in one hour. If anything happens, you know where to go," Anthony says, and leaves by the front door.

As soon as he's gone, Colt asks, "You hungry again?"

"Yes, no." My stomach is rumbling, but I'm not sure if it's because I'm hungry or sick about my brother.

"I'll get you some cereal."

"Please don't bother."

He stands up anyway and goes into the kitchen. "About what Jenna said earlier. You don't know the whole story."

"I only have one question," I say. "What did you do with the money?"

His face pales.

"Answer me!"

"I bought oDNA." His voice is quiet.

I wrinkle my nose in disgust. "So not only did you turn in an Original for cash, but then you bought an Original's DNA from the Institute knowing they're being imprisoned and tortured for it?"

"There's more to it than that. Let me—"

"I don't mean to be rude, really I don't," I say, holding up my hand, "but right now I don't want to think about it. I just want to focus on finding my brother. Maybe one day you can tell me, and maybe I'll understand, but for now, let's just get through the next little while, and then who knows? Maybe you'll never have to see me again, and none of this will matter anyway."

He reaches into a cupboard and removes a bowl. "If that's what you want." His tone is matter-of-fact, but there's a hint of something else. Sadness? Bitterness? I don't know him well enough to tell.

After a few silent moments, he asks, his voice still hard, "What are some things your father taught you?"

I'm not sure I like this topic any better than the last, but I answer anyway. Maybe I'll remember something that will help Max. "As much as he could, especially after my mom died. He was obsessive about it. First thing in the morning, at sunrise, he would make me watch these movies about all the different types of Primes, specifically their physical characteristics, including any distinguishable eye color. Then we'd go over their strengths and weaknesses. Over and over until I knew them as well as I did my father. Then for hours after he'd teach me to fight. Every kind of martial arts you could think of. Afternoons were saved for history lessons, role playing—"

"Role playing?"

"Yes. Like what to say in certain situations to get me out of tight spots. His lessons were nonstop. He said it was because I was at a disadvantage from everyone else. I think he was trying to put me on a level playing field, if that's possible."

"What about your brother?"

At this, I'm quiet. How can I explain Max? No one would understand. In this world, where everyone was considered exceptional, Max would be thought of as useless. Only my father and I knew how special he really was.

"Max is different," is all I say. "My father didn't teach him like he did me. I learned enough for both of us."

Colt hands me what looks like oats in a bowl but the coloring is different. "That must have been hard."

"It was all for Max, and me, too, I guess. But now I've lost him."

"We'll get him back."

I stare into the cereal for several seconds before I take a bite. The texture is similar to oatmeal, but it tastes sweeter.

Colt is quiet while I eat. He's looking at a magazine but every once in awhile he looks up at me. I'm almost finished when he sits up abruptly. His eyebrows are drawn together and his mouth is tight.

"What's wrong?" I ask.

He stands and looks around frantically.

"Colt?"

He's at my side and pulling me up before I can do it myself. The bowl of cereal falls to the ground, spilling milk all over the wooden floor.

"We have to go," he says.

"What's going on?"

"Someone's trying to break in." He pulls me into the kitchen.

"How do you know?" I ask. I tilt my head to listen for any strange sounds, but hear nothing.

"It's one of my things," he says as he glances all around. "There's got to be a way out of here."

"In the kitchen?"

Colt's opening bottom cupboards and knocking on the back paneling. A cracking sound has me doing the same, although I'm not sure what I'm searching for.

"Over here," he says from beneath the sink. He knocks aside several bottles of clear liquid. I crouch next to him and peer inside as he pushes a small lever at the bottom of the metal sink. The back wall of the cabinet slides open, revealing a narrow cavity.

"Get in," he says. Behind me the sound of a loud explosion rocks the whole apartment.

I hesitate. What if he's leading me into a trap?

"Please trust me," he says again, his eyes pleading. "I'm trying to make things right."

I clench my jaw, still unsure, but scurry in anyway. Anthony said I would be safe. I hope he's right.

I crawl quickly but have to drop to my belly as the circular, metal-walled tunnel narrows. Colt climbs in behind me; his arms are bumping my legs. As soon as we're a ways into the tunnel, the small door snaps shut. The sound is quiet but it makes my heart beat faster as if a gun just fired. I don't know the layout of this building. I don't know what lies ahead and this makes me extremely nervous. Plus it's dark and the space is small. I close my eyes and say it isn't.

"Keep going. And fast," Colt says, his voice low.

I scoot forward, careful to keep my head low so it doesn't hit the ceiling. Arm over arm, I army crawl. The walls smell like mold, a bitter earthy aura. This is the first time I've smelled something bad in this world. Sweat breaks across my forehead and in the small of my back. The tunnel seems like it will never end, and the tube suddenly seems tighter. When did that happen? My chest constricts and even my vision starts to blur.

"Breathe normal," Colt says. "Remember why you're doing this."

It's then that I realize my breaths have become shallow and rapid. I suck in deeply and think of Max. Several seconds pass before my lips stop tingling and the band around my chest loosens. I continue forward, focusing only on Max and not the small space.

Behind me, Colt grunts as he tries to squeeze his bigger body through the tube. I can only imagine what he must be feeling.

Just ahead the tunnel ends. "Colt?"

He grunts and slides his body forward. "What?"

"It's a dead end."

"No, it can't be. Bram wouldn't have built an emergency exit without an actual exit. Look for a—"

He's interrupted by a sound that makes my teeth ache: sharp nails scraping against metal.

"Go!" Colt says. "They've found us!"

Using all my strength, I pull myself forward as quickly as possible. "What's coming? Tell me," I demand.

"A Grater."

An image flashes in my mind: small, the size of a child, and human-like but with six-inch, razor-sharp claws on both hands and feet. They are fast and deadly. But I know its weakness. If I can get out.

The sound of claws scurrying in the tunnel after us grows closer. Colt is behind me. He won't stand a chance against it, not with how little he can move.

I reach the end of the tunnel and feel around the edges of the wall blocking our path until I discover a small raised button. I push it and a circular hatch opens. I slide out and spin around to stick the upper half of my body back into the tunnel.

"Grab my hands." I reach in as far as possible, my feet coming off the floor.

Colt scoots forward until he grabs me. I press my thighs against the wall and pull as hard as I can. A moment later he falls to the floor, the back of his black shirt covered in sweat.

I peer into the tunnel. The Grater has his head up and his eyes are glowing a bright yellow. He has a hairless human face. No eyelashes or eyebrows, and on his head are chunks of scales in place of hair. I swallow hard and push Colt, who was in the process of standing up, out of the way.

"Stay to the side," I say and glance up and down the hall where the tunnel has ended. It's empty, giving me nothing I can use as a weapon. I look back at the small metal door of the opening we just came through. It might work. I swing my leg up in a karate-like move and bring the foot of my heel down onto the door. It barely budges, but I'm pretty sure it's left a nice bruise on my foot. I go to do it again, but Colt stops me. He takes hold of the door with his hands and tugs until it rips from the hinges.

Ignoring his demands to tell him what it's for, I take it from him, and press myself to the wall. My head pounds as I wait; the sound of scraping blades only seconds away. One shot at this. If I miss, it could prove fatal to us both.

CHAPTER 11

I stay focused on the opening as I wait for the Grater. It's a terrifying task, remaining still when every part of me tells me to run. As soon as the Grater's deadly fingernails appear, I swing the sharp edge of the door down with all my strength. It chips his black claws, but doesn't break them.

The Grater shrieks, a horrible high-pitched sound that hurts my ears. It takes a swipe at me with its other hand, but I dodge it, just barely, and counter by swinging the door again. This time I'm successful and slice the claws on his left hand completely off. The Grater howls again and withdraws back into the tunnel.

"Come on!" Colt says and turns the other direction.

We race down the hallway toward a door leading outside. I go for it, but Colt pulls me into a different hallway before I get there.

"They'll be waiting for us outside," he says.

He runs a little further until he pushes on a door. A long staircase heads up. I shake my head. "We can't go up. We'll be trapped."

"Trust me," is all he says before he bounds up the stairs two at a time. I hesitate briefly before I hurry after him. How can I trust a boy who got me into this mess to begin with? Maybe there's one of those bridges on the roof we can escape onto and disappear into another building. This thought comforts me, and I continue on, but by the time I reach the thirteenth floor my muscles are spent, and I've slowed down considerably.

"Wouldn't an elevator be faster?" I ask through shallow breaths. Maybe Anthony was right about rushing after Max. My body isn't ready.

"No elevator," he says. "You've got to go faster. Any second now they're going to realize where we went."

As if they heard him, a loud crash echoes below us, like someone's taken a wrecking ball to the wall. I glance over the stair rail. A plume of dust and debris billows up the narrow stairway cavity. A moment later, a giant head appears and looks up at me. It's the same beast I bested at the hospital. He's what's called a Titan. I duck back and move up the stairs, but I still can't run any faster. There's no strength left in my muscles after having hung on to that cable under the bridge yesterday.

"Think of Max!" Colt says.

I flinch at the sound of frustration in his voice and try to move faster. For a few minutes I'm able to go up three more flights of stairs at full speed, but then my legs give out. No matter how much I want them to move, my muscles are shot. Tears sting my eyes, and I curse my body for being weak.

Colt sees me on my knees and comes back. I don't have a chance to apologize before he's picking me up and carrying me the rest of the way to the top. He's puffing heavy breaths through puckered lips.

To help balance my weight, I wrap my arms around his neck and my legs around his waist, much how Max had done with me earlier. My father had made me train with Max like this daily to build up my endurance. And to also train Max to hold on.

But I'm not Max, and I find the position awkward.

Colt wraps one arm around my waist to keep me from sliding off and uses the other to help propel him up the steps. I bury my head into his neck to prevent myself from seeing what's coming. The Titan's steps are loud, and I guess the stairs are too narrow for his body because all around it sounds like walls are caving in.

"Almost there," Colt says, taking a breath between each word.

I tighten my grip against him and imagine a bridge on the rooftop. There's got to be a bridge, some way for us to get away.

Colt pushes open a door and rushes outside. I lift my head. It's still dark but a rising orange and red fire against the horizon burns the night. I glance around and try not to panic. This rooftop is very different from the Institute's. There's no grass, only metal, and beyond its top there are no bridges.

"What are we going to do?" I say. I try to wiggle free to see if there's some way we can jump to the next building, but he holds me close.

"Don't let go," Colt says. "I know you're tired, but you have to hold on no matter what, okay?"

I nod my head, putting my complete trust in him because I don't know what else to do.

The ground beneath us rumbles. I look toward the door, which is still open. The hair of the Titan's head appears as he rounds the last corner to the top.

"Go!" I say.

Colt runs, although I don't know where he thinks he's going to go. The roof's edge is only twenty feet away. His left hand tightens on my back hard enough that I gasp.

Just as the Titan breaks through the door, sending twisted metal in all directions, Colt jumps. A breath catches in my lungs, and my stomach lurches into my chest as we fall from the roof.

Cold air rushes up at me, and I think this is the end. I shouldn't have trusted Colt. Surprisingly I don't think of Max, but of my father in the last few seconds of my life. Why didn't he prepare me better? Maybe give me some pDNA injections, anything, so I could've better protected Max. Now I've failed because I'm normal.

The thoughts are bitter, and I can taste them in my mouth. A horrible thing before you die.

CHAPTER 12

I close my eyes tight and wait for impact, but a tearing sound has me opening them back up. Colt's shirt is ripping in the back until it falls off completely and something dark unfolds itself from his skin. At first I think it's a parachute and I almost laugh I'm so happy, but when I see shiny, black, skin-like material expand fully, I forget that I'm falling to my death and instinctively push away. I regret it a moment later because now I'm falling even faster.

I scream and reach for Colt, who's in a dive position, two great bat-like wings arched high behind him. He catches my hand and pulls me to him. I scramble back into my holding position just in time for Colt to swoop upward, preventing us from hitting the ground.

I'm stunned. Shocked. Jenna had called him a Noc, but I didn't know what that was until now.

Colt flies between shiny rectangular buildings until we're several blocks away. He lands onto a roof of a smaller building, not near as high as the last one, for which I'm grateful. I expect the landing to be rough, but it is surprisingly gentle. He sets me down and steps away as his wings fold against his bare back.

I stare at him, completely fascinated. The muscles in his chest and stomach just above his jean line are as well defined as the twin arches of his hipbones. I walk behind him to get a closer look at his back. He doesn't move. The skin of his wings looks like leather, but shinier and so thin they would barely be noticeable under a shirt. I reach up and lightly touch the bones that border his wings. They are hard, more like wire than bone.

"Are you done ogling me?" Colt asks and turns around to face me.

"I'm not ogling," I say, my face turning red. "I'm just curious. My father didn't teach me about Nocs."

"That's because we're not supposed to exist. The government, or I should say the Institute, outlawed any kind of flying pDNA injections over thirty years ago. They saw it as a security threat."

"Then how are you here?"

I suddenly become painfully aware of my legs, which are shaky and weak. The adrenaline from falling from the roof must be wearing off. I lower to the ground and sit down, my legs stretched in front of me.

"I don't know. My mom was considered a Noc but didn't have these." He points to his back. "She had the ability to sense vibrations in the earth. She always knew when someone was coming ahead of time."

"That's how you knew about the attack at the apartment."

He nods. "And I have good hearing."

"What about your father?"

"He was a Rhine, like that girl Spit at the club, but he died when I was two."

"I'm sorry," I say, and wonder if he has inherited a Rhine's ability to never tire or weaken. Their endurance is something I wish I had. "And I'm sorry about not being able to run back there. I don't know what's wrong with me."

"You're exhausted. And out of shape. Staying at the Institute for weeks will do that to a person." He turns away from me, but at the last second I notice his face tighten in pain like he's stepped on a sharp pebble. He probably feels guilty, but I can't bring myself to say anything to ease his pain. Not yet anyway.

"Thank you," I say instead. "For saving me."

I slide my foot back and forth along the metal rooftop. With darkness receding, I'm able to get a better view of the area. All around us are buildings just like this one, but farther apart from each other, not like when we were in the heart of the city. There are more trees dotting the sides of the street here, and, if I squint hard, I can see the edge of a massive forest just beyond the last row of buildings a few blocks over.

Forests are everywhere, I remember, which is why they are so easy to hide in if you're an Original. With the world's population at such a decline, people slowly moved closer and closer to the cities, leaving nature to take over.

"What are we doing up here?" I ask.

Colt looks back at me like he wants to say something, but after a few seconds his gaze goes beyond me. "I live just below here. Anthony said if we ever get separated to come here. No one, not even Jenna, knows about it."

"So we wait," I say.

Colt comes and sits next to me, but not too close. "He'll be here soon."

"Are you cold?" I ask.

He stares straight ahead. "Nope."

I stare too and shiver when a cool breeze blows across my skin. The sun rises slowly, covering the city in a fiery haze. Sunlight twinkles on the shiny metal of the buildings, reminding me of the ocean. A longing deep inside my chest makes me sigh.

I risk a glance at Colt. He's deep in thought, his eyes focused on the bleeding horizon. I think of his life and what it might've been like living in the city. No parents and having to hide who you truly are. *Maybe I'm being too hard on him*, I think. But then I think of Max, trapped, alone, and probably terrified. Because of Colt.

Closing my eyes, I silence all thoughts and clear my mind. My father taught me how to do this to endure stressful times. "If your mind is clear, you can endure anything," he'd say. "Push the pain away." And that's what I need to do right now until I know more about Max: push the pain away.

I'm not sure how much time has passed, but the sun is fully on us when a scraping sound draws our attention. I turn around just as a small, square door opens on the roof floor. Anthony's head appears. The muscles in his face relax when he sees us. "You're here!"

"Where else would we be?" Colt stands and goes over to him. With two hands, he easily pulls Anthony onto the roof.

"I thought maybe the Institute captured you. I came back and saw Cleaners at the apartment. It looked like someone had destroyed it. What happened?" Anthony hands him a t-shirt as if he suspected he might be shirtless.

I grimace at the name. Cleaners are the Institute's cleanup crew when there's been an "incident" they don't want the public to know about. They're soldier-like with a hunger for violence and they never question authority—a bad combination. I move to stand, but it takes me a minute on account of my weak and sore muscles.

"The Institute came shortly after you left," Colt says as he pulls the black shirt over his head and around his chest. "They came with a Grater."

"How did they find us?" Anthony asks.

"I don't know, but we should probably check everything on us for trackers. What did Bram tell you?"

"Let's go inside and we'll discuss it."

I follow Colt and Anthony down the open hatch door and onto a ladder. Because my legs are shaky and weak, Colt stays to the side of the ladder and keeps a steady hand on me as I make my way down. Our eyes meet briefly, and I quickly glance away.

"You didn't get enough rest, did you?" Anthony asks me at the bottom.

"I'll be okay," I say and walk into a large room with wooden paneled walls. It's a stark contrast from Bram's safe house. There are only a couple of rusty metal chairs lying on top of worn, brown carpet. There's no kitchen, and off to my right is a single bathroom. But the biggest difference is what circles the room: weapons of all kinds, some I recognize and some I don't.

"What is this place?" I ask.

Colt brushes by me to get to the other side of the room. "This is my home."

Anthony grabs a small square-shaped device from off the wall. It looks familiar but I can't quite place it from all of the other electronics my father has taught me about. Anthony scans it up and down me, saying, "The Institute doesn't know about this place. In fact, they've condemned it. It's where we keep, well, weapons. It's the perfect hiding spot." The device in his hand beeps.

"You're clean," Anthony says to me. He turns to Colt. "I wish you wouldn't use your wings. They're going to be looking for you now just as hard as Sage. You know how they love Nocs."

"I didn't have a choice," Colt says as Anthony scans him up and down. "It was either fly or let them take Sage again. Besides it was still dark, mostly, and only the Titan saw me. They might not believe what he saw and think I had a parachute or something."

"I get it. It was a risk you had to take. I just wish it didn't have to happen."

All of a sudden the device beeps loudly, startling me.

"Got one," Anthony says. He swipes a small black sticker the size of a ladybug off the back of Colt's belt and hurries over to an electronic box hanging on the wall. Very carefully, he presses it onto a white pad on the front of the box and touches a button on its top. The white face lights up.

Colt growls. "I bet that Rhine at the club, Spit, snuck that on me when we left."

"Do you think they followed us here?" I ask, half tempted to climb back to the roof to check.

"This box is a scrambler," Anthony says. "Not only can it block different types of pulse transmitting within a quarter mile radius, but it can also send out false signals. No doubt the Institute has men scouring the area, but in about," he looks back at the box, "thirty seconds, they will receive a signal that shows Colt moving away from here. The signal will lead them on a ghost chase for about a mile before it drops off."

"This is a lot of close calls," I say, cringing.

"It's all worth it," Anthony says. "You're our priority."

His words twist inside me all sorts of wrong. Everyone around me is taking risks because they think I'm special. *Real special.* I can barely stand.

I go into the bathroom without saying a word. My back slides against the closed door until I'm sitting on the floor. For years I dreamed about being around Primes and living in their world, but it's clear I don't belong. I was so naïve. Someone's going to get hurt because of me. And even if I were mad at Colt for what he did, I'd never wish any harm coming to him.

I close my eyes tight before tears fall. Focus on Max. Nothing else.

After counting to sixty, I stand and go back into the wood-paneled room. Anthony and Colt are inspecting various weapons as if they're preparing for something big. I try not to think about it and ask, "Where's Jenna?"

Colt removes a gun with a long barrel and says, "Like I said, no one knows about this place. Not even her."

"She's at her mom's," Anthony says. He holds out a long stick-looking weapon. It's an older model, but I know its tip has the ability to shock people. "This one needs a new charge, Colt."

Colt walks toward him as if to take it, but suddenly he falls to the floor. At first I think he's tripped, and I'm about to help him up when his back arches and he starts shaking, his eyes rolling into the back of his head.

Anthony rushes to him. "Help me turn him on his side."

I drop to my knees and push him over, which is difficult because every muscle in his body is flexed and stiff. "Why is he having a seizure?"

"Just hold him still. It will pass in a couple of minutes."

Anthony holds his legs and arms, while I cradle his head, making sure it stays sideways. Colt's jaw is clenched tight and his rapid breaths force their way through his pressed lips. Sweat breaks all over his body and within seconds his clothes are wet. I hurt just looking at him.

"Is he aware of the pain?" I ask.

Anthony's quiet for a moment. "I don't know."

Colt's body jerks hard, and we tighten our grip. After another minute, his shaking slows and one by one his muscles relax. His eyelids close, and I lower his head to the floor. He looks asleep.

"Why did he have a seizure?"

Anthony withdraws his hands from Colt. "He has the Kiss."

My head snaps up. "What?"

"He's old, nineteen."

"That's not old! And besides, you're at least, what, seven, eight years older than him?"

"But I'm not as mutated."

I look down at Colt. How could he be dying? I reach out and gently stroke his black hair; my earlier anger toward him turns to sorrow even though I barely know him. He's so young.

My father had told me stories of how it used to be before humans tampered with their DNA. People living until the age of a hundred, having children, grandchildren, and often great-grandchildren. They went to college, had long careers, traveled. Experienced life to the fullest. There was none of that now. With so few years to live, the majority of humans rarely lived to fulfill their dreams. They took whatever job they could get to provide for basic comforts. Many didn't marry or have children. It was too painful for them to find love only to have it taken away from them so soon. It's no way to live life. If hell existed, that would be it.

"You say my father helped people. How exactly?" I ask.

"He never spoke of his research, but he found a way to temporarily heal human DNA, probably using his own DNA or yours."

I nod, remembering how he used to draw my blood once a month. "I wish I would've paid attention more to his work, but I was so tired from all his training that I never learned what he was doing. I regret that now. Maybe there's something I could have done for Colt."

"You have no reason to feel guilty. This," he glances down at Colt, "is the world we live in. We're used to death, but your presence gives us hope for the future. One day there will be a world where we can live to our full potential and death will come for us naturally, and not because of some scientist's experiments."

It sounds wonderful, but too far into the future. At least for Colt.

"You are so important, Sage. Do you understand?"

"I'm trying to, but I don't feel like my life is more important than any of yours. We can all make a difference in this world whether we live for five years or five hundred. It's just about what we choose to do with the time we have."

He's quiet for a minute, then, "My wife believed that too. The world was a better place with her in it. I was better."

I want to say more, but Colt makes a sound, a deep moan. I slide back a little to give him space. He rolls onto his back, flinching as if the movement hurts.

Anthony leans over him. "How are you feeling?"

"Like my mind exploded. Did it happen again?"

Anthony nods and sits back.

Colt glances over at me briefly but doesn't say anything. Neither do I. What do you say to someone who's dying?

Colt takes his time standing, but when he's up, he says, "What's the plan?"

Anthony reaches for a black bag against the wall. "Bram gave me some items we can use to go undetected inside the party tomorrow night. It should make things easier."

"What about extra help?"

"He has someone on the inside, but he wouldn't say who."

"That's it? One person?"

"You know how it is. Everyone who supports our cause is already being used."

Colt walks to the other side of the room, his scowl deeper than ever.

"So what now?" I ask.

Anthony's eyeing Colt, as if he's worried what he might do, but he speaks to me. "The most important thing you can do right now is rest. You're going to need it. And besides, there's nothing you can do for your brother until tomorrow."

Although I don't like waiting, he's right. I'm in no condition to confront others, and I need to be at my best if I'm going to rescue Max.

Anthony unzips the black bag and hands me two slices of bread from a clear sack inside. "I wish I had something better, but it's all I have for now. There's water in the bathroom. Eat and then get some rest. Blankets are in the corner."

"Thank you," I say and take a bite of the bread. It's dry and chalky in my mouth. I have to drink a lot of water to get it down, but by my last bite I'm fuller than I've ever been, making me think it's something more than simple bread.

I take my last drink from the faucet while Anthony and Colt speak quietly in the corner. They're talking strategy. I should be helping, but my eyelids are heavy. I unroll a blue mat and lie down, pulling a scratchy blanket up around me. I'll just shut my eyes for a few hours, then I'll get up. My last thoughts are of Max and my vow to raise him in a better world.

CHAPTER 13

My eyes open. The room is dark except for a small lamp in the corner. Colt is there, his back against the wall. He's reading a thin book in his hands.

I watch him for several minutes before I ask, "What are you reading?"

He startles. "Um, a book that used to belong to my mother."

"What's it called?"

"*Deliverance.*"

"It sounds interesting. What's it about?"

For the first time he smiles, changing his whole countenance to something warm and inviting. Its like he's momentarily forgotten his life. "Four men who go on a rafting trip, but then all this crazy stuff happens. It's a fight for survival."

"That's something we all know about, isn't it?" My anger toward him from yesterday has dulled. Either that, or my thoughts are too focused on getting Max back that I can't think or feel anything else.

"Unfortunately." He sets it down.

"What time is it?" I ask and stretch. My body feels better. I still have sore muscles but at least they're not shaking anymore.

"Almost twelve."

I sit up, surprised it's only noon. "I only slept for a few hours? But I feel so much better."

"Twelve, midnight. You've been asleep for almost fifteen hours."

Fifteen hours? A weight sinks inside my gut. I should've been preparing. "So the party is in less than twenty-four hours?"

He nods.

"Did you and Anthony get any sleep?"

"Both of us did. Slept most of the day."

The bathroom door opens. Anthony looks at me and blinks a few times as if he's not fully awake. "Good morning or evening. Are you feeling rested?"

"Much better, thank you."

"Good. We're meeting Jenna in an hour."

"How come you're always meeting at night?" I ask.

"Easier to go undetected. While the rest of the world sleeps, we plan how to save it." Anthony winks at me. He opens his bag and tosses me an apple and more bread. I eat them quickly.

In just a short time we're ready to go. Anthony and Colt both carry two bags; I carry one. It's filled with party costumes I have yet to see.

It's dark outside, the streets quiet. This area differs greatly from where we were before. The structures are still metal on the outside, but parts of them are rusted. The chipped sidewalks are a faded gray, and nearby two people sit close together against a doorway. They look as if they have nowhere else to go. It doesn't smell very nice here either. There's an aroma in the air that reminds me of potatoes that have been left in the sun for far too long.

I slide into the front passenger seat of a small silver car. It's not as nice as Jenna's. Part of the interior is peeling up near the base of the window. Anthony climbs behind the driver's seat, followed by Colt, who's driving.

"Back roads?" Colt says.

Anthony looks around. "That would be best. Fewer cameras."

"You really think they have me ID'd?"

"Possibly. Better to be safe."

"Does this car have a tracker on it?" I ask.

Colt swings the vehicle in the opposite direction and drives down a littered street. "Nope. It's an older model, before the government made it mandatory."

We pass many more buildings, several rusted on the corners and windows. A few are even partially collapsed. Every block or so, a few people huddle against a metal wall, a warming glow of light the size of their fists burning brightly at their center.

"Why is this area so run down?" I ask.

"It's the old part of town," Colt says. "It used to be nice, but then Junks appeared. The government attempted to get rid of them, but it was a slow process. All they managed to do was drive them underground, but by then people had already moved out, the important ones with money anyway. Ever since then, this part of the city has slowly rotted."

No wonder so many people have trouble making connections. They've been taught to move on from anything deemed broken. It's not long before the decayed buildings pass by us and give way to newer construction oblivious to the world it left behind.

We arrive at Jenna's house. She lives in a small subdivision just outside the city in a metal home, but the exterior is made to look like wood and rock. The forest is just beyond. I feel more comfortable here being so close to nature.

Jenna's waiting for us inside, typing on a flat keyboard built into a desk. She looks up and says, "It's about time."

I move into the room behind Anthony and Colt. A large, framed picture hanging on the wall overwhelms the small living room. It's a shadow of a ballerina, twirling beneath a full moon. There are fingerprint stains on the glass like it's been touched a lot.

Anthony drops his bags onto a nearby chair. "We took the back roads."

Jenna hushes him. "Mom's sleeping. Keep it down."

"Right, sorry," Anthony says, his voice lowered.

Colt drops onto a black sofa. "When are you going to update this place? A little color would be nice."

"I kind of like it," I say, surprising everyone in the room. The room is all black and white with splashes of red. Other than the ballerina picture, there is another painting of several red birds in a dive position over a smoking field. It's something I might pick out if given the opportunity.

"We might get along after all," Jenna says and slaps me on the back as she walks by me to get to Anthony. "What do you have for me?"

He opens one of the bags and removes a small container the size of my finger. "You're going to love this. I got one for each of you," he says and tosses one to Colt.

Colt examines it. "Is this what I think it is?"

Jenna looks up at Anthony, her eyes wide. "I thought these were illegal?"

I glance over Jenna's shoulder to see what she's looking at. "What is it?"

"They're contacts. Colored to be exact. This way you'll appear more like one of us."

"How did you get them?" Colt asks.

"Bram has a guy who secretly makes them."

Colt's eyebrows rise. "Wow. I had no idea he was in this deep. That's pretty brave considering the penalty is a minimum of fifteen years behind bars or worse. And us? At least ten if we're caught wearing them."

"I know I'm asking a lot," Anthony says, "but remember why we're doing this. We'll never make any headway if we aren't willing to take risks."

"What color are mine?" Jenna asks, seemingly unfazed.

"Jenna," Colt says. "Did you hear what I just said? Serious jail time. What about your mother?"

She continues to study the small box. "She doesn't recognize me anymore. I'd guess she only has a few weeks left to live." She looks up at Anthony. For the first time there's sadness in her eyes. "Once the Kiss finally takes her, I'll have no one but you. Your cause is mine."

Anthony moves to give her a reassuring squeeze on the shoulder, but she backs away. "No need to get all emotional about it. Sheesh. You act like you've won a popularity contest or something."

I shake my head, both disappointed and sad that Jenna can't allow herself even a small moment to feel something deeper than what lies on the surface. Anthony frowns too, like he's thinking the same thing.

"Where are my contacts?" I ask, suddenly realizing that Anthony only pulled out two boxes.

"You don't need any," Anthony says. "You'll be staying with

me in the car, monitoring things from the outside. Colt and Jenna will get Max."

I speak before he's finished. "No way. It has to be me that goes in."

Colt sits up on the chair. "You don't have a say. We're trying to save you, not throw you into the lion's den."

"But you don't understand. Max won't go with anyone else. It has to be me."

"We'll offer him a lollipop or something," Jenna says. "And kids adore me. He'll come."

I think of a way to explain Max, which is not an easy task. "Max isn't what you would call normal. Trust me when I say he won't come with anyone else. It has to be me that gets him or he will scream, and you guys can't risk exposing your position."

They look at each other as if trying to decide if I might be right. I pounce on their hesitancy. "Besides, I have those underground tunnels memorized. I can get us there faster than one of you trying to decipher a map."

Anthony tightens his mouth as if he's considering it, but Colt is still unconvinced and says, "Bad idea."

"What if she's right?" Anthony asks. "And the boy won't come with you? Then everything we're doing right now will be a complete waste and will surely get you two killed."

Jenna turns to me. "Can I keep the contacts when you're done with them?"

Colt glares at her, but I smile. "Sure."

"Then it's settled," Anthony says. He reaches into his bag and removes a small metal case. Inside are four pairs of what look like black dots. "We will all wear these on the inside of our ears. This is how we will communicate. Bram's guy inside will have a pair, too, but he won't be able to communicate with us, only listen. Jenna and I will monitor things from the outside, listening to various conversations from inside the center. If anyone is on to you, we'll know."

"Where are the costumes?" Jenna asks.

Anthony motions to the backpack on my shoulders. "In there.

You'll have to look at the dress. It should fit Sage, but it might be a little short. And you can do her hair, right?"

Jenna slides her fingers through my long hair, and for a moment I'm worried she might pull it. "No problem. She'll look just like them." She turns my chin until I'm facing her. "Just don't mess it up in the tunnels, got it?"

"I'll try not to."

Colt asks Jenna, "Did you pick up the meat?"

She snorts. "Of course I did. Can't you smell it? Why is it that I always get stuck with the crap jobs?"

"Because you're good at them," Colt says and relaxes back into the sofa.

Anthony glances at his wrist. "We have a few more hours until sunrise. Let's go over everything in detail until we have it memorized and then try to get some sleep. We'll wake at three in the afternoon, get ready, and get out of here. Got it?"

Our eyes all meet in silent agreement. There's a knot in my stomach, but I ignore it for fear it will tighten.

When it comes time to sleep, I'm ready. Anthony had each of us repeat the plan, including the layout of the tunnels and Center, so many times that I think my brain might return to mush. But when I lay down on a small bed in Jenna's basement, I can't sleep for several hours. I'm plagued with guilt for leaving Max. Memory problems or not, I should've sensed he was my brother, the most important person in my life. I am sick that I forgot him so easily.

Eventually I do fall asleep when I can't mentally take the guilt any longer, but it's soon after when I hear my name. Half asleep and half awake, I think I recognize the voice. It's the only voice I heard every morning for the last six years. "Sage. Sun's up. Let's go train."

I open my eyes and blink a few times. Not my father, but Colt. He is staring down at me, his blue eyes practically glowing in the darkened room. "Anthony's waiting for us upstairs."

I sit up and rub my eyes. "Is it already time?"

"I know. It feels like we've only slept for an hour. Food's upstairs." He leaves me alone in the basement.

I tilt my face toward the only window in the room, but sunlight, more cold than warm, barely filters through its dirty glass. I stand and stretch, then pump out fifty push-ups to get my blood pumping. Tonight is a big night, perhaps the biggest of my life. Tonight I am going to get my brother back.

CHAPTER 14

"Tell me again what you're going to do once you're inside," Anthony says. Papers are scattered across an oval-shaped kitchen table. It looks like he's been running various scenarios all day. My father used to do that.

I swallow the food in my mouth. "Change into the clothes, avoid cameras whenever possible, make our way to the ballroom where we wait for instructions from you."

"Correct. And don't forget to attach the heat sensor on the inside of your sleeve. That's how I'm going to tell you apart from the others in the building. It's going to give you a blue aura compared to the reds of everyone else."

"I still don't think that's a good idea," Colt says. "What if we get caught with them?"

"Highly unlikely. Besides, it's the only way I'll be able to keep track of you. I won't have you going in blind."

"It's fine," I say. "We won't get caught."

I already know that any type of weapons, including heat sensors, are scanned for at the initial entrance. Unless an alarm is set off, no one inside will be checked again.

"What about Bram's guy? What's his role in all this?" Colt asks. His complexion looks paler than usual, and I wonder if he's feeling well.

"He's there only as an observer. If something goes wrong he will be our eyes and ears."

"For what? To report back that we were all taken and killed?"

Anthony meets his gaze, his expression grim. "Yes."

"Awesome," Colt says and leaves the room.

"Don't worry," Anthony says to me. "It's not going to come to that."

"I know it won't. I'm getting my brother out of there."

"Listen to you, Tiger!" Jenna says as she walks into the kitchen wearing only a long t-shirt and underwear. She helps herself to a pastry on the counter, a cup of juice, and turns to face us. "You know there's like a five-percent chance of this plan actually working, right?"

I fold my arms. "It's going to work."

She lowers her glass, smiling, but it's not friendly. "Says the girl who can't cook a pizza."

"Can you just be nice for once?" Anthony asks as he gathers all the papers on the table. "And when you're done eating, will you help Sage with her hair?"

"Fine, but I have serious concerns that the dress you got for me won't fit her."

Colt reappears. "If anything it will be too loose."

"Stay out of this, Noc," Jenna says.

Anthony stuffs the papers into a briefcase. "I'm sure it will be just fine. We only have a few hours left, so let's get to it. Colt, you come with me."

"Where are we going?"

"Back to your place. There are a couple of weapons I should've grabbed, the kind that don't make noise."

Over his shoulder, Colt says, "Try not to kill each other, girls."

As soon as they're gone, Jenna says, "We better get started. I only have a few hours with you and, honestly, I don't think it's enough time."

I resist the urge to comment back, reminding myself that she's only thirteen years old. My energy shouldn't be wasted on her anyway. I inhale deeply and stand up. Just let her do her thing so I can focus on what really matters.

The process of prepping me for the party takes longer than I expect. Jenna bleaches my hair in blond stripes and has me shave my legs and arms twice to be sure I got everything.

"We need to make you as exotic looking as possible without having you stand out," she says, after twisting my hair into a design I've never seen before. Thin strips are looped in and out of each other into a giant heap on top of my head.

"Who taught you to do all this?" I ask, trying to hold still while she finishes painting my face.

"My mother. She used to do it for all the stars." Jenna brushes something onto my cheeks. "Everyone loved how she could transform a person. She was amazing."

I think of her mother, who's in the next room over, sleeping. On the way to the bathroom, I'd managed a quick peek in passing, the gentle hum of a ventilator having caught my attention. Mostly all I saw was a bunch of machines with tubes plugged into a pale woman with long dark hair. It made me wonder if it would've been harder to lose my mother slowly instead of all at once. I decided it would be. No one should have to watch someone they love suffer.

I say, "If she could do half of what you can do, then I'm sure she was amazing."

Jenna eyes me as if trying to decide how to take my compliment. "Thank you," she says, but quickly adds, "But there's only so much I could do for you. You don't have a lot to work with, so I hope it's enough."

A door downstairs opens and closes.

"That must be them," Jenna says and bounds into the hallway after them.

I stay alone in the bathroom for a moment, staring in the mirror. The reflection doesn't look like me. I'm someone else, except in the eyes. They are familiar. They have the same fire I often saw in my father's. I always wondered where the intensity came from, but now I know. The rising heat comes from a burning desire to protect the ones you love.

Before I go downstairs, I dress into the black pants and shirt Anthony got for me to wear into the underground tunnels. Then, as carefully as I can, I wrap a black bandana around my hair. Anthony's voice drifts up from downstairs. "Is she ready?"

"As much as she can be." Jenna's voice.

"Are you sure we're not making a mistake?" Colt asks.

"What else can we do?"

"We can make her go to Eden."

"But what about her brother?"

"We can save him later, but at least we will know that one Original survived."

"We're both going to survive," I say from the top of the stairs. "And so will you guys. I promise."

"You shouldn't promise anything. Ever," Jenna says. "It's a death wish. You look ridiculous, by the way."

"And you look scared," I say and breeze by her, snatching my backpack as I walk out the front door. I probably shouldn't have promised something so huge. It was a silly thing to say, but I know that if they don't survive, I won't either. What good will my promise be then?

I slide into the backseat of Colt's vehicle and stare forward as the others climb into the car. Anthony is behind the steering wheel driving west toward a setting sun; its light glitters against all the metal buildings, making the world around me look like a mirage. He leaves the city and drives into the forest. The windows are partially down, letting in a cool breeze that helps me breathe easy. No one says a word, but halfway there I wonder if they can hear my heart beating, specifically Colt, whom I now know has good hearing. A couple of times his eyes flicker my direction, but he doesn't say anything.

"Stop here," I say when I see a large boulder, taller than me, just off the side of the road. It's exactly where my father said it would be. The Center is maybe a mile from here.

Anthony slows the car and pulls off onto a road that looks like it hasn't been driven on for a long time. The pavement is cracked and chunks of it are missing.

I'm the last one out of the vehicle. My muscles are tight, like they are rebelling against what I'm about to do. Of all the creatures humans have mutated into, Junks are at the top of the list as one of the scariest. My mind quells the mutiny raging inside me, and I walk to the trunk of the vehicle where Anthony is unloading a couple of bags. He hands me my backpack, and I pull it over my shoulders.

From across the car, Jenna says, "You take care of that hair, Patch. It's one-of-a-kind."

"My name is Sage," I say but know it won't make a difference.

"This bag smells terrible," Colt says, his face puckering like he's chewing on something rotten. He finishes strapping a smaller, blue backpack to the front of him. "You better be right about meat distracting Junks, because this bag is making me sick."

"It will work," I say.

Colt swings a long black duffle bag holding several weapons onto his back. "How does your father know so much about Junks?"

This makes me pause. "I'm not sure."

A memory comes to mind. It's late spring. A thunderstorm has kept Max and me inside our small house for the better part of the day. My father's late. He was supposed to return the night before, but never showed up. This isn't like him, and I'm worried. But I don't let Max know this. Instead we watch television, a travel channel that shows exotic places filled with even more exotic-looking people. It's really late when I hear a sound coming from outside. I tell Max I'll be right back, thinking maybe a skunk has found our garbage again, but when I open the door, I discover a much bigger creature lurking beneath the thick canopy of our oak trees. It's tall and human-like but covered in something . . . the creature speaks. My name. And then asks for help. It's then that I realize it's my father.

I rush to him just as he collapses to his knees. He's covered in mud and has a deep cut above his forehead; blood runs into his eyes and down his face. After I help him into the house, he tells me he was in a car accident driving back from the city. He wouldn't give me any more details, but, as I am cleaning the wound in his head, I find the fractured half of a long and hardened, yellowed nail. My father mumbles something about it being bark, but I know better now. It belonged to a Junk.

Anthony finishes tightening the duffle bag to the back of Colt. "All set."

Colt turns around to face him.

"You take care of her, do you understand?" Anthony places his hands on Colt's shoulders, and his lips tighten like he's struggling to know what more to say.

"Don't worry," Colt says. "I've survived worse than this."

"Yes. Yes, you have. I'm so sorry." Anthony lowers his head in reverence.

I turn away, like Jenna, realizing this is a private conversation. The concerned look in Anthony's eyes reminds me of the way my father used to look at me right before he'd leave Max and me for several days. Like he wasn't sure if he'd come back.

They say a few more words until Jenna interrupts them. "Get going already! My life is short as it is."

"See you soon," Colt says to Anthony. He walks toward me. Each of his steps are confident like he does this all of the time. I wish I felt the same way.

"Ready?" he asks me.

I nod and follow him into the shadows of the rising trees, their limbs twisting and turning in and out of each other. Before we disappear entirely, I glance back over my shoulder. Anthony waves, but Jenna's staring straight ahead.

The trees are old in this forest, their branches so full of changing leaves that they block sunlight, preventing foliage from growing on the ground. This makes walking easy. Our pace is fast, and I almost have to jog to keep up with Colt's long strides. The wristpad Anthony gave me displays our GPS position and the time. I can also use it as a phone and to search online, but I won't be using any of those things for fear of being tracked.

"The entrance should be close," I say, remembering how my father had me draw this exact same path multiple times. Actually walking this path, knowing where I'm headed, turns my blood hot. If my father knew something like this was a reality, why didn't my father take us to Eden?

Colt stops and looks around. "What is it we're looking for again?"

"A tree trunk with a black skull painted onto the bark." I keep walking, my eyes scanning the terrain.

"There," I say and point. Not far away is a skull, partially faded, exactly where my father said it would be.

Colt goes to it first. He kicks at dirt and fallen leaves around the base of the tree until his foot hits metal.

"I can't believe you know all of this," he says, more to himself than to me.

I drop to my knees to help him unbury the hatch. "Let's just hurry."

Colt sweeps back a stack of fallen twigs and leaves with his forearm. "It looks like it was used recently, maybe in the last several weeks."

"How can you tell?"

"Because all of this has been strategically placed here. If this hadn't been used in a long time, roots and weeds would've grown over it."

"But who would deliberately go down here?"

Colt's gaze meets mine. "Why don't you ask the man who led us here?"

"I will when I find him." I'm surprised by the hardness in my voice. Maybe I'm angrier with my father than I think.

I bend next to Colt and grab a handle. I lift upwards, but it's too heavy. I sigh and let go.

"It's probably just stuck," Colt says, and I appreciate his efforts at trying to make me feel better. He grips the center handle. "Ready?"

I nod and step back, shoving all nerves and doubt to the shadows of my mind. They sit next to dark thoughts of my father.

Colt opens the hatch; it creaks and groans, and I worry about the sound it's making. Before it's all the way open, a stench punches me in the face, and I turn away before I vomit. The smell reminds me of a dead, bloated seal I'd found once on the beach. It made me throw up then, and it's all I can do not to throw up now. Colt is not so lucky. He turns his head and wretches next to the tree.

Wiping his mouth with the back of his hand, he says, "Sorry, but that's foul. I didn't think anything could smell more rotten than this meat I'm carrying."

"It's probably worse inside. Breathe through your mouth." I press a small button on my watch; a thin stream of light appears, and I point it down into the dark entrance. A rusted ladder leads to the ground.

"I'll go first," I say, but Colt stops me.

"Nope." He jumps in before I can protest.

I join him at the bottom. I was right. The smell is worse, forcing me to cover my nose with the sleeve of my shirt. Colt has the face of his wristpad entirely lit up, more so than the single beam from mine. It acts like a flashlight and illuminates a good portion of the path in front of us.

The tunnel is wider than I expect, more than the length of my arm span. It's held up by old wooden beams built into the ceiling every ten feet or so. Some of them are buckling under the weight, but at least it's tall enough that Colt won't have to duck.

Almost two centuries ago, these tunnels held large pipes as a way to deliver water to different parts of the city, but over the years, they were slowly eliminated when more efficient and cost effective ways were invented. For a time, many poor and homeless people lived in them, even improving their structure, but then Junks took over and the tunnels have remained theirs ever since.

"I don't hear anything," Colt says, "but there are vibrations." He bends down and places his hand on the ground. "We're definitely not alone."

I swallow. "How far away?"

"Not far." He straightens and tears off a strip of the inner lining of his jacket. He ties the material around the lower half of his face to cover his nose and says, "Have you ever seen a Junk?"

"My father had pictures."

"Not the same. Whatever you do, don't stare. Just remember your goal to save your brother. You want to cover your nose too?"

"I think I can handle it." I take a deep breath through my mouth and start forward. Colt joins me. He lets me lead the way, but I stop whenever he tells me to so he can listen and touch the ground.

I consider us lucky as we've turned three corners and have yet to see a Junk. "Maybe we'll go unnoticed."

The Center isn't far now. I'm about to suggest that we run when Colt grabs my arm hard and jerks me back into him. There's a faint sound in front of us. It's low and gargling, like the growl a pit bull might make if it were drowning.

Colt lowers his light toward our feet.

Another sound. The scurrying of feet. Many of them coming our direction. Snorts and more growls. My breathing quickens.

"Should we go back?" Colt asks.

My mind screams yes. I don't want to see what's coming, but I hear myself say, "No. Get the meat."

Colt unzips the backpack pressed against his chest.

"Here," he says and hands me a large, cold, wet slab of meat. By its texture it feels like beef, but by its scent it smells like road kill. Colt takes his own meat and steps in front of me, raising the light back into the tunnel.

The scurrying sounds grow louder, like we're about to be trampled, but then the frenzied noise stops, leaving only a silent terror that pains my ears. There's a corner up ahead. They are there, waiting. I don't need Colt's senses to tell me that. If we turn around and run, they will chase, but I can't run. I can only go forward, toward my brother.

I glance at Colt. Even in the dim light I can see the tightness in his neck and shoulders. His Adam's apple goes up and down as he takes a few steps forward. I stay close against his back. Very slowly, he turns the corner and shines the light, bathing the source of the quiet terror.

Light shines on three Junks, but there are more breathing sounds, soft, yet raspy, hidden within the shadows. The Junks are small, maybe to my waist, but their arms are long and almost to the ground. Their fingernails, however, do reach the dirt floor. They are thick, broken, and sharp, leaving a scar in the ground wherever they walk.

Pale, bloodshot eyes stare at me from inside sunken sockets. Noses are missing on all but one of them. Instead there's only a hole and lines of cartilage, white as bone. Their skin is gray, some of it flaking off, exposing yellowed bone. Two of them have patches of brown hair, the other is bald. One opens his lipless mouth, but no words come out, only the gurgling sound I heard earlier. A greenish, watery substance spills out onto his bloated chest.

"Breathe," Colt whispers.

It's then that I realize I'm holding my breath. I gulp a sip of air, wishing I would've remembered Colt's advice not to look at them. Their images will forever haunt my dreams.

When the hairless Junk closest to me takes a step forward, I toss the bloody slab of beef in his direction. His long arm shoots out and snags the meat with his jagged fingernail and the meat dangles back and forth. This catches the attention of the other Junks, the ones hiding in the shadows. They rush forward, surrounding the one with the meat. They poke and snap at him, like birds attempting to steal another's tasty worm.

"How are we going to get around them?" Colt whispers.

"Carefully and quickly," I say and step toward my future nightmares.

CHAPTER 15

L et me go first," Colt says, but I elude his grip and press my back to the wall. I need to share some of the risks. I slide forward, trying to be as quiet as possible.

The backs of the Junks are hunched over as they devour the meat. Small chunks are being tossed into the air only to be stabbed by the jagged nails of others. The light on my watch is dim, but I still catch splashes of red against gray skin. There's so much blood that I wonder if some of them aren't eating each other.

As visually disturbing as this is, the sounds are so much worse. It's not the tearing of flesh or chomping of teeth that pains, but all of that mixed with what sounds like retching noises from the constant stomach bile coming up their esophagi. It turns my stomach and almost makes me vomit.

"Watch your foot," Colt whispers.

I glance down. I'm within an inch of stepping onto the leg of a Junk who is on his belly. He is so still, I think he might be dead. I swallow and lift my leg over him, but just when I think I'm safe, my hand slides into a protruding chunk of dirt against the wall and dislodges it. It crumbles to the ground; the sound is enough to gain the attention of the Junks on the outer edge of the circle. They turn toward me, sharp teeth grinding against exposed jaws. One of them has blood dripping from his stained mouth.

My heartbeat skips and I freeze, afraid that even if I take a breath they will be upon me. A black tongue snakes out of a Junk's mouth and licks the side of his cheek.

Colt tosses another chunk of meat to the ground. A few of them take the bait and the distraction is enough to get me moving again. However, Black-Tongue is still staring. I think it is a girl by the amount of long, red hair still attached to her gray scalp. Her head cocks to the side, and I realize there is still a level of reasoning to her. Not like a human mind, but that of a predator. Unlike the others who seem to only care about survival, this girl sees the bigger picture.

Colt seems to notice too and pushes me to move faster.

The girl Junk with the black tongue takes hold of a nearby smaller Junk and steps toward us. My light flashes over the two, illuminating the fingernails of the smaller Junk, who also looks female, but I can't be sure. Its nails have been filed to sharp points.

"Move!" Colt says, his voice low, but he might as well be shouting.

I bolt into the darkened tunnel, forgetting all about trying to be quiet. Colt is close behind me. The light from his wristpad flashes back and forth upon dirt walls, a dirt ceiling and floor. It's all I can see and once again my chest tightens as the walls close in around me. I want to stop to catch my breath, but the scurried movements and liquid, ragged breathing of the two Junks behind us keep me moving.

"I hope you know where you're going!" Colt says as he tosses back another chunk of meat, but the two don't take the bait and continue their pursuit.

I take a left. I'm not consciously aware of where I'm going, but the layout has been so ingrained into me, I could do it in my sleep.

"We're almost there," I say, glancing over my shoulder.

Colt unsheathes two daggers from behind his back.

I take a right. It's a dead end, but I know this. I skid to a halt and turn around. Colt does the same, a dagger in each hand.

The Junks slow to a walk. The black-tongued girl, who has more human-like features than the other, is smiling. Her friend is making a yelping sound, almost like a hyena, and I wonder if it's laughter.

Black-Tongue pushes the other Junk forward. It stumbles toward us, hands raised, claws extended. It exhales, or sighs, and a mist of liquid sprays from its mouth.

Colt swipes a dagger at it, but it spins in the other direction.

"Dirty, disgusting things," he says.

A flap of skin on the Junk's forehead falls across its left eye. It reaches up and jerks it off before it lunges for Colt again. He jumps out of the way, but hits his head on the low ceiling, and the Junk almost catches the back of his leg. Colt swipes both daggers, this time nicking the Junk in the back of the head, but it's not enough to slow it down.

"Hand me one," I say.

Colt maneuvers in front of the Junk. "Stay out of this."

I huff and look around for something I can use. Only dirt. More than enough. I scoop up two handfuls. A flash of Colt's light catches the face of the black-tongued girl Junk. She's staying back, watching me with thoughtful eyes. I make a mental note to be aware of her position.

While Colt continues to unsuccessfully jab at the Junk, I carefully approach from behind. The Junk runs and slides between Colt's legs and closer to me. Colt moves to turn around, and, before I can react, the Junk slashes her hand just above Colt's pant line, cutting his shirt. Colt looks down surprised, but not in pain.

With the Junk's back to me, I shove the dirt in my hands down its throat. Combined with its stomach bile, the dirt turns to mud and the Junk coughs something fierce. Colt takes advantage and, just as I step back, stabs the dagger into the Junk's heart. A muddy-looking, bubbly mess spills from the Junk's mouth and onto her skinless chin.

It's in this moment, with Colt distracted, that black-tongue decides to attack, but I've kept my eyes on her. Just as her jagged claws are about to slice into Colt's back, I grab his left hand, the one holding a clean dagger, and jerk it backwards directly into Black-Tongue's gut. Her eyes widen and she stumbles to the ground. Blood puddles into her sunken stomach. She looks at me and, for a short moment, I catch a glimpse of the girl she might've been. The humanness in her pained expression makes me catch my breath.

What looks like tears rise in her scarlet eyes, but before they can fall Colt slashes the other dagger forward, cutting cleanly into her neck. Her head drops and rolls onto the ground, her eyes fixed on me. I turn away, trying to stifle the sob threatening to rack my entire body. What world has my father thrown me into?

"Are you okay?" Colt asks. He's wiping the blade of his dagger against his jeans. He doesn't seem at all bothered by what he's done.

I inhale a shaky breath. *Get my brother and get out. Focus on that*, I tell myself. "Let's just get this over with before more Junks come."

I hurry to the end of the tunnel and look up. There's a latched square door just above me, but I can't reach it.

"I've got it," Colt says and reaches up. He turns a handle and pushes. It groans but with a little more force, the small door opens. "I'll help you up."

I place my foot in his clasped hands and push up. When I can grab the lip of the opening, I pull myself up the rest of the way and sit on the edge. The faint light on my wristpad reveals a storage room that looks like it hasn't been used in years. Boxes are piled high to my right and metal shelving on my left holds more dust than anything else. The dirt on the floor, however, has been disturbed. Colt was right. Someone else has been here. It had to have been my father.

"Can I come up?" Colt asks below me. "The smell is killing me down here."

I move out of the way. A moment later Colt appears in a single leap. He closes the latch behind him and inhales deeply.

"So much better," he says. He removes his wristpad, places it on the ground, then presses a button on its glass surface. A light brightens the small room. "That was twisted down there, wasn't it?"

I remember the Junk's head rolling toward me. "I don't want to think about it."

I shrug the backpack off my shoulders and unzip it. Our clothes are still folded neatly inside. I use a disinfecting wipe to rub the meat juice and dirt from my hands before taking them out.

"You must really hate this world," he says, staring at me.

"Not hate. I just don't understand it. People have everything, and yet everyone I meet is in survival mode. Does anyone ever have meaningful relationships?" I hand him his clothes.

"Anthony did."

I unfold the dress from the backpack and remove the bandana from around my hair. "Good for him. I'm glad someone was happy."

He says nothing while he turns around and removes his t-shirt. His paper-thin, black wings are folded tightly to his back. I admire them for a moment before something red and dark on his side catches my eye.

"Colt," I say. "You're bleeding."

He lifts his arm and looks down. Blood drips slowly from two deep scratches just above his waist.

"Bloody Junks," he says, scowling.

I walk over to him. "Hold still."

"I can do it myself."

"Good for you." I press the bandana in my hand to his wound.

He flinches, but the motion seems to be more from my touch than any pain I might be causing him.

"You didn't mess up your hair," he says on an exhale. "Jenna would be proud. It looks good by the way. I like the blond stripes."

"Thanks." I move the cloth and inspect the wound, touching his back lightly. He jumps again, but not as much. "It doesn't look too bad. I don't think you'll need the med kit."

"Good. I'd hate for a Junk to be the cause of my death." He moves to turn around but I stop him.

"Keep facing that way," I say. "I have to dress."

"Then what's keeping you from watching me undress?"

"Nothing. Now hurry up."

Smiling, I turn around despite what I just said and undress quickly. The sleeveless dress, a red silky material, slides over me like water. The bottom sparkly hem reaches just above the floor, and I'm worried it might make me trip later. I smooth the dress over my hips. Even though it covers most of me, I still feel naked.

The last thing I do is place lilac-colored contacts into my eyes, indicating that I am a Ray, a Prime with a photogenic memory. It takes me a few tries, but eventually the contacts slide into place. Now I am one of them

I wait until I don't hear movement from Colt before I turn around. He's already facing me, with an expression I can't read. It's half curious and half something else. Whatever it is, it makes me uncomfortable.

"You look beautiful," he says. His eyes are no longer an electric blue, but a bright aqua color. I don't know what this means, and it bothers me. Colt being a Noc makes him a complete mystery.

"And your bowtie is crooked." I reach up to fix it, but he jerks backwards. "What's wrong?"

"You do a lot of touching."

"And?" I reach up again. This time he doesn't move.

"People don't touch each other," he says.

"Anthony touched your shoulders when he said goodbye."

"And it was weird."

I step back and admire my work. The tie is perfect other than being a bright purple. A strange color, I think, to go with his black suit. "Why are people afraid to touch each other?"

"They're not afraid necessarily, just worried about getting attached." He feels his tie. "How'd you know how to do that?"

"My father wore a bow tie every day. He said my mother loved them. Do you have the com devices?"

He blinks a few times like he's trying to remember what I'm talking about.

"Right," he finally says and reaches into his bag. A moment later he places four small black dots in my palm. "Put this just inside your ear."

I look at them closely. "These are so cool. My father showed them to me once." I press them into place and jump when Anthony's voice sounds in my ear.

"Are you there? Colt? Sage?"

"I'm here," I say loudly.

Colt laughs for the first time since I've met him. "You don't have to yell. You can whisper and he'd hear you." He puts the com devices in his ears and says, "Hey, Anthony." He scoops up his wristpad and secures it back onto his arm.

"What took you so long?" Anthony asks. "You were supposed to report to me ten minutes ago!"

"Junks," Anthony says. "But we survived. Thanks for asking."

"You can tell me about it later. Are you dressed?"

"Yes," I say, my voice more quiet.

"And have you attached the heat sensors?"

I look at Colt just as he presses something onto the inside of his sleeve. He reaches toward me, holding what looks like a small orange sticker. "Um," he says and hesitates like he doesn't know what to do or doesn't want to touch me.

I turn around and say, "Put it under the top seam of my dress."

A few seconds pass before his fingers brush against my lower neck. Goosebumps break on my skin.

Colt clears his throat. "All done."

"Good," Anthony says in our ears. "Now go to the door and look out carefully. Check for security."

Colt picks up our backpacks and stuffs them behind a shelf. "We know what to do. Relax."

"But I know you, Colt. You're reckless."

"Not now. I know what's at stake." His eyes shift to me.

I turn away, tired of the mantra of how important I am. While they continue to argue, I walk to a tall metal door. The door handle is long, running the entire length of the door, and when I pull it, it barely moves. I grab it with both hands and strain hard to get it to open a mere inch, just enough for me to look out.

Outside is a long hallway. Other than a thin strip of lighting lining the floor, it's dark. When I don't see any cameras, I wedge my foot into the crack and push it the rest of the way open.

"I'm leaving the room," I say when there's a break in their conversation.

"Wait up!" Colt says.

"No more talking to me unless you absolutely need to," Anthony says and then there's silence.

Colt crosses in front of me and stops at what looks like a long window built into the wall of the hallway.

"Check this out," he says.

I follow him to the other side of the hall and peer through

glass, but the room on the other side is dark. I even try shining the light from my watch into it, but the glass somehow blocks it. "I can't see anything."

"It's a lab of some kind."

"You can see?"

He points at his eyes. "Night vision. I bet this is where they make the oDNA serum."

I hesitate, wondering if we should destroy it. No more Originals will have to suffer for Primes if I do, but I bet the Institute has many more labs just like this one. Maybe after we save Max.

I leave Colt and walk down the hallway. Up ahead it turns left. This is as far as I know, and I wonder why my father didn't teach me the rest of the building's layout.

"I'm at the end," I say to Anthony.

"You know what to do," he says. "Be careful and let me know when you're upstairs."

Jenna's voice echoes in the background. "Ask about her hair!"

The com goes silent.

I glance around the corner real quick and spot a camera. It's pointed high and toward an elevator on the other end. If we go beneath it, we should go unnoticed.

"Here goes nothing," Colt says and nods me forward.

I hunch low and scurry along the wall just beneath the cameras. At the end is the elevator. Next to it is stairs. Both are in view of the camera. I glance back at Colt and shrug as if to say, "What now?"

He lifts his chin toward the elevator. I shake my head and point up at the camera.

Colt pushes me forward in direct view of the elevator and comes to stand next to me. My face goes red and I want nothing more than to punch him.

The elevator door opens. As soon as we are inside and I see that there is no interior camera, I turn on him. "Why did you do that?"

"There was no other way so relax. Besides, they didn't see our faces and by what we're wearing they'll think we just got lost. I'm sure there's another entrance down here."

"I hope so."

"Keep your head down when the door opens."

The elevator stops. I do as he says, and exit the doors to dive in with a crowd of moving people, my head still down. When I feel safe, I glance up. A woman with purple and pink hair combed straight up at least a foot past her head smiles at me. Her eyes are the same color as her pink lips. I smile back.

"I love your hair," she whispers and turns away.

I reach up and touch it self-consciously, hoping Jenna didn't overdo it, but when I step into the ballroom, I stop worrying. Everywhere I look there is someone else with brighter, higher, stranger hair than me, including some of the men. The only thing I do worry about is my dress. It's much more conservative than the other women's, and I hope it doesn't draw any attention.

"Over here," Colt says.

I follow him to the other side of the dimly lit ballroom, passing several ice sculptures in the shape of flames. I glance up. All along the ceiling are burning blue flames, much like what was at the dance club but a different color. If winter could burn, this is what it would look like.

I lower my eyes and try not to stare at the people we pass. It's not just their outfits and hair that are foreign to me. Each of them seem to have something unique about them, whether it is their height, their skin, or the occasional jewel on their face shining as bright as their eyes. I feel so plain and out of place just being near them. Ebony was right. I am unremarkable.

Colt stops near three grand pianos all being played in harmony together. The three men sitting at them have fingers that must be at least a foot long and instead of five, they have seven. Their fingers move faster than I think possible, and the music they play is the most beautiful sound I've ever heard.

A black curtain opens on a stage behind them and an exotic-looking woman steps forward. I gasp and stare. She has straight, white hair just past her waist and she's wearing a dress that looks like it's made of aqua-colored snakeskin. It twists around her until it reaches the floor where it spreads out behind her like a shimmering lake. She opens her mouth and begins to sing, but it isn't just one voice I hear. There is bass, tenor, alto, and soprano. Her voice is a whole choir. I forget what I thought earlier. *This* is the most beautiful sound I've ever heard.

I want to keep listening, but Colt's voice on the com says, "We're in position."

"Good," Anthony says. "Most of the heat signatures we're seeing are on the main floor with you. On the second floor there are fifteen people and six on the third."

"Have any of them not moved for an extended period of time or at all?" I ask, thinking of Max. He could sit still for hours if he was upset.

"I'm not sure. Give me a minute."

"What's that all about?" Colt asks me.

I just shake my head. The time for explaining my brother's actions would come soon enough. I go back to listening to the beautiful woman. The words she sings are in another language, but I can tell by the emotion in her voice that she's singing of great loss. When the music crescendos, my eyes tear. I quickly wipe at my eyes when I feel Colt watching me.

"There's one," Anthony's voice says on the com. "Third floor, east side. And whoever it is, they're alone."

I'm about to say it's Max, when an exceptionally tall, muscular-looking man in a lime-colored suit approaches us. His eyes match his suit, and he has slicked-back blond hair with olive-toned skin. He's smiling big, revealing a set of perfectly shaped white teeth. I can't place him as a specific breed of Prime, which means he hasn't had any synthetic DNA, but that didn't mean he isn't dangerous.

"I haven't seen you before," he says to me. His voice is deep, but smooth sounding, making me think of melted chocolate.

"She's with me, Tank," Colt says.

I turn to him. "You know him?"

Colt grimaces. "Everyone knows him."

"But I don't know you," Tank says. "Either of you." He looks back and forth at each of us.

"I'm Dick, this is Jane," Colt says.

Tank laughs. "Sure, okay." His eyes lower to mine. "You really don't know me?"

I study his face, strong jaw, butt chin. There is something familiar about him, but I can't place it.

"Sorry," I say and shake my head.

"Tank here," Colt says, his voice sarcastic, "is the world's best athlete. There isn't anything he can't do."

Tank laughs again. It's sweet sounding, making me feel at ease. "I wouldn't go that far, but I am good."

"Not for long," Colt says. "Another few years and," he drags his thumb across his own throat as if it's a knife, "it's lights out for you."

"Co—I mean Dick!" I say, quickly catching myself from calling him by his real name.

"The old man's right," Tank says. "But I plan on living every day to the fullest."

Colt straightens. "Don't call me old. We're probably the same age."

"I measure someone's age by their attitude, and you, *sir*, are an old fart." Tank punches his arm. I think it is meant to be playful, but Colt stumbles back.

"Would you like to dance?" Tank asks me.

"She's with me," Colt says.

"Let the girl decide."

I glare at Colt, frustrated by his negativity. "I'm sorry, Tank, but we have to go."

"One dance," he says. "I promise you won't regret it."

Colt steps threateningly close, regardless of the several inches of height Tank has on him. "She said no."

For the first time, Tank's smile disappears. A few people near us must sense the tension between us because they look in our direction. To prevent any further attention, I take hold of Tank's arm.

"One dance," I say.

Tank winks at Colt and guides me to the other side of the pianos where there's an open area for dancing. We join only a handful of other couples, and I'm very uncomfortable being this out in the open. Tank, on the other hand, seems to enjoy the admiring stares of those around us.

He stops in the center and pulls me into his arms as if I'm a feather, and I gasp at his strength. I rest my hand on his upper arm. My palm doesn't even come close to gripping it; his muscle is too big.

"I find it refreshing that you don't know who I am," he says. "How is that possible?"

"I'm not from around here," I say, my eyes on the singing, exotic woman. As much as I will miss her voice, I hope she stops singing soon so I can get Max.

"You're an alien. I knew it."

I look at him. "What?"

"From another planet. That explains why you don't know me, and why you're the prettiest woman in the room."

My face turns red. "Not in here. I've never seen such beauty."

"Neither have I."

I meet his gaze. It burns into mine and I turn away, speechless. Of all the lessons my father gave me, he never taught what to do in this situation. Should I fight him? Be flattered?

"What's your real name?" he asks.

"I don't know what you mean."

He stops dancing and brushes a stray hair away from my cheek. A chill spreads throughout my body.

"You can trust me," he says.

My heart races and I hope it's not because of his touch. "I better go."

"But I can help."

"I don't think so." I turn to leave, but he grabs my arm.

"I know about your brother."

My heart stops, and I look back at him, waiting for him to say more.

"I'm with Bram," he says, glancing around the room as if he's afraid someone might hear him. He pulls me back to him. "Keep dancing."

I do as he says, forcing myself to sway to the music. "If that's true, then what's my brother's name?"

Not even the Institute knows it. If Tank can tell me this, then I'd know that he's our guy on the inside.

Tank closes his eyes and taps the side of his forehead. "I know this. Give me a second."

While he thinks, I glance back at Colt. He's standing rigid with arms folded tightly to his chest. I motion him over.

"It's Mac," Tank says. "Wait, no. Matt."

When I narrow my eyes and take a step back, he stretches out his arm as if to stop me and says, "Max! It's Max. I remember now."

I exhale the breath I was holding. "Let's go."

I lead him back to the side of the ballroom where Colt is standing.

"Everything okay?" he asks. Colt stands close to me, closer then he's ever been before; our arms are almost touching. I wonder if the closeness bothers him.

"Tank is our man," I say, my voice low. "He knows about Max."

Colt is shaking his head. "That's what I heard through the com, but I don't believe it. It's a trick."

"It's true, old man," Tank says.

Colt leans toward him. "You're saying that the world's biggest sports star, who has these amazing abilities, supports a cause that wants to get rid of people like you?"

Tank smiles at Colt. "And people like you."

"Why?" I ask.

"Because there's so much I want to do with my life, with or without my enhanced abilities, but I won't live long enough to accomplish even a fraction of them. So I might as well help build a world where others can."

Colt scoffs. "Then why don't you use your position to get all of your buddies to help us out too?"

Tank shrugs in frustration. "I tried. A couple of years ago I was very vocal about what I thought, but I was laughed at. No one wants to be normal again. They think a world like that would be pathetic."

"I don't get it," I say. "You'd think people would be upset that everyone's dying so young. Why aren't they?"

Tank keeps his voice low. "For a couple of reasons. First, because they know their time is short, they want to enjoy as much of it as they can. Look around. Everyone here is young, most under the age of twenty-five. They don't want to spend what precious years they have left fighting a government who has ten times the resources they do. Besides, if you read our history, most uprisings were led by older men and women who had learned a better way through great hardship. Right now everyone's just having a good time."

"But people they love are dying."

"They're used to it. Party. Have fun. Don't get close to anyone. It's the world we live in. Messed up, I know." He shakes his head. "All we can do now is find and protect Originals, then hope that when their numbers are enough, they can make things right. If only I could live to see that day." He turns away, his jaw muscle clenches tight.

"It's a brilliant plan, if you think about it," Colt says. "As long as the population stays young while those in control grow old using serum made from Originals, they'll be able to control the population for centuries."

"Then we'll change things," I say. "Starting with saving my brother." Hot anger courses through me, igniting me with new energy. Everyone around me is so young, beautiful, and full of life, but within ten years they'll all be dead. So many deaths. There has to be a way to stop the Institute. I think of my father. With all the secrets he kept from me, he's bound to have a solution. I have to find him.

"Do you know Max's location?" Tank asks.

"Has the person on the third floor moved?" I ask Anthony through the com device. "I believe it's Max."

"He hasn't moved," Anthony's voice confirms.

Tank touches the back of my elbow. "I'll take you up."

"I thought you wanted to be an observer only," Colt says.

Tank doesn't take his eyes off me. "That was before I met her."

"I'm coming too," Colt says.

"No. It will appear suspicious with all three of us, but me wandering off with a pretty girl won't draw any attention." He smiles and winks at me.

I look at Colt, unsure of how I feel about being alone with Tank.

"You okay with this?" Colt asks me. "I can go with you."

I glance back at Tank. He's staring over my shoulder toward the exit. "I'll be fine. See you soon?"

Colt nods, his expression grim.

Tank grabs my hand and pulls me next to him as we walk out of the ballroom.

"Don't look so worried," he says. "The guards have to believe that you want to be with me, or we're going to get questioned."

"How do I do that?" I ask.

"Haven't you ever liked a boy before?"

"I've never been around a boy before until recently, other than my brother and dad, of course."

He doesn't stop moving, but squeezes my hand gently. "Just giggle and stuff. Stare at me and touch me a lot. That's what other girls do."

"I thought people didn't like to touch?"

"Oh there's plenty of touching, but there's no emotion behind it." He glances sideways at me.

"Then why bother?" I ask.

"Pleasure, my dear."

I turn away, embarrassed.

"Oh, come on now. You're saying this body doesn't turn you on?"

I scrunch my nose. "Turn me onto what? I don't understand."

He shakes his head and chuckles. "You've been living under a rock, haven't you?"

His words sting, and I once again realize how little I know of this world. I may be able to point out the weaknesses of just about every living species, or have the layout of buildings memorized, but I don't know much about how humans interact with each other. From what I've seen so far, I'm not real impressed.

Tank starts up a grand stairway, taking me with him. At the top are two men in white suits. Although they match several of the other guests, I know they are guards by their rigid stances.

"Remember what I said," Tank whispers in my ear as he wraps his arm around my waist.

I take a deep breath and nuzzle up against him, smiling big.

"Let's go have a good time, babe," Tank says and nuzzles me back.

When I giggle, the guard nearest me rolls his eyes, but he lets us pass without a word. As soon as we're out of their sight, Tank says, "I like when you cuddle up against me. Maybe we can do it again?"

I lean away but let him keep his arm around me since there's a camera nearby pointed in our direction. Still smiling, I say through my teeth, "Only under the threat of death."

"I can make that happen," he says, but nudges me playfully.

At the end of the hall a door opens. Tank pulls me closer to him. A woman, thin and a foot taller than Tank, steps out from a room and looks up. My heart beats a painful rhythm when my eyes meet with Ebony's, the Techhead from the Institute.

I'm so dead.

CHAPTER 16

"Mr. Bailey," Ebony says, "shouldn't you be downstairs celebrating?"

Tank laughs. Even though every muscle in his body is tense, it doesn't show in his voice. "I was just showing my girl around," he says.

"And which flavor of the week is it today?" Ebony's eyes start at my feet and slowly move up to my face. She frowns and narrows her eyes like she's trying to figure out a complex math equation.

I swallow hard. She's going to recognize me soon if I don't do something fast.

"I'm strawberry because that's his favorite flavor," I say and give him a big hug. "Isn't that right, baby?" I kiss him lightly on the cheek.

Tank squeezes me. "It sure is. I could eat strawberries all day long."

"You disgust me," Ebony says, lifting her narrow chin. She turns away from us and walks away.

"Love you, Ebony!" he calls after her. She doesn't acknowledge him.

When Ebony turns the corner and we are alone again, Tank opens a door toward the end of the hallway and ushers me inside a stairwell.

"That was close," he says as soon as the door closes.

I move two steps away from him and inspect the area. It's well lit with stairs going both up and down. I don't hear anyone, and I don't see any cameras either.

"Why did she make you so nervous?" I ask.

"Remember how I told you I tried to convince people that saving Originals was the only way out of this mess?" He starts climbing the stairs.

I nod and go after him.

"Word got back to Ebony and she had me called in for a little chat. I refused to go, but they used Titans to arrest me."

"Isn't that illegal?"

"Technically, but the Institute is never punished. They live by their own set of rules and no one ever questions them."

"So what happened?"

"She threatened permanent imprisonment or worse. Only when I convinced her that it was only a joke did she let me go. I'm not afraid of much, but that woman scares me."

"I know the feeling."

We reach the top of the stairs. My brother isn't far. It's all I can do to keep from breaking into a run to go to him.

Addressing the com, I say, "Anthony?"

There's a slight pause before he answers. "Yes?"

"How many are on the third floor now?"

"Only three. Your brother still hasn't moved, but there's two people just outside his door."

"Just two," I say, thinking. Between Tank and I, we should be able to get through them easily enough. I look up at Tank.

He is shaking his head. "I'm sorry. This is as far as I can go."

"What do you mean? My brother's just down the hall."

"I can't be discovered. My position is too valuable."

I clench my jaw until it hurts. "You mean you don't want to give up your fabulous life."

He takes me by the shoulders. "That's not it at all. HOPE needs the information I provide them. There's no one else with the connections I have."

I shrug off his hands. "But you're already discovered. As soon as they know my brother's gone, they're going to check the cameras and see that you were the last one with me."

Tank reaches into his pocket and pulls out a small syringe full of a clear liquid. "That's why I brought this."

"What is it?"

"It's a drug that will knock me out. When they find me, I'm going to tell them you injected me with it."

"And they'll believe you?"

"Easy. Everyone thinks I'm all brawn and no brains. It's a role I have to play." He looks at me for understanding, but I give him nothing.

"What if they capture me?" I ask. "Are you saying you won't help?"

"Of course I will. That's why I'm doing this." He raises his hand holding the syringe and injects it into his neck. "I can't help you if they suspect me too."

"I can't believe you just did that," I say, a shaky breath moving from my lungs.

Tank slumps against the wall. "I'm so sorry."

He slides to the floor slowly and closes his eyes, but he looks anything but peaceful.

I stare at him for a few seconds, shocked. What am I going to do now? Only two people stand between me and Max, but they are surely much stronger and faster than I am. The only thing I have going for me is my father's training. Hopefully I'll recognize whatever species they are so I can exploit their weaknesses.

"Everything okay?" Anthony asks into the com. His voice is hesitant, and I'm afraid he is close to calling the whole thing off.

"Slight set back, but nothing to worry about."

The com is silent again.

I breathe in and out, quick breaths through puckered lips, trying to summon some courage. *I can do this*, I think as I shake my hands in the air. I don't know why I'm so nervous. I escaped from the Institute, getting by more Primes than this, but that was before I had my memory. Now that I remember who I am, with all of my faults and insecurities, I'm not sure I can do it.

I think of Colt. He probably heard my conversation with Tank, but he won't know that he's lying on the floor unconscious unless I say something. But how will he get up here? He isn't anyone famous that no one will question. I won't risk his life any more than necessary.

It is up to me to save Max. I can do it for him. I have to.

At least I have a stunner. I lift up my dress and unhook it from the case around my thigh. It fits perfectly in my hand and should go unnoticed.

I take a deep breath and slowly open the door just a crack and peek out. Down the hall are a man and woman. They are both in white pantsuits like the other guards and have hair the color of seaweed. They have no distinguishing features for me to tell what type of species they are, which means I will have to wait until I see their eyes before I know how to react.

I'm going to have to get close.

Before I change my mind, I open the door and stumble out, laughing hard with snorts in between. My father taught me that when you act inebriated, people are more inclined to excuse outrageous behavior, giving you the opportunity to make a move. I'm hoping these guards will excuse my clumsiness enough until I can get close to them.

"Stop!" the woman says. "You shouldn't be up here."

I stumble forward, one arm swaying high. "Huh? I can't hear you."

"Go back," the man says. His voice is deeper than I expect. "You need to turn around and go back to the party."

I keep moving forward, searching the ground like I've dropped something. All the while I'm holding the stunner close to my stomach.

"You might have to help her," the woman says to the man.

I glance up for a fraction of a second, just enough to see his eyes. This time I stumble for real. One eye is dark brown and the other is a lime green. The woman's are the same. *Speeders.* They are almost impossible to fight in hand-to-hand combat. You blink and they appear behind you.

And I'm about to fight two of them. By myself. I swallow hard and lean against the wall while trying to remember if they have any kind of weakness. They don't.

The man approaches me and takes hold of my arm. "Let's go."

Better act fast before he does. Real quick, I jab the stunner into his chest and press a button at its top. The man jerks violently and falls to the ground.

"What did you do?" the woman asks. She blinks a few times until she decides to rush me, but I barely see her before her fist collides into the side of my face. I stumble along the wall, trying hard to keep my feet beneath me. My long dress makes this even more difficult.

Another blur of movement. All I can distinguish is a swish of her long seaweed hair before a blow to my stomach explodes air from my lungs. A fraction of a second later, the stunner is knocked from my hands.

"I'm going to break you now," she says, standing across from me with fists raised.

She comes straight for me, but I spin out of the way just in time. The stunner is ten feet away. If I go for it, I'll lose sight of her and that could be deadly. I stay where I'm at, every muscle tight.

The air stirs to my right and a flash of white comes at my head. I duck but not fast enough. The heel of her boot catches the side of my cheek, making me fall to the ground.

The stunner is only five feet away.

Glancing back, I kick hard where the woman is standing. The upper half of her body is already in motion, but I manage to graze her shin. She cries out and I scramble forward, tripping over my dress the whole time. Just as my fingers touch the stunner, something hard, probably her dumb boot again, smashes against the back of my head. Stars explode in my vision, and my body goes limp. Before my face hits the ground, the woman is jerking me up by the back of my hair until I'm upright with her standing behind me. Her other arm wraps around my throat, cutting off my air supply.

She whispers in my ear, "I'm not allowed to kill without permission, but I can break bones."

I attempt to fight, but the movement is only in my head. Without oxygen, I can't think or move. It's over. Maybe they'll put me in the same room as my brother. I hope.

Before I lose consciousness, the woman's arm leaves my throat, and I suck in as much air as I can handle. Unfortunately it's not much because now the woman is pulling my right arm backwards.

Any moment and I think the tendons in my shoulder will tear, but instead there's a strange gurgling.

The woman releases me, and I fall to the ground, gasping for air. As soon as my vision clears, I turn around to see why I was released. Colt is standing there, pressing the stunner to the woman's side. She's shaking violently while he holds her tight to his chest. The electric blue of his eyes shines through his contacts, and his lips are scrunched tight.

"Let her go," I say, but the words barely make it past my lips. I slide over to him. "Let her go," I say louder. Only when I touch his leg does he drop her to the floor. A whiff of smoke swirls into the air above her, and I smell something that reminds me of tanning animal skin, something I'd done plenty of back home.

Colt kneels next to me. "Are you all right?"

He takes the bottom of my dress and presses it to my cheek. If I'm bleeding I can't tell. My whole body is numb.

"I'm okay," I say and stand up, my head pounding. I stumble sideways, but Colt steadies me. He's breathing heavy. "How did you get up here?"

"I had to stun a few people."

"That was—" I was about to say "risky," but Colt's sudden, startled expression stops me.

"I can hear them. They've found the bodies, and they're coming up."

"Max!"

I run to the room Max should be in and open the door, all pains forgotten. It's a sterile office full of metal and electronics, a stark contrast to the rest of the building. On a white wall behind a silver desk is a tall painting of Ebony.

Behind me, Colt closes the door and locks it. "That should buy us some time," he says.

I search the rest of the room until I find Max on the other side of some metal shelving. His back is to me and he's sitting in a chair, staring out the window.

I hold out my hand to Colt to stop him from coming forward. "Give me a second."

"But they're coming! We need to hurry."

"I know, but I need a little time." I walk to Max and stand between him and the window. I bend down in front of him. His blond hair is combed straight and his skin is a perfectly white color, made even more so by the plain black t-shirt he's wearing. His pale blue eyes stare right through me.

"Max?" I say gently. I rest my hands on his small knees. He looks much younger than ten. "It's me. Sage. I've come to take you away from this place, but we have to go now."

He remains still, locked away in a prison I can't access. I notice there are marks on his arms. Tears burn the back of my throat.

"Max, please," I say again. "Remember the ocean? The shells, Max. We need to go to the ocean and gather shells. We'll count every single one of them."

This time he blinks. Behind him Colt is finding objects to press against the door. Already he's blocked it with a metal bookcase.

"Max?"

He blinks again, but he's not quite with me.

I say, "Do you remember that great big shell we found? The one with the tail that was twisted? We hung it on the porch and whenever Daddy would come home he'd blow it. Remember?"

Max's eyes shift to mine. He makes no sound, but his bottom lip quivers and he bites it. Tears fill his eyes and he wraps his arms around me. I return his hug and pick him up; his legs naturally go around my waist.

"I'm here. I came back," I say, rubbing his back.

Colt walks to the window and peers out. "I can break it and try to fly us out of here. I don't know if I'll be able to carry you both at the same time, though."

There are sounds outside the door. Two voices yelling. Max begins to squirm against me.

"Take him," I say.

"I'm not leaving either of you." He's looking around the office, probably searching for something to break the window.

A pounding rocks the door.

Colt picks up a silver, triangular-shaped object that looks like some kind of art sculpture and raises it above him.

"You have to take Max," I say again, my voice rising.

Max drops to the ground and runs to the corner of the room. "Max!" I hurry after him.

Colt throws the silver object and hits the glass, creating a spider-web like crack, but it doesn't break. He curses and picks up the object again.

I try and grab Max, but he avoids me and pounds his little fists on a bookcase engraved with animals along its trim.

"Stop it, Max," I say. "We have to go."

He takes hold of my arm and jerks it hard.

"Hey, what do you think—" I pause, a memory surfacing. Max only tugs on my arm when it's something really important. He did it once when he caught sight of a bear coming toward us along the bank of a river. I was too busy reeling in a fish. He saved our lives that day.

Glass shatters behind me.

"Let's go!" Colt yells.

The door to the office is shaking. They're coming in. I turn back to the bookcase, looking for anything that doesn't belong.

"What are you doing?" Colt shouts. Wind blows into the room, twisting up loose papers into the air.

I focus on an engraved shark at the corner of the border. It has wings. I press my finger against it and jump back, taking Max with me when the bookcase opens.

Behind it is a closed metal door with a keypad next to it.

Colt comes up from behind. "There's no time to figure out the code. We have to go now!"

Max lets go of my hand and goes to the keypad. He pushes a series of numbers until the door slides open.

Just then the door behind us explodes open.

"Everybody in," Colt says and pushes us inside what looks like a small closet. Men are pouring into the room, yelling for us to stop.

As soon as we're safely inside, the door closes and the room begins to move down. I exhale and rest my head against the wall, which is a shiny metal. My reflection is a mess. Hair tangled every which way, makeup smeared, and blood running down my cheek.

"Where do you think it's taking us?" I ask. My breath steams the metal.

"How did your brother know the code?" Colt says, staring down at Max.

"By paying attention."

The elevator jerks and I straighten, thinking it's going to stop, but it keeps moving down.

"Wherever it's going, we'll get through it," Colt says. "We've come this far, which completely surprises me, so maybe we've got a chance."

The elevator jerks again, this time stopping. Colt lowers into a defensive position.

I pick up Max and hold him tightly to my chest.

The door opens.

CHAPTER 17

I fully expect a whole legion of Primes to be waiting for me when the elevator doors open, but no one's there, and I exhale. Colt goes first into a darkened room.

"We're in the lab," he says. "Let's go."

I can barely see as I follow him through a series of long, narrow lab tables. When I pass a refrigerator with a glass door, I stop.

"What are you doing?" Colt asks, his voice tense.

I set Max on top of a nearby counter and click the light on my wristpad. After opening the refrigerator, I remove a case of six vials. Their labels read oDNA 748. I tuck them under one arm and pick up Max again.

"Let's go," I say.

I'm not sure why I'm taking the vials other than I know they are important to the Institute, which makes them important to me. Another lesson of my father's.

Colt opens a door at the opposite end of the lab, and together we sprint down the hall leading to the storage room. Colt looks up at the ceiling as if he's hearing something. "They're almost here."

I hurry into the room and set Max down so I can put the vials into the backpack I left behind. Colt closes the door behind us and pushes one of the shelves in front of it. Because there's no time to change, I tear the bottom half of the dress, giving my legs more movement.

"How much meat do we have left?" I ask.

Colt picks up his backpack and looks inside. "A few slabs. And we still have the daggers and a stun gun."

I kneel next to Max and look into his eyes, but I can tell by their glazed look that he's not really paying attention. This must be so scary for him. "I'm going to take you into a tunnel, but I don't want you to worry. We will be out soon, just keep your eyes closed, okay?"

He blinks but it could be an involuntary movement. I pick him up and hold him tightly to my chest.

"We're coming, Anthony," Colt says, just as footsteps hurry down the hall after us.

I open the square door leading into the tunnels and jump down. Max almost slips from my grip, but I hike him back up. Colt drops next to me and makes a gagging noise. "This smell is going to kill me."

"Not if the Junks get you first." Light from my watch spreads out before me. "Do you sense anything?"

"Nothing close. You want me to carry Max?"

"I've got him. Let's go." I begin to run. Max's fingers dig into my shoulder blades, and his body shakes. The sooner we get out of here the better.

Colt stays close behind me as we hurry through the tunnels. When we come to a cross tunnel I think I see movement, but I keep moving, holding tightly to Max.

"Go faster," Colt says.

I'm already sprinting, but I push harder, my legs burning from hip to ankle. Seconds later, I hear Junks, their strange gurgling sounds made worse by running. Colt tosses a slice of meat over his shoulder. Some of the sounds die off, but not enough.

"At least they're behind us," I say, panting. Two more turns and we'll be back at the hatch leading to the forest.

I glance back at Colt. The light from my wristpad catches his expression. His eyebrows are scrunched together and his lips are pressed tight, like when I was dancing with Tank, or when he took out the Speeder. He's either angry or worried.

"Anthony," Colt says, "we're in trouble."

I wonder what he's talking about, then we round the final corner. I skid to a stop. Directly under the hatch are Junks, at least ten of them. Behind Colt are three more running toward us. He pushes me to the side and withdraws a dagger. I look around. Just ahead is another turn that looks like the beginning of a partially constructed tunnel. I tug at Colt.

"This way," I say and run toward it.

"It's a dead end," Colt says.

"I know, but at least we can defend our backs better."

I rush to the end of it, which is only twenty feet or so off the main tunnel, and set down Max. Colt rounds the corner after me, but with each step he slows as if he's walking through thick mud. The light from my watch shows the muscles in his face have gone lax. He looks like he's about to fall asleep.

"Colt?"

He doesn't answer. His eyes glaze over and they shine. Then they roll up and show white.

"Colt!" I rush to him, but not fast enough to catch him before he falls to the ground, his body shaking uncontrollably.

The Junk's watery choking sounds change to what sounds like asthmatic hyenas. They are laughing.

CHAPTER 18

I tug on Colt's shoulders and dig my heels into the dirt to drag him to the back of the tunnel. Behind me, Max whimpers.

"It's okay, Max. I'm here. Just keep your eyes closed." I want to comfort him, but I need every ounce of strength I have to drag Colt.

I'm almost up against the tunnel wall when Junks appear. I roll Colt over and grab the last of the meat from his bag. I throw it hard, hoping to get it over their heads and far away from us, but it lands in the middle of the small swarm. They turn on it like a pack of rabid dogs, slicing and cutting at anything and everything.

With the Junks distracted, I turn to Colt. He's still shaking, his hands curled tight; one of them still clenches the dagger in a death grip. I hold his head to the side and look over my shoulder at Max. His eyes are closed tight and his hands are covering his ears. Any moment he may start screaming. I need to get us out of here and fast.

"Anthony," I say. "Colt's had another seizure. I need help. I'm trapped near the hatch."

"I'm almost there," he says into my com. He's out of breath.

A wet, tearing sound makes me look back at the wild pack. One of the Junks has ripped another with his claws. There is more blood than skin on his face. The bloodied Junk lunges at the aggressor, and the two roll away from the feeding frenzy. Razor-sharp teeth tear off an ear, and I look away.

Colt makes a sound. He's stopped shaking, but his eyes still swim in a murky sea of unconsciousness.

"Colt?" I whisper.

The two fighting Junks tumble closer to us. Max presses against my back and buries his head into my neck. I reach my left hand behind me and squeeze his leg, and pull Colt closer to me with my right. His legs lie only a few feet from the Junks. As long as they keep fighting, and the others keep eating, we may go unnoticed until Anthony can get to us.

I keep my head down and watch the two Junks out of the corner of my eye as they tear at each other with their long fingernails. All of a sudden, for no apparent reason, the Junks stop eating and the two near us stop fighting. They stand erect as if they're listening to something beyond my hearing capabilities. Several of them run back the way they came, but the two who had been fighting before turn toward us, sniffing the air.

I slowly untangle myself from Colt and Max, who's rocking back and forth, and remove the dagger from Colt's relaxed hand.

The Junk with the missing ear growls and steps forward. The other one hangs back, its eyes glancing anxiously between us. I remember the female Junk I helped kill earlier. How human she appeared at the end. I don't want to kill anything else, not if there is a chance it could be saved. The dagger shakes in my hand.

"I don't want to hurt you," I say, but Earless doesn't give any indication that he understands what I'm saying and keeps coming toward me, his hands extended. Blood gurgles in his throat; some of it sprays outside his mouth.

Just then there's a loud popping sound. A whole bunch of them. And voices shouting.

He looks back.

"Go on," I say. "Shoo!"

The Junk behind it runs away, but Earless hesitates for a moment longer until another series of pops echoes through the tunnels. It snarls once then disappears through the opening.

I exhale and drop the knife. "It's okay, Max. They're gone."

I want to go to Max, but I need to see what scared away the Junks. I peek around the corner. The area beneath the hatch is clear, but further down the Institute's guards are yelling and fighting with Junks.

I rush back to Colt and Max. We have one shot at this. It's now or never.

"Come on, Colt," I say. "Wake up!"

I sit him up by pushing against his back. He moans a little and his head sways, but at least he doesn't fall over.

I rotate in front of him and pat his face with my hands hard. "Look at me, Colt. Wake up!"

His eyes come into focus and stare back at me.

"I'm going to stand you up, but I need your help. We're in trouble, do you understand?"

His head lobs forward. I take that as a yes and slip my arms under his and press up. He struggles, but at least he's helping. In just a few seconds he's standing.

With my free hand I take hold of Max's arm and pull him forward with us. Stuck in his alternate world, he tries to resist, but I don't let go. I am practically carrying Colt and dragging Max.

The voices in the tunnel grow closer. There's no more shooting but a lot of yelling.

"Sage!" It's Anthony's voice.

"Anthony! Over here."

Anthony hurries in and comes to Colt. I let him take Colt, and I pick up Max.

"Is anyone hurt?" Anthony asks, looking us over.

"We're fine, but guards are coming."

"Let's go then." Anthony lifts Colt's arm and wraps it around his shoulders. "You've got to help me, Colt. Can you do that?"

Colt mumbles something unintelligible.

I carry Max ahead of them and jog back to the hatch. It's wide open, and I look up. The light from my wristpad shines through the darkness and onto Jenna's face.

"You completely ruined your hair," Jenna says from above. "And what did you do to the dress?"

"Improved it," I say and climb up the ladder.

As soon as I'm at the top, I set Max down and go back inside to help Anthony. Light flashes at the end of the hallway.

"Hurry!" I say.

Colt reaches for the ladder but misses. I hold his hand to

the ladder and do the same with the other. In his ear, I whisper, "Please. We're so close."

This seems to wake him up. He places his foot on the bottom rung and pushes up. I climb up with him, keeping a steady hand on his back.

"Stop!" a man shouts. He runs toward us. Two more appear behind him.

Jenna reaches a hand down. "Grab it!"

Colt takes hold and she easily lifts him out. They are all so strong.

"Go up, Sage," Anthony says. "I've got these guys."

He's holding the same dagger I had in my hand earlier.

"I'm not leaving you alone," I say.

"Three guys is nothing. I'll be fine. Go."

I look up toward where my brother sits waiting for me and then back at Anthony.

"Stop right there and we'll let you live," a guard says. He has a single spike sticking out of his otherwise bald head.

"Don't listen to him, Sage," Anthony says. "You're too valuable. Just go before they capture Max again."

This makes me move. I scramble up the ladder. When I'm at the top, I shout down, "Come on! You can make it."

He stares up at me through the narrow opening and smiles. "Change the world," he says just as an invisible blast knocks him to the ground.

CHAPTER 19

I'm staring at Anthony's unmoving body when Jenna shoves me aside and closes the hatch. She jams a long rod into the handle of the door and twists it around, preventing it from opening on the inside.

Max presses against me.

"He's not dead, right?" I ask, placing a protective arm around my brother. The night is cold and seeps through the thin material of my dress.

"It doesn't matter," Jenna says. "We have to get out of here."

"What do you mean it doesn't matter?"

She helps Colt to his feet, completely ignoring me.

"Answer me! Is he dead?"

She whirls on me, her golden eyes cold and cruel. "If I'm lucky that rod will hold for maybe five minutes, and then a whole lot of people, who none of us are equipped to fight, are going to come pouring out like locusts. Do you want all of us captured?"

I glance at Colt, but he's staring at the ground as if he's trying to remember what happened. "Fine," I say, and tighten my grip on Max.

"Can you run?" Jenna asks Colt.

"I think so," he stutters.

"Good. The car's this way."

She cuts into the forest, followed by Colt, who's half-running, half-limping. I stay as close behind them as I can but I'm not as fast. Max feels like he weighs a hundred pounds. But I don't stop. The burning in my muscles is nothing I haven't felt before. I'll go until my body gives out.

The forest is dark, lit up only by the fractured light of each of our wristpads, moving in sync with our swinging arms. Shadows stretch and break, bend and twist; the motion is nauseating if I don't stare straight ahead. We reach the car, which is a ways off the main road. There's a jagged trail behind the tires of torn-up earth and grass as if Anthony had been driving a hundred miles an hour before he stopped.

Jenna opens the passenger door for Colt, but before he gets there he falls to his knees and vomits in the dirt. I wonder if it's because he's pushed himself too hard after just having a seizure or because we left Anthony.

I unhook Max's arms from around my neck and place him in the backseat of the car before I go to help Colt. He waves me away.

"I'm fine," he says and wipes his mouth with the back of his hand. He stands up, stumbles a little, but then recovers. He still hasn't looked at me.

I slide next to Max while Jenna revs the engine to life.

"Is Anthony alive?" I ask again as the car shoots forward.

It takes her a few seconds to say, "He was only stunned. So, for now, he's alive."

"What will they do to him?"

Her fingers twist around the steering wheel. Her knuckles are bone white. "For the first twenty-four hours they will try to get him to give up the names of everyone involved and our locations. If they can't get him to talk, which they won't, then they'll drug him to get the truth, but even that won't work. He's built up a tolerance. We all have."

"Then what will they do?"

Her eyes meet mine in the rearview mirror. "They'll kill him."

When I suck in air, she adds, "Or they may choose to send him where everyone else goes who opposes the Institute: Purgatory Island, which is the same thing as a death sentence."

I've heard the name before but can't place it. "What's that?"

"It's an island that was set up as a prison over a hundred years ago. It came at a time when the population had exploded, which meant more bad guys. Prisons were so overcrowded that wardens had to start letting people go, the least of the offenders first. This outraged and scared a lot of people." Jenna turns the steering wheel, putting the car back onto a main road. I think we're heading in the direction of her mom's house.

She continues, "So the lawmakers at the time came up with an idea—a three-strikes-you're-out sort of thing. Except for murderers. They went straight to the Island. But for other criminals they were given a few chances. If they couldn't shape up, then they were shipped away."

"What's on the Island?"

"At first, absolutely nothing. They let people fend for themselves. The inmates had to find their own food, shelter, everything, so of course, the majority of them died within months of getting there, whether from starvation or each other. The only 'supervision' they had were eight guard stations a hundred yards off the coast in the water. They were connected together by strings of barbed wire that go all around the island to keep people from coming and going by boat without authorization." She takes a breath. So do I.

"Crime in America went down, but very few knew about the conditions of the Island. They were happy in their ignorance. This also happened to be during the boom of Prime DNA. Everyone was trying it, mixing it, shooting it. Eventually it found its way to the Island. All sorts of crazy things happened. Techheads that had been sent there survived by learning to manipulate human DNA so they didn't need normal food, but that changed a whole bunch of other things about them too. Unsupervised, they conducted all sorts of experiments, not only on animals but humans too. It was rumored that they had created some sort of monster race that could destroy all of society."

A shiver races up my spine and explodes on my skin. Max crawls onto my lap. I should ask Jenna to stop, but I have to know more.

"By this time, almost a century later, the human race had died off significantly thanks to pDNA, so the whole crowded prison thing no longer applied. This, combined with the rumors of a monster army, made the government shut down the Island, but that doesn't stop the Institute from still sending people there who threaten their way of life. They don't even bother shipping offenders out there. They simply drop them out of a plane with a parachute and hope they can figure out how to land."

I lean back into the stiff seat, my thoughts racing. *How do I not know any of this? My father taught me so much. Why not this?* I shake my head. None of that matters right now. I have one goal.

"We need to rescue Anthony," I say.

Jenna shakes her head. "Not going to happen."

"How can you say that? He's been like a father to both of you!" I look at the back of Colt's head, which is leaning against the window. "Colt?"

"Anthony's not a young buck," Jenna answers for him. "In less than a few years he'll be dead. You're in our world now, Patch, where survival means everything. Anthony knows this. Hell, he taught us this." She speeds up.

I stare at her, reminding myself that she's only thirteen. What a sad world she lives in. And the way things are going, her life isn't about to change.

"I'm sorry, Sage," Colt finally says. "Jenna's right. But we can fulfill his last wish—to make sure you and your brother get to Eden. HOPE was all he cared about."

"That's a lie! He cared about you two. And as for surviving your world, I'm glad I wasn't a part of it. Clearly it's made you forget the worth of a person's soul."

I say nothing else. Just hold onto Max until we pull into Jenna's garage. No one says a word until we are inside.

"I'm going to bed," Jenna says. "There's food in the kitchen if you want it." She bounds up the stairs without looking back.

Colt drops his backpack to the floor next to mine. "I'll crash on the couch. You and Max can have the downstairs." He sits down and rubs the back of his neck.

"Are you going to be okay?" I ask.

He nods. "Already feeling better."

"That's not what I meant."

"Loss is something I'm used to."

"That doesn't make it any easier."

He lies back on the couch, his eyes closed. "I'll be fine."

He doesn't say anything else so I take Max into the kitchen and get him some bread and milk. I even find some chocolate chips for him to snack on. All the while, my thoughts are on Anthony. Different scenarios flash in my mind, many of them dangerous. I weigh the risks and the benefits.

Max eats slowly, his hand never leaving mine. Despite my racing thoughts, I say soothing things to him, recalling our childhood. When I mention our father, his grip tightens.

"We'll see Daddy soon," I say and wonder if I'm lying. My father knew so much more than he ever told me.

When Max is done, I walk back into the darkened living room. Colt has one arm draped across his face. In case he's still awake, I whisper as I pick up both bags, "I'm taking these downstairs."

Holding Max's hand, I head to the basement and lay him down on my bed. "I'm so glad I got you back. You're such a bright boy, more so than anyone knows, but I see you."

I rest my head against his shoulder, breathing slow until my breaths match his. My hand strokes his head. His hair feels like silk against my fingertips.

The next words I say knot my stomach. "I have to go out for a little bit."

His eyes meet mine, but they reflect a calm serenity.

"I'll come back, but if for some reason I don't, Jenna and Colt will take you to Daddy. You can trust them."

His eyes close. I wish I knew what that meant. Part of me thinks he knows me better than anyone and that he understands my motives. The other part hopes he won't feel abandoned.

I wait a few more minutes before I straighten and sit on a chair across the room from him. In the moonlight barely filtering through the window near the ceiling, I sort through my backpack. I find the vials I took and hold one up to the light. The liquid is clear. I set it aside, along with my backpack, then look through Colt's.

I find a stunner and a small knife. Rescuing Anthony won't be easy.

CHAPTER 20

It takes thirty minutes to prepare. I stop a couple of times thinking it would be better if I stay with Max—I hardly know Anthony after all—but my thoughts always come back to the single fact that Anthony had saved my life. And he barely knows me.

I find a new outfit to wear to the party, cover my bruises with more makeup, and redo my hair into a different style to make sure no one will recognize me. As much as I can anyway. It's a huge risk, but I could never live with myself if I didn't at least try to save him back. Not only that, but Anthony is my best chance of getting Max and me to my father.

I glance at the time: 11:30. The party will continue long into the night. After stuffing a small purse with the stunner and sticking the earpieces back into place, there's only one thing left to do. I creep up the stairs, sneaking a glance at Colt. He's fast asleep, his chest rising and falling slowly, but with his enhanced hearing he may wake easily.

I tiptoe quietly down the hallway to Jenna's room and quietly open her door. The closet light is on. There are piles of clothes everywhere: covering a nearby desk, hanging from a curtain rod, and crowding the floor. The only part of the brown-carpeted floor that is exposed is the path leading to a messy bed. Jenna's on top of it, still in her clothes and curled up in a ball asleep. I maneuver my way to a dresser next to her, careful not to trip on anything.

It's got to be here somewhere, I think, looking over all the junk on top of the dresser. There are food wrappers, hair accessories, makeup, and books all stacked high in a precarious pile. I grind my teeth. This could take all night.

Unless.

I look back at Jenna. Her jean pocket. I squat next to her, trying to recall if she is right- or left-handed. I remember the way she did my hair. Definitely right-handed.

Gratefully, she's lying on her left side.

Very slowly, I feel the outside of her pocket and find the imprint of a key. I'm about to smile when a shaky breath escapes Jenna's lips, making me jump. I wait for her to settle back into a deep sleep before I attempt to sneak the key again.

My movements are quick and steady, and Jenna doesn't move when I slip the key from her pocket. One of my favorite lessons of my father's was learning to drive. He'd let me take his vehicle on an old country road near our home, but it was so broken up that I had to swerve a lot or risk harming the car.

I'm about to stand when I notice something crumpled in Jenna's hand. I gently pull back her fingers so I can remove it from her loose grip. It's a picture of her and Anthony in front of an office cubicle. Jenna's staring up at him and smiling big.

I lower the picture and look at Jenna. Her eyes are red and puffy in the faint light, and her pillow is wet. My heart softens. She's just a child thrown into a world that appears perfect on the outside, but inside is rotten.

"I'll get him back," I whisper, setting the picture atop her dresser.

I sneak back downstairs and leave a note. I write it quickly, not wanting to think about what it would mean if I didn't make it back. I barely know Jenna and Colt, but I have to trust them to take care of Max if something should happen to me. This is the hardest decision I've ever had to make, but Anthony risked his life for mine and that isn't something I can ignore. I don't care how many years he has left to live.

I slip out the door. Night's darkness is cold as it wraps around me, chilling my insides. It's a welcome distraction from the ache in my heart. I only hope Max will understand.

A few minutes later I'm driving away from Max, wiping at my eyes. I need to be strong. Stay focused.

On an exhale, I breathe out all doubt and fear. I need to remember my father's training and trust my instincts, the one thing I have going for me.

I recall the path Anthony had taken earlier and turn left when I reach the end of town. There are only the car's headlights to guide me, a stream of white light cutting its way through the darkness.

I go over my plan again. It could work, but only if I have the assistance of the only person who can help me. I'm not even sure if he's listening anymore.

I touch one of the electronic dots behind my ear to activate them and say, "Tank. I don't know if you can hear me or not, but I hope so. The Institute captured Anthony in the tunnels. Most likely he's still at the Center. I'm coming back to get him and hope you'll help me. I'm not sure what you can do, but I thought you should know." I take a deep, shaky breath. "I'll be there in twenty minutes. Please help me."

I say nothing more, knowing Tank can't respond if he wanted to. Two-way communication could be tracked if someone knew to look for it. Because of what happened, I'm sure the Institute has their tightest security in force.

Several minutes pass until I recognize the spot where Anthony had parked to let Colt and me off only hours ago. The Oscar Johnson Pavilion can't be far away. I keep driving through the overgrown forest, the road barely passable.

Because of the thick vegetation, the car's headlights can only shine so far. I imagine what may be lurking, hiding within the darkness. Primes could be watching me with their perfect eyes, and I would never know. My breathing quickens, and I wipe the sweat from my brow on the back of my arm.

I need air. Fresh, cool air. I quickly roll my window down and breathe in deeply just as I come to the top of a small rise. Finally there are streetlights, but I discover that I'm arriving at the side of the Center instead of the front gates. I'm still some distance away, but I can see several vehicles parked alongside a long circular driveway adorned with trees and tall statues.

I'm looking for a place to conceal the car when something crashes on its roof. I scream and swerve to the side, instant adrenaline coursing through my body. My hands grip the steering wheel until it hurts, and my heart beats fast. Do I run? Fight?

I jump when my door opens suddenly.

"What do you think you're doing?"

Colt.

I close my eyes and drop my shoulders in relief. After inhaling two big breaths, just enough to get my heartbeat back to a normal rhythm, I get out of the car and slam the door. Colt is standing shirtless, his arms folded to his chest, and his wings folded to his back.

"I'm doing what you won't," I say.

"And what exactly is your plan? They'll spot you in an instant."

"No, they won't. I'm in a completely different outfit, hair and all." He looks me up and down while I continue. "I plan on going through the front door. I'm fairly certain I can talk my way in."

"Then what? Fight your way to Anthony?"

"I have the stunner."

He's staring at me hard, not moving a muscle. "And how were you going to get him out? You have a costume for him too?"

"I will once I'm inside."

He narrows his eyes as if searching for a hole in my plan. He'll find lots of them, but I'm not worried. I have the one thing the Institute wants. The one thing to ensure Anthony's survival.

"And did you consider that Anthony might not be able to walk by now?" Colt asks. "What then?"

I lift my chin and look at him. "A trade. Me for him."

This makes Colt flinch, and he steps back. "You would do that?"

"Of course. Anthony saved me."

"But why? You get to live your whole life, probably until you're a hundred. Why would you risk your life for someone who has so little time left?"

I look up at the stars; each one burns bright. "This world of yours is so messed up. Man might have perfected a lot of things, made everything pretty and shiny, but in the process they've lost their human spirit. The part of them that will fight for those they love no matter the cost. It isn't about how much time any of us has left. It's what we do with that time that matters. If I die tonight, at least I will do it knowing it was for a good purpose and for a man who took great risk saving me and my brother."

Colt stares at me, moonlight reflecting in his blue eyes. He gives the slightest of nods.

"It's a choice I'm making. And I choose to help a good man in need. What are you going to choose?"

He turns and looks at the Center. "I'll help, but not using your twisted plan."

"You have a better one?"

"Yes."

CHAPTER 21

"Did you bring Anthony's heat signature gun?" Colt asks.

I open the door and reach behind the driver's seat where I saw Jenna place it earlier. "Here."

Colt takes it from me and raises it to his eyes to look through.

"Will it work this far away?" I ask. We must be at least half a mile from the Center.

"It's working," Colt says. "Most everyone is downstairs, but there's still ten or so people on the two floors above the party. I can't tell where they're keeping Anthony."

"So what are we going to do?"

Colt walks to the rear of the car and pops a latch. From within a metal box, he removes a circular object.

"What's that?" I ask.

"A distraction." He hands me the heat signature gun. "Keep watching. See who doesn't move. I'll be right back."

He sprints forward; his wings unfold huge and black, sweeping him into the darkness. If I didn't know him, the image would be terrifying.

I wait impatiently for several minutes, keeping a close eye on those inside the Center. Nothing looks out of the ordinary. So much for Colt's distraction.

"What are you doing?" I whisper in frustration. Every second we waste could cost Anthony his life.

Just then there's a loud boom, and I drop to my knees, fearing the worst. But when I look up, sprays of all kinds of colors light up the night sky. Several more follow. They're beautiful. I had only seen fireworks on television. I realize this is Colt's distraction.

I press the heat signature gun to my eyes. People, in the form of red, glowing shapes, rush outside. I glance to the second and third floor. Many more leave, some moving onto balconies, but on the second floor, on the south side, three men remain. One of them appears to be sitting down, but it's hard to tell since the shapes aren't well defined.

Colt lands in front of me, his great wings folding behind him. "Anything?"

"Second floor, south side. Take a look." I hand him the heat sensor.

"That's got to be him," he says. "I'll do a fly-by. Maybe we can get him out a window."

"There's a balcony. Take me to it."

"No way."

I point toward the Center. "There are two other guys in there. You're going to need my help. Quit arguing and let's get this over with while everyone is distracted."

"If you insist." He reaches into the truck and removes a backpack. "Put this on and wrap your arms around me."

I throw the bag over my shoulders, then link my hands around his cool neck and try to repress a shiver, but it comes anyway.

"Sorry I'm so cold," he says. "Part of being a Noc."

He wraps his arms around me and presses me tight to his chest. He looks into my eyes, our faces only an inch apart, then his wings spread and we are flying. My eyes are closed, but secure in Colt's arms, I open them and gasp. The stars look right within my grasp. For a moment I forget about everything else. Here soaring in the darkness, I have no worries, no fears; I am free.

I'm smiling when Colt says, "Hold on. I'm landing."

I barely feel it as he drops onto the roof. He releases me, and I walk to the edge and look over. The balcony of the room I think Anthony is in is two stories below me.

"You were supposed to get me on the balcony. Lower me down."

"Let me check it out first."

He disappears before I can argue. A noise near the corner ledge draws my attention. Most everyone is outside watching the fireworks and congregating near a lit-up pool. Several have already jumped into the water, clothes and all. They are laughing and celebrating, completely unaware that nearby a man is fighting for his life.

Colt returns a minute later and says, "You were right. Anthony's down there along with two Primes. One of them is the guard you zapped earlier and the other is a Mudder."

I moan. "That's bad."

I barely survived my first encounter with a Speeder, thanks to Colt, but to have to also deal with a Mudder? They're the strongest of the species, arms and legs like tree trunks and good at fighting. My only advantage is knowing their weakness. They tire quickly. However, between their strength and the quickness of the Speeder, I'm not sure how Colt and I can beat them.

"How's Anthony?" I ask.

A shadow darkens Colt's face, and he shakes his head. "Not good."

"Then let's hurry. We have the stunner and the knife. This could work."

"I don't think so," he says and moves his mouth like he's chewing on the inside of his cheek.

I cross the distance between us and take hold of his hand, which he immediately withdraws. I ignore the motion and say, "We have strength on our side, Colt. Not physical, but the kind of strength you get when fighting for a good cause. The Primes below us? They're only following orders, and will obey up until their lives are put in danger. Let's put them in danger and then save Anthony. Got it?"

Colt's jaw muscle bulges before he scoops me up and lifts me off the roof. He's careful when we land on the balcony and gently lets me go, but he's quick to step away from me.

I keep my steps light across metal planks and peer through a crack in the curtains. Two men in white suits talk by the door. Anthony's sitting in a chair, his back to me. At first I think he's better than what I suspected, but then I see blood. There's a dark puddle of it pooling beneath him.

146

I move away from the window and take deep breaths while Colt takes my position. It's my fault Anthony's hurt.

After a few seconds, I say, "We need to wait until they're closer to the window. That way we can surprise the Speeder with the stun gun. Together, we can take the other one."

Colt looks back at me. "You okay?"

"I will be when this is all over."

Colt leans to the other side of the window. "It's never over. Not in this world."

"Can you hear what they're saying?" I ask, pushing his comment to the back of my mind. The thought of constantly having to worry about my life or those I care about makes me ill.

"They're discussing the fireworks, trying to decide if it's someone's idea of a joke or if they pose a more serious threat."

A burst of blue and white explodes across the sky, making me look up. "This is the first time I've seen these in person. How long will they last?"

"At least another hour."

"They're beautiful."

Colt says nothing, and we stay like that for some time, going back and forth from watching the fireworks to peeking inside, waiting for an opportunity to present itself.

"This is taking too long," he says. "We might have to just go for it."

I'm about to agree when a loud noise echoes from within the room. Both Colt and I vie for position to peek in the crack, but in the end I win.

Inside is a flurry of movement. At first I think there are a bunch of people fighting, but when the Mudder falls to the ground, only two remain: the Speeder and Tank.

"It's Tank!" I say. "He's helping us."

Colt pushes down on my head so he can see over me and says, "I don't believe it."

Tank and the Speeder slowly circle each other. Tank is smiling, his hands curled into tight fists. I think the fight may last a while, but when the Speeder bolts faster than I can blink, leaving a white blur in its wake, Tank seems to predict the Speeder's move and kicks to the side. The action is deadly accurate and the Speeder cuts through the air and crashes into a wall. Tank smooths back his hair and goes to Anthony.

"Stand back," Colt says.

I scurry out of the way just before he kicks through the glass.

Tank looks up, not at all surprised to see us. "I was wondering how you'd get in. You must have some great gear to get on that balcony." Tank frowns. "Where's your shirt, Colt?"

"We had a few issues," Colt says and nods me forward to help Tank with Anthony. I notice he's being mindful to keep the wings on his back out of Tank's line of sight.

"What would've happened to Anthony if we came later?" Colt asks Tank.

"Then I would've secured him somewhere safe until you could retrieve him." Tank has one of Anthony's legs untied. I'm behind Anthony, working on untying his hands. It's a slow process because there's so much blood. I pretend it's water to get the job done.

"What about your precious celebrity cover?" I ask Tank, giving myself a distraction.

He looks up at me, pausing long. "I'm glad you came back."

"You didn't answer my question."

"I shut down the security cameras for exactly ten minutes, which wasn't easy. I had to knock a couple of brutes out to do it, so let's hurry this up. How do you plan on getting him out of here?" Tank doesn't show any signs of discomfort as he easily lifts Anthony to a standing position.

I don't look up at Anthony right away. I'm not ready to see the damage my actions caused.

"I guess there's no way around it," Colt says. He turns around and walks toward the window, exposing his back. "We're going this way."

Tank whistles. "You're a Noc! The real deal, wings and all. How about that? Never seen one before."

"I bet you don't feel so special now," Colt says.

"Anthony?" I place my hand on his back.

His head droops toward me, but he doesn't say anything, can't say anything because his lips are bruised and bleeding. Both eyes are a deep purple and swollen shut. Blood has dried just beneath his broken nose and onto his chin. His shirt has been torn open and on his chest there's a cut that starts at his right collarbone and slashes diagonally to the bottom of his ribs. I put a hand to my mouth to stifle a cry.

"He'll be okay," Tank says, his voice kind.

Anthony lets go of the side of Tank and finds my hand. He barely squeezes it.

"I'll take Anthony first," Colt says. He walks to him and turns him around slowly. "I'm going to strap you to me. Remember how we did it before?"

Anthony gives a small nod.

"Good."

After Colt and I guide him to the balcony, Colt removes a thick strap from the backpack and ties it around Anthony.

"I'll be back for you," Colt says to me. "Don't go anywhere." He looks at Tank and then back at me before taking off.

I watch them go, feeling sick at the sight of Anthony. Who could do this to someone else?

"Shocking, isn't it?" Tank says behind me.

I turn around. "What?"

"That we do things like this to each other when we live in such a beautiful world where 'peace' has reigned for decades."

"But it never existed at all, did it?"

"The war is just different now. It's man warring with himself, trying to combat what he thinks is imperfect. Unfortunately it's the Originals who get caught in the crossfire. Primes would do anything to get at one." He glances at the door. "I better go look busy and find a woman to entangle myself with. The Institute is going to know someone helped Anthony from the inside."

"Thank you for your help," I say.

Tank steps toward me. A breeze from the open balcony doors blows my hair. He catches it and smooths it back into place. "I'll do anything I can to help you. I hope I see you again." He drops his arm and exits the room, leaving me staring after him.

I shake my head to clear the red I know is on my face and

return to the balcony. I don't understand Tank's motives. To act so forward with someone you barely know makes me suspicious.

A scream comes from the pool down below as someone falls into the water. More laughing. A red firework lights the sky, making me catch movement—a dark blur moving quickly to my left. But when I glance over, it's gone. I focus my attention on the grove of trees where I saw whatever it was disappear. When a minute passes, I wonder if it was only my imagination.

Colt lands next to me and looks inside the room. "Where did Tank go?"

"Back to his celebrity status."

"Right where he belongs. Grab on."

I do as he says and wrap my arms around his neck. When we're in the air, I ask in his ear, "How's Anthony?"

"Hurt pretty bad, but he'll live. It's a good thing we came when—"

Just then Colt's body jerks hard to the left, and my grip slips. His hand barely catches mine, leaving my feet dangling in the air.

"Hold on!" he says. "I've been shot."

I glance up, squinting through my wind-blown hair. There's a tear in his right wing making it difficult for him to fly. With every downward stroke of his wings, we lower further to the ground.

I reach my other arm up to hang on tightly to Colt. We're far from the crowds, and darkness mostly conceals us, but that's the least of my worries. I look down. Directly below us, a man rushes after us, but the way he runs is more wolf-like. His hands hit the ground and his feet follow, propelling him forward, giving him ten-foot strides. And not far behind him, another creature follows after, his movements similar to the first. I wonder if it was one of them who shot Colt.

Another firework explodes, illuminating the face of the figure directly below us in a reddish glow. A strip of thick gray hair runs down the center of his head and two fangs fill his open mouth.

"Go higher!" I yell at Colt when my eyes meet those of the creature running toward us. They are a bright yellow, the color of the outer edge of a burning flame. He's a Canine and the last Prime I ever want near me.

Colt pushes his wings hard, lifting a little, but it's not enough. I let one hand go and reach into my pocket, my body swinging hard when Colt turns away from approaching trees.

"Your hand is slipping!" he says.

I grip the handle of the knife and pull it out just as the Canine leaps into the air, claws extended.

"Sage!" Colt yells and attempts to lift me.

I swipe down at the Canine, catching him just under his eye. He cries out and falls back to the ground, but at the last second, he manages to claw the back of my leg, his sharp nails cutting into my calf.

I scream as pain shoots up my leg. My grip in Colt's hand weakens, and my hand slips. The ground isn't too far below us. If I fall, I might not break a leg. My main concern is the Canine who I can't see anymore, but now that doesn't matter. He will find me now wherever I go.

Colt extends his wings again and flaps hard to get us back into the air. My eyes are closed tight, not because I'm worried about falling, but because of the Canine. He has my blood and now everything has changed.

CHAPTER 22

Colt lands by the car with a painful grunt and together we ease Anthony, who's sitting up against the wheel well, into the backseat. As soon as we're done, we scramble into the front, and before my door's even closed, Colt's pressing on the accelerator.

"You know what that was, right?" I say, but by his hurried movements I already know the answer. I reach down and press my palm to the back of my leg where blood is soaking through.

"A Canine." His voice is grim and the gravity of the situation fills the car.

I glance back at Anthony lying in the backseat. His breathing is labored, but his eyes are closed.

"We saved him," I say, trying to be positive.

"You did."

"Actually I remember you flying him to safety. I probably couldn't have gotten him out of the building."

"But if it weren't for you, I wouldn't even have tried." He glances at me briefly before returning his gaze to the road. Trees race past us, and the car vibrates from a speed it wasn't meant to reach.

"I don't believe that."

His Adam's apple moves up and down. "You were right about what you said back there. Our world has gotten so twisted that we've lost sight of what's important."

"Then we'll change it."

He shakes his head. "It's too late for that. All we can do now is save Originals and hope they can make the world right."

"You're wrong. There are still good people left. They just need to be shown another way. Look at Tank. And he figured it out all on his own. Others can too."

His hands tighten on the steering wheel. "If Tank is so super duper at everything he does, why did he abandon you in the stairwell? Seems like a coward's way to me."

"I'm not going to defend him, but he did come through for us in the end."

"As long as his precious identity isn't exposed."

I glance out the window, keeping silent. I may not agree with what Tank did, but I don't know him either. Maybe he is right, and his position within the elite's inner circle is crucial to the goals of HOPE.

"How's your leg?" Colt asks.

"Not bad. I'll bandage it later," I say, even though it's burning something awful. Right now we just need to get as far away from the city as possible.

Twenty minutes later we're turning down Jenna's street. Colt takes a deep breath. "As soon as we stop, we're going to have to hurry."

"I understand." I feel bad about Max. He'll barely have rested before I'm already moving him again.

Colt pulls into the garage. I'm about to open my door when he reaches across the seat and grabs my arm to stop me and then lets go. "I'm sorry this happened. Maybe if I'd done something different . . ."

"It's not your fault. Let's hurry. The Canine won't be far behind."

I hurry into the house. Colt starts packing a bag and grabbing a couple of blankets near the couch. I run downstairs and do the same, but first I have to change. I'm a little slow on account of my leg. The open wound is still bleeding so I quickly tie a cloth around it until I can dress it properly later. After I change into jeans and a t-shirt, I pick up the vials next to my backpack, wondering if I should take them. Space is limited, but these could prove valuable.

Nearby is a small blanket. I wrap the vials and stuff them into my bag along with random clothing from the closet. I don't even bother waking Max. I pick him up and carry him upstairs.

Colt is in the kitchen throwing food into a box.

"What's with all the noise?" Jenna says from the top of the stairs. She's rubbing her eyes, which are still red and swollen.

"Long story short," Colt says, "we went back to the Center and saved Anthony but a Canine snagged Sage's leg. We have to leave now."

Jenna jogs down the stairs. "You saved Anthony? Where is he?"

"The car. He's hurt pretty bad."

Jenna runs outside.

"Do you have medicine and bandages?" I ask.

"Already got it. What else do you think we might need?"

I open my mouth to speak when Jenna bursts into the house and wraps her arms around me and Max.

"Thank you, thank you, thank you!" she cries.

"Let's do this later," Colt says. "We have to get out of here."

Jenna lets go and looks from me to Colt, sniffing and wiping at her eyes. "What? Why? Anthony's in no condition to move."

Colt picks up the box of food and carries it into the living room. "Didn't you hear? A Canine is on to us."

Her eyes widen. "Oh no."

"Exactly." He pushes open the door leading to the garage with his foot.

"I'm coming with you," she says after him.

"No. The Institute doesn't know about your involvement, I don't think anyway, and besides, you still have your mother."

"Who will be dead in a few weeks. I've already said my good-byes. There's nothing left for me here but memories. I'm going."

"But who will care for her?" he asks.

"A nurse will be here in the morning."

"Then pack your stuff fast," I say and walk outside after Colt.

The fact that she could leave her mother in her last hours disturbs me. I don't think anything could drag me away if a loved one of mine was dying, but then again I didn't grow up in this world.

It takes us a minute to reposition Anthony to where we can all fit in the car. He moans a couple of times but doesn't say anything. I stay in the backseat next to him, Max curled up on my lap.

"Should I go in and get Jenna?" Colt asks, but just then she appears, carrying two big bags.

"You've got to be joking," Colt mumbles and presses a button to open the trunk.

A moment later she slides into the front passenger seat. "So where are we going? Have you even thought this through?"

"Out of the city. South," he says.

"That's all you have?"

Colt doesn't answer until we've backed out of the driveway. "If you haven't noticed, the one man who knows where we should be going can't talk, so until he can, we're driving."

Jenna leans over and looks at the dashboard in front of him. "You have half a charge."

"That's enough to get us to Providence. Save your energy and sleep, which means don't talk. It will take us at least two hours to get there."

"What about Anthony?"

"I'll bandage him up," I say, already opening the medical kit at my feet.

"Don't hurt him," Jenna says.

Colt turns to her and moans. "Because that's exactly what she wants to do—save him then hurt him. Go to sleep, Jenna, *please.*"

"Fine. Whatever." She leans her head against the door.

Colt glances back at me. "Make sure you get your leg, too."

"What about your wing?" I ask.

He's quiet for a few seconds, then, "There's nothing in there that will help."

I wish I knew how to help him, but I have no idea what his wings are made of. Maybe nothing can help but time. Inside the medical kit I find the same cream Colt had put on my hand earlier. I tighten my hand, feeling very little pain from the blisters. I'm amazed at how well it worked. We had medicine back at our home in Maine, but nothing that worked this quickly.

I squeeze some of it onto my fingertip and gently press it to the wound on Anthony's chest. He doesn't move, not even flinches. It takes some time since the cut is long, and I'm trying to be careful, but eventually I have the wound dressed and can turn my attention to his less serious wounds.

After I finish with him, I examine my leg. It's worse than I thought. The cut is deep, and blood has soaked through my pants and run into my shoe. It squishes between my toes when I curl them. Very carefully, I remove my shoe and dress the wound properly. It takes a lot of control not to flinch in pain every time I touch it. I'm acutely aware that Colt keeps spying on me in the rearview mirror.

I attach the last strip of tape onto the wide bandage, and glance at Max, who is curled up in the seat, a blanket loosely on top. I tuck it tight around him and stare out the window, my eyelids growing heavy. I can't remember how much sleep I've had in the last twenty-four hours. Jenna is snoring softly in front of me.

It's dark outside, but I can still make out an outline of trees as they push themselves against the road. Not many people travel like this anymore—drive from city to city—not since the human race started dying off anyway. Smaller towns were abandoned as people moved to bigger cities to find jobs. This gave the forest free rein over the land, and it consumed it like wild fire. Only major highways were maintained, mostly, but all other roads only received the attention of tree roots and other natural elements. These are the roads we're on now, and Colt has to drive slowly around broken-up chunks of gravel or deep potholes.

"Is it possible?" I ask through a yawn.

Colt looks at me in the rearview mirror. "To what?"

"To outrun a Canine." Of all the Primes my father taught me about, they were the ones he told me to avoid the most. They only had one weakness, but unfortunately it wasn't one that could easily be exploited. Canines hate bright lights.

"It's next to impossible."

"But my father did, right? Otherwise he would've been caught by now."

Colt doesn't say anything for a long time. He shifts in his seat like it's suddenly too small. "Your father didn't outrun it," he says. "I killed it."

This startles me. "When?"

"About a week after the raid on your house. Of course I didn't know it was your house at the time. I just knew a Canine was after the founder of HOPE, the man I had turned over to the Institute. For months and months I searched for the Canine. His name was Erik, and he had been working for the Institute for over five years. Whenever I heard about his whereabouts, I'd try to find him, but I never could get the jump on him. Eventually I found out where he lived, and decided the only way I was going to get him was if I waited for him at his house. He was rarely there, probably because he was always tracking your father. After spending weeks in front of his house, I finally got lucky. He showed up and we fought." He swallows and takes a breath. "I obviously won, but just barely."

I'm too stunned to say anything. My mind is racing, swirling all sorts of directions. He turned my father in for money, but ended up saving him? Everything I think about him is so confusing, and it's giving me a headache.

"I know you may never forgive me," he says, "but I am sorry. I was at a dark place in my life when I did what I did. I know that's no excuse."

"Thank you for stopping the Canine from getting my father," is all I can say.

Colt doesn't say anything after this, and neither do I. In a few minutes, my eyelids grow heavy and finally close.

I don't dream, which makes me think I haven't been sleeping long when a frantic voice wakes me. The sun is up, just barely, and its light filters through the breaks in the trees. I bolt awake when I realize Anthony's hands are grasping at the air, and he's struggling to sit up.

"Hold still," I say. "It's okay. We're in the car."

"Water," he says and coughs.

I unzip my backpack and open a water bottle. Very carefully I pour it though his cracked lips. After a couple of gulps, he pushes my hand away.

"Thank you," he says.

"How are you feeling?" I ask.

"A little better. Where are we going?"

Colt takes a few minutes to tell him what happened. During

157

this time Jenna wakes up and swivels around in her seat to listen. Max is breathing peacefully next to me. I reposition his head to make him more comfortable.

When Colt finishes, Anthony shakes his head. "You shouldn't have come back for me. The Canine would never have known about you otherwise."

"But then you would've been shipped off to Purgatory Island where you would surely die," I say.

"But you and your brother would be safe."

"Oh shut it, Anthony," Jenna says. "Patch did what we wouldn't, even though she had more to lose." She turns to me. "I'm only saying this once, so listen good. You showed more bravery than anyone I've ever known. Thank you. You taught me something, big surprise I know, but you did. I wish I would've had the courage to do it."

"I only did what I thought was right," I say, not even bothering to correct her on my name. "What's our next move?"

"What direction are we heading?" Anthony asks.

"South," Colt says. "Toward Providence so we can charge the car."

"Good. From there we can go to New York City. There's a safe house there where I'm told your father is staying." Anthony shifts uncomfortably in the seat, favoring his left side.

"But what about the Canine?" Jenna asks. "He won't give up until he finds Patch, which means we're all in danger."

Anthony takes another sip of water. "We need to get far enough ahead of it that he loses her scent. As long as he doesn't come within a hundred miles of her, she'll be fine."

"Unless he goes looking for her," Colt says.

I close my eyes, thinking how I might need to be on the run for a very long time. What would that mean for Max? I need to find my father, let him take Max to be sure he'll be kept safe, and then I can figure out what to do about the Canine.

"Why don't we just kill it?" Jenna says. "Use Patch to lure it in and then slice its head off."

"Because Canines never come alone. The Institute's Prime army will be right behind it," Anthony says.

Jenna begins to argue, saying something about tricking the Institute, but I can't listen anymore. I lean back and snuggle against Max. Bad things are coming for me; it's only a matter of time.

CHAPTER 23

Max finally wakes. I'm surprised he slept through all the arguing. I stayed out of the conversation, lost in my own thoughts of how I can protect those around me. Canines are ruthless, driven more by animal instincts than human emotions.

After some time, the others grow tired of the debate and fall into an uncomfortable silence. Max tugs on my shirt.

"Are you hungry?" I ask and smooth his messy hair.

He pats my arm.

I reach into my backpack and remove a cereal bar. I open it and hand it to Max. Colt's muttering under his breath, his back muscles tight.

"What's wrong?" I ask him. We're in another city, my guess Providence. It looks similar to Boston, but smaller and shinier, if that's possible.

"Colt?" I ask again.

"I can't find an active charging station," he says.

I look at the screen on the dashboard. Where I'd normally see images of many small, lit-up batteries on the map, there's nothing. "Maybe the dash screen is broken?"

Jenna sits up in her seat and looks around. Anthony's eyes are closed, and I wonder if he's fallen back asleep.

"It's not. I drove by a couple. They're all shut down." Colt's fingers twist around the steering wheel then straighten. "Do you know the odds of that happening?"

"What are you thinking?"

Colt pulls over on the side of the road, parking in front of a newer-looking, blue home with shiny, black metal trim. He swivels in the driver's seat, his expression grim, but when he sees Max, he smiles. "Hey little man. We haven't properly met. I'm Colt and this moody girl is Jenna. Don't worry about remembering her name. She's very forgettable."

"Ugh! I can't stand you!" Jenna says then turns to Max. "Don't listen to this mean guy. I'm the nicest, smartest person you'll ever meet." She ruffles Max's hair, but he immediately withdraws into me.

I wrap my arm around him. "Max doesn't like to be touched."

"Then Max and Colt will get along well," she says.

Anthony moans and looks around. "Why are we stopped?"

"I can't find a live charging station," Colt says.

No one says anything, making the air feel thick and heavy.

"What's going on?" I ask.

Jenna collapses back into the seat, her head dropping back. "We are so screwed."

"We don't know anything yet," Anthony says, but his hands have tightened into balls. "Go to the north side, on the outskirts. They might be active there but not showing on the city's map."

Colt faces forward and maneuvers the car back onto the road while Jenna turns on her wristpad and expands a virtual keyboard into the air. It's good one of us has one. Colt had ours deactivated after the party to make sure we wouldn't be tracked. Jenna types fast, soundlessly clicking and swishing through various screens.

"I still don't understand what's going on," I say again. My heart is pounding, telling me that whatever it is, it's bad.

"Charging stations are on their own power grid. My guess is someone has shut it off," Anthony says. He's staring straight ahead, looking stronger somehow. Maybe it's because he's leaning forward, seemingly oblivious to the wound on his chest.

"Does that happen often?"

"They're off," Jenna says. "The announcement is all over the net. The government is claiming they don't know what happened, but promises to restore power as quickly as possible. In the meantime, if someone needs a charge they can go to one of five battery-operated stations provided by the Institute."

I turn to Anthony. "They did this, didn't they? To catch us?"

"But how would they know what direction we went?" asks Jenna.

"The Canine," Colt says and turns a corner too fast. I rest my arm against the back of the seat to keep Max and me from sliding into Anthony.

"And Providence is the closest city to Boston," Anthony says. "They probably guessed we would be driving."

I reposition myself into the seat, holding tightly to Max. "How much charge is left?"

Everyone's quiet, waiting for Colt to answer. "Maybe another thirty minutes."

Jenna shakes her head. "What are we going to do? If we stay, the Canine will find us in a matter of days."

"We keep traveling to New York," Anthony says.

Jenna's mouth drops open. "Are you crazy? New York City is 180 miles away, and what with the little charge left, we'll only make it another twenty or thirty miles before we have to hike through the woods and no one does that!"

"Why?" I ask her. The thought of returning to the forest is the best news I've heard in a long time.

She scowls. "Because that's where wild animals live."

"They are no more wild than the Primes I've met."

"It's our only option," Anthony says. "What supplies do we have?"

Colt glances back at the trunk as if trying to remember what we had packed. "A few blankets, food for a couple of days, but not much water."

Anthony taps his fingers against the seat in front of him. "We need to stop somewhere and get a few more things. If we can walk three miles an hour for ten hours a day, then we could be there in five days or so."

Jenna folds her arms and says, "I said I would go with you to New York, but I didn't say I'd run around in the forest, sleep on the ground, and live off the land!"

Colt presses a button, making Jenna's door open even though we're still moving.

"Then get out. Right now."

"Are you crazy?" she asks. Wind tears through the car, stirring up Jenna's hair and a few papers that are near her feet.

"Close the door, Colt," Anthony says, his voice tired-sounding.

Colt does as he says. "I don't know what moron lowered the adult age to twelve. It's obvious you're still a child."

Jenna faces forward and sinks into the seat, mumbling, "You're the child."

All the commotion has made Max scramble on top of me and bury his head into my shoulder. I hold him tight and say to Jenna, "The woods aren't that bad. I promise. Besides, I'm sure Anthony will let you get one of those air mattresses to sleep on."

Her head lifts. "Like on the commercials?"

Colt lets out an exaggerated moan, but before Jenna can react, I say quickly, "Yes. They're lightweight and small enough that it won't take up much room. We can spare the room, right, Anthony?"

"Fine," he says, "but Jenna you're going to have to buy our supplies. The Institute has probably flagged all security cameras to detect our faces, but it will take awhile for them to connect you to me."

Jenna sits up straight and smiles. "I can do that."

Colt glances at her sideways. "You can only get what we need."

"Sure. Right. No problem," she says but is smirking.

"Is there a sports store nearby?" Anthony asks.

"Almost there," Colt says and turns right at a stoplight.

A few minutes later he parks in front of a huge shopping mall at least six stories high. It's the most architecturally interesting building I've ever seen. On the roof are several tall twisted, cone-shaped spikes that spiral many feet into the air, and the entire structure is covered in the same shiny metal as the other buildings.

"Don't take forever," Colt tells Jenna as she reaches for the door.

"Wait," I say, stopping her. "Isn't there some kind of portable battery charger we can buy?"

Anthony shakes his head. "They stopped making them years ago when flying became the main means of transportation between cities, but you can still find them occasionally on the black market.

Had I known this was going to happen, I would've been more prepared."

"None of us thought any of this would happen," Colt says.

"Any last requests?" Jenna asks, placing her hand on the door handle.

Anthony hands her a list of several items he's written down on a sheet of paper. "Get these."

"Can I add one thing?" I ask.

Jenna hands it to me. I borrow Anthony's pen and scribble the words "Universal Snaring Pack" and hand it back to her. She reads it and wrinkles her nose. "I don't even think this is a real thing."

"Just ask someone."

After she leaves, I turn my attention to Max, who keeps pushing his head into my shoulder. I think he wants out of the car. So do I. Fresh air sounds so good right now, but we can't risk it.

To calm him down, I talk about our time in Maine, specifically when we would go fishing with our mother and father. This works and his whole body relaxes. Anthony has fallen back asleep. Colt, who has slid into the seat, his head against the headrest, has fallen asleep too, but every once in a while his eyes open and then close.

Almost an hour later, Jenna returns, pushing a full shopping cart.

"She's back," I say.

Colt sits up and looks over. "I'm going to kill her."

This wakes Anthony. He groans a little when he sees how much stuff Jenna has purchased. "Don't say anything to her, Colt. Let's just get on the road." He rolls down his window. "Wow, Jenna. You sure got a lot. Was that everything on my list?"

Jenna smiles big. "I picked up a few extra things I thought we would need."

"Put what you can in the trunk," Anthony says and nudges Colt.

Colt presses a button to pop the trunk. "This is stupid."

It takes some time for Jenna to squeeze most everything in, but what's left over has to come up front with us, which is already cramped.

Colt doesn't say a word, even though his mouth is constantly working like he wants to.

When he pulls back onto the road, Jenna turns around and says to Max, "I got something for you." She opens her hand. Inside is a small figurine of a bear.

"How thoughtful," I say, surprised. My eyes flicker to Colt. Even he seems surprised.

"I thought it would remind you of home," she says and moves it closer to him.

Max doesn't look at her but very hesitantly he reaches up and then snatches it.

"Thank you, Jenna," I say.

Max turns it over in his hands. The others probably don't see it, but I recognize the look in his eyes. He's smiling.

Jenna turns back around in her seat and pops open a drink. "So how many miles do you really think the battery will last for?"

"Maybe forty if the roads aren't too bad and if I drive fast," Colt says.

Jenna puts her foot on the dash. "Then for once, don't be a pansy and speed."

Colt presses the accelerator, and the car jumps forward. Jenna squeals as pink liquid spills down the front of her.

CHAPTER 24

No one says anything as we speed away from Providence. Jenna has her back to Colt while she plays with her wristpad, and Anthony's staring out the window. Every once in awhile he shifts like he's still in pain.

Max plays with the bear across my raised knee, raised because it's resting on all the junk Jenna bought. The car's too crowded and growing hotter by the second. I wipe sweat on my forehead with the back of my hand, telling myself that any minute now I'll be able to get out of the car. Trees and bushes are practically on top of us, even more than they were outside of Boston. Roots have broken up sections of the road, which probably haven't been driven on for decades. I crack the window and suck in cool air.

"You okay?" Colt asks. He's looking at me in the rearview mirror.

"I will be." I force myself to think of the pain radiating in my leg. It's sharp and burns. My heartbeat pulses around the wound.

"You said you lived by the coast?"

I nod and take a deep breath. "Max and I would often spend the night on the beach during the summer."

"Did you go fishing in the river or the ocean?"

So he was listening earlier. I take another breath. "River."

"How about hiking? You do much of it where you lived?"

I realize he's trying to distract me. I attempt to ignore the tightening band around my chest and answer his questions. The words come slow at first, but soon I'm telling him all about the trails and what Max and I would do for fun. Eventually the suffocating feeling goes away, and my heart rate steadies. It's not long after when Colt slows the car.

Jenna looks up from her wristpad. "What are you doing?"

"I only have two minutes of charge left. Anthony?"

I glance over. He's fallen asleep again so I nudge him gently.

He opens his eyes and takes a second to orient himself. "How far did we get?"

"Only twenty-seven miles."

"It will have to do. Let's hide the car."

I wrap my arms around Max as Colt pulls off the road. The car bounces us up and down. I'm careful not to bump against Anthony, who's already groaning in pain. Once we are a hundred yards into the forest, Colt stops and turns the engine off. Behind us, the road is nowhere within view.

Anthony opens his door. "We need to move quickly. We didn't cover as many miles as I would've liked, and we lost a lot of time at that sports store."

"It's not my fault they were having a sale," Jenna says and follows him out.

As soon as I step onto the forest floor, mindful of my leg, I inhale deeply. The smell of rich soil and autumn leaves makes me feel at home. Max seems more relaxed too. He's standing several feet from me, staring up at the tree limbs above us.

I limp over and kneel next to him. "It's like home, isn't it?"

He places his hand on my shoulder.

Behind me, the car's trunk opens, and I turn around. Colt starts pulling out items and I go to help.

"There's no way we can take all this," he says. "Why did you get so much, Jenna?"

"I didn't want to forget anything." She grabs a pink sweater and pulls it over her head. "Besides, that might've been the last time I ever get to shop."

"Nonsense," Anthony says. He turns to me. "Can you help me with this?"

I take hold of the full backpack in his hands and help him pull it over his shoulders. "Are you sure you can carry it?"

He nods and grimaces at the same time. "I think so."

"Here's your snare-thingies," Jenna says. "The guy at the store had to get it out of storage."

I take the package from her and inspect it. There are four snares in different sizes, exactly what I need.

"Do you know how to use those?" Colt asks me.

"Since I was nine." I unzip my back and stuff them inside for later.

Ten minutes later we're ready to go. Both Colt and Anthony are carrying two bags, mostly food. Jenna packs a small rolled-up tent and a few sleeping bags on her back. I'm packing our clothes and some cooking gear. I also know I'll have to carry Max much of the way.

Before we begin, I bend down and lift my pant leg. There's a splotch of red seeping through the white bandage on the back of my calf. I'll have to keep an eye on it as it will probably take at least twenty-four hours for the medicine to take effect.

"Are you okay to walk with that?" Colt asks. He's snuck up behind me, too quiet to hear.

I hurry and reposition my pant leg. "I'll be fine."

"So listen," Anthony says a ways in front of us. "Our pace is going to be quick. I know that's going to be hard with Max, but we will just do the best we can. Are you listening, Jenna?"

She looks up from her wristpad. "Quick pace. Got it. So what are we waiting for?"

Anthony shakes his head. "Let's go then."

I take hold of Max's hand and follow Anthony and Jenna. Colt walks beside us, lost in his thoughts. The forest is overgrown; gnarly branches twist every which way and tall bushes block our path, making us go around them. I worry that we're going too slow, but I can't go faster. As it is, I'm having a difficult time concealing my limp from the others. I don't want to be the one holding us up.

Only an hour passes before Max tugs on my hand to be carried. I pick him up.

"I can carry him, if you think he'd let me," Colt says to me.

"Maybe we can try later," I say, hoping Max will let him. Not only will it help me, but I know it's important for Max to get used to other people. In case something happens and I'm unable to care for him.

In front of me, Jenna trips and stumbles forward.

"You can walk better if you weren't staring at your wristpad," Anthony says from the front of the line.

"I could walk better if there were actual paved paths or even a trail. This is ridiculous!"

"What has got your attention on that thing anyway?" he asks.

Jenna glances behind her and looks at Colt. "Remember a while ago? When I helped you with that problem?"

"You didn't help me with anything," Colt says.

"Of course I did, numb nuts. Remember? I hacked into the Institute's system to try and help you track the Canine."

Anthony stops moving like someone's jerked the back of his shirt. He turns around, glances at me and then at Colt, looking extremely uncomfortable. "We can talk about this later, Jenna."

"No need to be secretive," Jenna says. "Patch knows all about Colt's betrayal."

And there it is. I hate being reminded of it again.

Anthony's eyebrows rise. "Oh." He looks at me like he wants me to say something, but I remain silent, staring just beyond him.

"So you helped me. What about it?" Colt asks. His tone is sharp sounding and bitter.

"My access was never closed," Jenna says, her voice low.

"To the Institute's communication system?" Anthony asks.

The corners of Jenna's mouth turn up slow and deliberate. "I kept it open, figuring we'd need it one day. And what do you know? I'm a bloody genius. I'm able to see their announcements, their movements—"

"You mean you can tell where they're going?"

She nods, still grinning.

Anthony walks over to her. "Where are they now?"

"Ebony just sent a notice to all Fronters to focus their efforts to the south."

I cringe at the name. Fronters. The name the Institute gives to Primes who act as their secret soldiers. They could be your neighbors for all anyone knows. I think they are the worst kind of people, deceptive right to your face.

Anthony says, "Good. That means we'll have some extra time."

"It's dangerous to keep that connection open," Colt says. "They could discover it and feed us false information."

Jenna starts walking again. "Only if they know to look for it and the only way they will do that is if they discover my connection to Anthony. That could take them weeks of interviewing all of the MyTalk employees."

"It's a big risk," Colt says walking after her. "I don't think you should be doing it."

She shrugs. "Too bad. I think the advantages outweigh the risks. This way we'll know when they come."

"Jenna's right," Anthony says. "We need a heads up."

I hurry after them, taking up the rear. Max squirms in my arms to get a better position.

Colt moves next to Anthony. "But if they find out the connection sooner than you think, they could feed Jenna false information, giving them time to track the signal back to us."

"You're such a pessimist," Jenna calls up to him. "The world isn't always falling apart. Besides, I'm lucky, everyone knows that."

"Lucky as a dog with fleas."

"How about we don't talk for awhile?" Anthony asks.

"Fine by me." Colt slows and waits for me to pass before he continues on.

"Best thing to happen all day," Jenna adds, quickening her pace.

After traveling for only an hour, I give up trying to walk normal. It takes too much effort to ignore the pain while carrying Max. He lets me set him down to walk occasionally, but after ten minutes he needs to be held again. Our pace is too fast and the terrain too difficult for him to navigate. If my father hadn't trained me for hours on end, I probably couldn't do it either. As it is, I'm barely able to keep up, especially with my limp.

I feel bad for the others having to wait on us. They aren't even winded, including Anthony who, despite his visible injuries, moves freely without wincing. If only I was stronger, we could probably run through the forest, but my physical limitations hold us back. They may even get Max and me captured again and the others killed.

But, assuming I'm not captured, I get to live longer.

I sigh and wipe the sweat from my brow. What good is living until I'm an old lady if everyone I become friends with dies decades before me? There's Eden. Maybe there are others my age I can connect with. I look up at Jenna and Anthony and then glance behind me at Colt. I would miss them, though, despite only knowing them a short time.

"I wish he'd let me carry him," Colt says to me just as I'm picking up Max for the fourth time. Colt has made many attempts to connect with him but not had any success.

"He'll come around," I say. "It just takes time."

"We really need to take care of your leg."

"It's fine. I bandaged it in the car. It can wait until we stop for the night." I shift Max to my right hip and focus on the color of the changing leaves, the dark reds and brown. Anything to draw my attention away from the pain.

It's well into the afternoon when I realize I can't hear Colt's footsteps behind me anymore. I turn around. Sunlight spills through the cracks in the trees; a long ribbon of light shines on half of Colt's face. He's standing a ways back, his eyes wide and expression frozen. I've seen that look before.

"Anthony!" I call and set Max down.

I run toward Colt, but he falls backwards before I can catch him. I drop to the ground and turn his head to the side while his whole body seizes. Anthony comes to the ground next to me to help hold him.

"They're becoming more frequent," Jenna says from behind us.

We ignore her and tend to Colt. His body is tight and rigid, eyes rolled back into his head. I stroke his hair softly and whisper encouraging words to try and soothe his pain. No one should live like this, with death on their back. Max stays away from us, his gaze focused on the branches above me; yet I have a distinct impression he knows exactly what's going on.

After a full ten minutes, Colt's eyes come into focus. He

immediately scoots away from me and says in a hoarse voice, "Don't touch me."

I stand up and brush the leaves from my legs. "I was only trying to help. Are you okay?"

Colt rubs his head with his palm, and then thumps it a couple of times as if trying to reset whatever isn't working. He stands up slowly, his footing unsteady. "I'm fine. Let's go. We've wasted enough time."

Anthony nudges Jenna forward after Colt. I trail behind. Maybe my father knows of something that can help him. He helped Anthony's late wife; surely he can help Colt. I hope so because I don't think Colt has much time left.

CHAPTER 25

"We'll stop here for the night," Anthony says.

The sun is just beginning to set, but the forest is so dense, very little light finds its way through the limbs above. We will need to start a fire soon. I lower onto a nearby fallen tree between two thick branches to give my leg a rest. Max wiggles off my lap and sits next to me, the toy bear in his hand.

Anthony drops his backpack and bends down next to it. To me, he says, "You, Max, and Jenna can sleep in the tent." He unzips the bag and removes several packages of food.

"I'll set it up," Jenna says and shrugs off her own backpack.

I move to get up, my muscles groaning. "I can help."

"I got it," she says. "You look like you're about to collapse."

I push myself up, ignoring the aches and pains. "I'm fine."

"It's not like it's hard," she says and pulls out a small roll barely four inches thick with a single button at its center.

I raise my eyebrows, wondering how it's going to fit three people.

Jenna presses the black button and tosses the roll to the ground. It clicks three times and then begins to unfold on its own until it's a dome as tall and wide as Anthony. My father had a tent the same size, but it required thin poles to set it up. Something like this would've been much easier.

"See," Jenna says. "I told you not to get up."

I sigh and turn back toward Anthony. Colt is squatting next to him, sorting through the food.

"What about firewood?" I ask. "Can I gather it?"

Jenna laughs. "For what?"

Colt looks up at me. "We have an auto-stove."

"What about to keep warm?"

"It will do the job."

Max takes hold of my hand and squeezes it gently.

"We want a fire," I say, standing firm. No auto-stove can give the kind of comfort a real fire can provide

Anthony shrugs. "All right. Go get some wood."

"Not until you take care of that leg," Colt says. He looks up and our eyes meet briefly. "Sit down."

I do as he says and roll up my pant leg to inspect the wound. The bandage I put on earlier is soaked through with blood.

"You're going to get an infection," Colt says. He opens a small box and sifts through the contents while I rip the tape and bandages away from my leg. He flinches when he sees the wound. "Why didn't you say it was this bad?"

"It's not too bad," I say and accept an antiseptic wipe from him. I grit my teeth as I carefully wipe at the blood.

"Let me help," he says. He kneels in the dirt next to me and is about to touch my leg, but his hand stops suddenly like he's afraid to touch me.

"What's your problem, Colt?" Jenna asks.

I look over at her, wondering how long she has been watching us.

Jenna tosses a small bag into the tent. "It's not like you haven't touched people before. Unless you're afraid you might have feelings for Patch? Is that it?"

My eyes go to Colt, but he's staring down at my wound.

"You are such a bratty little girl, Jenna. No one ever takes you seriously," he says. A second later, he takes hold of the back of my calf and with his other hand blots the blood. The action is rough and I wince. He doesn't say anything, but he is gentler after that.

"I can get the rest," I say to ease him of his embarrassment. As if Colt could ever have feelings for me—a weak girl with plain hair and plain eyes.

Colt wipes at the last of the blood and then straightens. He hands me a small tube. "Put this on the wound before the bandage. Your leg should feel a lot better by morning. And don't even bother with the firewood. I'll get it."

"Thanks," I say, but he's already walking away.

That night, as I cuddle up to Max, listening to the dying embers of the fire expel their last breath, I think of the past and the future. The world has changed so much, but since being back in the forest, I'm reminded of how much it hasn't changed. More like parts of it have been forgotten. The good parts like the importance of human connections. It's those bonds that help people see outside themselves, that make them want to be a better person and make the world a better place for those they care about. My mother called this hope in action. And without hope people merely exist, experiencing no joy or love. No wonder Colt's so bitter and Jenna's apathetic. Only Anthony, who gave himself to love once, seems to hope for a better world.

Morning comes quickly. The cold stinging my cheeks keeps me snuggled inside my sleeping bag. Next to me Max is already awake. He's staring at the top of the tent. There's a flap partially open where he can see through to the tops of the trees. Red leaves are bright against a gray sky. They are still and unbending in the slight breeze. This place feels hallowed, unaffected by the turmoil that exists outside it.

A single leaf detaches and drifts back and forth until it lands on top of the tent. Max sighs. I kiss him on the cheek and whisper, "Time to get out of bed."

He wiggles into the sleeping bag until his head disappears. I smile and slide away from the warmth of the bag. The cold air brings all my senses alive. I peel back the bandage on my leg. The wound is still open but the edges aren't nearly as red. I swivel my ankle. And just like Colt said it would, it doesn't hurt as badly.

"Fine," I say, "but when you smell breakfast you need to get up."

On the other side of him, Jenna groans and turns over.

After I pull on my shoes and sweater, I open the tent and step out. Anthony's bed is empty and Colt is sitting next to a small fire, staring into the flames. His shirt is off and his black wings are folded against his back. He doesn't notice me until I sit on a log next to him.

It's another minute before he says, "I've never been by a real fire before. I mean, one that isn't out of control."

"What do you mean?"

Still facing the fire, he says, "When I was little, a fire destroyed the school I attended. It was one of the oldest buildings in the city. No one even tried to save it. Just let it burn. Three kids died."

"I'm sorry."

"I've always hated fire since then. I saw it as something that destroyed life, but now I realize it just needs to be controlled. Seeing fire like this . . . I can't look away."

I stare into the burning flames with him, watching them dance in and out of each other. After a minute, I ask, "Did you get any sleep?"

"A little."

"Aren't you cold?" I ask, running my hands up and down my arms to stay warm.

Colt shakes his head.

Anthony appears from within the forest. "Good morning," he says to me. "How are you feeling?"

"I wish as good as you look. You look amazing, considering." His cheeks are red from the cool morning air, but there's no trace of the bruises that had been on his face yesterday.

"Great DNA," he says and smiles. He walks by me and slaps the side of Jenna's tent. "Get up, Jenna."

"It's too cold!" she says.

"It won't be once we start moving, which will be in ten minutes with or without you."

"Do we have any eggs?" I ask. "I can make breakfast."

Anthony opens a backpack near Colt and pulls out several silver pouches and a smaller version of the wand Jenna had used to cook the pizza we ate earlier. "Don't worry about it. I've got breakfast right here."

A minute later I'm eating what looks like scrambled eggs and bacon, but it tastes more like mushrooms and salty tree bark.

"Have any of you ever had real scrambled eggs?" I ask.

Colt pulls a shirt on over his head. "Once at a restaurant. They tasted funny."

Anthony laughed. "That's because you're used to this terrible garbage. My family had a couple of chickens when I was little. Nothing beats the real thing."

"Where did you keep them?" I ask.

"In our backyard. We lived in a subdivision that allowed smaller farm animals. We were one of the few who did."

"Are there any real farms any more?"

"There's a few really big ones back west, but most of our food is manufactured now. The Institute lobbied for that decades ago, convincing the government that Primes needed special food to ensure optimum health." He takes a bite of his food. "The Institute is out of control."

My eyes go to the fire. Colt is looking too. The embers burn a fiery red, frayed by black, jagged edges.

It is twenty minutes before we're moving north again, thanks to Jenna and her inability to be rushed. Max walks at first, but after a while the cold gets to him, despite being bundled in layers of clothing. The poor child needs more fat on him, but for some reason his body doesn't produce it like everyone else's.

Max doesn't ask to be picked up when I finally do, but he's shivering so violently I figure it's the only way he'll get warm. With the weight of Max and the backpack, the pain in my calf returns, as does my limp. Soon I'm quite a ways back on the trail.

"Hurry up, Patch!" Jenna calls.

Anthony turns around and walks backward on the trail. He's carrying a large backpack and another on his front. "Do you want to stop for awhile?"

I shake my head and in between breaths say, "Keep going."

Colt, who was out of view in the front, comes back and walks next to me. "How are you doing?

"Not as strong as you guys, that's for sure." I hate that I'm drawing this much attention.

"Being physically strong isn't what's important."

"Right now it is."

Colt looks down at Max. "Hey kid, I want to show you something."

I set Max down. He's warm now, but it won't last for long. If only the clouds would part and let sunlight through.

Colt takes off his shirt and hands it to me. "Will you hold this for a second?" I take it while Colt says, "Watch this, Max." Colt turns around and unfolds his wings; his right one still has a small tear near the base. The wings span out at least eight feet on each side. I watch Max's eyes. They glance at the wings, then up, then back again. Colt has his attention.

Colt folds them back up and spins around to face us. He bends down in front of Max. "I can fly, kid. You want to go for a ride?"

"But your wing," I say. "You're not all the way healed."

"I'll be fine as long as I don't fly too high or too long."

"What about the Institute? Won't they detect you?"

"Not if I keep below the tree line. It's not too congested here so I should be able to fly between them for a bit."

Anthony calls back to us, "What are you guys doing?"

"Give us a minute," Colt says. "We'll catch up in a few." He looks back at Max. "What do you say? You want to go for a ride?"

Max looks up at me, not directly but close enough. I nudge him forward. "Remember the birds back at home? You used to love watching them. Here's your chance to be one. Go on. I'll be right below you."

Max won't go toward Colt until I guide him, but he doesn't protest either.

"Turn around," Colt says, "and I'll hang onto you." Max does as he says and Colt wraps his arms around him so Max is facing out. "Five, four, three, two, one. Blast off!"

Colt rises into the air, his wings flapping, creating gusts of wind all around me. Leaves swirl and twist and my hair rises in the commotion. Max's eyes are big and he's actually smiling, not just in his eyes.

I follow beneath them as Colt maneuvers through the trees, sometimes diving toward the ground and pulling up at the last second. Max giggles, a sound I haven't heard for a long time. My eyes tear, and I wipe at them with the sleeve of my sweater.

Colt flies for another ten minutes before the trees grow too thick and he's forced to the ground. He pats the top of Max's head. "Just wait until we get into open air, then I'll really show you something."

"Thank you," I say. "I haven't heard him laugh like that since our mother died."

Colt bends down and looks at Max. "My mom died when I was younger, too. I'm sorry."

Max reaches out and places his hand on Colt's cheek. Colt doesn't move for a second, looking back and forth into Max's eyes, but then he straightens and clears his throat. "You're a good kid, and you have an amazing sister. I'm glad I met you two."

The way he says it, his voice soft and full of sincerity, warms my insides.

"Come on," Colt says to Max. "I may not be able to fly here, but I can do the next best thing."

Max steps forward without being coaxed, and Colt lifts him into the air and runs toward Anthony and Jenna, calling, "Here comes Jet Boy!"

Max laughs out loud, a sound that is sweeter than any bird's song.

By the time twilight comes hours later, everyone is hungry. I shrug my pack to the ground and collapse into the grass, but at least I didn't have to carry Max. He stayed with Colt for much of the day, and with a little effort from Anthony, Max also warmed to him.

"I'll get firewood," Anthony says, after he's set up the tent for Jenna and me.

Jenna's been occupied with her wristpad all day. She looks up from it now. "The Institute sent out a notice a few minutes ago. They're asking Fronters to keep an eye out for you guys, specifically on the west side of Providence."

"The Canine," Colt says. "It's only a matter of time before he tracks us here."

"And hopefully by then we will be in New York City," Anthony says.

"To the safe house," Jenna says. "But then what?"

"There's a good chance Sage's father will still be there. Plus they have a lot more resources in the city. They may be able to fly us out. Maybe all the way to Eden."

Colt sets Max down. "And the Canine? What about him?"

Anthony is quiet for several seconds before he says, "Something will have to be done about him. Otherwise, you'll never be safe." He looks at me, but I glance away. As long as the Canine lives he'll always come, which means everyone around me is in danger.

"What do you guys want for dinner?" Anthony asks. "Fake chicken or fake fish?"

Jenna moans.

"How about rabbit?" I ask. I've already seen several of them in the forest. They are the easiest animals to catch with a snare. "I bet I have one before you guys have a fire started." I unzip my pack and search for one of the smaller snares.

Anthony's eyebrows rise. "You have a deal."

Jenna scrunches her nose like she's tasting something foul. "Rabbit? I didn't know you could eat those."

"You can eat anything with meat," Colt says.

"Humans have meat. Are you going to eat me?"

"I'd rather die."

"That can be arranged."

I walk in between them, hoping to break up their argument. "I'm leaving. Anthony, is it okay if Max stays with you?"

Max is sitting next to him, watching Anthony as he breaks up little twigs in front of him.

"Of course. I couldn't ask for better company."

"Thanks. I'll hurry back."

"Wait!" Colt says, turning away from Jenna. "I'm coming with you before Jenna attempts to murder me."

Jenna says something in return, but I'm already too far into the forest to hear what.

Colt catches up. His movements are far quieter than mine, even though I'm trying hard to move soundlessly across the forest floor into a steep ravine. I grab onto large rocks and thin trees as I make my way down to where I think the most rabbits will be.

The sun is beginning to dip behind the tree line. I need to find a rabbit soon, before darkness comes; otherwise it will be impossible to spot one. I search the landscape, focusing on bushes where I might find a rabbit trail.

After a few minutes, Colt says, "I always wanted to hunt when I was younger."

"Then why didn't you?"

He shrugs. "Never got around to it, but I'd go into the forest sometimes just to be alone. People thought I was crazy. They couldn't understand why I liked it."

Up ahead, a branch of a bush moves as if an animal's ducked inside. I squint my eyes, trying to see through the fading light. I stop moving and wait for the movement again.

"What do you like about it?" I say, my voice low.

"The world feels normal out here. It hasn't been tampered with like people have." Colt pauses and points to the right of the bush I'd been staring at. "It's over there."

I look at him. "Huh?"

"The rabbit. It moved over to that bush." He continues to point to the right of me.

"How do you know it's a rabbit?"

"First I heard it, but then I saw it. Briefly. It's black with big ears."

"Right. I keep forgetting you're a Noc. Stay here." I walk through the woods until I reach the bush Colt had been pointing at earlier. Sure enough there is a small trail moving in and out of the forests undergrowth. I set the snare nearby, placing old apple peels and an extra ripe banana at its center, then hurry back to Colt a good distance away.

"I'm glad you can forget what I am," Colt whispers. "I wish I could."

I keep my eye focused on the bush, my breathing even, and wait for a glimpse of the rabbit. "I'd give anything to have your abilities," I say, my voice as low as his.

"You can't mean that."

"Maybe not, but I feel like such a burden to the rest of you. I know you all could travel a lot faster without me and Max."

"But this isn't about us. It's about you."

I don't say anything else. The whole thing makes me uncomfortable. Colt is silent too, seemingly deep in thought.

At least ten minutes pass, and I'm considering walking back to camp. I can check the trap in a couple of hours or even in the morning. Usually my snares work quickly, but I'm in a new, unfamiliar area.

Just then a rabbit jumps out of the bush and sniffs the air. He waits a few minutes before hopping toward the snare. I hold my breath. *Almost there.*

"Got it!" Colt says.

I walk through the trees to the rabbit that is struggling to free itself from the wire around its neck. I pick it up gently and grimace. "I hate this part."

Before thinking about it any further, I snap the rabbit's neck. "Thank you," I whisper.

Colt grips my arm suddenly, startling me "What is it?"

"Something's coming."

A breath catches in my lungs. "The Institute?"

He shakes his head. "I don't think so. I don't recognize the sound, but whatever it is, it's big."

"From where?"

He points to the left of us and slowly backs up. "It doesn't sound human."

"An animal probably. Could just be a deer."

"Its steps are too heavy."

"Mountain lion?" I hope that's what it is because I don't want to think of the alternative.

"I don't think so. It's heavier."

"Come on. Let's go," I say, but a deep, throaty growl stops me. I know the sound.

"What is that?" Colt asks.

I scan the forest around us, but it's too dark to see anything. It could be anywhere. Running is no longer an option, and the forest is too thick here for Colt to fly. A tree with lower limbs is about forty feet away. We should be able to climb it to get high enough away from the beast.

Maybe there's a better option. To our side, closer than the tree, is a rocky face set into the side of a hill. There's a thin crack we may fit into.

I whisper, "Slowly back up to the rocks, and whatever you do, don't run."

Colt does as I say, just as another growl rumbles through the forest. A shiver races up my spine and across my skin.

"Is that what I think it is?" Colt says.

Before I can answer, a grizzly bear stomps its way forward from a thick grove of trees and bushes. Over a century ago, the east coast only had to contend with black bears, but with the population decline and the ever-growing forests, grizzlies had expanded their territories all across the land.

Colt turns to run, but I take hold of his shirt. "Move slowly. There's a crack in the rocks behind us."

The grizzly bounds toward us until it's twenty feet away. It rises up on its hind legs and lets out a monstrous roar that shakes every bone in my body.

We're almost to the split in the rocks. Colt glances over his shoulder. "You go first," he says.

I take one giant step back and attempt to squeeze through the narrow crevice. The jagged rocks scrape against my skin, but I keep moving as far as I can, which is only about five feet into the small opening.

Colt moves to follow me when the grizzly bear charges. Colt has just enough time to slide in next to me before the bear reaches the rocks. Its massive paw swipes into the crack, barely missing Colt's leg. The bear smells terrible, almost as bad as the odor in the tunnels.

"I can't believe this is really happening," Colt says, his voice higher than normal. He lifts his leg to avoid another blow from the bear's razor-sharp claws.

I want to offer some words of comfort, to tell him that the bear will go away soon enough, but there's a growing pressure on my chest. The space is too tight, and I can't breathe. My fingers claw at the rocks as if to break through them. I gasp for air, but my lungs feel like they're closing off. My eyes close tight. My breathing is too quick, and my lips begin to tingle. I need to get out of here before I pass out.

"Hey," Colt says. "Look at me."

I barely hear him over the sound of my heartbeat drumming in my ears.

"Sage. Look at me," his voice commands.

I open my eyes.

"Take deep, slow breaths. In and out."

The bear roars again, vibrating the rocks, and I'm afraid the whole mountain will collapse on top of us.

I'm not sure how Colt does it in the tight space, but he finds my hand. He squeezes it tight. "You need to breathe. Relax. We're going to get out of here." He rubs my palm with his thumb. The touch is tender and for a moment I forget that I need air.

The bear snorts and swipes at the ground in front of the crevice, but after a few seconds, it turns and slowly saunters away. It glances back at us a few times until the trees and shrubs swallow the bear whole.

As soon as Colt's sure the bear is gone, he steps out of the crevice, pulling me with him. I collapse to my knees and suck in as much oxygen as my lungs can handle.

Colt stands near me, eyeing the forest like he's afraid the bear might return. "Are you all right?" he whispers down to me.

I wait until the tingling leaves my body before I answer in a quiet voice. "Sorry I panicked. I'm not one for small spaces."

"I've noticed."

I laugh uncomfortably, wishing he didn't know that part of me. "You probably think I'm a coward."

"Um, we just faced a bear. I would've run if it weren't for you. As far as I'm concerned, you are the bravest person I know."

"I wouldn't say that." Despite my shaky legs, I walk toward where the rabbit's body lies in the grass and pick it up. Colt comes next to me; his hand, the one that had been holding mine, is balled tight, and I wonder how hard that must've been for him, touching me like that.

"My fear of tight spaces began when I was seven," I say and head toward camp. "I fell into a crack in a cave near our home when I was out exploring. I was there for almost two days before my father found me." I shove a branch out of my way. It's almost completely dark now and the air has turned cold.

"I can't imagine what that must've been like." Colt walks beside me, oblivious to the cool air.

I shrug. "We all have fears to overcome."

He doesn't say anything, simply stares straight ahead. I rely on his good eyesight to guide us back to camp. When we arrive a fire burns brightly. Max runs up to me and takes my hand.

"I beat you," Anthony says.

"Only because we were attacked by a bear." Colt drops next to him on the ground.

Anthony's eyes widen; fire reflects in their glassy surface. "A what?"

Jenna laughs. "That's the funniest thing I've heard all day!"

Colt ignores her and tells Anthony all about it. His version sounds much more exciting than what really happened. Thankfully, he doesn't mention anything about me freaking out.

I smile and listen while I gut and skin the rabbit. Max watches intently, every step of the process. It's something he's familiar with. Thirty minutes later everyone, including Jenna, is licking their fingers.

"That was delicious," Colt says.

Anthony tosses a small bone into the fire. "Just like I remember."

"Not bad," Jenna says. "A little tough maybe."

Colt leans over and looks at her. "Not bad? It was perfect."

She shrugs. "I might've given a better review if there was more of it."

Anthony laughs. A second later the rest of us join him. Even Max is smiling.

I lean back on my hands, warm and content. In just a few more days, we will reach New York City. My father will be there, I just know it; then we can put all of this behind us.

Jenna sits up, looking at her wristpad, and says, "Good news."

"What is it?" Anthony asks.

"The Institute. They've called off the search."

Colt stiffens and looks around as if he expects us to be surrounded. The forest is quiet except for the occasional popping of a dying fire.

Anthony holds his hand out. "Let me see."

Jenna removes her wristpad and hands it to him. He reads something on its lit-up screen. "It's true. Yesterday they searched Providence and when they found nothing, they called off the search. However, they did ask the authorities in all nearby cities to watch out for us." He looks up. "We did it. We're going to make it."

Colt stands. "No way. It's a trick. They know about Jenna's tap into their security. I told you this would happen!"

Jenna kicks out her legs and leans back into a tree trunk. "You're being paranoid as usual."

Colt ignores her and turns to Anthony. "Come on, Anthony. You have to know this is a trick. We have to leave now."

Anthony's lips are pressed tight as if he's thinking hard. "And go where? Whether it's a trick or not, and I'm not saying it is, the only way we're going to help these two is if we get them to New York City as quickly as possible."

"Then let's go now."

Anthony looks at each of us then shakes his head. "We've already pushed hard today. Let's get some rest and then we'll leave early. If we go fast tomorrow and into the night, we'll be there in two more days."

I scoot Max next to me. "What about the Canine?"

"He'll do what the Institute says. They'll probably send him to different cities to see if he can pick up your scent. Don't worry. Just get plenty of rest. You're going to need it." Anthony says all this, but the lines in his forehead are more prominent. He stirs the fire, lifting bits of ash into the air.

Colt kneels down next to Anthony, a pleading look in his eye. "I can fly. Take them out of here. One by one if I have to."

"Your wing isn't healed all the way for a flight like that. It will tear within the first ten miles and you know it."

Colt straightens and looks away, every muscle in his body flexed tight. The fire's flame casts moving shadows across his face.

I don't know what to believe. I want to believe Anthony is right and that we are safe, but Colt has a point. Why would the Institute give up so easily?

"No one worry," Anthony says again but doesn't make eye contact. There's tension in the air, and it crowds the space between us.

"Come on, Max," I say, trying to keep my voice steady to protect my thoughts. No one can know what my mind is suddenly spinning. It scares even me, but I can't take any chances with Max's life. "Let's get you to bed."

"You two can have the tent to yourself," Jenna says. "I'm going to sleep out here."

"Are you sure?"

She nods. "The Institute is finally off our backs. I'm going to relax by the fire and enjoy it."

"You're delusional, Jenna," Colt says and walks off into the forest.

I take Max away from the tension and get him inside the tent. While he pulls on a sweatshirt, I look through Jenna's belongings until I find what I'm looking for: my inactivated wristpad from when I was in the tunnels. I latch it around my arm and climb into the sleeping bag next to Max, my heart thumping within my chest.

"You're going to be okay," I whisper. "I promise. Soon you'll be with Dad. Just remember that everything I do is to protect you." I kiss him on the cheek and lie down, my breathing quickening. I don't want to do this, but deep down I know Colt is right about the Institute, and the only way Max is going to be safe is if I'm far away from him. It's the only way any of them will be safe.

As soon as Max is asleep, I sit up and check my pack. A sleeping bag, food for a few days, and a knife. There are also a couple of snares at the bottom. While I rearrange it to make room for water, I think of how me leaving will affect Max. Will he let the others help him? He and Colt have bonded, but I don't know if that's enough. I can only hope there's a small part of him that will understand how right now I am his biggest threat.

CHAPTER 26

A couple of hours pass. The air is cool, almost freezing, and it stings my skin. I peek outside the tent; the others are finally asleep. I feel around for my jacket, and tie it around my waist instead of pulling it on. I need the cold to keep me awake and force me to run faster.

I quietly slip my backpack over my shoulders and touch the screen of the wristpad. A soft glow lights its face, and I search for the option to only activate the GPS. In just a few seconds, a map projects onto the side of the tent, showing my location. I scan it briefly, making the decision to head west before I turn south to New York. Hopefully by the time I reach there, my father will have already taken Max far away.

My plan is to contact them later through my wristpad, after I figure out a way to get rid of the Canine. Until then, no one around me is safe.

The last thing I do before exiting the tent is scribble a short letter to Anthony, pleading that he deliver Max safely to my father. I thank him for everything and write that I hope I will see him soon. I consider writing a note to Colt, but for some reason the thought of saying goodbye to him causes an ache in my heart I've never felt before.

I fold up the note and place it on my pillow. Max's hand lies next to it. I squeeze it gently, wishing things were different. Before I dwell on the "what ifs," I leave the tent.

Hot coals are all that's left of the fire, glowing a reddish-orange in a sea of black. Anthony and Jenna sleep next to it peacefully. I glance around looking for Colt. I find him on the other side of camp, sitting against a tree. His head is slumped forward. Again I feel the hurt.

Time to go.

I slip into the forest and only when I think I'm a safe distance away do I start running. My pace is quick but after thirty minutes I slow down. Not because I'm tired, but because I can't see through the tears clouding my vision.

I am alone.

And as long as the Canine is after me, that's how it has to be. I need to think of a way to stop him or this will be my life forever. I wonder if my father felt the same way all the weeks he was away from us. I feel sorry for him in that moment and wipe at my eyes. At least I'm in a world that is familiar.

When I expect dawn, it doesn't come. The sun's light is trapped behind dark clouds, further dampening my spirits. It's going to rain. Wind tears through the trees, howling as it goes as if to warn the forest of the approaching storm.

I should find shelter but decide to press on. I need as much distance as I can get between Max and me. The others will be awake by now and notice that I'm gone. I worry how Max will react. Hopefully he will understand.

After almost an hour of walking, the rain, which began thirty minutes before, forces me to stop. I find the biggest tree I can and press myself against it while I rummage through my backpack, searching for a poncho. I find it at the bottom and carefully unfold the slick, thin material. It's just big enough to cover me while I'm balled tight, arms wrapped around knees. I tuck the covering beneath my feet and behind my back, trapping me in a camouflaged, plastic cocoon.

I don't think about the deep ache in my gut, because if I do I know the feeling will spread to the rest of my body. The last thing I need is to feel hopeless.

Instead, I transport myself to another time. I imagine the sights, the sounds, the smells of my home in the woods. My mother is still alive. We are making an apple pie together while another cooks in the oven. The aroma of cinnamon fills the cabin and pours out the open window. It brings my father through the front door. He's holding a folder overwhelmed with papers. Max is sleeping in a bassinet in the corner.

My reminiscence of better times seems to last forever. I don't want it to end, but all of a sudden the poncho is torn off me, shattering my memories. I quickly stand and press myself to the tree trunk, but when I see who is standing in front of me, I slump back down.

"Did you really think I wouldn't find you?" Colt asks. He's completely drenched, and although the heavy downpour has slowed to a drizzle, I can tell by the patterns of moisture on his forehead and chest that most of it is sweat. His bare chest heaves up and down.

I shake my head. "What are you doing? Go back. Please. I need you to help Max. Besides, you know what's going to happen if you stay with me."

He squats down in front of me and hesitates briefly before taking my hands in his. They are surprisingly warm. He stares down at our hands, his brow furrowed. This is the second time he's initiated physical contact with me. I wonder if that's more than he's done with anyone in his lifetime.

He looks up at me. "I get why you left, I do, but it wasn't smart going alone."

"I don't want you to get hurt."

"Why?" He searches my eyes.

I'm not sure how to answer him. I barely know him, yet I can't bear the thought of something bad happening to him. "You've already risked so much for Max and me, Anthony and Jenna, too. It is enough."

He straightens and pulls me up with him. "I'll tell you when it's enough."

"How is Max?"

"You mean when he found out his sister deserted him?" He must've seen my hurt expression because he quickly says, "I didn't mean that, sorry. Honestly, he seemed to take it much better than I did. I think he knows he'll see you again, but I wasn't so sure."

"Is that why you came after me?" It's my turn to search his eyes.

He clears his throat. "All of us agreed it would be a good idea if I went with you."

My face falls and I turn away, feeling silly for thinking he might say something else.

"My wing is almost better," he continues. "If we can just stay ahead of the Institute, it won't be long before I can fly you to New York City. And then, who knows? Maybe we'll catch up to the others before they go to Eden."

I start walking. Must keep moving. "But there's something you've failed to acknowledge."

"What's that?"

"You found me. A little too easy, if you ask me. Just imagine how much easier it will be for the Canine."

"We don't even know they're on to us yet."

I glance at him over my shoulder. "You don't believe that, and you know it. I saw yours and Anthony's expressions when Jenna told you about the Institute's announcement. They're coming."

He doesn't dispel or confirm my suspicions, but when I pick up my pace, he matches it.

"We just have to keep moving," he says.

"That's what I'm doing."

"Have you eaten yet?"

"I will."

Colt swings the backpack off his shoulders in front of him while still walking. He rummages through the bag. "Here. Eat this."

I take a breakfast bar from him and tear into it. "Thanks."

The rain finally stops falling, and, as if someone's taken a knife to the sky, light breaks through the gray. I glance over at Colt. Although, he's taking a big risk by being with me, I'm glad he's here. I don't feel so alone.

"Do you have any dry clothes you can change into?" he asks.

I glance down, surprised to see that I'm shivering. Sometimes my thoughts distract me from physical ailments, a trick my father taught me. "I have some in my backpack."

"Good. And if you need more, I brought something that will fit you."

I stop moving and turn to him. He's staring straight ahead, his expression serious. I wish I could read his thoughts. "Thank you."

He doesn't look at me. "I'll wait over here."

It takes me several minutes to peel the wet clothes off my body. Once I'm dressed, I roll my damp shirt and pants into the poncho and stuff them into my backpack. At some point I'll dry them.

Colt turns around when he hears me approaching. He has pulled on a white t-shirt. "Feel better?"

I nod.

"Good, because we need to run now."

My heart skips a beat. "Are they here?"

"Maybe."

"What are you sensing?"

"Could be nothing, but the forest is too quiet. Usually I can hear deer or rabbits, something, but nothing's moving."

I inhale deeply then swallow the cold air. "Let's go."

We run fast, me trailing behind Colt. I used to run along the beach for hours so running through the forest, even jumping over the occasional log, isn't difficult. It helps that my leg is feeling better and that I'm not carrying Max.

After two hours, Colt stops in a clearing. "Let's take a break."

I nod, unable to catch my breath enough to speak, and fall back into the still damp grass, my arms spread wide. My body hums as if charged with electricity; sparks of it shock my legs. It is a good feeling.

Colt's looking down at me, but it's not a relaxed look. More pained than anything else.

"What?" I ask.

"I just want to apologize again. For putting you and Max in danger. I was a fool."

I sit up, trying to remember what he's talking about, but then it comes to me. Me forgetting must mean I've forgiven him "You don't need to apologize again. I for—"

"They're here."

His words cut off my forgiveness. I scramble to my feet. On the far side of the clearing, the Canine stands still. His stance is more predator than human.

"Can we run?" I whisper.

Colt tucks me behind him. "We're surrounded."

"I've got them," the Canine says, but to whom I'm not sure. I can't see anyone else. He wipes saliva off his hairy chin.

As if on cue, the forest becomes alive with sounds of machines—the same roaring sound I'd heard when we were driving away from the charging station. I glance around, but am unable to see anything through the trees. How did they manage to approach us without me hearing? They must have some kind of noise filter.

Colt turns to me and takes me by the arms. "I'm going to fly us out of here, got it?"

"But your wing—"

"Is fine now. It's the only shot we have."

"There's no way. They'll shoot you down before we've even begun."

He works his jaw, staring back and forth into my eyes.

"It's okay," I say. "It's me they want. I'll bargain for your release."

"Me? You think that's what I'm worried about?"

I glance behind him. Prime men and women with all kinds of guns trail behind the Canine and circle wide around us. They are different shapes and sizes, some extremely skinny with white hair, some muscular and short with red Mohawks. Others have multi-colored hair, but one thing they have in common is they are all deadly. There's got to be a way out of this, but nothing comes to mind. My father never prepared me for something like this.

The circle of Primes comes together. Over their heads, a tall figure walks toward us. I hoped I'd never have to see that face again, but there she is—Ebony, her hands clasped together in front of her and her chin tilted up.

Two Primes break the circle, allowing her to pass. Just before the circle closes, I notice a quick movement behind the line. Some-one is on the outside of the circle, pacing back and forth. I squint my eyes to discover who, but the circle grows tighter.

Ebony walks alongside the Canine. She isn't smiling, nor does she look angry. Her lack of emotion disturbs me more than anything else. A person incapable of feeling is the cruelest of leaders.

She stops a short distance from us. "You have cost us a lot of money, Original, and one way or another, you will pay us back."

"She's not a commodity," Colt says. He keeps one hand in front of me as if to protect me.

Ebony looks at him for the first time. "I am surprised to see you here, Colt."

I turn to him. "How does she know your name?"

Ebony smiles, but it's not a happy, genuine one. It's full of venom, the kind that kills you with one bite. "You haven't told her, have you?"

Colt looks at me, his eyes sad, and then I know what she's talking about.

I answer for him. "I know all about Colt, and what he's done. He's not that same man anymore."

"Oh really?" Ebony asks. "Then why was he in my office six weeks ago looking for work? He even said nothing was beneath him. Colt goes where the money flows."

I shake my head and say, "I don't believe you."

"Don't insult me," Ebony hisses. "Techheads have no reason to lie. They are the truth in this world, sometimes the only one telling it."

"Your version of the truth," I say.

Her left nostril rises. "I should cut out your tongue for even suggesting such a thing."

"Stop!" Colt says to her, then turns to me. "What she said is true, Sage, but that's not the whole story."

His eyes bleed an emotion stronger than any storm. Pain is at the center, and I sense his desperation to be understood, like everything he's fought for is slipping from his grasp.

"I'm afraid there isn't any time for your pathetic story," Ebony says and moves closer to us. The Canine follows, his eyes fixed on me like I'm a hambone. "It's time to go, Original, and then we're going to go find that dumb brother of yours. He's got to be around here somewhere."

"You're not going to touch her or him," Colt says.

"And how will you stop us? Look around, Noc. You're surrounded."

In my peripheral vision, I see Colt looking up like he's considering flying. I can't let that happen. They'll shoot us down before we're ten feet off the ground, and as confused as I am about Colt, I couldn't bear the thought of anything happening to him. I'll save him if I can, and then walk away forever if I need to.

I speak quickly, "Let Colt go and I'll go with you."

"No, Sage," Colt says.

I don't look over at him when I take a firm step forward. I'd escaped once before. Maybe I can do it again.

"Take her," Ebony says to the Canine. She turns around and walks away.

The Canine approaches me, grayish foam bubbling at the sides of his mouth. His hands, claws extended, open and close like he's about to fight someone in a boxing ring, but what does he expect me to do? Fight him? I hardly have the skills—but I do know his weakness.

I glance up at the sun. It's just above us, shining bright against a blue sky, completely oblivious to the scene unfolding beneath it. I hold my wristpad just right so the light shines upon its shiny surface and turn it toward the Canine's yellow eyes. He immediately recoils and hisses as if doused with fire.

Ebony turns around. Her thin eyebrows pull together and her equally thin lips turn down. "Must this be so complicated? She's an Original! Someone shoot her through the arm and get this over with."

A man with a violet complexion raises a weapon I don't recognize and points in my direction. His finger presses on a button. I dive to the side just as a sound louder than any thunder cracks through the air.

"No!" Colt yells and jumps in front of me.

Something hits him in the chest and his body flips in the air until he's lying face first in the dirt. I drop to my knees in front of him, unsure what to do. "Colt?" I shake him gently. He doesn't respond. "What did you do to him?"

The Canine comes next to me. His sweaty palm closes over

the back of my neck and lifts me until my feet dangle. Switching me to his other hand, he turns me around to face him. His breath, smelling of rotten teeth and sour milk, warms my lips when he says, "Chasing you has been the most fun I've had all year, but to lick the blood off my claws again," he moans, "would be the highlight of my life."

"Enough," Ebony calls from the side of the clearing. "I have work to do."

He sniffs me. "Another time, perhaps," he says and carries me like I'm a dead rabbit. I try to look back at Colt to see if he's moving, but the Canine's tight grip on my neck prevents me.

We are about to disappear into the shadows of the forest when a whirling sound appears out of nowhere. It's followed by a gust of wind that tears through the clearing, twisting my hair up into my face. Above us, a great sphere blocks the sunlight and plunges us into darkness.

"What is going on?" Ebony demands but no one answers.

A square section of the bottom of the sphere opens and a familiar, blond-haired man pokes his head out and grins. "Having a party without me?"

"Tank?" Ebony asks. It's probably the first time in her life she's ever been confused.

"That's me, babe." His hand lowers out of the bottom of the aircraft. He's holding a wide-barreled gun and shoots in our direction.

A burst of air, traveling faster than sound, knocks us to the ground and sucks the air from my lungs. Tank shoots again in the opposite direction before anyone can react. Soon everyone is lying on the ground, all gasping for air.

I claw at the ground, desperate to take a breath, but it's like there's an invisible weight crushing my lungs. Bursts of red and blues cloud my vision.

"We've got you," Tank's voice says, and I feel myself being lifted.

A second later he's leaping, and instantly the temperature warms. He must've jumped back into the sphere. I can't see much, the reds and blues turning to black, except for blinking lights.

Every part of me is cramping, straining my muscles to the point I think they might snap and curl up into tight balls.

"You need to relax and breathe, Sage." It's Anthony's voice. How did he get here?

"Come on, Patch," Jenna says. "Quit acting like a baby and relax. You'd think you were dying or something."

Jenna and Anthony's voices brings me great comfort. That means Max must be here too. I concentrate hard on loosening my muscles, but my chest continues to constrict. Take yourself to another place, my father's voice echoes in my head.

I imagine I'm swimming beneath the ocean's often turbulent surface. It's another world under the sea, one that is quiet and makes sense.

I sit up, sucking in a deep breath, my eyes wide.

"There you go. Just breathe in and out real slow." Anthony rubs my back in slow circles.

I take another breath and my vision clears. Tank's perfectly shaped face comes into focus. He's directly in front of me, flashing his flawless teeth that look like sculpted pearls. Jenna's behind him, sitting on a swivel chair picking at her fingernails.

"Where's Max?" I ask, gasping for air. My lungs still haven't fully expanded.

Anthony points to my left. Max is there, bouncing the toy bear along the arm of another chair. He looks content and happy. My shoulders relax. For all of two seconds before I panic again. "Colt! We have to get him. They shot him and—"

Tank covers my mouth with his large hand. "Calm down, woman. He's in the next room."

I scramble to my feet and rush through an oval-shaped metal opening. Colt is lying on the floor, his chest exposed. A girl in a white lab coat with long, straight black hair is bent over him, tapping a bandage to a wound near his left shoulder.

I drop next to him. "How is he?"

She looks up at me, and I startle. Her eyes are all white, not even black pupils. She's a Spotter, which means she has a gift for sensing poor health in others. Because of this, they often go into the medical field.

"He will live," she says. "A short time, anyway. He had another seizure. A small one, but it was bad."

I smooth a black curl away from his forehead. It could be me lying there, but he saved me. I don't believe what Ebony said. Colt is a good man.

"When will he wake?" I ask.

"Maybe in an hour. I gave him something to help with the pain in his shoulder. That's probably what caused the seizure."

"Thank you," I say.

"It's my pleasure." She stands and goes to a metal sink built into an all-black cabinet to wash her hands. "My name's Ash, and you are the first Original I've ever met."

"And I'm Sage, and you're the first Spotter I've ever met."

She smiles and dries her hands.

This room is cooler in temperature than the one I just came from and circular in shape. There are black shiny cabinets built into all the round walls. One of the cupboards is wide and tall, making me wonder if it pulls out into a bed. By the temperature and how clean this room is, I assume it's some sort of medical area.

"We'll make him more comfortable in a few minutes," Ash says. She opens a nearby cupboard and places silver medical instruments inside.

Above me is a skylight. White clouds rush by and it's then that I remember that we're flying, which surprises me because I feel no vibrations from the motion.

"Where are we going?" I ask.

Ash turns around. "We arrive in New York City in two hours."

"It takes that long?"

Anthony clears his throat behind me. "We're making a wide circle to approach the city from the south to hopefully avoid detection from the Institute."

"Excuse me," Ash says and passes by Anthony and through an oval opening.

"Thanks, Ash," he calls after her. He looks back at me and crosses his arm to his chest. "You left us."

I place my hand on Colt's forehead. It's warmer than I've ever felt him before. "I didn't want the Canine to catch up to us. They would've taken or killed you all, and I couldn't live with that, especially knowing it's me they're tracking."

It's a long moment before Anthony says, "Colt didn't do so well when he realized you left."

"I didn't mean to worry anyone."

"I get why you did it, but I wish we could've talked about it first. We could've come up with a plan, one that wouldn't have given Colt a panic attack. But I am glad he found you."

"I'm not. He would be okay right now if it wasn't for me." The words are bitter in my mouth, and when I swallow them my stomach churns.

"You need to be careful, Sage." His voice holds a threatening note.

I look up at him. "What are you talking about?"

"Colt isn't like you, not even close. You have a whole population of Originals waiting for you, other people with whom you can form relationships. Don't get hung up on one of us."

I try to process his words, but I'm not sure what he's saying. "I don't understand."

His expression softens. "You're caring too much. Nothing good will come of it."

His meaning becomes clear, and my face burns red. "I'm just concerned is all. He's saved my life a couple of times. I don't know how I will ever repay him."

"You owe him nothing. He was doing his job and only his job. Remember that." He walks away, leaving me alone with Colt.

I place my hand in my lap. *He was only doing his job.* That's all it was, because we're different. I make my mind believe Anthony's truth, despite the feelings of my heart.

I stay with Colt a little longer before I return to the room I came in from. It looks similar to the medical room, but one wall has a bunch of electronics and blinking lights. I recognize a few of the monitors: satellite feed of the landscape, heat detectors monitoring areas we pass over, and a running feed of various conversations that must be going on within a certain proximity of us. Tank probably has it flagged to look for anything that has to do with us.

I don't see Jenna and Anthony, but there is a closed door directly in front of me. My guess is they are behind it.

Max is still in his chair, holding the toy bear, but his eyes are on the screens and blinking lights. Although others don't know it, I know his mind is unraveling everything he sees and placing it in easy-to-remember blocks. He can solve the hardest puzzle by doing this. As far as I'm concerned, Max is far smarter than any Techhead ever to exist.

"I'm glad you're okay."

I whirl around. Tank is sitting in a chair, looking up from a book in his lap. Just the man I was looking for. "Why did you do it?"

"Do what?" he asks.

"Give up your anonymity to save us?" My eyes go to Max. He's back to bouncing the toy bear along the armrest.

Tank shrugs, and I'm afraid the motion might make his huge muscles rip the sleeves off his shirt. "I knew years ago that I was different from others, and not because of my DNA, but my way of thinking. I was always looking for a better and more efficient way to accomplish tasks. I think that's one reason why I'm so good at sports. People think it's because of this amazing body I've been given," he flexes his chest muscles and winks, "but it isn't. It's my mind that makes me powerful. I believe this is true with most, if people would only exercise their minds instead of letting it become weak."

"But that still doesn't explain why you're helping us."

Tank swivels back and forth in his chair, like he's bored. "Anyone using their brain and who is willing to look at the hard truth will admit that our world is dying. Only pride stops them. Men thinking they are gods, trying to eradicate what they see as weakness. It makes me sick! As soon as I heard about HOPE, I joined and used my position among the elite to help any way I could, but I always knew there would come a time when I'd have to give up my current life and start a new one. And I'm quite pleased that the timing happened to be when I met you."

I glance down, embarrassed by his confession.

"Don't misunderstand me," he's quick to say. "I'm not into you like that, though you are quite striking for an Original, but when I heard that you escaped from the Institute and then saw your performance at the party the other night, I knew you were the one."

"One what?"

"The one who would tip the balance between Originals and Primes. The Originals have been waiting for someone like you, someone to prove to them that they stand a chance. Many thought it would be your father, and although he's a brilliant scientist, he lacks the courage that's needed to face the Institute."

"He may be smart, but his training was cruel," I say before I can stop myself. It's the first time I've admitted this even to myself.

A tall shadow falls across the light at my feet. I look up. Colt is leaning against the doorway, the bandage on his shoulder a dark red.

"Looks like Sleeping Beauty's awake," Tank says and stands up to go to him. "That was some move you made out there, protecting the girl and all." He slugs Colt in his bad shoulder, making Colt moan. "I'll let the others know you're awake."

Tank crosses the room and presses a button. A door slides open and closes behind him.

"Before you say anything," Colt says, "I have to explain."

For a second I'm confused, but then I remember. His meeting with Ebony. "Is it true?"

"I only did it to try and find out more about their actions. I hoped it would lead me to the Canine." Colt shifts his position so he's leaning against the other side of the door. Blood stains the bandage on his shoulder. "And there's something else. I did use the thousand dollars to buy oDNA. My seizures had gotten so bad that I got scared for my life, and that made me desperate. I only had two doses, though, before I gave the rest of it away."

"Why?"

"Guilt. I knew where it came from and had heard the rumors about what the Institute did to Originals. I didn't want to be a part of it anymore, even if it meant my life."

Max reaches up and takes my hand. He squeezes it hard, but I ignore him and say to Colt, "I believe you."

"That easily? After everything I've done?"

"That is why I believe you. Your actions have proved to me that you are trying to do what's right. The past is in the past."

"Then you forgive me?" Colt winces and rolls his hurt shoulder back like it's bothering him.

I lift my gaze to his. The blue in his eyes does not burn bright, but is softer now, like the color of the ocean against an orange horizon. I brush the top of Max's head. He doesn't move, just continues to stare at the running feed of conversation on the screen. I couldn't have saved him without Colt's help.

I cross the room until I'm standing directly in front of Colt. "Of course I forgive you. How can I not? I have no idea what you endured as a child, what desperation you must've felt. All I have to go on is the person in front of me."

His jaw muscle moves as he swallows hard. "How can you forgive me so easily?"

"Is this another virtue your world lacks?"

He takes a full breath and closes his eyes. "Not anymore."

I reach up and touch him lightly on his shoulder. "Are you okay?"

His eyes open and he smiles. It's small but it's there. "More than okay, but what about you?"

This time when I meet his gaze, I startle and have to look away. Probably because he's staring at me deeper, like the way someone looks when they have discovered a whole new world.

He seems to sense my discomfort because he says, "So Tank rescued us?"

I nod, my eyes downcast. I don't want to look at him, to see that new strangeness in the blue horizon that seems to go on forever.

"Did anything happen to you after I blacked out?" he asks.

"Tank came shortly after, and wind blasted everyone. Nothing happened."

"Then what are these?" He reaches up and gently pushes my hair away, exposing my neck.

I touch where he's looking. My neck is extremely tender and probably looks something awful if Colt noticed. "It's nothing, really. The Canine used me as his rag toy is all."

I laugh uncomfortably, still unable to meet his gaze. A trail of blood running down his chest catches my eye.

"You're bleeding," I say and attempt to get past him into the medical room. At first he doesn't let me by, forcing our bodies within an inch from each other. The heat from his bare chest warms my skin and yet I shiver, a pleasant tingling that spreads to my limbs.

Finally he moves, and I can breathe again.

I look through several cupboards until I find a bandage. I turn around and practically run into Colt. He has snuck into the room without me hearing, or maybe my mind was distracted by other thoughts.

"I'll try not to hurt you," I say. I start at the bottom of the blood's path near his belly button and drag the cloth upwards, absorbing the crimson color from his skin. My fingers go over every ripple of his muscles until I reach the bloodied bandage on his chest. Carefully, I tear it off and press the cloth to the wound while I reach for a fresh dressing.

I feel Colt's eyes on me as I open the bandage using my teeth and free hand. After I tape it securely to his skin, I move to take a step back, but he gently takes hold of my hand and pulls me to him. His eyes burn the color of blue fire, something I'd only seen in my father's lab.

"Are we interrupting?"

Colt lets me go, and I step back. Jenna's smirking in the doorway. Anthony's behind her, not looking pleased at all.

I don't look at Colt as I walk between them to get back to Max. Jenna follows after me, but Anthony stays behind with Colt.

"So who's flying this thing?" I ask Jenna.

She drops into a nearby swivel chair and whirls it around. "It mostly flies itself once coordinates are put in, but Tank is the one who lands it and stuff. Are you hungry?"

"A little."

Jenna pushes a nearby button on the wall. "Hey Ash, you have anything to eat on this rig?"

"Food's up here," Ash's voice says through a speaker.

"Can you bring it to us?"

"Get it yourself. I'm not a stewardess."

Jenna slides further into the chair and lets her arms fall to the side. Her moan is as long as it is deep. "Fine."

It takes her a few seconds, but she manages to get to her feet and opens the door.

I peek in quickly. It's a much larger room with lots of windows. We are high in the air. The door closes, leaving just Max and me. The faint voices of Anthony and Colt echo from the next room.

"I'm glad we're together again, Max." I squeeze his hand. "And soon we will be with Dad."

We sit alone, the many blinking lights our only companions. Max stands and walks to the wall of monitors. His finger starts at the top, and he touches each one until he ends at the monitor scrolling conversations. He taps it over and over, even though he's not looking directly at it. More out of the corner of his eye.

"What are you looking at?" I move next to him as he continues to tap on the screen. Words scroll past, most of them meaningless conversations about if the Institute is hiring or where the Institute will be distributing their next round of oDNA. Tank must have this program listening for any conversations with the word "Institute" in them. Every so often the word *Original* pops up, but it's used in the context of something like, "Is this the original version or the remade one?" It's nothing specific to me. My guess is that he also has it looking for Anthony and Jenna's names and probably his too. And when all or even a part of the words are used close together, an alarm will go off.

"Do you like the words, Max? The way they scroll down?"

He taps them again, harder this time. He really wants me to see something. I read the conversations, every word, instead of skimming them. Every third line the conversation seems to skip like it's interrupted by another frequency.

"That's weird," I whisper. In one of the lines, the word "Original" appears and my heart skips a beat. I focus only on every third line and stumble when I realize what it says.

We're not as safe as Tank thinks we are.

CHAPTER 27

I wait for the Institute's message to cycle through one more time to be sure I'm right. As soon as it does, I yell, "Tank! Get in here now!"

Anthony and Colt come into the room first. Both of them don't look happy, but I don't have time to wonder about it before Tank rushes in followed by Jenna, who's holding a plate of food. Ash comes last.

"What's wrong?" Colt asks.

I point at the screen. "Have you seen this?'

Jenna takes a bite of bread and says, "They're called letters, Patch, and when said together they form words."

"Look at what they're really saying, every third line." It takes them a few minutes to notice the loop as every sentence runs in a different order than the first time it appears.

Anthony is the one to say it out loud first. "An Original girl and boy travel in your direction in a hover-plane. Shoot it down and take them alive. Kill everyone else on sight."

"Can they do that?" Jenna asks. "I mean how many hover-planes are coming into New York City today? Ten? They can't shoot us all down."

"Of course they can." Tank leaves the room and goes to the front of the plane where windows are the walls. Everyone follows, except for Max. Tank presses a code into a keypad, and although I don't feel it, the plane stops in midair.

"What are we going to do?" Jenna asks.

I glance at Colt, but he doesn't look at me. He's tense again, not at all relaxed like he was in the medical room.

Tank stares out the window as if searching the skies for an attacker. "The Institute must've guessed I'd be listening to conversations and delayed their message feed. They even guessed words I'd be flagging. Maybe I'm not as smart as I'd like to think I am." He straightens and turns around. "How did you catch it?"

"It wasn't me," I say. "Max saw it."

Everyone turns and looks through the opening at Max. He's back to skipping his toy bear across the arm of the chair.

"How close are we to the outskirts of New York City?" Anthony asks.

"Ten miles," Tank says. "I can get us as close as possible and then we're going to have to land, but even from there the safe house is on the other side of the city, which is another forty miles."

"Hold up," Jenna says, her arms raised. "Are you saying we have to travel that distance without transportation? Because I am so done hiking!"

Tank sits on a high-backed chair and takes control of the steering shaft. "Then you can stay behind and be this plane's guard dog. I don't want anything happening to it."

"I am no one's dog."

"Then you're going to have to hike. Now shut up and help me land this thing." He barks out several orders. Jenna and Ash jump in to help. Anthony hangs back, shifting back and forth and waiting to be told what to do.

Colt slips from the room, and I go after him. After pulling on a shirt, he takes a backpack and starts shoving items into it from nearby drawers. It looks like dried packs of food, clothes, anything we may need.

"You okay?" I ask.

"Fine," he says. His voice is hard and cold like the first day I met him. He walks into the medical room without looking at me. Anthony must've warned him like he did me. And he's listening.

I go after him, wanting to tell him that Anthony's wrong, but the words get all mixed up in my mind. Probably because I'm not sure if Anthony is wrong at all. I barely know Colt.

He shoves more supplies into his bag. "You need something?"

Yes, I do, I realize. "Look at me."

He keeps moving.

"Stop, Colt." I reach out and take his arm. He immediately withdraws.

"Don't. I should never have . . . we can't . . ."

His eyes have returned to a softer blue. And then I know. I do feel differently around him, like I'm in front of a never-ending burning fire, all warm and cozy inside. I wish I didn't. I wish my heart froze at the sight of him. It would make things so much easier for when I went to Eden, a place not meant for Primes.

I back away, giving him the space he needs.

He brushes by me. "We have to get ready. We have a long walk ahead of us."

I don't follow him right away. There are so many thoughts and emotions colliding inside my head, making me feel more confused than ever before. My mother once told me that emotions could change a person's goals and desires. Sometimes for the better, but not always. This is one of those times. There's only one goal that matters right now, and I can't let whatever I feel for Colt get in the way. I have to get Max to Eden where he'll be safe.

Anthony's voice carries over from the next room. "Do you have everything ready to go, Colt?"

"Just about."

I join them in the other room. Jenna's standing inches from the door as if she can't wait to get off the plane.

Anthony asks me, "You and Max good to go?"

I glance over at Max. He's sitting still in the chair, the bear nowhere to be seen. "We're ready." I grab my backpack nearby, the one I had taken when I left everyone at camp. Tank must've grabbed it when he saved Colt and me.

Anthony takes his turn gathering supplies, mostly weapons, and shoves them into a duffel bag. "We're moving quick when we land, so be prepared."

I walk to Max and hold still like he is. I know a lot about New York City, the biggest city in all the United States. Because of its size, the country's capitol was moved here over fifty years ago. I always thought I might visit it one day, but never did I think that when that time came I'd be sneaking inside.

After several minutes, Tank calls from the windowed room, "We're landing in ten seconds. Brace yourselves."

I grab onto Max to steady him, but I barely feel the jolt when the hover-plane lands.

"Let's move," Anthony says. A door lowers as if on command. Anthony and Colt follow Jenna down the ramp. I walk down it, slower than the others while I wait for Max.

Tank remains inside, speaking with Ash about flying the plane somewhere just outside the city's boundaries. The way he's standing next to her and touching her on the elbow makes me think she means more to him than a mere conspirator in HOPE. My suspicions are confirmed when he tenderly kisses her on the forehead before he leaves the plane.

"We head north," Tank says as he walks by me and toward Max. "I'll take the kid."

Colt blocks him. "No, I've got *Max*." He bends down in front of him and says to Max, "Want to go for a ride?"

Max lets go of my hand and takes a step forward. Colt scoops him up and swivels him onto his back.

"Thanks," I say. His eyes meet mine briefly and he nods.

I walk behind everyone, taking in my surroundings, analyzing every detail. If danger presents itself, I need to know the strengths and weaknesses of the landscape. This will help me to know whether it would be better to run or fight.

I sigh and tie my hair back. No matter how far I am from my father, his voice is always ringing in my head.

The landscape is full of hills and rocks, some of them as tall as me, making walking a challenge, but the canopy of trees above us is thicker than it was in Providence, which will help hide us should the Institute fly over. Most of us keep our heads on swivel, listening and watching carefully, but Jenna shoves ear buds into her ears. She probably listens to screaming music, something loud and chaotic.

It's not long before the others decide to run so I pick up my feet to follow after. Thankfully, the pain in my leg is mostly gone. Colt's carrying Max in front of me, holding him as I would. Every once in a while Max's gaze falls upon me, but his focus leaves moments later.

After a few hours of jogging, I become winded and my pace slows despite my mind screaming to go faster. My body is a traitor, and one day I'm afraid it will cost me my life.

"You want me to carry you?" Tank calls over his shoulder. "My muscles will barely feel your weight."

I take a deep breath to make sure I have enough air to answer. "I think your muscles are busy holding up your ego."

Colt looks back, the corner of his mouth slightly turned up.

Tank laughs. "There's always room for a pretty lady."

I want to retort, but I only have enough lung strength to keep jogging. I manage to go almost another hour before I say between breaths, "I need a break." My voice isn't loud, but Colt hears and calls up to the group.

"Let's rest for a bit." He lowers Max to the ground.

Tank jogs back to us. "Why are we stopping?"

"We need a break," Colt says.

Tank looks confused until he notices I'm sitting down, gasping for air. "Right, fine, but only for a few minutes."

"Slowing us up again, eh Patch?" Jenna says and drops her pack onto a large boulder.

Anthony comes next to her. "Lay off, Jenna. I'm tired too."

"Sure you are," she mumbles.

I pretend not to hear and do all that I can to regulate my breathing.

"How much further?" Colt asks.

"If we're fast, we can be there by nightfall," Tank says.

Colt's gaze flickers in my direction. "Let's go slower and make it there by morning."

"No way," Jenna says. "I want a comfortable bed tonight."

Tank stretches his arms up and around. "Look, if this is about Sage, I can carry her. My offer still stands. In fact, I think I might enjoy it." He winks at me, but I roll my eyes, knowing he's only teasing.

"You don't need to carry her," Colt says. "She just needs a little more time than the rest of us."

"We could split up," Jenna says. "You know, some of us go ahead, get a car and then come back for the rest of you."

"It didn't go so well last time we did that," Anthony says. He's pacing back and forth, not the least bit winded.

"What are you talking about?" Tank says. "It went exactly as I had planned."

Colt takes a threatening step toward him. "You planned on me getting shot and Sage getting strangled?"

I stand up. "Enough! I'm fine. Let's just keep going and if I get tired, then you guys can go ahead."

"No one's going ahead," Colt says.

Jenna throws her pack back over her shoulders. "I am. Love you, Sage, but I'm so over this."

Tank follows after her. "Think about it," he calls over his shoulder in my direction.

Anthony pats me on the back. "Don't push yourself. Just do the best you can." He trots away.

"I feel like such a charity case," I say and grab my bag. In a mock voice, I say, "Poor Sage. Can't do much of anything."

"No one thinks that," Colt says and picks up Max again.

Our fast pace continues. I manage to keep up but it's not long before I need to stop again. Several blisters have formed on my feet, and my legs are shaking. I slow to a walk, not even bothering to say anything.

Colt calls to the others. "Let's take another break!"

This time, surprisingly, Jenna doesn't complain. "Good. I need to pee."

"Don't go alone," Anthony says. He leans up against a tree and pulls down his shirt to inspect his wound. My eyes widen at how much it has healed.

"I don't need anyone to hold my hand," Jenna says.

Anthony readjusts his shirt. "No one goes out alone."

"I'll go with you," I say.

"Oh, goodie! We'll visit the dirt toilet and powder our noses with pine needles." Jenna heads into the forest. "Try to keep up, Patch."

I turn to Max and ruffle the hair on his head. "I'll be right back. Stay with Colt."

Dipping under a low hanging branch, I scramble up a small

rise, my feet slipping on wet earth. It's a difficult path Jenna has chosen, probably deliberately. I inch my way around thick foliage while trying to keep my hair from being ensnared by prickly limbs.

When I'm close, Jenna looks over her shoulder. "Seeing how we're doing the whole girl bathroom thing, we might as well gossip too."

"About what?"

"First on the list is what's up with you and Colt?"

I almost trip over a fallen log but manage to catch myself. "Nothing, why?"

"Oh come on now. You can be honest with me. I saw you in the medical room. Colt was standing all close to you, holding your hand. And if there's one thing I know, Colt doesn't like to be touched. Ever. So what's the deal?"

"He's nice."

"What a dumb answer. Let me try again. Does he make you hot?"

I glance away, embarrassed

"Maybe you don't know what I'm talking about. You did live like a caveman after all." Before I can refute her, she says, "I'm not saying I've been around the block or anything, but I know a few things about men and women." She pats me on the back. "I think it's time we had *the* talk, Patch."

I shrug her arm off my shoulder. "I'm not an idiot. I know what you're talking about. As for Colt, he's very handsome, that's all."

"But you know it can't work, right?"

I remain silent.

Jenna continues, "We're trying to save your kind, not breed more Primes."

"Who said anything about breeding? I just want to know him better." The forest grows dark the farther we go, and I look up. The trees are older here, their branches more full, making it seem more like night than day. "Are we going too far?"

Jenna keeps walking. "You need to think big picture here. Colt's like the first guy you've met and, in my humble opinion, a Junk would be a better companion. Besides, how do you know there isn't some hottie Original back at Eden?"

"I really don't want to have this conversation with you."

"Fine, but don't say I didn't warn you when your dream guy in Eden doesn't like you because you're hung up on some Noc." She turns left up a steep ravine, sending a few birds from their nests, their wings flapping against red leaves.

I take wide steps, pressing my hands against my knees to help me up the hill. "Can we just stop already?"

"At the top. I want to make sure we're far away from Tank. He'll do anything to catch a peek at a girl."

"I think that's just an act," I say, remembering how he was with Ash.

"I don't."

A few minutes later, we crest the top. I glance behind us, surprised at how far we've come. I can't see or hear the others.

"I'll be over here," Jenna says and moves to my right.

I quickly do my business then return to the top of the hill to wait for Jenna. I inhale deeply, and smell the forest's rich earthy aroma. Jenna's approaching footsteps are loud as they snap twigs and other woodsy debris.

Too loud. There should be other sounds this time of day, like birds chirping or the singing of cicadas, but there's none of that. Something's frightened them, which means we should be frightened too.

I rush after Jenna, catching her just before she ducks behind a thick, blackened tree trunk.

"Get away, Patch. You haven't washed your hands—"

I quickly cover her mouth and whisper. "There's something out there. Be quiet." I press both of us against the tree and strain my ears. "Do you hear anything?"

She cocks her head to the side. "I think so." Her eyes go big. "It's not a bear, right? Please tell me it's not a bear."

The sounds I'm hearing are heavy but too quick for a bear. "I don't think so. Just stay still."

For the first time, she does as I ask. We stay huddled together, pressed against the tree. As the sound draws near, I determine that two people are walking, one of them much heavier than the other. Occasionally one of them speaks, but I can't hear their words yet.

I peek around the tree trunk and can just barely make out their forms as they move easily in and out of the trees. One of them is massively tall and thick, like a tree trunk that has lost all its limbs. And it's walking toward us.

The other man is a little taller than me and thin. His arms seem unnaturally long, his hands almost reaching his knees. I think hard until I recall their species. To Jenna, I whisper, "One is a Plank, the other a Twiggy."

Her grip tightens against the bark on the tree until it snaps off. "We are so screwed."

"Maybe they won't notice us," I say and lower myself to the ground, taking Jenna with me. We're slightly positioned down the slope so there's a chance they might not see us, especially with all the shadows crowding beneath the leafy umbrella above us.

I slowly breathe in and out to make sure I don't hold my breath. I need to keep a clear mind. Jenna's fears are not unfounded. Planks are similar in strength to the tall Titan I faced at the Institute, but Planks don't lack intelligence, nor do they have the same weakness of bending at the waist. A Plank's only weakness, common to their species, but not definitive, is poor eyesight. Twiggy's, on the other hand, are fast runners and have a death grip if they catch you, but their movements are awkward in hand-to-hand combat. Alone, each species can be dealt with, but simultaneously they're a deadly combination. Something tells me they know this and aren't traveling together because they enjoy each other's company.

"—not stupid. I know I saw it land," the Plank is saying. His voice is deep and smooth, each syllable running into the next.

"Then where are they, Ted?" the Twiggy asks and Jenna and me cringe at the same time. His voice is high and sharp, like the sound I'd imagine a rat would make if rats could talk. I'm glad they don't because there are a lot more rats than people.

"Quit talking and maybe we'll hear them, horse-face," Ted says.

"What if someone else already found them?"

Ted doesn't answer. His footsteps come closer, crushing everything beneath his massive feet.

"Can you imagine if we get the reward?" Horse-face says. I'm not sure if that's his name or if Ted was insulting him. "I'm going to move out of my sister's house with my share. How 'bout you?"

Jenna nudges me. She points down the hill and mouths the word "run." I shake my head vehemently, knowing the Twiggy will catch us.

"I'm going," she whispers, determined lines set in her forehead.

"Did you hear that?" Ted says. They stop moving.

I glare at Jenna and shake my head. She scowls and mouths the word *what?*

"I didn't hear anything," Horse-face says, "but I sure smell something, like perfume. It's nice, better than what my sister wears."

Jenna nods her head as if thinking, "Of course it is."

"Who's out there?" Ted calls.

Jenna looks like she's going to bolt, so I take hold of her arm hard to keep her still.

Several seconds pass before Horse-face says, "Someone's passed by here recently. You think whoever it was came from the plane you saw land?"

Ted starts walking again. "I thought you said I was seeing things?"

Horse-face laughs, a horrible grating sound, and I'm convinced that a rat's laugh would be much more pleasant. "I was just messing with you. I saw it too."

Ted's not far away, passing by us. "Shut up, Lenny." I guess his name isn't Horse-face.

When they are some distance away, still within earshot, but out of sight, Jenna says, "I'm out of here."

"No! Wait," I say, my voice as quiet as possible. The Primes have moved on too quickly, I think.

She looks back at me as if she's considering whether or not to obey, but decides against it. "You better follow me if you know what's good for you." She hurries down the slope almost to the point of tripping.

I don't move, despite the fear of being alone. Jenna's almost to the bottom, and I think maybe I was wrong, when I hear the faint sound of something running through the forest. Because the steps are light, I imagine a deer, but when the figure comes into view I'm not surprised that it's the Twiggy, Lenny the horse-face. I am surprised, however, by the way he's moving, all orangutan-like, but graceful and really fast.

Jenna looks over her shoulder and doesn't even have the chance to scream before Lenny's huge hand sucks itself around her neck. He lifts her above his head like a rag doll and races up the hill, smiling big, which seems to widen his narrow face.

"I've got her! I've got her! Wahoo! We're rich!" he yells, and if it were possible for him to jump and click his heels while running upwards, I have no doubt he'd do it.

I press myself against the tree as he runs past, but he's too happy with his prize to notice me. I try to catch Jenna's eye, but her body's bouncing so violently that she can't look over. Not far, the sound of heavy footsteps, like an elephant on steroids, crashes through the forest. Ted has arrived.

"Let me see," he says to Lenny.

I carefully peek around the tree. Lenny sets Jenna down, who wobbles precariously. Once she balances herself, she punches at Lenny. "What the hell? You can't just grab people like that!"

Lenny pushes her away with his long arm, making her fall to the ground. "You see that, Ted? She's like a wild dog."

Jenna scrambles to her feet. "Nobody calls me a dog."

She rushes him, but he stretches his arm and stops her progression with his hand to her forehead. Jenna's cursing and swinging her fists at him, but he's at least a foot away from her much smaller arms. He laughs.

"She seems awfully feisty for an Original," Ted says. "Let me see her eyes."

Lenny spins his hand, forcing Jenna to turn around, despite her angry words, half of which I don't recognize. Ted bends down until his eyes are level with Jenna's. A second later he straightens, his expression anything but jubilant.

"You moron, Lenny! This isn't her."

While Lenny takes his own turn to examine Jenna, I drop my head back into the tree. Ted had said "her." They are looking for me, which means the Institute has a lot more people searching for us than we expected. And since they're offering a reward, it will be impossible to know whom to trust.

"Where is she?" Ted says to Jenna.

"Your mom?" Jenna asks, innocently. "She left you when you were a baby, don't you remember? She couldn't stand your face."

"Don't get smart with us."

"Impossible," she says.

Ted hits her hard, making me flinch. A blow like that would've knocked me unconscious.

Jenna wipes her mouth with the back of her hand. "My cat hits harder than you."

Ted cocks back his fist. "Where is the Original? Tell me or next time you'll see stars permanently."

Jenna raises her chin. "That doesn't even make sense."

Lenny grabs her neck from behind and lifts her up, shaking her hard. "I want my reward! Tell us where she is!"

When he's finished, his grip lightens, giving her a chance to respond. She gasps for air, then says, "I don't know any Originals!" There's no humor in her voice now.

"Of course you do," Ted says. "Why else would a little girl like you be out here, within thirty miles of where I saw a plane land?"

"I saw it land too and was curious," she says.

This gives the men pause.

"You looking for the Original too?" Lenny asks. He lowers her to the ground.

She runs with it. "I sure am. I'm going to use the money to buy me those new Nike shoes. You see them? The ones that let you walk on water?"

"My sister has a pair," Lenny says. "They don't work all of the time." He lets go of Jenna's neck.

"Don't they? That's too bad."

Ted's watching her closely. "If you know about the Original," he says, "then you heard the announcement, right?"

My mind races. Announcement? The one we deciphered on

the plane? But it said nothing about a reward. Jenna's probably thinking the same thing.

"My com was low, but I heard all the important stuff. Original and reward. That's all I need to hear and I'm like a Canine." She growls and shows her teeth.

Lenny laughs.

Jenna looks at him. "Don't do that."

"Huh?"

"I don't believe you," Ted says.

"I don't care what you believe. You guys have wasted enough of my time, and it's only a few more hours before dark." She turns to leave, but Ted grabs her by the arms.

"I don't think so. Not until you pass my test."

"I'm dyslexic," she says.

"There's no reading involved. Just me smashing your head in three times. If you don't tell me where the Original is, then I figure you're telling the truth and you can live, if you're still alive by then."

"I don't know of any Original," she says. Her loyalty touches me. I wouldn't have guessed she had it in her.

Ted continues to hold her with his left hand, while he raises his right fist. "We'll see."

Jenna's eyes close tight.

"Stop!" I call and step out of my hiding place.

The men startle and settle into a defensive position.

Jenna opens her eyes and groans, "Balls, Patch! What are you thinking?"

"I'm thinking I want you to keep your face. Let her go," I say. "I'm the one you want."

"Raise your hands and walk toward me," Ted says. "I want to see your eyes."

I move out of the shadows and come toward them, my hands above my head. They both stare into my eyes.

"Eww," Lenny says. "Her eyes are ugly. Definitely an Original."

"You are so dumb," Jenna mutters to me under her breath.

"There's supposed to be two of you." Ted says. "Where's the boy?"

I turn to Jenna. "You're the one who bolted when I said not to, remember?" To Ted I answer, "Just me. The broadcast was wrong."

Lenny thumps his long arm into the ground. "I ain't sharin' the prize with nobody."

"Neither am I," Ted says. "I say we make the Original scream. Maybe the boy's hiding in the forest just like she was."

"There's no one out there," I say, but I know he's not going to believe me. I motion toward Jenna with my head. "Let her go and then worry about securing me. You can look for the boy later."

Lenny laughs, which makes my teeth grind. "Secure you?" he says. "My hand will secure you. There's not a thing you can do to us."

"It's not for protection from me, but from other Primes who surely saw my plane land too. They're probably coming right now and when they see me with you, they're going to want to fight."

Ted and Larry look at each other. They know I'm right.

"We can split up," Lenny says. "I'll take the Original, you look for the boy."

"No way. You'll take her straight to the Institute and cash out on the prize yourself. I'll take her."

"I'm not letting her out of my sight."

While the two continue to argue, Jenna leans over and whispers to me, "You can't seriously leave with them."

"Don't worry. When an opportunity presents itself I'll get away. You just make sure Max makes it to my father safely." Much louder, I say, "You better hurry and make a decision, boys."

"I've got a better idea," Jenna says. "Remember how you wanted to know what my special ability was?"

I look at her questioningly.

"You might want to cover your ears." She sucks in air through puckered lips, and then opens her mouth wide. The sound that comes out is nothing short of an atomic vocal bomb. I clamp my hands over my ears and drop to the ground. The men do the same. My eardrums feel like they are on fire, a burning inferno of excruciating pain.

Jenna continues to scream until she runs out of air. By the time she's finished, I'm curled into a fetal position, unable to produce a single thought. As much as I want to close my eyes and take myself to a happy, pain-free mental place, they remain open.

Ted and Lenny are struggling to get up. Jenna does her best to make sure they stay down. She kicks them each hard in the stomach and then follows it up with a blow to their faces. She's saying something and by her expression, the words can't be pretty or nice.

Jenna manages to hold them off for a short time, but soon they gain the upper hand. Lenny swipes his long arm at her feet, knocking her to the ground. A second later Ted presses his foot to her chest. I can't hear her but by the way her eyes look like they might pop from their sockets or the way her mouth is forming the shape of a large O, I know she is screaming.

I try to crawl over to help her, but the smallest move is excruciating. It's a horrible feeling, the helplessness of the situation. Jenna will die because I'm normal.

Two figures streak across my line of vision. The largest barrels into Ted's chest, knocking him off of Jenna, who quickly scrambles to the side. It takes me a second to realize the person is Tank. Colt comes right behind him, aimed at Lenny, who looks thoroughly confused. Just before Colt reaches him he turns like he's going to bolt, but Colt doesn't let him. He tackles Lenny to the ground and, while Lenny's face is pressed into the dirt, Colt leans over him and says something into his ear. Then he slowly moves off Lenny's back, and Lenny jumps to his feet and runs fast into the forest. Ted and Tank are in an epic battle the kings of the forest would be jealous of. Tank is smiling like it's the most fun he's had in a long time.

While they continue to trade Titan-sized blows, Colt comes and kneels in front of me. His eyebrows are drawn together and his mouth is moving. I can't hear him, but I know he's saying my name. The pain in my ears is so sharp I wonder if they are bleeding.

"I can't hear," I say. At least I think I'm saying it aloud.

Colt points his forefinger upwards and mouths the word *up*. I attempt to get on all fours, but an intense dizziness comes over me and I fall back down. Colt's lips tighten and he presses his palm to my back.

I glance away from his concerned stare and look for Tank. He's in the middle of tossing Ted over his head. Two trees have already been knocked over from their fighting. Ted crashes into a third; the tree snaps at the base. This time when Ted shakily comes to his feet, he shakes his head and follows Lenny's escape route. The victor, Tank, raises his arm to the sky and runs a victory lap. Colt looks at him sternly and says something to make him stop.

Both Tank and Jenna come over to me. The three of them stand together, discussing something I really wish I could hear, especially because I'm sure it's about me. Colt shrugs off a small backpack and opens it up. I try again to get to my feet but fall over. I'm so nauseated that I think I might vomit.

Almost a full minute passes before Colt turns around. His expression is as solemn as the others. They have the look of someone who is about to put their family pet to sleep, so when Colt kneels down and brings his hand forward, revealing a needled syringe, my eyes go big.

"No!" I say.

Before he stabs it into me, I think he says, "Trust me." He raises his eyebrows like he's waiting for me to answer.

I nod my head, assuming that whatever's in the syringe will heal my ears and get me back to walking as soon as possible. If two Primes saw the plane go down, there are most likely others. We need to get out of the forest and quick.

Colt gently presses the needle to the crook in my arm. I barely feel the sting when he pushes it into me. He gives me an encouraging smile. I wait, expecting any moment to feel better, but I don't. Instead I grow sleepy. Now I panic. My eyes go wide and I shake my head as much as the pain in my ears will allow. I don't want to go to sleep.

But I don't have a choice.

My eyes close, and I'm greeted by a suffocating blackness.

CHAPTER 28

There's nothing pleasant about a drug-induced sleep. It takes away a person's control, specifically mine, so when my eyes finally open, I wake in a bad mood.

I blink a few times and attempt to orient myself. Nothing looks familiar.

I'm sitting with my back pressed against the wall of a tall metal structure, surrounded by litter that smells of pizza and dog urine. Not more than ten feet across from me is a building, the side rusted, making it more copper than silver. I'm in a long, narrow alleyway. The sky above me is a dark blue. It won't be long until nightfall, which means I've been out for at least a couple of hours.

"About time," a voice says.

I turn my head and for the first time since waking realize that my ears no longer hurt, and I'm not dizzy. Tank looks at me for just a second before turning his back. He's peering outside the alleyway.

"Where are we?" I ask.

"New York City." His voice is serious, which worries me. Tank is never serious.

"Where are the others?" I ask, thinking specifically of Max.

"They took a different route."

I scoot next to him and look around the corner. "Why? I thought we were supposed to stay together."

The streets are busy. Vehicles, most of them older-looking compared to the ones in Boston, speed down the street, making it a suicide mission for any pedestrian thinking of passing, which, by the worn expressions of the people huddled together under faded and worn awnings, could be a serious possibility.

"We were spotted by a few Primes about an hour ago," Tank says. "With people after us we thought it better to split you and your brother up to increase our odds that at least one of you will make it to your father."

"It's got to be Max," I blurt.

"That's what we thought you would say, so I took you and went straight into the city to act as a decoy, especially for the Canine, who probably arrived around the same time we did."

I try hard to prevent it, but a shiver shakes my whole body. *The Canine.* Something has to be done about him or I and everyone around me will be at risk.

Tank seems to read my mind. "Don't worry. I'm working on what to do with him. Truthfully, I thought we'd be well through the city by now, beating even the others, but I had no idea it would be this difficult. See, look." He points to his left.

I lean out a little farther. There's an electronic billboard attached to a walkway that crosses over the busy road. It's looping the words, "Boy and girl Originals loose in city. Call Institute immediately for reward. Last seen with—" then the screen flashes a picture of Tank, the most well-known sports hero in America.

"The signs are all over," he says. "For the first time in my life, I regret being famous."

I slide back into the alley. "Can I see my pack?"

Tank moves with me and removes the bag off of his shoulder. "It will probably be a little easier from here on out, now that I'm not carrying you, which is what blew our cover in the first place."

While I search my bag, I ask, "How was Max doing last time you saw him?"

"Really good. Colt has a way with him. I think Colt wanted to be the one to take you, but Max wouldn't go to anyone else."

"I'm glad he's with Max." I find what I'm looking for and pull out a black pen and the rain poncho I used earlier.

"What do you need those for?"

I don't answer right away as I'm busy tearing at the yellow poncho until it's shaped into a large square. "Come here," I say.

"We need to give you a disguise." I fold the square material in half so it's the shape of a triangle and stands up. "You're too tall. Bend over so I can get at your head."

He gets on his knees and still has to lower his head for me to reach him. While I secure the makeshift bandana over his hair, he says, "I doubt this will work. Everyone knows me, especially women. They'll spot me a mile away even if I'm invisible."

I cinch the ends of the bandana tight at the base of his neck. "You don't have to do that with me."

He straightens. "Do what?"

"Act like that." I take the pen and start darkening his blond eyebrows.

Tank's quiet for a moment, then says, "How do you know it's an act?"

"I saw you with Ash. You care for her. A lot."

His eyebrows draw together, making me nearly give him a unibrow. "Don't tell anyone, okay?"

"Why do you do it?" I say. His eyebrows relax, and I return to the task of transforming him into someone else.

"I found early on that when I act like a chauvinistic pig, people tend to dismiss me. It has helped me fly under the Institute's radar."

"Well now that you've run right through it, you can drop the act. I'm sure Ash will appreciate it as much as the rest of us."

He smiles. "I'll work on it."

I lean back and take a look at him. With his bright hair covered and his brows darkened, he looks like he could be a relative of Tank's. "Not bad."

He stands and looks at his blurry reflection in the side of the metal building. His black pants are tight, but not as tight as his white shirt. I don't know how he wears clothes like that. It would drive me crazy.

"It might work, but what about you?" Tank asks.

I'm already pulling my blond-streaked hair into a high ponytail. "I still have the colored contacts, and I'll wear my sweatshirt with the hood up. It'll have to work."

"No hood. It will draw attention. Your picture isn't out there yet so you should be fine with colored contacts." I put them in and he looks me over. "You have anything better to wear? You look like you just rolled out of bed."

I glance down at my blue long-sleeved shirt and black sweat pants. Not a whole lot I could do to make them better.

"Try this," Tank says. He takes hold of my right sleeve and tears it off, exposing my shoulder.

"Hey!" I say, but he's already tearing at the other one.

He hands the torn material to me. "Take these sleeves, roll them up, and wear them as bracelets. As for your pants, can you push them up to your knees?"

I do as he says, tearing off the bandage from the back of my calf as I do so. The wound is almost healed. I glance down at my entire outfit. "It looks dumb."

"Fashion these days is dumb, but at least you'll blend in," he says. "How are you feeling?"

I stretch my arms. "Not bad."

"Good. We're going to move fast but inconspicuously. It's about three miles to your father." My heart skips a beat. "The others should be waiting for us. Ready?" He moves to turn around, but I stop him.

"What about the Canine?"

He looks at me, his eyes serious like he's trying to decide whether or not to tell me the truth. I make it easy for him. "I won't go if there's a risk to the others."

"Then we'll have to draw him out. The trick is getting him away from the Institute's henchmen who will surely be with him. There's no way I'll be able to fight them all. Let's go." He pulls me onto the street. I walk quickly to catch up to him, eyes downcast.

"Try and act normal," he says. "Not so . . . you."

I clear my throat and raise my chin. Act like someone else. Be someone else. I say these words in my head over and over until I think I believe them. The sun is all but gone from the city. Its fading light reflects off the sides of metal buildings, sending rays of sunshine bouncing through the streets. I meet people's gaze as I pass. I am one of them. A few smile back at me. I belong.

"If we can get the Canine alone, I know I can kill him," Tank says after we've traveled a few blocks.

It's less crowded here. By the looks of it, we've migrated into a business district with warehouses that have already shut down for the day. A smell like rotting meat fills the air, forcing me to breathe with my mouth open. Off to my right is a food recycling plant, most likely the source of the putrid aroma.

"It will probably take me a few minutes though," Tank continues, "which we won't have. Not only that, but it will draw attention we don't want."

"We need to become invisible. The Canine too." I look around, my mind working quickly. What would my father suggest? I step over a sealed manhole and stop.

"What is it?" Tank asks.

"The underground tunnels. I need access to a computer." I hurry over to the nearest building and peek in a dusty window. I can barely make out what looks like machines for an auto mechanic shop.

"The tunnels?" Tank says over my shoulder. "You're not thinking of going in there, are you? Because that would be suicide."

I step back and glance at the next building over. A sign above the door reads: Mike's Packaging and Shipping. "It's not suicide. I've done it before," I say and walk over to the door.

Tank follows after me. "But that was in Boston. New York is a whole other beast. There are more Junks and who knows what else living down there."

"The Mutant Alligators," I say as I turn the doorknob. "They're a legend." The door's locked.

"You don't know that, but even if it is, Junks are real and there's probably hundreds if not thousands down there."

I turn around, almost running into him. "Can you open this for me? I need to get inside."

Tank glances around before settling his gaze on me. "You're not listening."

"No, you're not listening. Just trust me on this. I only need five minutes with a computer. If I can't find a way to make my plan work, then we'll move on." He searches my eyes as if looking for ways to break through my resolve. I lift my chin to let him know it's impermeable.

He reaches behind me and turns the knob until it snaps, along with three other locks that must've been holding the door secure. It's a good thing Tank is with me since I don't think even Colt could've opened it.

"Hurry," Tank says. "Who knows when the Canine might show?"

I nod and rush inside to the nearest metal desk. I slide my fingers across the top until a holographic blue screen appears in front of me. An electronic voice says, "Say password."

I don't need to see the company's files. I cross both fingers tightly and say, "Bypass. Go online."

I breathe a sigh of relief when the screen spins, a spectrum of translucent colors whirling in front of me, until it settles onto several 3D images of cats. Some are walking in tight loops while others lick their fur. A plain brown one, smaller than the rest, is chasing its tail.

It strangely reminds me of myself.

"What a stupid home screen," Tank says over my shoulder.

With a swipe of my finger, the cats disappear. "Search tunnel blueprints of New York City," I command to the computer.

The holographic screen spins again. When it stops, the electronic voice says, "Tunnel blueprints displayed by date." A long list appears. The most recent one is from thirty years ago. I click on it and then expand the next screen as wide as it will go, which is the whole length of the desk and almost as tall as Tank. I stand up to get a better look at the image.

Tank moves close and, after inspecting the screen, says, "I think we're somewhere in here." He points to the top left of the screen.

"How can you tell?"

His finger moves to the bottom. "See this giant circle? This is the city's water storage. And up here, where there are fewer manholes," his hand moves through a series of what look like long pipes, but I know are really tunnels, "is the business district. If I were to guess, this one," he taps on a small yellow circle, "is the manhole just outside this building. Or maybe this one."

I study the map. The business district has several tunnels

crossing in and out of each other. Each manhole is almost half a mile apart. "Can you tell where my father is located?"

Tank snakes his finger around the holographic screen and stops at the bottom, near the center. "Here. About two miles away."

"And the Canine will be coming from the direction we just came from." I walk around the desk and look outside the only window in the room. Night is fully upon us. We can use it to our advantage.

"What are you thinking?"

"I say I confront him outside."

"What do you mean 'I'? What happened to 'we'?" He motions his hand back and forth between us.

I return to the blueprints. "Just go with me on this." I point to the manhole just outside the building. "I wait for him here. When I see him coming, I'll make sure he sees me too. Then I'll jump in the manhole and run to this one, where you'll be waiting to pull me out."

"And then I'll kill the Canine when he comes through? I don't get it. It won't give me any more time than if you were to run on the street toward me."

"I'm not looking for more time. I'm trying to make the Canine disappear."

"By trapping him in the tunnels." He considers this for a moment then says, "There's a chance the Canine will have a tracker on him so even if he goes into the tunnel, the Institute can still find him."

"I'll take that chance. Besides, it'll be a dead body they find." I cross the room and open the door.

"How can you be so sure? Junks could be on the other side of the city."

"Not when I'm finished. In a couple of hours, the tunnels will be drowning in Junks."

CHAPTER 29

"This is such a bad idea," Tank says, while he lowers down another bucket of rotten meat into the manhole.

I'm not looking when I take it and almost drop the foul mess of unrecognizable animal parts, but I manage to steady it again. My heart's pounding, and my head is on a swivel, always on the lookout for approaching Junks. This is my fifth bucket of slop from the food recycling plant just down the street. Already the tunnel smells of something dead and bloated. I quickly walk a short distance past the manhole and dump the bucket onto a growing pile of rancid meat. The tunnels are much nicer here than they were in Boston, if it's possible for a tunnel to be considered nice. They are made entirely of concrete with ceilings twice my height and even include lights every few yards or so. A lot of them aren't working anymore, but any amount of light in a place like this can sure comfort a girl who's stupid enough to climb into a Junk-infested tunnel. My only complaint, if I'm allowed to have one, is that the space is too narrow; my arms can't stretch out all the way before the walls stop them.

"How do you know Junks won't get you first?" Tank asks as he hands me another full bucket.

"I don't, but I figure the first one dropping through this hole has the advantage." I keep talking while I move to empty more rotten slop. "When the Canine or any of his buddies come after me, Junks will have to get through them to get to me. By then, I fully plan on being at the other manhole where you'll be pulling me up. And as soon as I'm out, you seal the tunnel."

"What about this entrance? Who's going to close it?"

"No one. Junks will make sure that no one's getting out this way."

"I just wish I could fit in there," Tank says. "If anything goes wrong—"

"It won't." I accept another bucket and walk down the narrow tunnel, feeling strangely deflated. "I hope," I whisper and add the congealed contents to the growing pile of gruesome guts. My plan had seemed like a good one when I came up with it over an hour ago, but the more I think about it, the more I see its fatal flaws. The only reason I haven't called the whole thing off yet is I can't think of a better solution. All I know is I can't let the Canine track me to where Max and the others are hiding. And even though Tank still has enough power on his wind gun for one more blast, we don't know how many Primes might be traveling with the Canine, and we can't guarantee they will all be standing close enough together for the gun to have any effect anyway.

Tank lowers more garbage gruel. I wish New York City had more people sensitive to the HOPE movement for us to turn to, but it doesn't. Of all the states, Tank tells me it has the least, which makes me wonder why my father chose to meet us here and not somewhere else. Regardless, our lack of friends makes it so I have to turn to our common enemy—Junks. They will unknowingly help me. Or eat the flesh off my body.

A faint sound, like the rustling of steps through dirt, comes from down the tunnel. My heart stops for just a moment, and I suck in air to get it beating again. They're here. I hurry back.

"Up, up, up," I say, reaching toward Tank. I can't see anything, but the rustling grows louder.

Tank scoops me up and pulls me through the manhole. I'm in such a rush that I'm kicking my legs as if doing so would help me get through faster. As soon as I'm out, my flailing legs knock over the barrel of remaining rancid food. It spills everywhere, splashing upwards and onto my pants.

"No!" I say and brush at my legs, but the smelly liquid has already absorbed into my sweats.

Tank unzips his backpack and removes a small cloth from the first aid kit and blots at my pants. "This isn't good."

"As long as I'm fast, it's not a big deal."

Tank straightens, his face scrunched into a worried look.

"You should probably get out of here," I say, acting like it's no big deal that I smell like Junk's favorite food. "The Canine could show any time."

"Right." He looks down the road, his chest filling with air.

"I will be fine. I'll communicate with you the entire time. Go." I touch the small black earpiece behind my ear. At least we can talk to each other. If only we had enough of them that I could talk to Colt and ask about Max.

"Let me at least give you this." He reaches behind his back and pulls out the wind gun. "If you get into trouble, use it. It will buy you some time."

I take it from him and tuck it in the back of my pants. "Thanks."

"We'll give it a few hours. If the Canine doesn't show up, then we've got to move on."

"I'm not going back to Max until I know we can't be tracked."

"Let's just see what happens before we have that conversation." He pats me on the back. "See you soon," he says and jogs away.

I watch him until the darkness swallows him entirely, leaving me alone. The street is quiet and still. I don't like it. There should be sounds of life somewhere in the city: a dog barking, the scurrying of a rat, a horn blaring, but there's none of that. It's like the city is holding its breath, like the way a person would just before witnessing someone suddenly jumping from a high cliff.

A single streetlight not far away provides some light, but it's not comforting. Instead it casts shadows all around, making me worry that something might be hiding inside, watching me. I hate the unknown. I would rather face a twenty-foot monster than a mouse concealed by darkness.

A gurgling noise from underground replaces my current gloom. I get on my knees and firmly plant my hands on the outside of the manhole so I can lower my head and look inside. Three Junks are tearing at the rotten meat, eating it so fast they often have to stop to keep from choking. It won't be long until more Junks come.

I straighten and walk to the side of the street to hide myself within the shadows where I won't feel so vulnerable. The Canine will find me regardless. No need to stay in the light feeling like an exposed deer in headlights.

"You okay?" Tank's voice says in my ear.

"I'm good. A few Junks have already arrived. They're downing the food as if it's candy."

"Good." He's silent for a moment, then, "Remember what we talked about. If the Canine doesn't show up before the food runs out, we have to move."

I glance up into the night sky. A few stars twinkle, their light going off and on as if they can't make up their mind whether they want to be light or dark. "We'll talk about it later." He doesn't say anything further and neither do I.

Time passes. Deathly slow. A couple of hours at least. I've been alone before, sometimes for days while I was out hunting in the backcountry of Maine when my father was able to stay with Max, but this is so different. I was the hunter then, in a position of power, but now I'm the prey, weak and vulnerable. And the willing prey at that. No animal I know of does this.

A hissing sound to my left startles me, and I back up, my hands sliding along the metal building behind me. I'm no longer alone. Another hiss, like the kind a snake gives right before it strikes. The sound is followed by heavy footsteps, but on the opposite side of the street. That means there are at least two of them. I glance around, searching the dark for more.

I want to run. It's a natural response for prey to ensure their survival, but it's not my survival I'm worried about. This thought gives me courage, and I step out of the darkness and into the light. I don't stop moving until I'm standing in front of the open manhole, concealing it from whoever's out there. Beneath me are the faint sounds of what could possibly be dozens of Junks.

The Canine appears first, or the silhouette of him anyway. I know it's him by the way he moves: less human and more animal. He's slightly hunched over, his arms arched at his sides on account of massive biceps. I almost say something to Tank through the earpiece, but decide against it.

"Looks like you finally found me," I call, though I probably could've whispered it and he would've heard. Movement within the manhole gets my attention, and I glance down. There are two Junks looking up at me with yellow, blood-shot eyes; their faces are covered in bits of torn flesh and blood. I quickly glance away to keep my eyes on the Canine, but I'm worried. Why are those Junks not eating? I need them *away* from the opening. My brain works several scenarios, but it's my nose that solves the problem first. *The smell.* I look around at the spilled contents of the leftover stinky sap. The Junks can smell it. The fetid food below must be getting low.

"You made this too easy," the Canine says, his voice deep and coarse-sounding like he just gargled gasoline.

"One thing I am not is easy," I say.

The Canine looks around as if expecting others to suddenly appear.

"There's no one else," I say. "I'm here alone, but I can't say the same for you."

Movement to my left catches my attention. There's a figure swaying in the darkness, almost weightless as if it's a body hanging from the gallows. A low hissing sound follows. I think it may be a Serpen, a human with snake DNA. I don't let myself think of the severe consequences this could mean, especially when a third figure appears to my right.

It's a woman, mostly normal-looking with long, dark hair and pale skin, but her eyes are all-black. No whites to be seen. I think she's a Rhine, or possibly a Trix. It's hard to tell without seeing her up close, something I definitely don't want to do, especially now that she's pointing a tranquilizer gun directly at me.

"We prefer to work alone," the Canine says, "but Ebony doesn't want any mistakes. We're taking you back tonight. You can come willingly or, my personal favorite, fight."

His use of the word *we* confuses me. Does he mean him and the other Prime's with him? I inch closer to the manhole, despite the Junks below. Just beyond the Canine, a shadow shifts. The movement is familiar, but it disappears before I can place it. How many more Primes are hiding in the shadows?

"I bet it makes you feel real tough to fight someone like me," I say.

He snorts. "I don't do it to feel tough. I do it to spill your blood, one of the many benefits of my job. There's nothing better than the taste of an Original's blood."

The Serpen's lifeless-looking body moves away from the darkness and toward me, but it stops at the shadow's edge, hissing. Any closer and the poison from its mouth will render me useless if it spits. But so will the gun in the girl's hand. I better act fast.

"I hate to disappoint," I say, "but it's not *my* blood that's going to be spilled tonight. Besides, I think there's someone who likes the taste of blood more than you do."

The Canine looks back and forth at his fellow Primes and nods as if to say, "get her." Before anything else can happen, I take one step backwards and fall into the manhole. My hands catch the lip of the circular opening, leaving my legs dangling just above the two Junks. I swing my body fast and only let go when I'm able to jump past them. As soon as my feet hit the ground, I'm running.

"I'm coming toward you," I say to Tank.

"Hurry," his voice says back.

I glance over my shoulder. The two Junks who were camping out at the bottom of the manhole are scurrying after me, the knuckles at the end of their long fingers bouncing off the dirt floor. Just beyond them, where the spoiled food wanes, a mound of Junks fight, clawing and biting at whatever they can. A few of them have spotted me.

The woman with the gun momentarily blocks my view of the Junks. I'm surprised that she is the first one through. She sees me running away and raises the gun along with a smile that suggests she has the upper hand. That hand is swiped clean off her body by a stubby Junk with long claws. She screams and falls to the ground, clutching her bleeding, handless arm to her chest. I turn the corner before seeing what happens next, but when the woman's screams are cut off suddenly, I can guess what happened.

The hallway is darker here and more narrow, but it's clear of Junks, which was the plan. I run fast, pumping my arms back and forth to stay ahead of the Junks that are still chasing after me. The cold metal of the gun at my back is a comfort. In a bind, I can use it. So far this plan is going better than I expected.

A few pops echo through the tunnels. The Canine and the Serpen have most likely joined the fight.

Half a mile. That's how far I need to run. Three minutes if I'm super fast. I turn another corner and glance behind me. There are now five Junks in pursuit, their expressions twisted into a blinding hunger with wide, bloodshot eyes and crowded teeth in bloodied mouths. Stay in front of them; that's all I have to do.

Sounds all at once fill the tunnel. Some are high-pitched squeals accompanied by a sort of hissing–spitting noise that I can only assume is the Serpen. A series of small explosions shake the earth beneath me, making me stumble to my knees. I scramble to my feet and keep running even when the claws of one of the Junk's just misses tearing off my foot. I reach for the gun. I didn't want to have to use the wind blaster this soon, but I may not have a choice. The Junks are so close now they may as well be my shadow.

If I can just go a little faster. *Push!* I give it all I've got, every muscle working together, doing their part until my strides lengthen. This seems to do the trick and soon the Junks are back within a comfortable distance. I'm so close. There are no more explosions, no more screaming. Even though I'm sprinting, my breathing and heartbeat become steady. I'm going to make it.

"That was a dirty trick you pulled!" the voice of the Canine calls. His voice is loud in the small tunnel, startling me, and I almost stumble again.

A tight knot forms in my throat. The Canine is still alive. I glance over my shoulder. There's not enough light for me to determine how close he is to me. Only the Junks are there, but two of them have stopped, probably to attack the threat behind them.

A moment later my eardrums are accosted by a terrible ripping sound of flesh and bones, followed by a spray blast, as if someone has thrown a bucket of water into the wall, but I know it's not water. Something moans long and deep.

I turn the corner. One more bend and I will be out of this mess. "Are you there, Tank?"

"I'm in position."

There's more light where I'm heading, a bright curtain of safety. I look behind me one last time. Beyond my shadowing Junks is the Canine, his face torn and bloody but still alive. And just beyond him are several more of the mutated creatures.

Light envelopes me as I turn the last corner and for the first time since dropping into the tunnels, I take a deep breath. Tank's head is lowered in from the manhole.

"Hurry!" He stretches out his long arm.

I'm still sprinting, more from joy than fear now. Soon Tank will pull me up and seal the manhole behind, leaving the Canine with hungry Junks. My only task before freedom is to blast the Canine, temporarily immobilizing his body, giving Junks a fabulous feast.

The light above me flickers and dust falls from the ceiling as if something huge has shaken the tunnel. The few Junks are still behind me, followed by the Canine. They don't seem to notice the disruption.

I look at Tank at the same time a monstrous roar fills the tunnel, shaking me until I think my bones might crumble. I have to catch myself against the wall to keep from falling over. I hurry and glance behind me to make sure I won't be attacked by Junks. They, too, have frozen in place, and they no longer look like bloodthirsty animals, but more like startled fawns. Their yellowed eyes can't get any wider. They stare beyond me at something hidden within the shadows. The Canine is the only one still moving forward, seemingly unaware of the danger. Or maybe he just doesn't care.

"What was that?" Tank asks.

I don't answer. There's a massive shape moving toward us. The side of its body slides against the walls, sounding like sandpaper.

Tank turns his head toward the sound. A second later he says, "You better move. Fast."

But it's too late. The creature is already moving beneath Tank, who is covering his nose. Instinctively, I hold my breath and raise the gun in my hand. I flash it back and forth between the Canine and the unknown monster, not sure who I should shoot. The

Junks still aren't moving, despite the Canine coming up behind them dangerously close.

The far reaches of the light finally touch the creature, and I suck in air. It's so disfigured that I don't know what deformity repels me the most. Its arms are short and positioned awkwardly on the front of its hairless body that's gray in color, except for the parts that are blood red where it looks like his leather-like skin has fallen off. The creature is at least two heads taller than Junks but still shorter than me. The most abnormal feature about it, if I had to choose just one, is how wide it is, like it's just eaten a horse. And by the blood dripping from its flat, long chin, that might be a likely possibility.

"Shoot it!" Tank yells.

I turn around at the sound of blades slashing through skin. Behind me the Canine has torn the Junks in two, painting the walls in red. Just beyond him is a crowd of Junks huddled together at the back of the tunnel with hungry, eager faces.

"What are you waiting for?" Tank calls again. His hand is stretched long as if he can reach me.

The monster is getting closer, slowly because of its size, but with purpose, like he wants to use me as a palate cleanser after eating that horse. I can shoot it, jump over it, and get to Tank. The Canine will do the same, but will most likely not survive once we seal the manhole. Junks will be upon him in a matter of seconds.

There's one huge problem, and it's the reason why I'm hesitating. I can't be sure he *won't* survive unless I stick to the plan. I steady the gun on the Canine. He proceeds forward not flinching in the least. Until I make him flinch.

I pull the trigger.

The sound of a windstorm rushes out of the gun's barrel, knocking the Canine backwards. Before his body can hit the ground, I'm placing each hand, downward facing, on the sides of the walls and lifting up. My feet spread too to help push me up toward the ceiling.

I scramble as high as I can go just as the monster and its foul smell reaches me. The creature's stench burns my nostrils, and my stomach churns, making me gag. It looks up at me, the motion pulling sagging, rotten skin down away from its sickly, yellowed eyes. It attempts to reach me, but it can't jump, only bounce like an overfilled water balloon. Another roar almost makes me lose my footing; one foot slides off the tunnel's wall and brushes the top of the creature.

"Careful!" Tank calls.

The monster lets out one more terrible growl then moves on to feast on the Canine, who looks supremely frustrated as he's still struggling to get up. Several of the Junks have come forward, clawing and snarling at the Canine, but they slink back to the shadows when the creature roars again.

I move to lower myself on the ground, thinking I'm safe, but all of a sudden something whips up over the monster's face and snaps me on my thigh, tearing open my pants and a good chunk of skin. A second later, the frog-like tongue returns to his mouth. I cry out and fall to the ground.

"Run!" Tank yells.

I scramble to my feet, despite my stinging leg, but the monster doesn't turn back like I expect. Instead it continues on to the Canine. I limp toward Tank and reach up my arm when I'm beneath him. He pulls me up as if I'm a bucket of water. The last thing I see is the monster tearing into the Canine while Junks snap and snort not far away in hopes of feasting upon a strewn bit of meat. The image is gruesome and stains my mind. It's not something I'll easily forget.

Tank sets me to the side and shoves the metal covering back over the manhole. "Why didn't you shoot that thing?"

It takes a second for my heart to start beating again. "Because I had to be sure the Canine wouldn't survive."

"Did you get cut?" Tank asks. He's looking down at my left leg.

"Not really. That monster whipped me with his tongue, like a frog." I examine the wound. There's a long red mark on my lower thigh that's barely open; a slow drop of blood runs down my leg. It doesn't look that bad but it sure stings.

"His tongue?" He shakes his head. "I've never seen anything like that. Does your leg hurt?"

"Not really. How much farther?"

He turns to his left. "A mile and a half, I think. We can take our time now that we aren't being tracked."

"Let's hurry. I want to get back to Max." I walk past him in the direction he was looking, trying to even my breathing. If I don't focus on Max then I'm afraid I might have a panic attack. I've never seen so much blood or heard those kind of bone-breaking sounds before. It was so brutal and vicious.

The sting in my leg spreads.

Tank catches up to me. We're still in some sort of business district, but the buildings here look newer and are well kept. I read their signs, forcing them to memory, every detail. Anything to replace what I just witnessed.

After a few minutes, Tank asks, "Are you okay?"

"I'm not used to seeing such brutality." I want to say more. That what I have witnessed the last several days has created a darkness inside me that's threatening to suffocate my heart. No wonder Primes choose not to feel.

Tank rounds a corner at a small diner. Only a man and woman sit inside, six booths apart. They don't look at us as we pass.

"This is a hard world to live in if you aren't used to it," Tank says.

Despite the late hour there are several people walking the streets, looking as if they don't know which way to go. Just wandering aimlessly, too afraid to go home to a place where no one feels emotions, where no one loves. Or maybe that's just how I see them.

"But is anyone really living?" I ask. "Life should be about making connections with others, learning to love them to the point where you would sacrifice your own desires for even a moment to make that person happy."

He doesn't say anything, only continues on, pulling further away from me. I limp to catch up to him. My left leg is on fire and becoming useless. I rub my palm against it, willing it to get better.

"No one thinks like you," Tank finally says. He's staring straight ahead, appearing to be deep in thought.

"That could be a good thing," I say. The strained sound of my voice smothers my attempt at humor.

Tank turns around. "Why are you limping? Is it the cut?"

I rub at my leg again, but even as I do so, the invisible flames spread to my other side. "Something's wrong. My leg's burning and it's getting difficult to walk."

Tanks drops to his knees and examines the wound. I don't look with him. His concerned expression is enough for me to know that there's something seriously wrong.

"You've been poisoned."

"Do we have anything for it?"

He shakes his head. "I don't know what 'it' is. The creature was nothing I've ever seen before." He straightens. "We better hurry and get you to your father. He's probably the only one who can help you now. Think you can run?"

"I'll try."

"This way. We're almost there." He darts into a nearby alley-way, away from prying eyes, and jogs fast.

I sort of keep up by doing a weird skipping motion, but then something happens. The burning sensation changes to an all-out inferno on the bottom half of my body, and I cry out. Tank turns back while I collapse to the ground, unable to take the pain any longer, and shove the back of my hand into my mouth to keep from screaming.

"Hold on, Sage," he says and scoops me up into his arms.

He runs fast, turning corners and jumping over fences. I try to pay attention to where he's going but the searing heat has moved to my abdomen. I scream and bite into the flesh on my arm. My eyes squeeze tight.

When I manage to open them, Tank is tapping his finger into a specific pattern upon the circular image of Eden's tree that's etched into the side of a three-story metal building. A moment later a door appears when a section of the building sinks backwards.

Tank steps across the threshold just as I stifle another scream. The burning sensation reaches my arms, rendering them as use-less as my legs, not because they've gone limp but because every muscle is flexed tight, only adding to my misery. Tank is running up a staircase past several voices that are calling out to him.

When the pain reaches my chest, I can no longer hold in my terror. Never have I felt such pain! "Help me! Please! Tank!"

My screams come one on top of the other until I can barely catch my breath. Tank hurries into a room and shouts, but I can't hear him. Holding me with one arm, he uses his other to swipe books, papers, and a lamp off a desk and sets me on its top. My legs are extended, feet and toes curled tight, but my arms are twisted unnaturally to my chest, cramped muscles deciding their position.

My lungs still burn but the fire reaches my vocal cords, shutting off any sounds I was making. All I can do now is gasp for air. I thrash my head back and forth. A few people I don't recognize look me over. Tank disappears through a door, leaving me alone with strangers.

"Don't go!" I say, but it's only my mind calling out to him. Meaningless, desperate thoughts in a world that seems to have none, unless they involve self-preservation.

Hot tears add to my burning pain. I blink through them, staring at the empty doorway and sucking in quick short breaths.

The two men in the room are talking about my leg.

"Never seen a wound like this."

"It's clearly poison."

"There's no way we have an antidote for something like this. It's a shame we have to lose an Original this way."

"Hush, you two," a woman with short blond hair says. "The girl can hear you."

The room goes quiet. I wish they were still talking. Their voices, no matter what they were saying, was a slight distraction from the inferno tearing through my body like a fire across a dry forest. I think of my brother and father. Are they here? This has got to be the location for HOPE that Tank was talking about. Then where are they? Maybe something happened to Colt and the others. Maybe the Institute found Max.

These thoughts on top of my pain are more than I can bear. I'm about to close my eyes when I catch movement in the doorway. It's Colt, but it's not how I expect to see him. He's coming in on an electrically assisted chair. His black hair is disheveled and one of his eyes is dark purple and swollen. How did that happen? And why isn't he walking?

Our eyes meet.

"Slow your breathing," the woman says to me. "Deep breaths."

I don't know what Colt sees in my eyes, but despite being in obvious pain, he struggles to get out of the chair. He almost falls but catches himself on the arm of the chair. He forces a smile and limps to my side.

"You look worse than I do," he says and smiles.

I'm hurting too bad to smile back. Tears run down the sides of my face as I fight for every breath.

"Sage!" a familiar voice calls from beyond the doorway. A second later my father, who I haven't seen in over a month, appears at my side. He looks me up and down and then smooths my hair. "Hold on, Sage."

I have mixed feelings about seeing him. Part of me is angry that he lied to me about so many things, like what he was doing all those times he disappeared. The other half of me wants to bury myself in his arms. I can let go now. He's here and will take care of everything.

My father addresses the others. "What do we have, Dex?"

Dex, a man whose head is mostly shaved except for a long ponytail that's both black and blue, says, "A laceration on her thigh. Whatever cut her was laced with poison and it's spreading fast. I'm not sure we can stop it without knowing what it was that poisoned her."

"I know what it was," my father says. "Get me the vial labeled EN437 from the back of the freezer. Heat it to room temperature and bring me the biggest needle you've got."

He stares down at me. His face looks the same as when I last saw him, but there's something different. I wish I could figure out what, but the pain radiating across my body keeps me from thinking beyond the surface. He speaks fast, more to the others than me, something about keeping my circulation going.

I don't hear all of it because Colt is speaking in my ear.

"I'm so sorry I left you. Maybe this wouldn't have happened

if," he pauses. His face is pale and sweat dots his forehead. "I went with you instead of Tank. Max would've been fine with him. I don't know what I was thinking."

I wish I could ease his mind instead of making these silly, quick breathing sounds. I attempt to give him a reassuring look, but I don't think my face muscles are working anymore so I'm probably staring at him like a frozen corpse. Not reassuring.

My father's still talking while poking me along my arms as if checking for a good vein.

"Your dad's not so bad," Colt says again in my ear. "He's kind to me when he shouldn't be. I told him about what I did. I expected him to throw me out, but he didn't. I don't understand you Originals. You've got me thinking all kinds of crazy thoughts."

Dex appears near my father holding a vial and a syringe. "It's ready."

My father takes the syringe and fills it with purplish liquid from the vial.

Colt whispers, "Max did really well. He went undetected the whole way here thanks to you. The only problem was Jenna talking too much like usual. Even Anthony was ready to boot her, especially when she made us stop so she could buy a pair of shoes." In his highest voice possible, he says in a mock-Jenna voice, "We're in New York City! I can't come here without buying shoes!"

"That's not how I sound!" a high voice from the doorway says.

I can't move my head anymore, but my eyes look upward. I can just barely see the top of Jenna's head.

My father places his hand onto my shoulder and presses the needle to my arm. "This might hurt, but something tells me you won't mind."

Before he can inject me, my body spasms suddenly and my eyes roll to the back of my head, taking the light with them.

"She's seizing! Hold her still!" my father shouts. Hands press down all over my body. "Get that arm! Steady. Good. It's in."

I never even felt the sting of the needle.

"Now what?" Jenna's voice asks.

My body stops shaking, but my eyes remain firmly embedded into the back of my head where the pain doesn't seem as bad.

"We wait," my father says.

"Do you think she's still in pain?" It's Colt.

They must think I'm unconscious. What I wouldn't give to be unconscious right now!

"I don't know."

"How did you know what to give her?" Jenna asks.

The room is silent for what feels like a very long time, especially to someone like me. Pain is never patient.

"I've been through those tunnels more times than I'd like to admit. One time when Benton, my old lab partner, and I were going through them, the same creature that attacked Sage tonight attacked us. I barely got away but only because Benton sacrificed himself." His voice is pained, a sound I've only heard when he would speak about my mother. "I saw how the thing killed him and knew it was through poison. Several hours later I returned to the spot and managed to get a tissue sample on what was left of Benton's body. Through it, I was able to isolate the toxin and come up with an antidote."

"But what was it?" Jenna asks. "And are there a lot of them?"

"Three at least that I've seen. As far as I can tell they are genetically mutated Junks, which doesn't make sense because where would Junks get new pDNA injections?"

"Someone's doing it to them," Colt says and the room goes quiet. "Probably the Institute."

Footsteps come into the room. "How is she?" Tank's voice.

"I think she'll make it. How's Max?"

"He's staring at a clock on the wall," Anthony's voice says. "I tried getting him to do something else, but he won't budge."

Max. My heart aches to see him. I need this poison out of me so I can go to him. He's probably so nervous by everything that's happened that he's retreated into his mind, to a place that's far better than this world. Sometimes I wish he could take me there too.

"Why are you looking at me like that?" Tank asks.

"She could've died out there," Colt says. "Why would you ever concoct a plan that put her in such danger?"

"It was Sage's plan, not mine. I tried to talk her out of it, but she was determined to get the Canine off her back. She was afraid he would track her here and she was probably right."

"None of that matters now," Anthony says. "Let Sage rest. She's going to wake soon and then we're going to have to leave this place. Just because the Canine isn't tracking her anymore doesn't mean the Institute has given up. Let's go. We have a lot to plan."

"I'll stay with her," Colt says.

"No. I'll stay with her." My father's voice is firm.

"Right. Okay." Colt stands. I can tell by the sound of his movements that it takes him great effort. He must've had another seizure. After a few seconds, the whirling sound of his chair leaves the room.

My father doesn't say anything, but his hand presses against mine. After several minutes of silence I fall asleep.

I dream of monsters. Deformed, hairless, with teeth the size of railroad spikes. They are tearing through the flesh and bones of a body, the first of many. A long line of humans, standing erect, each waits their turn to be feasted upon. Their eyes are open, yet they don't run.

After each ravaged body, the monsters glance back at me as if to make sure I'm watching. No matter how hard I try, I can't look away. The blood of their victims runs together and pools at my feet, rising higher and higher until I'm almost drowning. When the copper-smelling blood reaches my lips, pours into my mouth, my eyelids snap open and I sit up screaming.

"Whoa! Calm down. You're safe."

The room is dark and warm. I don't think it's the same room Tank brought me into earlier. I'm lying on a hard cot pressed against a wall. A lamp is in the corner of the room, turned on a dim setting. There's a table ... my eyes narrow. Maybe this is the same room I was in. The table is the same length as me, but there are books and papers back on its top. There's no window, which bothers me. I really want to see the moonlight. I want to know there's light out there away from the dark images carved into my mind like a branding.

"Lay back," my father says. He helps lower me onto a pillow. "How are you feeling?"

I turn my head and stare at him, at the scruff on his face, at the deep lines etched into the corners of his eyes, at the way he is looking at me in the same way he looked at my mother. I throw my arms around his neck.

He squeezes me back. "I've been so worried about you. I just kept praying that you'd remember your training."

My body tenses, and all the nostalgia I was just experiencing turns rotten at the mention of what the last several years of my life have been like. I let him go and drop back to the pillow. I can't hide the bitterness in my next words. "You taught me well."

He raises his hands like he's preparing to stop an attack. "I know I was hard on you, but it was for your own good. I couldn't take care of you forever."

"You left us," I say.

He drops his hands and sighs deeply. "I didn't want to, but there were too many of them. If I tried to fight back then we all would've been captured."

His explanation leaves a bad taste in my mouth even though his answer is logical. Maybe that's the problem. "Why didn't you try to find us?"

"I knew you were at the Institute, but I had no way to get you out. I had to trust that you'd remember your training."

"You could've tried."

He shakes his head. "I couldn't risk it. I'm the only scientist left in the HOPE movement who has any chance of finding a cure to the Kiss or at least a way to prolong the lives of Primes without using oDNA. We must fix the human race. This is the priority."

"There's a lot more wrong with humans than their DNA. All people care about anymore is surviving, and you fixing their DNA isn't going to change that." My chest begins to ache right where my heart is. "You've become like them, Dad. You knew the layout of the Institute just as well as I did. You could've saved us, but instead you cared more about your self-preservation."

"That's not fair," he says, but that's all he says.

Across the room, I spot my backpack. I take a moment to stand. The pain in my leg is gone, but I'm shaky and weak.

"Nothing is fair in this world," I say and walk to the bag. I fish through it until I find the vials I'd taken from the Institute's lab. With two hands, I remove all eight of them, careful not to drop them. "I took these. Maybe they can help with whatever it is you do."

He stands and flips on the overhead lights. I flinch and lower my eyes. The bright lights make my head pound to an unpleasant beat.

"Where did you get these?" he asks as he takes them from me.

"Some lab in the basement of the Oscar Johnson Pavilion."

He holds them up to the light, wonder turning to excitement. "I can't believe it! Do you know what these are?"

"I think it's the latest and greatest oDNA serum the Institute has been advertising."

My father's smiling big, turning them over in his hand. "I've been trying to get my hands on these for months! I snuck into their lab from the tunnels a couple of times to find them, but they were never there. They've got something in here that's helping humans live longer than ever before. At first I thought it was extra phosphate causing the mutation, but that proved inaccurate." He chuckles to himself, an inside joke I will never know.

I glance toward the doorway, wondering about Max. My father keeps talking about possible mutations, gene therapies, until I tune him out altogether. I don't remember his obsession being this bad. Before, when he was with us, he was *with* us, but he's barely noticed I'm back.

"Maybe it has something to do with the MT-TL1 gene," he says and finally looks up at me. His eyes blink twice. He sees me. "This is going to help so many people. I must get working on it right away. Do you understand?"

Save the world or comfort your recently discovered daughter? "Of course. Do what you've got to do."

He hugs me briefly. "I really am glad you found your way back to me. I never doubted."

246

He turns and disappears, leaving me alone in the room. A room that is suddenly very small. The walls squeeze toward me, and I suck in air at the suddenness of the movement. I force myself to move before I start to hyperventilate and go out the same doorway my father just exited, taking my backpack with me. There's a long hallway with a few doors on each side. I walk to the first one but find that it's locked. The next one, however, opens. Inside are a bunch of boxes, cabinets—not what I'm looking for.

The next few doors have a thin window at their tops, allowing me to peer inside. Jenna is in one of them. She is sitting on a bed, staring down at something in her hands while bobbing her head in time to music that plays low. Anthony is in another room, but he's fast asleep. I'm getting close.

After two more rooms, I find what I need. Max. He's lying in bed with the lights turned low, but he's not alone. Colt is asleep on a chair shoved into the corner. His legs stretch long, and he's so far slumped into the chair that I'm afraid he'll fall to the floor.

I quietly slip in and close the door. No one stirs. After placing the backpack next to the wall, I pick up a small blanket at the foot of Max's bed and drape it carefully over Colt. He inhales deeply, and I think he's going to wake, but his head flops to the other side, eyes still closed. Something bad must've happened to him. I clench my jaw. He's sacrificed so much for us. They all have.

The sooner we get to Eden the better.

I slowly climb behind Max on the bed and rest my hand on his arm, which seems bigger somehow. I try not to think about what he might've gone through, but these thoughts are forceful and invade my sleep only moments later.

Max is being hunted by the creature in the tunnel. He's running fast, alone and scared in a never-ending maze. I'm a witness to his terror, a useless ghost unable to offer even a word of encouragement. I think all is lost when a tall figure of a man appears at the end of the tunnel; light from behind silhouettes his muscular frame. Slowly and deliberately, pointed wings unfold from behind his back. The relief I feel is instant. Max is no longer alone.

My eyes open. Gray light squeezes through a dirt-stained window. It's morning, probably only six o'clock. Max is tucked safely in my arms. His breathing is slow and steady. I lift the edge of the blanket and tuck it around his arms, leaving mine exposed. The hairs on my arm rise, and I look up.

Colt is sitting up in the chair, watching me. Our eyes meet, but we don't speak. Eventually I fall back asleep.

When I wake again, it's because Max is shaking my arm. I throw my arms around him, and he does the same to me.

"You do that so easily," Colt says.

"It's what you do when you love and care for someone." I keep hugging Max, but loosen my grip. Max curls into me like a cat in front of a fireplace. When I glance at Colt, he averts his gaze and stares into a shaft of sunlight, illuminating a sea of dust fairies spinning and twirling through the air. He looks deathly pale.

"What happened to you out there?" I ask. He doesn't seem to have heard me. I give him a moment longer to answer, but when he doesn't, I add, "Thank you for keeping Max safe. It's what I wanted."

Colt's chest rises and falls as he takes one giant breath. He slides to the edge of the chair and pushes himself upright. It takes him longer than it should. "You two need to eat. We'll be leaving soon."

This surprises me, and I swing my legs to the side of the bed, taking Max with me. "Why the rush? The Canine is dead. We should be safe for a while."

"We can't be sure of that. It's better to get you two out of here as soon as possible." He turns and leaves the room.

"Wait!" I go after him, but his strides are so much longer than mine that he's at the end of the hallway and around the corner before I have a chance at stopping him.

A door opens suddenly, and I jump, nearly dropping Max.

"Just because you were raised in a forest where you didn't have to worry about your loud mouth, doesn't mean you can shout here." Jenna is standing in the doorway, rubbing her matted hair. "People are trying to sleep."

Another door opens on the other side.

"Sure you were," Anthony says. His hair is wet like he just showered. "How are you feeling, Sage?"

"Much better, thank you."

"And how about you, Max? I bet you were glad to see your sister." He goes to rub Max's head but stops himself. "Is Colt already up?"

I nod. "He's eating."

"Good. He needs it." Anthony walks away. "See you guys at breakfast."

"I swear that's all they think about," Jenna mumbles and turns back into her room. She drops onto a mess of covers crumpled on her bed.

I follow her in and close the door. Max clings tightly to me. "So, um, can you tell me what happened? Why is Colt so messed up?"

"Because you've messed him up."

"What do you mean?"

Jenna moans and turns over, kicking at the mound of blankets until they are on the floor. She tucks her hands behind her head and looks at me. "We ran into some trouble. A lot of it actually. Some Rhine spotted Max and was yelling in the streets until a whole pack of Primes, and not the good kind either, were hunting us like turkeys on Thanksgiving Day. Colt didn't want them discovering this place so he took them on while the rest of us escaped."

"How did he get away?"

"He didn't. When he didn't show up after about an hour, Anthony went looking for him. He found him in an alley in the middle of a massive seizure, probably brought on by having the crap kicked out of him."

My legs weaken, and I drop to the foot of her bed. My arms go limp too, but Max doesn't fall. His arms are firmly entwined behind my neck.

"Anthony brought him to your father, who was able to bring him out of it, but just barely." Jenna sits up. "I know how you feel about Colt, but it's better if you face reality now before it explodes in your face. Colt is dying, Sage. One more of those and he's worm food." She rolls back over. "Now get out of my room. I want to sleep more."

I don't feel myself moving as I stand and leave the room, even Max feels weightless. Maybe that's how people in this world survive, by feeling numb. I don't want to get like that. Stop all emotions just so I can survive.

I think of what Colt must have endured just to protect Max and the others. I let myself feel emotions of all kinds. Anger toward the men who hurt him, fear for his life, frustration that I couldn't be there to help. Tears burn my eyes.

It hurts a dark and ugly pain when I think of his suffering, but then I feel something unexpected. A beautiful comfort that I have someone in my life that would sacrifice so much for others.

I follow the sound of voices until I reach the kitchen. It's bigger than I expect. Three long tables divide the room evenly. On the back wall are a short counter, sink, and refrigerator. Colt is sitting next to Anthony at one of the tables. A few others who had helped me the night before are engrossed in a conversation at another table.

I set down Max and say, "One second."

Colt turns toward me and stands when he sees me coming toward him. I don't stop moving until I throw my arms around him. "Thank you."

His arms stay limp at his side, but after a few seconds they slowly come around me. "You're welcome."

The room has gone quiet, but I don't care. The warmth of Colt's body, his scent of autumn leaves and apples, and the way his fingers are gently going through the back of my hair soothes the ache in my heart.

"What's this?" a familiar voice asks.

Colt's arms drop, and I step away. My father's standing in the doorway, dark circles under his eyes. My guess is he didn't sleep at all last night.

"I was just telling Colt thank you for taking care of Max," I say.

My father scoops up Max. "Yes. We are forever in your debt, Colt. Whatever you need, just say it and I will try and make it happen."

Colt clears his throat. "I'd like to get Sage and Max to Eden as quickly as possible."

I close my eyes briefly, unable to ignore the sting of his words. Maybe he doesn't feel the same way as I do.

My father looks from Colt to me. "I think that would be wise as well. They can leave as soon as the group is ready to go."

I flinch. "They? Aren't you coming with us?"

He walks over to me. "I want to, really I do, but I need to be here. There are a lot of people relying on me."

I'm stunned and not even sure what to say. Eventually the words leave my mind and out my mouth. "And what about your own children who you haven't seen forever, who have been locked up for weeks, who have come close to dying multiple times?"

He takes me by the arms. "I raised you with all the knowledge I have of this world. I trained you, sometimes hard I admit, but it was all for this day when you would have to go it alone. You don't need me anymore nor does Max. I love you both, more than you could possibly know, but there's a whole world that needs my help. Do you understand?"

"I get that you are important, and that you want to help everyone, but why does it feel like this decision is super easy for you?"

This makes him pause. He exhales and lowers his arms. "It's not easy, but I guess I just don't let myself think about it or it will hurt too much."

Over his shoulder I see Colt. His eyes are on the floor, and his jaw muscle is flexed. "You've become like them, Dad. Mom would be so disappointed."

This makes him bristle. "You're probably right, but she never had to do the things I've done."

"Regardless, it's a choice you make. To shut yourself off from feeling."

"You sound like your mother." He chuckles quietly as if thinking back to another time. "Look, I'll make you a promise. You go to Eden now with your brother, and I promise to come as soon as my work is done. Besides, you'll like Eden. There are so many others like you that you won't even miss me or anyone else here. Life will go on, Sage."

And there you have it. He has no intention of following us. *Life will go on.* For everyone. And I'm expected to just forget what I feel, as if my feelings never mattered at all.

"I'll be ready shortly." I pick up Max and leave before anyone can stop me. Tears sting the back of my eyes, but I won't let anyone see. I walk quickly down the empty hallway back to Max's room.

There will be people like me at Eden.

Original humans.

Complete strangers.

Tears run into the back of my throat. I thought things would be different when I found my father, but I was wrong. He is part of this world now.

I slip inside Max's bedroom and close the door. My back presses against it, and with Max I slide slowly to the floor. Maybe I'm being naïve, and it really is better that I go to Eden sooner than later. Had I been in this world as long as my father, maybe I'd have stopped caring too.

Max drops his head to my shoulder. He is all that matters now. I have to protect him and the only way to do that is get him to Eden.

I give him a gentle squeeze. "You ready to go on another trip? I think you'll like it. There are people like us, but more importantly we'll be safe."

I hold him for several more minutes before I set him on the bed so I can change into a pile of girl clothes someone has left near the door. Probably my father by how perfectly they fit. And the color of my shirt, a dark turquoise, is my favorite color. Max is already dressed in fresh clothes most likely given to him last night.

All that's left to do is check our pack. I set it on the bed and rummage through its large pockets. It could use more food. And, if possible, a new outfit for each of us. The ones in it are dirty and in desperate need of a wash.

My door opens and Jenna appears. "So I hear you're leaving soon."

I unfold a shirt from the pack and shake it hard. "Looks that way." Dirt billows into the air.

I expect Jenna to say something sarcastic, but instead she says, "You're better off at Eden, you know that right?"

I don't answer because I don't know what's better for me anymore. I straighten and grab Max's hand. "We're ready."

"Before we go, your father wants to meet with us."

"I thought he was busy with his experiments."

"He's going to tell us where Eden is, and I don't know about you, but I'm dying to know. I bet it's underground somewhere."

I kneel down and speak to Max. "Wait here. I'll be right back." I kiss him on the forehead and follow after Jenna.

She guides me to a part of the building I haven't been to yet. Only a few lights are on in the narrow hallway. Parts of the plastered walls are broken and crumbled, exposing rotted wood. There's a moldy smell that makes me hold my breath, but Jenna doesn't seem to notice it. She's humming softly.

"It's up here," she says.

The room we go into isn't much better than the hallway, but at least there are more lights. Around a metal table sits my father, Colt, Tank, and Anthony. They are speaking quietly until they see me.

"So where are Max and I being shipped off to?" I ask.

Tank whistles. "Those Original boys don't stand a chance."

Colt shakes his head. "Shut up, Tank."

Jenna snickers and sits down next to Anthony, who seems especially quiet. He's the only one who hasn't looked at me yet.

"Have a seat, Sage," my father says before Tank and Colt can get into a further argument.

"I'll stand."

He tightens his lips, but continues. "What I'm about to tell you must stay confidential. Not many Primes know the location of Eden and it has to stay this way. I can't stress the importance of this."

"We get it," Colt says. There is color back in his face, which makes me feel a little better.

My father looks at him sharply. "No, you don't. I'd rather not tell you this secret, especially knowing your past, but you saved my children."

"So where is this place?" Jenna asks. "It's underground, right? Some hidden bunker or maybe a giant cave in a mountain."

Anthony's head rises. "Too obvious. The Institute's already scoured every mountain and used thermal imaging to look underground. It's got to be in a place that the Institute would never go to. A place where even if they did look and saw people, they *still* wouldn't go there. "

Jenna frowns and taps the top of the table with her fingernails. "Where's that?"

"There's only one place the Institute avoids, and you can't be thinking of sending her and Max there," Colt says. "There's no way." His face is pale, and I think he might throw up.

"What? Where?" I ask.

Jenna slaps the table. "Clueless here! Fill us in already."

"Purgatory Island," my father says. There are more lines on his face than normal. Creases of worry and concern etched deep into his skin. I want to focus on those lines, to pretend I hadn't heard those two words, but they're like flies in summer and refuse to be ignored.

"So you're sending me to hell?" I ask, but Jenna's voice comes at the same time and is much louder.

"What brainless idiot would put a bunch of Originals on the most dangerous place on earth?"

"I would," my father says. "Yes, it's dangerous, but once they reach the compound they are completely safe."

I rub the back of my neck, where the muscles still ache from my earlier seizure. "Compound? You mean the prison? The one that has been overrun with mutated Primes?"

Colt stands suddenly, knocking his chair backwards. "This is insane. I can't even believe we are discussing this. Anthony?"

Anthony is staring down at the table.

"You knew, didn't you?" Colt asks.

"I found out last night."

Colt turns away and walks to the other side of the room.

Tank leans forward, his fists tightened. "Why can't Sage hide out with Max in the forest? She did just fine for years and the Institute never found her."

"But they did eventually," my father answers.

Colt whirls around. "Because you led a Canine right to them!"

This time my father stands. "Actually, I believe that was your fault, Colt."

"How long has Eden been there?" I ask before the tension in the room explodes into something physical.

"A little over forty years."

"Forty years?" I ask. "How is that possible? You're fifty-years old!"

"Forty-seven," he corrects with a frown. "And it was my father who started the project with a few others. Eden is safe, I assure you."

"But getting there isn't," Tank says.

Jenna leans back into her seat. "Well, I'm not going."

"You don't have to," my father says. "In fact, none of you are going, not the whole way at least. There will be a few Originals waiting as soon as you get them to the bay. They know the island better than anyone."

Colt places his hands on the table. "I'm not leaving them alone until they get inside this supposed safe compound."

"You're not in any condition to be doing anything," my father says. "Now sit down."

"I'm just fine."

"Not for long," Jenna mumbles and the room grows quiet.

Colt looks around the room at each of us. I'm the only one who will meet his gaze. His normally bright blue eyes appear dull and lifeless.

"I'll be in my room," he says. "Come get me when it's time to go."

As soon as he's gone, I turn to my father. "The serum I stole from the Institute. What does it do exactly?"

He seems taken off guard by the question, but quickly recovers. "It temporarily masks the pDNA, tricking the body into thinking it's repaired, but eventually it wears off and cells begin to die again. The whole process can take several years."

"And what are you trying to do with it?"

"In a nutshell? Take out the toxic pDNA altogether so humans can live as long as they did before."

"Hello varicose veins and arthritis," Jenna says and lowers her head to the table like she's bored.

"If you think it's possible," I say, "why hasn't the Institute done it yet? Surely their big brains are more than capable."

"They *can* do it," Anthony says before my father can answer. "But they won't. They found that by reverting the DNA back to what it was, Primes slowly lose their special abilities, making them like Originals, or really just normal humans. I think the thought of that disgusts Techheads."

"But it's not just that," my father adds. "The Institute holds all the power. They are controlling people with promises of new DNA or threats of withholding their technological advances."

"We are at their mercy," I say, finally understanding the Institute's motives. As long as they are the ones developing the drugs, we will always need them.

"How long until you develop a cure from the oDNA Sage gave you?" Tank asks. He props his legs up on the table. He is the only one who doesn't seem affected by this news.

"It will take time, possibly years."

"I don't care about that right now," I say, warranting the confused looks of everyone in the room. Even Jenna lifts her head. "Colt has the Kiss. I want you to give one of the oDNA serums to him. This will temporarily save him, right?"

"I have so few—" my father begins but I interrupt him.

"Do this one thing for me. *Please.* I'm about to walk out of your life, and you may never see me again. Grant me this one wish."

His gaze lowers to the table, and he shakes his head. "We have to think about what's best for the future. I need every vial you gave me for the experiments."

Anger wells inside me, a burning inferno I fear might explode from my head. There may be logic in his words, but I'm too mad to care.

"Hell balls, William!" Jenna says, surprising everyone. "Give your daughter this one thing. It's not like she hasn't earned it."

"I agree," Anthony adds. "Both she and Colt have sacrificed so much to get you those vials. It's the least you can do."

Although bringing the vials to my father was an afterthought, I'm glad Anthony made it seem like the oDNA was our first priority. This type of logic resonates with my father. I glance at Anthony appreciatively.

My father's shoulders sag as does his countenance. "You don't understand. If the trials fail then I'll have no backup serum, and, as you already know, it's very difficult to come by."

"I'll get you more," Tank offers. "Save bat boy."

"Look at me, Dad," I say. His gaze rises to mine. I'm so full of desperation that I pray he can see it bleeding from every pore. I need Colt to be okay. I can't go to Eden knowing otherwise.

My father closes his eyes. "Fine, but if I do this, he's going to have to stay under my supervision for at least forty-eight hours. Those injections make a person severely ill before they get better."

Tank lets out a low whistle. "There's no way you're going to get Colt to stay here while you and Max leave, Sage. You know this."

"But if he doesn't stay, he'll die," Anthony says. "One more seizure will kill him."

I stand, feeling stronger than I have in a long time. "Leave it to me. I'll get him to stay one way or another."

CHAPTER 30

I'm in my father's lab, a room I've never been in before. It's in the basement of the old, rundown building, yet is the brightest, cleanest room I've seen. It has been strategically designed with all the modern conveniences. By my father, I have no doubts. It's a much larger version of the lab he had in our home, right down to the lab rats in glass cages in the corner of the room.

"What are we doing in here?" Colt asks.

I turn around. His face has some color to it. Not because he's feeling better, but because it took great effort for him to take the stairs getting here, though he'd never admit it. He casually wipes sweat from his brow like he gets it all the time.

"I wanted to show you my father's lab," I say. "He's close to finding a cure for the Kiss."

Colt picks up a nearby beaker and stares at the crimson fluid inside. "That's what people have been saying for decades."

I stare at the red liquid too as Colt swishes it around inside the glass. It's probably blood, but I don't want to think about it. I'm here for one purpose. I shake my head and say, "It's for real this time. That serum I stole from the Institute has the ability to prolong a man's life for at least another five years. My father believes he can use it to get rid of the pDNA, which will make man's DNA become pure again."

"Why are you telling me all this?" His eyes narrow. "Don't think for a second I'm going to take an oDNA injection, especially not right now."

His posture has become rigid. I'm going to have to proceed slowly so he doesn't suspect.

"Of course not." I walk to a nearby cot and sit down. "Will you sit with me?"

He remains still. "There isn't time for this. We need to get you and Max out of here."

"But there is time. Please. Just for a minute." I pat the nylon material next to me. When he still looks conflicted, I add, "I need to tell you something important before we leave."

This time he comes. He sits next to me, our legs brushing, igniting a warm chill across my skin. I close my eyes briefly and then open them. I don't want to do this, but I can't think of any other way.

Very slowly, I slide my hand over his. Air escapes between his lips as if I'm causing him pain.

"This world," I say, "is all about illusions. Your cities are shiny and new, the people are beautiful, smart, strong, exceptional. It all seems so perfect. But who decided that this was perfection? There is nothing beautiful about perfection. It's the flaws that give character, that give true beauty."

I tighten my grip on his hand. "Have you heard of the Mona Lisa?"

"That was a painting the Institute destroyed decades ago, right?"

I think back to the replica that had hung in my room for as long as I could remember. "It was flawed, they said. In their eyes the woman wasn't beautiful. They thought she represented everything wrong with Original humans. They had spewed this rhetoric for so long that no one cared when they finally destroyed Leonardo da Vinci's greatest work. That's what 'perfection' has brought this world. Apathy."

I slide off the cot and move to kneel in front of him. A shiver passes over him, and at the same time I quiver, but I ignore the feeling. I have to. For in this moment, I can't let myself feel. To save his life.

I continue, "People don't want to see past the illusion, because once they do they will realize how rotten their world is. They will see the decay and death beneath their perfect cities; they will see how they are still imperfect despite their perfect appearance. And this awareness will make them start to care again. Care to make things right." I let go of his hand and raise my hand to his cheek. Very slowly, I brush my fingertips over the skin on his jawbone.

"I have seen past your illusion," I say. "You are kind and gentle, loyal and brave. But you're also stubborn, reckless, and temperamental."

"I'm not—"

My thumb brushes over his full lips, silencing his protests. "All of this is perfection to me."

I don't mean to pause, but I can't help it. I never realized how deep my feelings went for him until this moment. My hand lowers to his chest, where it rests just above his rapidly beating heart.

I finally look up at him. "You're dying, Colt."

I expect some kind of emotion on his face, but there is nothing.

"We all die," he says, but when I open my mouth to speak, he adds, "but not all of us die at peace."

It's his turn to take my hands. There is no hesitation in his action.

"You speak of beauty," he says, his eyes burning blue, "as if it actually exists in this world. I didn't believe that until I met you." He takes a breath. "You've made me feel things I never thought possible. It's like my heart is beating for the first time, and even though I know my life is about to expire, I can say what most others cannot—that I will die happy."

Warmness spreads through me, turns hot when his fingers caress the underside of my wrists.

"You don't have to die," I say.

"I'm not going to do anything until I know you and Max are on that island safely. Nothing else matters."

The look in his eyes is firm. He will never stay. He would rather die. All for me.

I hate what I'm about to do, but I see no other way. Moving slowly, I let go of him and slide my right hand behind his neck to pull him toward me. Our foreheads touch first, and I pause. Colt nuzzles his head against mine. His mouth parts just barely, but enough that the breath escaping from his lungs warms my neck.

Don't feel don't feel don't feel.

He turns his head a fraction of an inch, and I turn mine. His lips graze my jawbone, slide softly to my chin. His hands trail up my bare arms, every fingertip igniting a fire beneath his touch. The burn goes bone deep, searing doubt and fear from my heart and mind, and I know I will never be the same. Especially when his lips meet mine.

His mouth moves slowly, carefully, as if he might shatter me, but when my lips part and I press hard to him, his kiss turns deep and desperate. The suddenness of it brings me back to reality. I have a job to do.

While we continue to kiss, I slip my left hand into my pocket and remove the syringe my father gave me. In one swift motion, I jab it into his neck and inject the medicine that will make him fall asleep within seconds. He jerks back, his eyes wide.

"I'm so sorry," I say, "but I can't have you die. It would kill me."

He mumbles some sort of protest before his eyes close, and his head falls back.

I carefully lower him onto the cot and lift his legs until they are lying with the rest of his body. He is safe now. My father will give him the Institute's serum, giving him at least another five years of life. It will be a life where he will most likely hate me, but I'm willing to take that risk. Besides, I may never see him again.

I lean over him and lightly kiss him on the forehead. "Goodbye," I say. It's the most painful word I've ever said.

CHAPTER 31

Upstairs Tank, Anthony, and Jenna are waiting for me, standing around a small table with papers scattered on its top. They stop talking and look at me expectantly.

"It's done," I say.

"Good," Tank says. He hands me two small daggers. "You might need these. Do you know how to use them?"

I nod and slide one into each of my boots. My father taught me how to fight with knives, but it has been awhile. Hopefully, I won't need them.

Jenna swings a backpack over her shoulder. "Maybe the new DNA serum will fix Colt's face."

"Not now, Jenna," Anthony says and walks away.

We follow after him, down the hall and back into the room I arrived in. We are greeted by two men and one woman, all dark skinned. The woman is just as tall and muscular as the men. From behind I probably couldn't tell them apart, but her feminine features, high cheekbones and pouty lips, give her away. All three have black hair with a single blue stripe down the middle. They are Dresdens, incredibly strong and skilled in combat.

My father's there too, kneeling down and speaking to Max in a quiet voice. When he sees me, he straightens and comes over to me to give me a tight hug. He is cold and smells like chemicals.

"I'll take care of Colt," he says. "I promise." When he releases me, he motions to the newcomers. "Meet Tori, Summa, and Rowdy. They will guide you to the Originals who will take Max and Sage to Eden."

Anthony nods at them. They do the same back.

Tank slaps the nearest one on the back, Summa, I think, and says, "I didn't know we had Dresdens on our side. Spectacular!"

"Don't touch me again," Summa says. He speaks with a beautiful accent.

Tank smiles and raises his hand as if they put a gun on him.

"Great," Jenna says and crowds past me to exit the room. "More moody people. Bloody fantastic." Anthony and Tank follow after her along with the Dresdens.

It's only me, my father, and Max in the room now. I place my hand on Max's small shoulder.

My father looks down at us, his expression a mix of emotions I can't place. Is he worried about us? Is he anxious to get started on his work? I hate that I can't tell. "Take care of Max, Sage. And take care of yourself. I'll see you when I can."

I wait for some type of emotion to come, but it doesn't so I take Max's hand in mine and leave.

The Dresden Tori drives us to the edge of the city where the shiny metal ends and the wild country begins. Trees, tall and wide, stretch and twist toward the sky. Beneath the canopy of trees, an endless darkness stretches on. It's a darkness I'm familiar with.

Tori parks the vehicle. "We're here. Everybody out."

I do as she asks, taking Max with me. Before I have a chance to ask our location, the Dresdens disappear into the forest.

"They are the most boring Primes I've ever met," Jenna says, her voice low. "I almost fell asleep in the car. Or died. I would've been happy with either."

Tank rounds the backside of the vehicle. "I'll pay you twenty dollars if you can get one of them to smile."

"Deal." She slaps the top of the car and hurries after the Dresdens.

"Let me know if you need any help with Max," Tank says to me before he goes after her.

The path through the overgrown forest is well tread, sometimes dangerously so. Where it dips and turns, huge chunks of earth have slipped into steep ravines, and I have to inch carefully just to stay on the trail. It brings me some comfort to know that so many Originals made this journey before me.

Max is clinging to my chest, my arms wrapped around him tightly. He's been whimpering softly for the last ten minutes. It's not a sound I'm used to.

"What's wrong with him?" Anthony asks. He's walking just behind me.

"I'm not sure. He's upset about something." I whisper encouraging words to him and caress the back of his head while my other arm holds him up.

"Maybe he misses Colt," Anthony offers.

My chest tightens at his name, and I quickly push images of Colt to the fringes of my mind where painful memories wait to be forgotten. But I won't forget. I will return for him, to see again the contours of his face, the way his eyes look into mine as if he might slip into them forever, and feel the way my skin ignites beneath his touch.

"It's going to snow soon," I say. Clouds crowd the sky in grays and blacks. It's cold, but I'm much colder on the inside.

Up ahead, Jenna is trying to engage one of the male Dresdens in a conversation, but he's having none of it, which I can tell is really bothering her. She keeps trying different topics from celebrity gossip to politics. Tank is behind her muttering and swiping at branches as he passes.

Everyone seems on edge. Even I'm feeling apprehensive, but I don't know if it's because of Max's continuing whimpers or the fact that I'm moving to a new home with others like me, and I'm not sure if that's what I really want.

It's for Max, I remind myself and squeeze him tight.

As the day wears on, I begin to limp on my leg that was stung. There's not much pain, but I just can't get it to do what I want. It's like the monster's poison is still inside, threatening me even now.

Anthony offers to hold Max, but Max won't let him, so I alternate between carrying Max and making him walk. By late afternoon, his cat-like protests have grown louder.

"Can't you do something about that kid?" Tori calls. She's several yards in front of us, standing to the side of the trail. Her skin is stretched so tight over her high cheekbones that it looks like wax.

"Leave them alone," Tank says.

Her waxy face chunks into a scowl. "How are we supposed to go unnoticed with that wailing?"

"How am I going to keep from driving my fist into your face?" Jenna says. She takes an equally threatening stance, even though she's at least a foot smaller. Behind her, Tank chuckles.

Anthony pushes past me. "Enough. Max just needs a break. We'll spend the night here and push on in the morning." He unzips his backpack and begins to set up camp, giving them no time to argue.

"About time," Jenna says, dropping herself onto a nearby tree stump. "Hey, Patch, we can tent together. It will be like old times. Except don't ditch me this time. I like having you around."

I look up at her, surprised, as does Tank and Anthony.

"You're friends with an Original?" the Dresden man, Rowdy, asks. He moves closer to her. This is the first time I've heard him speak.

Jenna winks at Tank and me, then turns to Rowdy. "What? Me and Patch? We go way back. I've been protecting her, for like, forever."

Rowdy joins her on the stump. "That's really brave of you. Not many Primes would risk their lives like that. Personally I think we need to sacrifice all that we can to protect Originals."

"Me too," she says. "Hell, I'd cut off my own arm and feed it to her if she needed it."

Tanks curses under his breath and walks to the other side of camp where he unrolls his bedding. I just shake my head and take Max into the forest to gather firewood.

Nightfall comes quickly, a bluish gray that fades to black just before I have the fire started. The Dresdens sit close, both fascinated and mesmerized by the dancing flames.

"It's much better in real life, isn't it?" Tank asks them. His back is against a tree, his legs straight in front of him.

"It's beautiful," Rowdy says.

Jenna scoots closer to him. She looks small next to his tall and wide body. "Mind if I get a little closer? I'm cold."

Tank coughs or gags, and I stifle a laugh, but Max doesn't. He giggles softly into my chest. I'm not sure if it's about Jenna or something else, but either way I love it.

Max has been much calmer since we made camp, even wandered around a bit on his own. This helps me relax too, and I take some time thinking about Eden and what it will be like, if I will fit in.

"How's your leg?" Anthony says to me, his voice quiet among the others who are still talking about the fire.

I rub my palm against the wound. "It's better. I think I just needed to rest it."

He nods thoughtfully. "You made the right decision, you know. About Colt."

The bite of food in my mouth turns sour. "I just hope he can forgive me one day."

"He will. And I think a lot of people will do things they never thought possible, if you keep doing what you're good at."

"What's that supposed to mean?" I lean back against a tree. Keep doing what I'm good at? All I've been is a liability.

"There is strength in words," he says. "Primes aren't powerful because of their unique abilities. What makes them truly powerful, for good or for bad, is their ability to get others to not only believe in a certain ideal, but to sacrifice all that they have for it, even their very life."

Max takes hold of my hand as I say, "I don't understand."

Anthony turns his head and looks me directly in the eyes. "I would follow you to my death."

I'm so stunned that I don't know what to say. Follow me? A seventeen-year-old girl? But I'm nobody.

"Just be who you are, and people will follow," he says then turns his attention to the conversation around the fire. The others are talking about the Institute's latest drug and pondering the implications. I try to listen, but Anthony's words have created a storm of doubt and confusion in my mind.

It's not long after that I realize Max's breathing is slow and steady. I don't want to leave the warmth of the fire, but I know it's going to be a long day tomorrow, and I should probably get all the rest I can. I rise and carry Max to the tent.

"Have a good night, Patch," Jenna calls. "I'll be in soon!"

I freeze, unable to take her pretend affection any longer. Over my shoulder, I say, "Don't forget to take your medication, Jenna. You know how that rash can get out of control."

Tank laughs out loud while Rowdy says, "What rash?"

I duck inside the tent before I hear any more, but I'm smiling.

It takes a few minutes to bundle Max before I tuck him into bed. Darkness has brought a bitter cold that stings my fingertips. The others won't feel it, not like we do. At least where I'm going there will be others like me who feel the world as it really is.

I climb into my sleeping bag and lie down, but I cannot sleep. Colt's surprised and betrayed eyes will not let me.

CHAPTER 32

The sound of footsteps crunching against hard grass wakes me. Gray early light filters through the top of the tent where ice crystals sparkle on the mesh opening.

Jenna has her back to me, sleeping. Max is awake and staring up. I nuzzle my cold nose to his cheek.

"Good morning."

He turns his head and looks me directly in the eyes, something he doesn't do very often.

"What is it?"

He opens his mouth like he wants to say something, but that's impossible. I've never heard him say a word before.

I sit up, leaving the warmth of my bag. "Max?"

He draws his eyebrows together and strains hard, his mouth still open. A hoarse sound comes out, and his eyes widen. He seems as surprised as I am.

"Are you trying to talk?" I ask.

He tries again, but when nothing happens, he closes his mouth tight and looks up; the blank stare in his eyes has returned.

Did that really just happen?

"Max?"

He doesn't respond. The moment of clarity is gone.

I dress quickly in layers and then prepare Max for the cooler temperature. Outside the tent, Anthony has a fire burning bright. The Dresdens are awake and surrounding the flames as if they are cold, but they are only wearing black, long-sleeved shirts and pants. I don't see Tank.

I grab Max's hand and work our way between the Dresdens to

get closer to the heat. My leg is stiff, but it's not as weak as it was yesterday. Maybe it's getting better.

Anthony hands Max and me several wrapped food bars. "Eat up. We need to leave camp soon to make the drop-off point in time."

"Did you sleep well?" Rowdy asks me. His features are softer than the others'. Even his mouth is more pleasant with the corners turned up at the sides.

"Well enough. This weather makes it hard though."

He looks around as if noticing winter's touch for the first time. "I never thought about that. Does the cold affect all Originals?"

"Of course it does," Tori snaps. Summa, the third and taller of the three Dresdens has yet to speak since we entered the forest.

Rowdy seems unaffected by Tori's curtness and asks me, "Would you like to use my jacket? I won't be needing it."

I'm surprised by his thoughtfulness. "Thank you, but I'm fine. Max could use it though."

He shakes off his backpack to retrieve it.

"What's your story?" I ask.

"My story?" He hands the jacket to me.

"Where are you from?"

"New York City, but my story is the same as everyone else's."

"No, it's not," I say.

"Of course it is," Tori says. "Parents dead, working till we die, which will be within ten years, probably go childless."

Rowdy nods as if it's true.

"But no one has the same life," I say. "We all experience things differently. Just because your parents are dead"—I turn to Tori—"doesn't mean that Rowdy felt the same way as you did at their passing. Maybe he had a good relationship with them. Maybe he had a happy childhood where you didn't. Maybe his favorite ice cream flavor is chocolate where you love strawberry. Everyone has their own story, and it's important we know each others."

"Why?" Rowdy asks.

Anthony is smiling at me, but I glance away and say, "Because then you will see each other as individuals. And you can relate to them in ways other than sadness and death. And then, finally, humans can start caring again—for the actual soul of the man and not the shell."

No one says anything except for the fire, which spits and hisses. I look down, embarrassed. My foot twists into the hard ground, creating a wavy pattern into the dirt.

Sounds of footsteps come toward us, but no one moves. The steps are familiar.

"The path looks clear," Tank says when he emerges from the forest. "Let's get going."

Thirty minutes later we are well onto the worn path, parts of it wet and slippery. The sky is a mess of purples and grays, and a cold wind finds its way through my layers and to my skin. I'm holding Max so that helps a little, but holding him is also affecting my leg, which is stiff again.

The air smells both salty and fishy. We must be close to the ocean.

In front of me, Rowdy and Jenna walk side-by-side, talking about something I can't hear on account of the wind. Every once in awhile Jenna throws her head back and laughs. Tank is in front of the line, followed by Tori and Summa. For some reason Anthony is lagging behind. Every now and then I glance behind me to make sure he's still there.

Max is calmer today. I think I am too. I made a decision, and that choice has put me on a path I can't change. I can only go forward.

It's afternoon. My limp is more pronounced. There's still no pain, just tightness, like my muscle has died and rigor mortis has taken over. Others have asked if they can help me, but because Max has managed to walk most of the way, I haven't needed assistance.

I think Max recognizes that I'm struggling. He's not even walking by me right now. He's several feet ahead, his small body navigating the rough trail with ease. Something's different about him. Maybe he's—a shout behind me makes me jump, and I turn around.

Anthony comes running out of the forest. "Run!"

I don't stop to ask why. I scoop up Max and run hard, straight up a steep hill after the others. Anthony is behind me before I'm at the top.

"Hurry, Sage," he says, not even out of breath. "The Institute. I don't know how, but they've found us."

This makes me move faster.

At the top of the hill, Anthony calls to the others. "Run! We've been discovered!"

The Dresdens and Jenna take off, but Tank hangs back until I reach him.

"Give me Max," he says.

Before I have the chance to hand him over, Max swivels toward Tank and goes to him without protest. Tank sprints ahead, leaving Anthony and me.

"No matter what, Sage," Anthony says while we run hard, "you have to leave us behind. The drop-off point isn't much farther. We'll hold them off."

I'm not sure I can do that: leave them behind.

But I can't think about that right now.

Just go.

Not far away, the tree line ends sharply and opens into a grassy meadow. I slow up, not wanting to be exposed, but Anthony pushes me forward.

"We don't have a choice." This time he sounds out of breath, but I don't think it's because he's fatigued. He's scared.

Out in the clearing, the Dresdens are waiting. As soon as I pass them, they start running behind me. Tank and Jenna are almost to the other side of the meadow. Tank hands Max to Jenna before turning around to come back for us.

The wind blows fiercely in this wide-open space. Not far off, grass gives way to rocks, and rocks give way to a sudden drop. Dozens of feet below, the ocean must be clawing at the cliff's edge as if it might climb up and swallow us whole. Snowflakes swirl through the air.

Just then there's a loud explosion, almost knocking us off our feet.

"What was that?" I ask.

No one answers, but no one moves either.

A whizzing through the air has me searching the sky.

"There!" Rowdy says and points.

A small, circular object is coming right for us. It lands in front of us then makes a series of clicks until it opens. A light shoots straight up and swirls and pixelates until it forms a tall figure. When the image finally comes together, Ebony and her protruding forehead stand before us.

"Going somewhere?" she asks. She's wearing a long gray dress, and her hands are clasped together at her slender waist.

Anthony puts his hand in front of me and pushes me back.

"Let us go, Ebony," Tank says. "These children deserve to live a long life, not be blood slaves to the elite."

"How rich coming from you, Tank. Have you forgotten that you were one of the elite? How many pDNA and oDNA injections were you given?"

Color drains from his face. "That was a long time ago."

Ebony's lip twists up into an ugly sneer. "How convenient that you have a change of heart *after* you become a perfect being." Her gaze leaves Tank and turns to the rest of us. "Surrender now and no harm will come to you, other than imprisonment of course. And if you're lucky it won't be Purgatory Island."

No one speaks or moves. I scan the edge of the forest searching for Jenna and Max but can't find them. Hopefully they are long gone.

Ebony laughs. "Did you really think you would make it to Eden?"

Anthony jerks in surprise. Even the Dresdens seem taken off guard.

"You didn't think I knew, did you?" Ebony asks.

Anthony's jaw tightens. "How?"

"It's okay, Anthony," Tank says. "She doesn't know where."

"Don't I?" For the first time, Ebony smiles, exposing a row of perfectly white teeth. Her incisors are unnaturally pointed, making me think of monsters and death.

Behind her, the forest comes alive. Bushes shake and tree branches move.

They're coming.

"Last chance," Ebony says. "Give us the Originals."

Tank cracks his knuckles and shifts his weight back and forth. "I've been waiting years for this. I want to make you bloodsuckers bleed."

While Tank and Ebony continue to exchange verbal blows, Anthony turns to me and grips my arm. "You need to run. Follow after Jenna. She'll take you where you need to be."

I shake my head before I speak. "I can't. I won't leave you guys here to fight."

He smiles kindly. "Join your people, Sage. Let us deal with ours. Your turn to fight will come soon enough."

I glance over his shoulder; the blood drains from my face. A familiar figure has exploded from the forest amidst a flurry of white snowflakes. I know his run, I know the way his fists pound into the ground just before his hind legs propel him forward in great bounds, but more than anything else I know the hungry look in his eyes. He wants me.

But it's not possible.

He should be dead.

"Anthony?" I say, but only the last syllable of his name is audible.

He turns around, and his whole body tightens. "How is this possible?"

"I can't leave now," I say behind him, frantic. "He'll track me straight to Eden."

The Canine slows but his gaze remains fixed on me. At least a dozen Primes jog behind him; three of them are Titans. Several of the others have guns. We are greatly outnumbered and outgunned.

"You look surprised, Original," Ebony says.

"Explain to me how he's still alive," I say, knowing she won't be able to resist a teaching moment.

Ebony raises her hand, making the Canine and the others come to a screeching halt. Dust and bits of torn grass billow behind them.

The Canine snarls and spits at me, then snaps his powerful jaws several times. Fear courses through my veins like poison, burning from the inside out. My only comfort is knowing that Jenna has Max far away from all of this.

Ebony clears her throat. "I realized years ago the value of Canines. They hunger for the hunt. It overrules any sort of moral reasoning, which makes them the perfect soldier. However, if one is killed, our trace on an Original is lost."

"You talk too much," Tank says. I notice he's reaching into his pocket out of view from Ebony.

Ebony glares, her features all sharp lines and points. "Don't interrupt me."

"Let her finish," Anthony says as he wipes a large snowflake from his eyelashes. He's as curious as I am to find out how the Canine is still alive.

Her voice lowers like she's about to reveal a great secret. "It was my idea to find twins. Two is always better than one."

I stare at the Canine. That's when it hits me. He's the one I kept seeing whenever the other Canine was around. The second figure running after us when Colt was shot in the wing, when Ebony surrounded us in the forest, and that night I jumped into the tunnels to stop the first Canine. His twin brother was always there, waiting and watching for his turn.

"Impossible," Rowdy says. "There hasn't been a documented case of twins in over a century."

"Not among Primes, but Originals can have them fairly easily with the right drugs. And breeding Canines made sense—twins will actually work together and share blood." Ebony says the words slowly, deliberately.

It's hard to process what she's saying, but when the wheels in my brain spin enough, I understand. They're not just taking Originals for the marrow in their bones, they're mating them too. And probably doing all sorts of experiments on them. I grow nauseous and fight the urge to collapse to the ground.

I'm the first to speak. "What you're doing is illegal. You can't force pDNA injections."

"Who will stop us?"

"You are the worst kind of person," I say and step past Anthony to get closer to Ebony. "Your twisted, over-inflated view of your kind has destroyed humanity and all that was once good about this world."

She opens her mouth to speak, but I stop her.

"I'm not finished. Your kind has polluted this planet for far too long, and I swear to you, one way or another, you will pay for your crimes."

Ebony's normally calm expression cracks and twists into something dark and ugly. "Nobody threatens me." She glances behind us and calls, "Kill them all, including the boy, but leave the girl barely breathing. I'm going to pump her so full of chemicals, she won't recognize her own face." She motions forward with her hand, and, as if on a springboard, the Primes behind her shoot forward.

"Now, Tank!" Anthony yells.

Tank removes a small black device from his pocket and presses a button. A loud pop vibrates the air, and a puff of smoke bursts from all Primes' guns. Tank's has rendered them useless, giving us a fighting chance. This distraction slows down some of the Primes but not all.

I barely have the knives pulled from my boots before I'm knocked back by the Canine. I land hard on the cold ground and gasp for air. The Canine is growling over me, spit foaming in the corners of his mouth. I swing the blade upwards, but he takes hold of my wrist and squeezes until I think my bone will snap.

I scream just as Anthony slams into his side, knocking him off balance. I quickly scramble backwards, keeping the knives, the only form of self-defense I have, firmly in my hands. Off to my right, Tank has taken on two Speeders, while the Dresdens engage the others.

The Dresdens are excellent fighters and their ability to jump unnaturally high proves to be their greatest asset. Summa takes down two Primes with back-to-back blows with a curved short sword from each hand. He must've hit a major artery in the neck of one of them because blood sprays into the air, turning the falling snow red.

I jump to my feet and rush to help Anthony, who's lost the upper hand with the Canine. The Canine leaps into the air and rains a heavy blow with the back of his hand into Anthony's face. Anthony falls to the ground, blood spurting from his nose. The Canine senses me coming and whirls around to pursue me. Just before we meet, I drop to the ground and slide along the wet grass. I swipe hard and fast, cutting into his leg. He cries out and spins around, teeth bared and gleaming wet.

Anthony leaps over me and attacks him again. He's strong, but the Canine's movements are more accurate. Anthony manages to get a clean punch to the Canine's jaw, but the only reaction from the Canine is to retaliate with a kick to Anthony's gut.

I'm already to my feet and running back to help, but I'm stopped by a short and stocky Peccarian. They aren't the best fighters of the Primes but their thick skulls and leather-like skin make them difficult to take down.

"All I've heard for the last week is how great your blood tastes," he says. His voice is hoarse, like he eats wood chips for breakfast.

"Get in line," I say and swing the butt end of the knife for his throat, but it hits the base of his head instead. It makes a dull thudding sound against his skull. The Peccarian barely flinches.

He punches me in the stomach, dropping me to the ground gasping for breath. While he laughs, his weakness comes to my mind.

I wait until he's standing above me then I thrust the knife hard in an upward motion. The knife slides just under his jaw, where the meat is soft and tender, and doesn't stop until it reaches the top of his skull.

I'm relieved by the quick results until he falls on top of me. While I struggle to push him off, I glance over at the others. There are at least five lying dead on the ground. Not surprisingly, three of them are behind Tank. He's tearing through them, one swipe of a blade after another. He's too fast and strong for most of them, until he reaches two of the Titans. Their size alone makes them worthy competitors. I know Tank thinks this too because he's smiling wide.

In the middle of the fray, Ebony's virtual image appears calm, her hands clasped together at her waist, but she's shouting orders. I know she's smart enough to realize that no one can hear her, but she can't help herself.

Finally I'm able to wriggle free from the Peccarian, who reeks of onions and alcohol. Not far from me, Anthony is pinned beneath the Canine. His arms are bloody from trying to block the Canine from slashing open his head.

I rush to him, my knife raised high. Expecting the Canine's heightened senses to detect my approach, I tuck and roll at the last second. Good thing too because he turns around just as I reach him and swipes five razor-sharp claws directly where I would've been standing.

His eyes widen in surprise. Exploiting the moment, I lunge the knife forward, hoping to at least draw blood, but he rears back like a cat doused with water. His head lifts and his gaze meets mine before he runs the opposite direction.

I lean over Anthony and extend my hand. "You okay?"

"I'll survive." He wipes blood away from his eyes.

Together we rush after the Canine, but a tall Prime knocks Anthony away, leaving me to contend with the hungry predator alone. I run fast, taking a small detour toward Ebony's projected image.

She sees me coming and holds up her hands. "Stop! You are under the authority of the Institute and will be—"

I stomp on the small, metal transmitter. Ebony's image shimmers until it fades into nothing.

"Thanks, Sage!" Tank calls, and I'm surprised he even noticed. He and a Titan are rolling across the grass, exchanging blows.

I search the open space for the Canine. He's standing a short distance from me, not far from the edge of the cliff. His mouth is open in a partial smile. One of his sharp incisors is rubbing against his bottom lip, slicing open the pink flesh. Blood runs onto his hairy chin.

"My brother shared your blood with me," he says.

I walk toward him, the knife firmly in my grip. Using my peripheral vision, I take in all that I can, searching for something I can use against him. I have nothing to temporarily blind him with, unfortunately, and the thick cloud cover prevents me from using the sun in any way.

There's a stick nearby.

It will break.

A few scattered rocks.

He will dodge them.

A hundred-foot cliff.

He'll take me with him.

I have to try. To end this once and for all.

I lunge for the Canine, hoping to get him down low, but he swipes his hand backwards. The back of his hand connects with my jaw. The force of it knocks me to the ground, and stars explode behind my eyelids.

The whole side of my face feels like it has been rammed by a wrecking ball. He's too strong.

From across the meadow someone calls my name as if saying it will somehow make me stronger. I think it is Anthony, maybe Tank.

Sorry, guys, but I'm not strong like you.

The Canine nears me. I lash out at him but am too slow. He kicks me hard. The sound of my ribs breaking is as bad as the pain that ripples throughout my body. I can't fight him like this, blow for blow. I'll lose.

I try a different strategy and say, despite the pain when my lungs expand, "I'm sorry about your brother."

He hesitates for a moment then says, "You shouldn't be. Splitting a salary was burdensome. Killing my brother made me a rich man, so really I should be thanking you."

Because appealing to any sense of brotherly love he might've had didn't work, I try a different approach. "Why are you doing this? You used to be one of us, an Original."

"And I hated every second of it. How do you stand it? The feeling of inadequacy? The weakness? The pain?" He stomps hard on my foot and twists.

I cry out and almost drop the knife. Just beyond the battle continues. One of the Dresdens is lifeless on the ground, snow slowly blanketing his body on a sea of red. There's too much of it,

I think, but then I notice there's a pair of legs beneath him. Two dead.

Tank is on the other side of the clearing, moving slower than usual and no longer smiling. He's fighting three Primes, and his yellow shirt is partially red in the back. I only see Rowdy and Anthony trying to work their way back to me, but a sudden new wave of Primes slow their progress.

"Answer me!" the Canine says, bringing my attention back to him.

As soon as I catch my breath, I say, "It is difficult to live in this world where everyone is stronger and prettier than me—"

"A living nightmare."

"—but that doesn't make them better than me." I lift quickly at the waist and slash the knife. It slices into the meaty part of his thigh where I know he is the strongest.

The Canine drops to his knee and growls. I scramble away from him and get to my feet. He breathes heavily through his wide nostrils like a bull facing a matador. This is not an optimal position.

I glance to the left and right of me, searching for an escape. There are only two options: back into the fight with the others or over the cliff. I'd consider the cliff if there was water directly below it, but there's only a short, rocky beach.

Back to the fight it is.

I'm about to run when someone yells my name—a sweet, child's voice, almost angelic. I turn around slowly.

Max.

He's standing at the edge of the forest where Jenna had disappeared with him minutes earlier. His chest is rising and falling, and his little fists are clenched at his side.

My eyes go to the Canine. He sniffs the air and smiles at me.

Before I can stop him, he turns around and bounds after Max.

"No!" I scream. I take off after him, ignoring the pain in my foot and the burning in my ribs.

Max doesn't seem to see the Canine. He's staring only at me with wide, terror-stricken eyes.

"Run, Max!" I yell again. There's no way I'll get to the Canine in time.

The knife.

I raise my arm and aim the best I can. I only have one shot at this. Thinking back to my father's teachings, I inhale deeply and exhale. Focus. Block out all other stimuli. See your target. I flip my arm forward and let the knife fly. It spins end over end through falling snowflakes until it hits the Canine in the back. He falls face forward.

I keep running and jump over the Canine, who I'm pretty sure is still alive. A blow like that, although harmful, most likely won't kill him. I reach Max and scoop him up.

"Are you okay? Where's Jenna?"

He points behind him.

Jenna appears just then, racing up a hill. "That little twerp! He kicked me and ran away!"

Max smiles big. A snowflake lands on his nose. Who is this kid?

"Look out!" Jenna shouts.

I know what's coming. I drop Max just as the Canine's open hand knocks the side of my head. My body flies through the air several feet and into a tree. More cracked ribs. When I land, all I can do is inhale tiny sips of air.

But I can't give up.

The Canine has Max by the throat with one hand, and with his other he takes Max's arm and bites it hard. The consequences of what just happened pains me more than anything else. He's had Max's blood now and will be able to track him anywhere. I no longer have a choice. I know what has to be done.

I struggle to my feet, determined to save Max, even though I know there's nothing I can do from my position. Jenna, however, can. She swings a big stick, hitting him directly on his wounded leg. When he drops to his knees, she reverses her swing and hits the knife still firmly embedded into the left side of his back. This makes him let go of Max.

This new, more clear-minded Max knows he needs to run. He turns to come toward me, but I point back the way he came.

"Get out of here!" My words are leaving half-full lungs, so they are barely audible. Max may not have heard me, but he sees the direction of my pointed finger and goes that way.

Jenna manages to hit the Canine two more times before he finally catches the limb in her hand. He twists it from her grip and stands tall.

Jenna opens her mouth to scream.

"No!" I yell, finding enough oxygen for the short word. If she does that it will render everyone within a twenty-yard radius useless, and if Tank and the others somehow lose the battle, Max and I will easily be dragged off. I can't give up that control.

Instead of screaming, Jenna kicks at the Canine. She's strong, but her movement barely affects him. In return, he picks her up and tosses her to the side, then snaps his head in my direction. Foamy, blood-tinged saliva bubbles in the corners of his mouth.

He walks toward me, mindful of his injured leg. His left shoulder drops unnaturally.

I hobble backwards out of the tree line and back toward the edge of the cliff, all the while searching for some kind of a weapon. I bend over and snatch up as many rocks as I can hold, almost slipping on the wet ground in the process.

The Canine's breathing is ragged, and by the sound of it there's fluid in his lungs, which means one of them is punctured.

I draw my hand back and throw a rock hard and fast. He easily dodges it. I do it again. This time I hit him in the shoulder, but the rock bounces off of him like it's rubber. This is just stupid, but it's all I got. I throw the rest of them and glance behind me. The edge isn't far. It's my only weapon, but one that can easily be used against me, too. It's worth the risk for Max. The Canine has to die.

Beyond the Canine, the fight has grown fiercer. There's not many standing. Tank is there. And Tori. I panic when I can't find Anthony, but then I see him. He's on the ground, dragging himself away from an approaching Titan. Blood runs down the side of his face.

I want so badly to help, but I can't as long as the Canine is in my path. I glance behind me again. Only a few feet to the edge.

"Nowhere to go," the Canine says.

It's difficult and painful to speak, but I have to. Words are all I have left. "I can jump, and all my precious blood will be spilled on those rocks below."

"You wouldn't do that."

"Of course I would, but if you promise to end the fight and let the others go, I'll go with you peacefully."

His gaze flickers to the edge behind me. He's probably trying to decide if I really would jump or not. He doesn't know me at all.

"Fine," he says. "Give up now, and we'll end this."

I hold out my wrists. "Take me."

He comes directly in front of me, and stares down at my outstretched hands. "I'm not stupid." He reaches inside his leathered vest and removes a syringe from his pocket. "You're a much better prisoner unconscious."

Before he can do anything further, I make my move. The only one I have left.

Using both hands, I grab his good arm and roll backwards to the ground with as much force as I can, taking his body with me. I continue the momentum by raising my legs up, effectively flipping him directly over me and off of the cliff. The motion is so fast that I'm brought to my feet, completing a perfect backward somersault, my back to the sea.

I look over my shoulder. I did it! The Canine is falling to his death, his hands outstretched and mouth forming a giant O. Surprising myself, I laugh out loud, despite it hurting every part of my chest.

I go to take a step forward to help the others, but the edge I'm standing on doesn't agree. The fragile earth gives way and my foot slips, followed by the rest of me. I claw at the dirt, my nails digging hard into the ground, but there is nothing to support my weight, and I fall even faster until there's nothing beneath me but air.

CHAPTER 33

I've never felt heavier. Or more helpless.

The ground rushes up at me. I will be dead soon. At least Max will be safe.

I close my eyes, a natural instinct, when all of a sudden my body is plucked from the air. My arms and legs jerk forward, and I grunt.

My eyelids snap open. Somehow I'm flying just a few feet from the ground. When a small section of sandy beach opens, I'm let go and fall the rest of the way. I roll a few times before I stop. Pain radiates from my chest to the rest of my body, but I'm alive. That's all that matters.

But how?

I roll onto my back. A dark figure, black wings spread wide, circles above me, cutting through the swirling snowflakes like a fallen angel.

Colt.

He flies toward me then lands a few feet away. His wings fold behind him, completing the motion just as he kneels in front of me.

"Are you okay?"

I'm shocked beyond words. He shouldn't be here!

"Answer me." His expression is serious, but his eyes are concerned.

"What are you doing here?"

"Where's Max?" he asks.

"Safe with Jenna. Now answer me. What are you doing here?"

He looks up like he's about to fly away. I take hold of his arm. "You shouldn't be here. Why are you here?"

He turns back to me. "What you did to me, taking away my agency, wasn't cool, but I get why you did it. So I hope you can one day understand what I did."

"What's that supposed to mean?"

His jaw flexes.

"You're all that matters, Sage." He reaches into his back pocket. "Take this." He shoves a small, metal device into my hand. His fingers linger over mine, making the pain in my body just an annoying distraction.

"I have to go help the others," he says.

I latch onto his hand. I don't want him to go. It's so selfish of me, but I don't. The feeling overwhelms me, bringing tears to my eyes, especially when I see sweat dotting every pore on his face. Some of it is tinged with blood.

"Please don't go," I say.

Colt brings his forehead down to mine. "You could never truly love me if I stayed."

He kisses me hard on the mouth before pushing off the ground and flying into the air, leaving me crying after him . . . for all of two seconds before I mentally slap myself. I have to get up there to help.

All around me is a sheer cliff wall, but a long way down the beach the cliff lessens. I take off running, more like skipping, since the pain is intense, but I mentally push past it. The metal sphere Colt gave me is cold against my tightened hand. Hurry!

I curse him several times. Why didn't he take the oDNA? Sure, he just saved my life, but in exchange for his own?

Up ahead I spot four figures. I squint hard through the snow-flakes landing on my eyelashes. One of them is Max. The other is Jenna. They are talking to two adults near the shore. They must be the Originals we are supposed to meet. They turn toward me, and Jenna waves her arms back and forth.

The beach is rocky here, slowing my progress. Not much further and I'll be able to work my way back to the fight.

A loud explosion goes off behind me, shaking the ground,

and I almost stumble. I glance behind me. Smoke at the top of the cliffs billows into the sky. My heart lurches inside my chest, and my gut twists something awful.

I run faster.

The only pain I feel now is in my heart.

I begin to cut up a steep, yet passable, incline to the top when Jenna calls my name. At first I ignore her and continue to climb, but then she yells again. She sounds frantic. I glance back at her.

She's waving her arms along with the other two adults. Max is sitting on the ground. Something must be wrong.

I change directions and scramble down the rocky face to run toward Max. There's not enough time. If I could stop the earth's rotation if only for five minutes, I could save everyone I love.

But time has no master.

I'm gasping for air by the time I reach Max. I go straight to him and ignore the others.

"What's wrong?" I ask.

Max shrugs his shoulders.

"What's this about, Jenna? I have to get back to help the others. You should come too."

"You're not going anywhere," a deep voice says behind me.

I turn around. My first thought is that he's the oldest man I've ever seen. His hair is almost all gray, but his face appears younger. Only a few wrinkles gather at the corners of his eyes.

"I mean no disrespect, sir, but I'm going back."

"You can't," the woman next to him says. She looks younger, but would still be considered old by many Primes. "The Institute will have this place surrounded within five minutes. We have to get you and your brother out of here right now. It's your only chance."

"But we can't just leave them!" I turn to Jenna, my eyes wide, my expression pleading. "Jenna?"

She exhales. "You have to go, Patch. Take Max. I'll go help the others."

"But Colt—"

"I know. I saw him. Don't worry about him. He's a survivor."

A bubbling sound in the ocean draws my attention. A ways off the beach, in deeper waters, a submarine emerges.

The older man takes hold of my arm. "Let's go."

I knock his hand away. "Don't touch me!"

"Sage," Jenna says, using my real name for the first time, "think about Max."

My eyes lower to my brother. He's staring up at me, his eyes matching the blue of the ocean's water. He's taken his shoes off and has buried his toes in the sand, just like he used to do before our lives changed forever. When things were simpler.

"We can't waste any more time," the man says. "We're leaving with or without you, but it's your choice."

"Please," the woman says. "Come be with your kind. There's a good life waiting for you."

Good life? The words twist inside me all kinds of wrong.

Max stands and takes my hand. I follow his gaze across the ocean that seems to go on forever. At the horizon, sunlight breaks through the grays and blacks of the snowstorm. Max smiles.

"Is this what you really want?" I ask.

My new seemingly clear-minded brother nods.

It's hard to say the words, knowing I'm leaving without checking on the others, but I say them anyway. For Max.

"Let's go." I look back at Jenna.

"I don't hug," Jenna says like she thinks I was going to try. I was.

"Take care of yourself," I say to her. "And please take care of the others."

"I will."

After I pocket the device Colt gave me into the waterproof pocket in my pants, Max and I step into the ocean to go after the man and the woman. The water is cold as it fills my shoes. I pick up Max to keep him from getting wet for as long as possible.

"My name is Audrey," the older woman says over her shoulder. "And that's Tom."

Tom is already past the waves and swimming to the submarine whose latch is now open.

"Can the boy swim?" Audrey asks.

"He'll do fine."

A small swell reaches my thighs. The sea is calm today, soothing the storm raging inside me. I feel like such a traitor, leaving the others like this.

Tom reaches the submarine and yells to someone inside. A small flotation device appears at the top. He takes it with one arm and tosses it to Audrey, who's already swimming.

She pushes it toward me. "Use this."

The water is at my chest when I grab it. I don't think I'll need it, but as soon as I start swimming, a searing pain in my ribs stops me. I grab onto the tube along with Max and kick hard.

There's no sign of Jenna behind me. Or anyone else. Even the smoke's gone. It's like they never existed.

Audrey has one hand on the black submarine and the other is stretched toward me. I take it, and she pulls us aboard.

"Climb in," she says. "There are warm clothes and blankets down below. I'm a nurse and will take a look at your wounds when you're ready."

"Thank you," I say. Because it's too difficult for me to lift Max, I'm about to ask for help, but Max scrambles by me and climbs up and into the hatch all on his own.

The inside of the sub is surprisingly large. There are four sections divided up by narrow metal doors. Audrey leads us back to an octagonal-shaped room with bunk beds all around. She hands us each a prepared bundle.

"There's a shower room to your left," she says. "Take your time. Your new world is going to take some getting used to, but you'll fit right in. I promise."

"You want to go first?" I ask Max after Audrey leaves.

He nods and cradles the cotton bundle to his chest and walks to the bathroom, but I stop him.

"Wait a second, Max." I take three steps to him and lightly take hold of his chin, tilting it up toward me. His blue eyes look directly into mine. There is no avoidance, no shifting, no awkwardness. "What happened to you?"

He shrugs and turns back around. I stare after him as he disappears behind a closed door. Should I worry? Maybe this is only temporary, moments of clarity brought on by the stress of our situation.

While Max showers, I retrieve Colt's device from my pocket and study it. It looks to be some kind of earpiece. I push it into my ear and suck in air at the sound of Colt's voice.

"Sage," he says, "if you're listening to this, then that means you're safe and on your way to Eden." He takes a deep breath. "And I probably won't see you ever again."

I drop to the nearest bed, my legs weak. He is silent for several seconds. Wind blows in the background like he's recording while flying.

He starts up again. "I only have a few minutes since I just found out the Institute somehow discovered your location. I just hope I get to you in time."

The wind picks up so he speaks louder. "What you did to me earlier, I get why you tricked me, but I don't know your motives. Did you mean anything you said or were you just saying it so I'd get the injections because you're a good person and you would do it for anyone? Did the kiss mean anything? I may never know."

He hesitates. "But that's okay. I know how I feel about you, and I can admit it now. You changed me, Sage. You gave me back my humanity and for that I will be forever grateful.

"I have to tell you something I overheard. I debated on whether or not you should know, but if it were me, I'd want to know. When I was coming to, I heard your father say to one of the other scientists that he gave Max some kind of injection. He said he was trying to make him better. This made me mad so when he came near me, I decked him hard."

My father injected Max? Acid churns in my stomach.

Colt keeps speaking, "I know he's your father and all, and he was going to help me, but I couldn't stop myself. Besides, there's nothing he could've done to convince me to get those injections anyway. Not until I saw you safely to Eden, even if it meant my life." He swallows hard. "Which may just happen, but I'm okay with that. You see, Sage, I began dying the day I was born. The world held nothing for me. No parents, no siblings, no friends. No love. My heart was sealed shut like so many others.

"But then I met you. I knew there was something different about you the moment I saw you. I thought it was because you were an Original, but it didn't take long for me to realize that it was much more than that. There was this fire in your eyes, a burning passion for life. And then you spoke of compassion and hope. Two things no one speaks about, let alone believes in."

He's quiet again. His silence makes the beating of my heart louder.

"I know the next time I see you will be my last," he says. "If I mean anything at all to you, I want you to promise me that you will live a long life in Eden. That you will discover a world you hoped this one would be. And I promise you that if I survive this last journey, I will return to your father and get those injections, if he'll still have me. If, by some higher power, I'm allowed to survive the Kiss, I swear I will bring back hope to this world. A world that maybe you can return to one day. Who knows? Maybe we will see each other again." His voice grows quiet. "I hope so."

"Goodbye, Sage."

I listen to the recording a little longer to be sure there's nothing else. There isn't. I remove it from my ear and push it back into my pocket.

The air in the submarine is cold. I take a shaky breath, several of them, and drop my head into my hands. An ache twists my heart, and I don't think it will ever right itself.

Max comes out then and rests his hands on the top of my head.

"Sage," he says.

I look up at him. "I don't know what Father did to you, but I do like hearing you speak."

He smiles and then opens his mouth like he wants to say more, but nothing comes.

"It's okay," I say. "It will come in time."

He throws his arm around me, giving me a tight hug.

I return it with just as much feeling.

"We're going to be okay, Max." And I mean it.

We will go to Eden where I will recover and where Max will be happy and safe.

But then I will return.

Somehow I will find a way to take down the Institute. All I need to do is find the right curtain and tear it down to expose the filth beyond the shine.

I will not live my life confined to a secret island. I will not live my life without love. And I will not live my life in a world without hope.

I'd rather die.

THE END

Glossary

pDNA (prime DNA): DNA that has been eradicated of all impurities. In addition, pDNA can be altered to give any human their desired traits, i.e. height, strength, physical characteristics, etc.

Prime: A human with pDNA.

oDNA (original DNA): DNA from a human that has not been altered in any way.

Original: A human with pure DNA who has never had an injection of pDNA.

Techhead: A Prime with the extreme intelligence. They are defined by abnormally long foreheads and tall height. They do not function well under chaotic situations, which can be used against them. Techheads control the majority of the world's technology as well as medical knowledge. Because of this, they are the governing force.

Noc: A rare Prime with the ability to fly and see well in the dark. Nocturnal pDNA injections were outlawed by the Institute decades ago, but the offspring from some Nocs survived.

Canine: A Prime with an insatiable desire for blood. Once tasted, they can track their victim anywhere. They are identified by their yellow eyes and sharp claws. Only known weakness is an aversion to bright lights.

Junk: Primes who became addicted to all kinds of pDNA injections. Over time, they mutated into smaller creatures void of any kind of human reasoning. The Institute attempted to eradicate them, but they took refuge into the cities tunnels.

Rhine: A prime with all-black eyes and distinguishable spikes on their head. They don't tire easily and can endure long stretches of physical activity. They have excellent hearing.

Titan: An abnormally tall Prime with massive muscles and low intelligence. The majority of them work as soldiers for the Institute. Characterized by narrow, black eyes and unusually small legs.

Mudder: One of the stronger Primes with excellent fighting skills. Eye color varies, but they can be defined by their high cheekbones and narrow jaws. Their only weakness is they tire easily.

Speeder: The fastest of all the Primes, characterized by one green eye and one brown. No known weaknesses.

Ray: A Prime with a photographic memory and distinguishable lilac-colored eyes.

Dresden: Tall, strong Primes who are trained in combat on account of their size and natural abilities. They can also jump unnaturally high. Defining mark is black hair with a blue stripe in the middle.

Spotter: A Prime who has the ability to sense poor health in others through an abnormal sense of smell. They are characterized by all-white eyes.

Serpen: An unusually thin Prime with snake DNA. Their spit contains poison that is toxic to others. They do not function well in the cold.

Peccarian: They have thick skulls and leather-like skin, making them hard to kill. Characterized by abnormally large heads. Tissue is softest beneath their chin.

Trix: A Prime with all-black eyes and dark hair. Their bones and joints can be stretched unnaturally, but not for long periods of time.

Purgatory Island: An island off the state of New York. It was used as a prison for Primes, but was later shut down when the world's population declined. It is overrun with severely mutated animals and some Primes. The Institute still uses it occasionally for Primes they consider to be violent criminals. HOPE also secretly uses the island as a refuge for Originals.

Eden: A sanctuary for Originals hidden on Purgatory Island. It was built by Sean Radkey, Sage's grandfather, forty years ago.

HOPE (Helping Originals Protect Eden): A movement started by William Radkey in an effort to protect Originals and Eden. They believe Originals are their future and must be protected at all costs.

"Continuous effort—not strength or intelligence—

is the key to unlocking our potential."

Winston Churchill

About the Author

Rachel McClellan is the author of the bestselling Devil Series and the young adult Fractured Light trilogy. When she's not in her writing lair, she's partying with her husband and four crazy, yet lovable, children. Rachel's love for storytelling began as a child when the moon first possessed the night. For when the lights went out, her imagination painted a whole new world. And what a scary world it was . . .